ALSO BY KEN

All the King's Men
The Kingmaker
The Rebel King
Queen Move

Hoops
Long Shot
Block Shot
Hook Shot
Hoops Shorts
The Close-Up

Soul
My Soul to Keep
Down to My Soul
Refrain

Grip
Flow
Grip
Still

Bennett
When You Are Mine
Loving You Always
Be Mine Forever
Until I'm Yours

Standalones
Reel
Before I Let Go

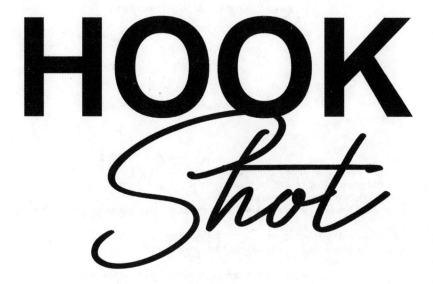

KENNEDY RYAN

Bloom books

To those living with invisible pain
and fighting so hard to be free.
Don't stop healing.

Published by Bloom Books, an imprint of Sourcebooks
P.O. Box 4410, Naperville, Illinois 60567-4410
(630) 961-3900
sourcebooks.com

Originally self-published in 2019 by Kennedy Ryan.
Cataloging-in-Publication data is on file with the Library of Congress.

Printed and bound in the United States of America.
VP 10 9 8 7 6 5 4 3 2 1

CONTENT WARNING

Hook Shot tells the story of one woman's healing journey from childhood sexual assault—how she finds joy and her happily ever after. There is a flashback to the incident in chapter 30.

Though not graphically depicted, it can be skipped by any readers who might find it triggering.

Thank you for reading and please take care of yourselves.

"Give yourself permission to let it hurt,
but allow yourself permission to let it heal."
            —*Nikki Rowe, Once a Girl, Now a Woman*

PROLOGUE
LOTUS

I GREW UP BELIEVING THE SKY SPOKE TO ME. THE BOOMING voice of thunder. The sharp retort of lightning. Every storm a conversation. A volatile exchange. But today, there's a rainbow. Skittle-colored stripes airbrushed overhead in a rain-washed sky.

"You remember what the rainbow means?" MiMi, my great-grandmother, asks.

Like so many things she has taught me, the answer is ingrained, woven into my fibers. I don't even have to think about it.

"A rainbow is the bridge between heaven and earth," I reply, my voice coming out strong even though my insides quake.

"Hmm. Somebody's trying to get into heaven." She considers the sky, eyes wise beyond her eighty-some-odd years. "Not today."

We stand shadowed by one of New Orleans's famous oaks in the cemetery, watching the few assembled mourners disperse. There are no tears for the dead. There weren't many who loved Ron Clemmons. He was a man only a mother could love.

His mother and mine.

My pulse stutters at the sight of Mama. I last saw her when I was twelve, four years ago. She is today, as she was then, standing by Ron, but this time he lies in an open grave. I snap my lips tight against the word screaming in my head, determined not to speak.

Mama!

Even though I don't say her name, she looks up as if I have. Her eyes widen through the short black veil that looks like something fashionable women wore years ago when burying their lovers. "Vintage," Mama used to say instead of "thrift store." Classic, not secondhand. She always wanted the finer things and clung to any man who promised them. Except Ron never promised her much, and Mama still clung like it was a habit she didn't know how to break.

The fine arches of her brows snap together, and her gaze ricochets between me and MiMi and then darts to the open grave. There are few cemeteries in New Orleans where they bury folks underground. This is one of them. For the poor and unloved, unclaimed. That's what this is. That's what Ron is.

She touches the black silky chignon plaited at the back of her head and takes a few steps in our direction but freezes mid-stride. I glance at MiMi, who shakes her head gravely, telling Mama not to come any closer. It's acceptance, not shock, on Mama's face as she turns away and follows the trickle of mourners leaving the cemetery. It's not the first time she has thought to see me, but MiMi knows I don't want to see her.

If anyone knows, MiMi does.

Gravediggers take the place of the few who'd stood around while the clergyman read from his little book of ceremonial prayers. Weddings, baptisms, funerals. A verse for everything.

"It's time," MiMi says, her mouth grim.

We make our way across the grass to reach the men shoveling dirt. One of them glances up, catching sight of MiMi, and elbows the other. They pause in the shoveling.

"Madam DuPree," one of them drawls, his Louisiana accent thick as swamp water. "What can we do for you?"

"Leave." MiMi waves a hand at the grave. "Don't worry. You don't have to go too far or wait too long. We just need a bit of privacy. Then you can do whatever you want with his body."

Her eyes drift to the open mouth of the ground swallowing Ron whole, and she smiles. "It's his soul I'm here to discuss."

You've never seen men scurry like these two at her words. Their shovels drop. They take off. It was a two-hour bus ride from St. Martine, our small parish town, to the city, but even here folks know MiMi. In a world full of phonies, she's the genuine article. And when she says leave, you go.

We stand over the grave, and though the casket is closed and splattered with the first clumps of dirt, I shiver as if Ron might sit up and climb out.

"There's nothing to fear," MiMi assures me, her face aged and eyes ageless. "Take my hand."

She extends her arm to the side for me but trains her eyes on the coffin.

"Feel my words in your mouth," she says, and I do. The syllables she utters vibrate on my lips, tremble on my tongue. "Feel my power in your veins."

She squeezes my hand, and the lightning that split the sky hours ago strikes through my blood. She spares me a quick glance and a smile of satisfaction from what she must see on my face.

Awe.

"It's the power of the unbroken line," she says with a gentle smile. "Two women from our lineage together. There's power in that."

She turns her attention back ahead and glances up at the sky, now quiet and awaiting her wishes.

"You know who I am," she says, her words, her voice, bold, confident. "I'm here to make my judgment known. This man's soul hangs in the balance."

At MiMi's words, a chill descends in the summer air.

"I'm here to lay a stone on the side of hell. As he begins his journey, I send him on with these words."

Her eyes open wide, and she slowly turns her head to look at me, and it's exactly as she said. I feel the power in my veins. And her words, I feel them on my tongue, and we say them in shocking simultaneity.

"No peace," we say together.

In the years to come, I will ask myself many times if I really believe we consigned Ron to hell that day. Like so many things I gleaned from MiMi, I have no explanation. I only know that once our words are spoken, that rainbow, the multicolored, promising path from heaven to earth, is nowhere to be found.

"Wild women are an unexplainable spark of life. They ooze freedom and seek awareness, they belong to nobody but themselves…
She'll allow you into her chaos, but she'll also show you her magic."

—Nikki Rowe, *Once a Girl, Now a Woman*

CHAPTER 1
LOTUS

THEY SAY IF YOU CAN MAKE IT HERE, YOU CAN MAKE IT ANYWHERE. New York City is a beautiful bitch dipped in glitter, giving you the finger while walking the runway in her Louboutins. The best, brightest, and beastliest grind here.

When I moved from Atlanta to New York two years ago, it felt like I was embarking on an improbable adventure to an open frontier. I was like that Pioneer Woman on television, but instead of churning my own butter, I made clothes from scratch. My bare necessities were three garbage bags stuffed with all my belongings, my great-grandmother's sewing machine, and a knockoff Louis Vuitton Neverfull bag. I fancied myself Carrie Bradshaw. The girls eating lunch with me in Bryant Park right now? They're my Charlotte, Miranda, and Samantha, all rolled into two.

"So I've got some news," Billie says, her eyes darting between me and my roommate, Yari. "Paul's getting a divorce."

I give something dark in my grilled chicken salad an investigative poke to make sure it doesn't move but otherwise don't respond. Yari, looking inappropriately unimpressed, slurps the last of her Pellegrino through a straw.

"Uh, *bitches…*" Billie says, disappointment darkening her green eyes. The flush climbing her cheeks is embarrassment, anger, or ninety-five degrees of New York summer. Either way, her temperature is rising.

"Oh, sorry. That's great," I finally say, not bothering to inject much enthusiasm or faith into my words.

"Doesn't he get a divorce, like, every month?" Yari asks, fake curiosity on her face. "Seems like he decides to get one every time you give him a blow job."

If anything, Wilhelmina Claybourne—Billie to her friends, of which we are the closest—blushes even redder.

"No, he doesn't," Billie replies, suddenly preoccupied with the turkey roll on her Styrofoam plate.

"Were you or were you not balls to jaws last night?" Yari's eyes are serious, but her lips twitch at the corners.

"I don't see what that has to do with any—"

"Balls to jaws. I rest my case." Yari bangs her water on the table like a gavel. "I think it's sad that I understand Paul better than you *and* his wife do."

"It's not a real marriage," Billie protests weakly.

"That must be why he never gets a real divorce." I stand and gesture for them to do the same. "Come on. We need to get back to work or we'll be late for the meeting."

The green umbrella covering our table sheltered us from some of the unrelenting sunshine, but as soon as we toss our trash and start walking the few blocks to our office, it beats on our heads.

"They don't even sleep together," Billie tries again.

"Why would he need to sleep with his wife when he's fucking you?" I ask, keeping my tone nonchalant. I actually get pissed as hell every time we have this revolving door of a conversation.

"Forget I brought it up." Billie sighs, walking between us with her eyes trained forward.

"I'm sorry, Bill, but you're having an affair with another woman's husband," Yari says, taking the elastic band from her wrist and pulling her long, dark hair into a messy bun. "This is the circle of trust and truth, and we're your best friends. If we don't call you on your ratchet ways, who will?"

Billie looks over at me, waiting for me to weigh in. As though she doesn't already know where I stand.

"She's right," I say. "You're thinking with your heart and your vagina."

"Gimme a break. You like sex more than Yari and me combined," Billie fires back.

I don't unleash on her because I know we're riding her hard and she needs to score a point. "I actually think I'm done with dick for a while," I say a little too casually.

My words create a tiny cone of stunned silence even as the frenetic urban soundtrack continues playing around us.

"Sorry." Yari bangs an imaginary hearing aid. "This damn thing doesn't always pick up bullshit. What'd you say?"

The three of us laugh, but I sober with each step that takes us closer to the design studio where we work in the Garment District.

"I'm serious," I tell them. "I love dick, true, but I feel like I need...I don't know, a break."

How do I explain how complex sex is for me? I've always compartmentalized it into a purely physical connection. I scratched the itch on my terms, letting men into my body but allowing no real intimacy. Lately, though, not only has it left me unsatisfied, but it's left me depressed. Empty. Bleak. Something in me wants more than what I've had, but true intimacy is a risk I'm not willing to take.

Not to mention the fear. The last time I had sex...

I'm not sure how to articulate to my friends what I don't fully understand myself? Nothing I've been feeling makes sense. And telling them now would be like starting in the middle of a story they've never heard before. Maybe I could at least *try* talking to them about it.

"Whoa." Billie stares at her phone with her mouth hanging open. "Did we know there's a *Hi, Felicia* Bitmoji?"

Okay. Maybe not talk to my friends about this.

"Sorry," she says, sidestepping a construction worker. "What were you saying about swearing off dick, Lo?"

"I think I want to take a sex break."

Both of them stare at me as we approach the entrance to JPL Maison, the design studio where we work.

"I don't understand the words that are coming out of your mouth," Yari finally replies.

"I don't know," I say with a shrug. "It feels…empty."

"Then find a bigger dick," Billie says. "One that'll fill you up."

The three of us share a grin in the lobby of the building with the renovated loft that houses our offices.

"I'm serious. I think this"—I gesture to my pelvic area—"needs to be man-free for a while."

"Remember that time I tried to quit smoking and gnawed through the strap of my purse?" Billie asks. "I feel like that's how you'll be if you don't come on a regular basis. You might also gain ten pounds. I did."

"Who said anything about not coming?" I ignore Yari's snort. "I have a diverse and quite capable fleet of vibrators."

The freight elevator stops, and we walk onto a floor displaying bolts of vibrant fabric, several tables with seamstresses and sewing machines, and rack after rack of expensive clothing in various stages of completion.

"What about Chase?" Yari says of our boss's favorite photographer and my latest fuckboi. "He won't be happy about your little sex break."

"Already told him, and you're right. He wasn't happy." I snort. "What can I say? I got a golden pussy. It's a curse."

They laugh as I knew they would, distracted by the sass I use to cover my confusion. It was that last time having sex with Chase that pushed me to this decision.

"But Chase knows he's got about as much say over my body as he has over the price of tea in Chinatown," I continue. "He'll be fine."

We climb the iron stairwell to the top floor housing our offices and the conference room. I take my spot at the long table, a slab of repurposed slate unearthed from an old quarry. In every meeting, I sit immediately to the right of Jean Pierre Louis, founding designer of JPL Maison.

Two paths couldn't have been more unlikely to cross than mine and my boss's. I offered to style a shoot for a friend at the last minute in Atlanta. I wasn't even officially working in fashion. It was a side hustle to help get me through college. My major at Spelman was business, but I often considered opening my own store or doing something in fashion later.

JP and I hit it off right away. I was the only one who understood his tirade of French when he saw the "blasphemy" of his creation being so poorly styled. I stepped in, fixed the hot mess the stylist had made, and soothed the beast with the Louisiana French MiMi taught me. Apparently, it was good enough because by the end of the day he was telling me dirty jokes in French and offering me a job.

We've only gotten closer over the last two years. He recommended that I enroll at FIT, which is not far from the studio. It kicked my ass, getting my associate's degree in fashion design while working full-time and often *overtime* at the atelier, but it was worth it. I've been sitting at JP's right in every meeting for a long time now.

"Wearable wonder," JP says without preamble, his French accent thick. "That is our theme for this season."

He gestures for everyone at the table to gather around him and his sketch pad. He could design digitally and share it so we all looked on our iPads, but JP is surprisingly old school. His fingers are often smudged with charcoal from his pencils, and the notepad perennially tucked under his arm is always full.

"Feast your eyes," he says with a dramatic flourish, "on spring."

Sketch after sketch comes alive with the vivid colors he's used to articulate the clothes on paper. There are easily a hundred sketches, but only a portion of them will actually make it to the runway for Fashion Week in September.

"All of you know what a purist I am," JP says. "But like we always say, fashion is first art, then commerce. And commerce is where Paul comes in."

Our collective attention turns to Paul, JPL CEO and Billie's boss/adulterous love interest.

Yari elbows me, and we silently mouth *bastard* to each other.

"Yes, well," Paul says, adjusting the glasses Billie finds so sexy. "The possibilities with a theme like wearable wonder are endless. Our marketing team has been working tirelessly, and I think we've hit pay dirt partnering with Bodee, a sportswear company with a smaller share of the market than Nike, Reebok, or Adidas but looking to make big moves.

"Of course, you've all heard of wearable tech," Paul continues. "Fitbit, the Apple Watch, et cetera… We see a potential marketing intersection between our theme, wearable wonder, and wearable technology."

"Watches," JP says triumphantly. "Bodee has asked me to design a line of watches."

"They'll still be JPL designs," Paul says. "Some of our models will even wear them in the September show."

"And I have the perfect spokesperson," JP chimes in with what can only reasonably be described as heart eyes. "Chase actually brought him to my attention."

Oh, this should be great. Chase does have a good eye, obviously.

"He's a professional athlete," JP says, his voice going higher with his eagerness. "A basketball player. His body is…"

JP clears his throat and visibly tries to calm himself down. I should offer him a wind machine, à la Queen Bey, to cool off.

"As I was saying…" JP's voice is only slightly more subdued. "He's a basketball player."

"I thought I had a picture here somewhere." Paul flips through his stack of papers. "But at any rate it's Kenan Ross."

I don't need a picture. I have perfect recall for six feet and seven inches of dark-bronze skin, flexing muscle, regal bone structure, and a smile more stunning because it's so rare. I last saw *him* when Chase accompanied me to a San Diego Waves Christmas party. Kenan plays basketball with my cousin Iris's husband.

I keep my face serene and vaguely interested, but inside I'm doing a face palm and cursing in two languages. Just as I decide I'm giving up men while I figure out what the hell is broken in me, the sexiest man I've ever met dribbles into my life? Hard to avoid him if he's our new spokesperson. And I *have* managed to avoid him in the past. The few encounters we've had were charged with an intensity that made one thing clear: The rules I set for other men—casual, easy, simple—do not apply with Kenan Ross.

No, thank you.

"We've been in talks with his agent, but he still hasn't agreed," JP says. "I thought it'd be nice to meet him in a more relaxed environment. Something not work-related. He's here for the summer and would probably enjoy meeting some people. I've invited him to Vale's party tonight."

Vale, JP's assistant, and her husband, an influential fashion magazine editor, throw legendary parties. I've been looking forward to their yacht party for weeks. They don't own a yacht but have generous friends in high nautical places.

"Aw, man," I say, making sure to look appropriately disappointed. "I don't think I can make it tonight. I've got this other thing."

"What happened?" Yari frowns. "This morning you said you were, and I quote, 'here for this.' What thing do you have now?"

"It's a new thing," I tell her through a teeth-clenched smile.

"Don't be a party poop. It'll be fun." JP breaks out his grown-man pout, bottom lip pushed to capacity. "Please, Lo. We're all going."

"You must come," Vale says from the end of the table in her lilting Swedish accent. "Keir asked the caterer to add those olive hors d'oeuvres to the menu specifically for you."

"Oooooh," I moan. "Not the crostini?"

"Yes," she replies with the reverence those appetizers are due. "The crostini."

"And what, pray tell," Yari says, "would you be doing that's better than sailing down the Hudson with New York's flyest?"

"All our friends will be there," Billie urges. "And one of Anna Wintour's minions has been invited."

"Second or third minion?" I demand sharply.

"Second," Vale confirms with the aplomb of a woman assured of victory.

Dammit. I've been wanting to meet that second minion.

"Think of the fabulous people," JP says.

"The delicious food," Vale adds.

"Don't forget the entertainment," Billie pipes in.

Their food is only matched by their fun. They have a penchant for games we all play with rolling eyes and exasperation but enjoy by the end.

It's not any of their arguments that ultimately persuade me, though. Kenan Ross is one man. Since when did I allow *any* man to deprive me of something I want? Much less the mere threat of being attracted to him? I'm stronger than that.

"Okay." I finally yield with a smile to everyone watching and waiting for me to cave. "I'll come."

"Well," Paul drawls as my friends squeal their excitement, "with *that* settled, let's get down to business."

"You're right, Paul. Down to business," JP says, clasping his hands under his chin. "So what are you all wearing?"

I laugh with everyone except Paul, and get caught up plotting my Instagram-ready outfit for the party. How could I have considered skipping it? Sure, Kenan is devastatingly handsome. And yes, this virile man comes at a time when I've sworn off men altogether, but so what? I've never met a guy I couldn't resist.

How different could Kenan Ross be?

CHAPTER 2
KENAN

"Did you say *arm porn*?"

I hope I heard my agent, Banner Morales, wrong.

"Uh, yeah," she replies, and even over the phone I hear her amusement, though she tries to disguise it. "It means—"

"Stop." I grab my wallet and keys from the dresser and head for the door. "I don't want to know."

"Okay, but you *are* going to the party tonight, right?"

"What party?" I ask, grinning and locking up. "I just got to New York. I kinda want to chill tonight, and you know I hate parties."

All true.

"Kenan, come on. It'll be fun. A great way to meet new people in a new city. And a great chance to network."

"Network?" I ask disparagingly. "It's like you don't even know me, B."

"I know if left to your own devices, you'll be holed up in that apartment all summer working out in your home gym and listening to jazz."

Damn. She *does* know me.

I wait for the elevator to come, grimacing because I don't want to have this discussion. "I'm leaving for the party now."

"Oh good." Banner sounds relieved. "There should be a car downstairs waiting. And heads up, some of the Bodee folks will be there, too."

"Just a small gathering of friends, huh?" I ask dryly.

"Work is play, and play is work. You know many a deal begins over dinner and a drink."

"I know, I know." I step onto the elevator and chuckle. "And I may be going to this party, but I haven't made up my mind about this arm porn thing."

"Okay, seriously. He just likes your…arms and thinks you'd be great for this new line of watches he's designing with Bodee, that activewear company."

"But I don't do shit like this. Body armor, tennis shoes, sports drinks—I'm down. But fashion? Me?"

"He's a fashion designer, but don't think of it as fashion per se," Banner says, using that cajoling tone I've heard a thousand times in all the years she's represented me. "Bodee is on the come-up in sportswear. They're making moves to increase their market share and compete with the big boys. This partnership with Jean Pierre, who's a pretty big deal in the fashion industry by the way, demonstrates they understand the power of cross-marketing."

"Are you done with your little pitch?"

"My *little pitch* is something you should pay attention to. You're in the home stretch of your NBA career, Kenan."

"You think I'm not financially prepared for retirement?" I ask, a little offended because that's far from the truth. "You know better than anyone how well diversified I am. The businesses I own, the investments I've made."

"I want you to be *relevant* for years to come," Banner says. "Thirty-six is almost the end of your NBA career, but so young for everything else. You have a lot of life ahead of you after retirement—decades—and while business interests and investments are great, these are most ballers' highest-earning years by far. Off-court opportunities will help us stockpile."

I'm poised to tell her I don't give a damn about being relevant and will welcome the return of my privacy with open arms when she pounces and plays the card she knows always works.

"Think of your daughter."

I've done nothing *but* think of Simone. She's the whole reason I'm in this city. I don't even like New York that much. I prefer the pace of the West Coast. This is the city that never sleeps. I like sleep. I sleep eight hours every night and have for as long as I can remember.

"What about her?" I take Banner's bait, as she knew I would.

"You've amassed a fortune playing basketball, and that's great, but the more opportunities we consider and create, the better for your future and for hers."

I'm silent, processing her words. The elevator doors open, and I stand there for a few seconds. My professional life is pretty incredible, but my personal life has been a war zone the last few years. My ex-wife, Bridget, made sure of that, and I'm afraid our only child, Simone, is the biggest casualty. She's my weak spot—the jugular Banner goes for whenever she really wants me to do something.

And it works every damn time.

"I'll think about it." I catch the closing door with my arm and walk into the lobby of my new apartment building.

"Just go to the party," Banner says. "Hang out with Jean Pierre. Have fun. You're rich as hell. An eligible bachelor. It's New York. Live a little. And don't be all growly for the next three months."

I *am* growly. She's right. I present a controlled front to the world, but it feels like I've been angry for the last three years. And the control it requires for me to *not* show the world that anger, that frustration, is exhausting.

"I'm sorry, B." I make eye contact with a man parked outside my apartment building leaning against a black SUV.

"Mr. Ross?" he asks.

I nod and climb in the back seat when he opens the door.

"Chelsea Piers?" he asks, voice quiet and polite, no doubt because I'm on the phone. I nod again and raise the partition separating us. Last thing I need is some driver selling stories about my private life.

"Kenan, you still there?" Banner asks.

"Yeah. The driver just picked me up, and we're on our way to the party. Satisfied?"

"I'll be *really* satisfied if you loosen up and enjoy your summer in New York."

"I shouldn't be here. Simone shouldn't be here. I don't give a fuck where Bridget wants to live, but she didn't have to drag my daughter with her across the country so she can do some reality show about being a baller's wife when, thank God, she's not even my wife anymore."

Banner is abruptly silent in the face of my mini-tirade.

"Okay," she says with a little laugh. She's one of the few people who has seen me truly lose my temper. She knows how to give me space to recover it.

"I'm sorry." I release a weary breath and run a hand over my face. "I'm so tired of Bridget's games, and this is the most immature, selfish one yet. Not just inconveniencing me, but uprooting Simone, and I'm pissed about it. So enjoying New York is not really a priority."

"I get that," Banner replies. "Bridget has made life hell for you."

For years, I add silently.

"But at least you got your divorce and didn't lose half your money."

"Thanks to you." Banner can't see my grateful smile, but I want her to know how much I appreciate all she's done for my career while protecting me financially.

"Hey. I'm just glad you hadn't married her before you signed with me," Banner says. "There are a lot of ballers' college sweethearts walking around with half the paper."

We'd just graduated from college when I was drafted to the NBA. Bridget was pregnant and moving with me to Houston, my first team. When I signed with Banner as my agent, she insisted on a prenup and personally oversaw many of the details to ensure there were no loopholes.

"Most men would not have been as generous as you were,

Kenan," Banner says. "You gave her more than you had to in the divorce."

"She's the mother of my child. Even if we aren't married, even though she cheated on me, even though she held up our divorce forever demanding more money, that still means something."

"It wasn't just about the money, though, was it?"

"No, she *claims* to want me back, but that's some shit. She's the one who threw the marriage away."

"Maybe she regrets it," Banner says softly, a hesitant note in her voice. "I don't excuse cheating, by any means, but people do make mistakes."

"Yeah, well, she made a big one. I never cheated on Bridget, not even before we were married. I can't ever trust her again, so she can forget this reconciliation she's fantasizing about."

"Maybe focus less on Bridget's drama and more on yourself. Have a summer fling."

"I don't fling."

"Then have a summer fuck."

Banner's tough as nails and crude as hell when she needs to be. Representing some of the alpha-est males in the NBA, she often has to be to hold her own.

"Now *that* I might consider." I won't tell her how long it's been. We do have *some* boundaries.

"Who knows?" Banner continues. "You might meet someone you really like."

An image, one I've suppressed for months, breaks the surface. Petite, slim, curvy. Platinum-blond hair. Cinnamon skin. Dark, defiant, sultry eyes that can look right through a man and show him nothing at all. Lotus DuPree. I know she lives here in New York, but each time we've seen each other in the past, she's made it clear she wasn't interested. Her, I would summer fuck. Her, I might even summer fling, but she was with another guy when I saw her at the team Christmas party. Maybe she's taken. As interested as I am in her, I'm not sure she reciprocates, and I doubt I'll get the chance to find out.

"Uh, yeah. Maybe, but I'm not gonna hold my breath." I take in the glimmering lights against the city backdrop.

"Well, be open. And remember, no growling or scowling at this party tonight."

"But those are two of my favorite things."

"And don't agree to anything," Banner adds sharply. "If Jean Pierre presses you, tell him your agent will be in touch with an answer."

"Which will probably be a hell no."

"Glad, come on," she says, abbreviating my on-court moniker "Gladiator."

The irony is I'm so tired of fighting. Not on the court, but after all the drama with Bridget, definitely tired of fighting off the court.

"Okay. No growling. No scowling. No committing to anything. Got it." I drop my head back against the leather headrest. "Can I go now?"

"Yes. Let's debrief tomorrow."

"Bless you. Bye, B."

"Bye, Kenan."

As soon as she hangs up, I close my eyes and try to absorb the quiet into my very pores. Extended conversations, even with people I love, sometimes leave me feeling drained. I'm an introvert. The things that refuel me don't involve people at all. I love being alone.

"Children and bored adults need to be entertained. Grown men living with purpose require time and quiet and energy."

That's what my dad used to say.

God, I miss him. Thinking about the wisdom he always shared with me, sometimes welcome, sometimes not, sears me even a year after his death.

"Son, fuck her, but don't keep her. The two of you are oil and water and will make each other miserable."

He said *that* when he met Bridget.

"You weren't wrong," I mutter to no one but myself. That was probably why, even after more than a decade of trying, Bridget and I didn't work out. She craves the limelight. I shun it. I believe in fidelity. She had an affair with one of my teammates, a supposed close friend. Just minor philosophical differences.

Now she has the audacity to join this new reality show *Baller Bae*… I need to stop thinking about this or I'll be walking into that party growling and scowling, in direct opposition to Banner's orders.

We drive through the city, which hums with some force I've never experienced anywhere else. I can't quite place it, but it feels like potential energy—like you could toss a ball from any spot here and it would travel around the world. No wonder people come here to dream.

The partition rolls down. "We're here, Mr. Ross," the driver says.

I peel off several bills and offer them through the opening.

"Oh, it's taken care of," he says, even though he's eyeing the cash.

"I take care of myself."

I give him the money, flash the briefest of smiles, and climb out. While I walk toward the massive boat moored to the pier, I rehearse social cues like smiling, nodding, and feigning interest. A tall, dark-haired man and a woman with a snowy-white bob stand at a velvet rope greeting party guests approaching the boat.

"Mr. Ross," she says with an accent I can't quite place. "I'm Vale, Jean Pierre's assistant. We spoke on the phone."

"Oh, hi." I accept her hand with a smile. "Thanks for sending the car."

"No problem," she says warmly. "And this is my husband, Keir."

"How do you do?" he asks.

"Fine. Thank you for inviting me."

"Mr. Ross!" a man says from a few feet away.

He claps his hands once, and his eyes roam from my shoes to my head. I have no idea whether this short man with dark hair, an open smile, and the beginnings of a paunch is Jean Pierre, but he's wearing an ascot and has a French accent, so there's a good chance he could be.

"Or should I call you Gladiator?" he all but purrs.

"Don't do that." *Judging by the look on his face, that came out wrong.* "What I mean is my teammates call me that, but not many other people do. Kenan is fine, and you're Jean Pierre?"

"Yes, well, my"—he does air quotes and winks—"*'teammates'* call me JP, and you're welcome to as well."

"Okay. JP then."

A pretty blond woman walks up beside JP, her blue eyes assessing.

"Well, hello there," she says. "I'm a huge fan of the game and *you* in particular. We're so glad you could make it."

JP frowns at her, but she either doesn't notice or doesn't care because she keeps staring and batting fake lashes at me. Nothing against fake lashes. I just don't like it when the woman blinking them is fake, too. I've had one of those already.

"Kenan, this is Amanda," JP says. "One of my favorite stylists."

"*One* of your favorites?" She affects an affronted look. Or maybe it's real. I can't tell.

"Don't be a greedy little so-and-so," JP says, defusing the chastisement with a smile.

"You're the last guest to arrive," Keir says smoothly, unclamping the rope and gesturing for us to walk the short board to the floating boat.

The yacht is huge, and everyone seems to be spread over two decks. A DJ plays everything from house music to hip-hop to '80s and '90s pop. Servers bearing trays laden with food glide between clusters of guests. We're moving so slowly on the water I barely feel it, but the pier has drifted farther away every time I glance back. The skyline, dotted with glittering buildings against the velvety night, keeps distracting me from the conversation.

"You hungry?" Amanda asks. She'd take a bite of me if I was down, which I'm not. I've had enough experience with man-eaters to last a lifetime. She'll find someone else to devour. I'm sure any reasonably attractive millionaire will do.

"Uh, nah. I've eaten." I shake my head and tap my leg with twitching fingers. My workout regimen has been thrown off the last few days transitioning into my new place and moving. I can tell I have a lot of pent-up energy. They probably don't have anything I can eat anyway. The key to me playing as long as I want to and going out on my terms is playing smarter, not harder. Smarter means living like a monk year-round, if you're a monk who works out twice a day, soaks in ice baths, and can still have sex.

That *could* be why I'm twitching. Bridget and I may have been on opposite sides of every issue, but we slept in the same bed, and shame on me, I fucked her long after I stopped loving her. But my vows were sacred, at least to me, and she was my only option. No sex was *not* an option.

And yet...here I stand with twitching fingers and pent-up energy. I could definitely use the summer fuck Banner suggested.

"Drink?" JP asks.

Not usually, but alcohol does help me smile when I feel like scowling. "Sure. Wine's fine. Red."

I avoid the hard stuff as much as possible, even in the off-season. Besides, if I plan to make it off this boat without Amanda taking advantage of me, I need a relatively clear head.

JP grabs a glass of red from one of the trays and introduces me to several more people. They may as well be the same person as much as their names and faces compute.

"It's a lot," a pretty redhead with green eyes says. "*We're* a lot, but we mean well. I'm Billie, by the way."

"Nice to meet you, Billie," I say.

"The games will help you get to know everyone," JP assures, as if *that* assures me.

"Games?" I ask. I play one game. Basketball. Anything else, I can't be bothered.

"They always have games," Billie says dryly, offering a commiserative glance. "You don't have to play, but it usually turns out to be fun. We've played hide-and-seek."

"Pin the tail," JP adds jovially.

"Dodgeball." Amanda laughs.

"We broke a twenty-thousand-dollar vase that night," a male voice says from behind me. "Needless to say, no more dodgeball."

I turn to face the voice and immediately recognize the guy who goes with it. The dark-eyed, petite, sexy-as-fuck pixie I can't stop thinking about was with this dude the last time I saw her.

"Chase, right?" I ask, making a conscious effort to unbend my eyebrows because I can *feel* the scowl forming. "I think we met at a Christmas party a few months back. You're a photographer?"

You were with Lotus is what I think but don't say.

"Yup, great memory." He smiles, and I want to snatch the dirty-blond man bun from his scalp hair by hair. I recognize it's an extreme reaction, but that is the only way to describe how I feel when I'm around that woman. Extreme.

"Chase is the reason we found each other," JP says, giving him a pleased smile.

"How so?" I ask. This alliance is looking less likely with every passing minute and each revelation.

"Your arms." Chase nods to my forearms, exposed by my short-sleeve shirt. "Remember at the party I said you had great arms?"

He says it like that should explain everything, but I raise both brows meaningfully, silently encouraging him to elaborate.

"When JP told me he was looking for a watch spokesperson," Chase continues, "I thought of you."

My mind latches on to a vague improbability. "Do you know Lotus, too?" I ask JP directly.

"Know her?" JP laughs heartily, shaking his little paunch and straining the buttons on his silk shirt. "She works in my atelier."

Note for later: google *atelier*.

I'm not one to believe in fate, but my first week in a city this big I have a six-degrees-of-separation with the one woman I'd summer fling *and* summer fuck. When fate knocks, you answer.

"So is she…"I clear my throat. "She's not here, is she? On the boat?"

"Why?" Chase asks, suspicion lacing his voice now, the easy friendliness from minutes ago gone.

None of your damn business is what I want to say, but Banner's still in my ear.

"We have mutual friends," I say, eyeing him as closely as he's eyeing me.

"I didn't realize that," JP says. "I wonder why she didn't mention you know each other?"

"Know each other is a stretch," I tell him with a humorless grin. "Like I said, we have mutual friends. One of my teammates is married to her cousin. We've met a few times before."

"She's here somewhere," JP says, scanning the deck.

Considering that at the Christmas party she basically fled the scene as soon as she realized I was there, I wouldn't lay odds on actually getting to speak to her. She'll probably jump overboard. Knowing she's here, though, shouldn't make me feel this way. I barely know the woman. Correction. I do *not* know the woman, and she has made it clear she doesn't want to know me. Amanda wants to know me. Bridget claims to want me back. I could find a dozen—no, more—women tonight who want me.

And perversely, I'm drawn to the one who doesn't.

"I'll find her," JP interrupts my inner monologue, "and call her over."

"That's not necessary." I say it half-heartedly because I don't plan to stop him.

"Yari," JP calls across the deck. "Where's Lo?"

An attractive Latina woman—maybe Puerto Rican, Dominican—turns her head from the person she's talking to. Her eyes drift from JP to me and back again.

"Upper deck maybe?" Yari answers with a shrug.

"Be a doll," JP says drolly, "and go get her for me?"

She says something to the person standing with her and then disappears up a set of stairs.

JP, Chase, and Amanda continue talking, moving on in the conversation. I'm tuned into the discussion with half an ear and a quarter of my attention. I'm starting to believe Lotus really did abandon ship rather than see me, when her friend Yari returns.

And Lotus follows.

Somehow she looks different every time I see her, but there is something about her that never seems to change. I've seen her with platinum braids and hair cut so short it framed her face, but I should have known better than to think I could predict her.

The petite woman who descends the stairs is another incarnation of the one who fascinated me from the first look we shared in a hospital room two years ago. My teammate August, her cousin Iris's husband, had a concussion. She came to visit while I was there, and it felt like a horse kicked me in the stomach when she walked in. It knocked the air out of me, out of the room. Such a small woman completely commanded a space doing no more than stepping through the door.

She does that again now, but this time there are no braids. Her hair isn't cropped, nor is it platinum. It's a halo of textured curls, her natural hair, layered in shades of honey and wheat and gold, contrasting with her skin. She's a little darker than the last time I saw her, like she caught the summer sun and trapped its warmth inside her skin until she glowed. Her wide mouth, though unsmiling, is still soft, the curves lush and tempting. There's something feline about Lotus. The careless grace of her movements. The heart-shaped face with its pointed chin, flared cheekbones, and tipped-up eyes. She pushes her hair back, and I see a trail of gold studs dotting the fragile shell of her ear. In the other ear she wears one oversize gold hoop. A sleeveless blood-orange sundress flows over her slim curves like fire and water. She looks like a sun-kissed gypsy.

She doesn't look away. I've been rude as hell when we've met in the past, staring at her like I had no home training. Most women would clear their throats, roll their eyes, snap their fingers in my face. Something to indicate *what the hell, man,* but not Lotus. She's stared back every time. Not like she was studying me as closely as I studied her, but more like she was allowing me to look my fill.

And I do.

By the time she makes it to JP's side, I'm braced and ready to maintain my cool and not make an ass of myself…again. We've only seen each other a few times and never for very long. Up close with time to study her, I see new details I missed before. The thin straps of her sundress bare more of her than I've seen in the past, and several colorful, intricate tattoos decorate her burnished skin. Script kisses her collarbone, but I'm not close enough to read it. Moons adorn three fingers of her right hand—a crescent on the ring finger, half on the middle finger, and full on the index.

She's wearing flat sandals tonight instead of heels, and her head doesn't quite reach my shoulder. God, as big as I am, I could crush her if I wasn't careful. Not that I'll ever get the chance to be careless with her. The look on her face says it, that long-suffering unyield-ingness, that eloquent silence tells me in no uncertain terms my interest is duly noted and not reciprocated.

"You needed me, JP?" she asks, the warmth of her voice chilled to room temperature, probably for my benefit.

"You didn't tell me you knew Kenan when I mentioned him in the meeting today," he says with gentle accusation. It's obvious he's fond of Lotus.

Long lashes drop to cover her eyes before she lifts them to boldly meet mine. "We don't really know each other," she says with a little lift of her slim shoulders. "His teammate is married to my cousin. Good to see you again, Kenan."

It's the first time I've heard her say my name. It's quiet for a few seconds while the various people in the tight circle slide looks between Lotus and me, no doubt trying to figure out what's really up.

While *I* try to figure out what's really up.

"Good to see you again, too," I say, forcing a small smile.

"How were Iris and August when you left San Diego?" she asks, snagging a few of the olive hors d'oeuvres from Chase's small plate.

"Good. Working on the nursery."

She goes still for a moment, a natural smile curving her mouth, before she turns to her friend Yari who walked her over.

"So how do I convince you to wear my watches, Mr. Ross?" JP asks.

All the attention falls on me. "Let's play it by ear," I reply and sip my wine.

"Well, you do have great arms," JP points out again. "It'd be total arm porn."

I wince because that still just doesn't sound right.

"You have no idea what that is, do you?" Lotus leans over to whisper. She's in my space, and she smells fresh and sweet and spicy, like she dabbed drops of her personality at her wrists and behind her knees.

"Um…it sounds like some freaky shit."

She laughs, and it's the first time her openness, the freedom of who she really is, has been unleashed on me. I've seen it from a distance with Iris and her daughter Sarai, but Lotus's dark eyes shine with humor and her lips twitch even after she's done laughing.

We don't have time to go deeper because Keir grabs a mic and verbally herds everyone into the yacht's main saloon.

"Thank you all for coming tonight," Keir says, spreading a warm smile around the room. "It wouldn't be a party without one of our legendary games, now would it?"

He and Vale laugh when the crowd lets out a collective exasperated groan.

"Tonight, in honor of our special guest, Mr. Kenan Ross," Vale says, gesturing over to me, "we'll play a new game."

Not wanting to be the center of attention for long, I offer a brief, probably awkward smile and hope they'll get on with it.

"You can thank me later," I whisper to Lotus once they've moved on, taking a chance that the ease that existed a few moments ago might linger.

"You're a Drake fan?" she asks.

"Huh?" I run the conversation over in my head. Why would she ask me—

Oh, the Drake album *Thank Me Later*.

"Not really," I reply honestly. "I mean he's all right, but he's not, like, top five."

I'm about to ask for her top five, considering this is the longest she's ever spoken to me, when the word "kiss" arrests my attention.

"What'd they say?" I turn to ask Lotus, but she's not there. She's gone and is standing with Chase and nibbling off his plate. He bends to whisper something in her ear. She shakes her head, starts to walk off, but then steals his plate first before joining Billie and Yari a few feet away.

"He said we're playing Hook Shot," Amanda says with a look I think is meant to be sexy.

"Uh…that's a game?"

"Yeah, in your honor. You know the hook shot in basketball, when you—"

"Yeah, that part I get." I point to myself. "I'm a basketball player, so yeah, hook shot, but what's the game?"

Vale approaches, her Icelandic blue eyes cool and smiling when she proffers a leather bag.

"Pull," she says with an encouraging nod.

"Pull?" I ask, still wondering what the hell is going on.

"Yes." Her tone is patient, and she shakes the little bag. "It's a drinking game."

Even more lost.

"So," she continues, slowing her words like that might help me, "you pull your icon."

"Icon?"

Now I feel stupid. Every answer she gives me spawns another question.

"Pull," she repeats, and at least she's laughing. "And I'll show you."

I reach into the leather bag and feel several smaller silky bags. I grab one and look at her for what's next.

"Open, but don't show." She offers the bag to Amanda, who does the same.

There's a small boot in my bag.

"It's a boot," I say.

"Shhhh!" Vale hisses and laughs even more. "It's a secret."

Several people didn't get the memo because when I glance over to Lotus's crew, she's comparing hers with Billie's and Yari's. Hers is a button she shoves quickly back into the bag.

"Someone else has the same icon as yours," Vale explains. "You will both take a shot of tequila. That's the 'shot.' And you kiss the person who has the same item you pulled. Like a hookup. Hook shot, but you don't actually hook up. It can be a quick kiss."

She laughs, waggling her brows suggestively. "But it's more fun when it's not."

"Kiss?" I huff a *fuck that* laugh.

"It's like spin the bottle," Amanda adds with a shrug. "Like you played in high school, but...older and with better kissing."

Dammit, Banner, you owe me big-time.

"Nah." I shake my head. "I don't think so."

"But it's zee game," Vale says, dismayed. "In your honor. Hook Shot is a real game. We did not make it up. Just added fashion."

"It can be *zee* game all it wants," I tell her, grinning to soften the absolute truth that I'm not interested. "I'm not playing."

Games always have me doing stupid shit, and then when I resist doing stupid shit, I look difficult.

"It's fun, right?" JP asks when he walks up. "Hook Shot. Get it?"

I don't want to kiss him or Chase or whoever has the other boot. The only person I'd want to kiss has a button. And I'm tired of watching Chase run after her all night. Even now he's caressing Lotus's bare arm and sliding his hand down her back as low as it can decently go without grabbing her ass. He's agitating me.

"No one *has* to kiss. Only those who want," JP says, leaning forward and inviting me to laugh with him. "Some like to watch."

"Yeah, JP, I think I'm gonna…" I stop when I see what he clutches loosely in his hand.

Maybe this night is salvageable.

"So you asked what you need to do to sign me for the watches, right?"

The speculative gleam in JP's eyes brightens, and he nods slowly.

"*Oui*," he replies with a grin. "Tell me how."

CHAPTER 3
LOTUS

"Chase, I said no." I inject some steel since he doesn't seem to be getting the hint.

"Why not, Lo?" He cages me against the bathroom counter with his body.

"I don't have to give you a reason except I don't want to." I shake my hands dry since he's blocking the towel. "I've tried to be nice, but you following me in here is not okay."

"We had a good thing." He kisses my neck and cups my breast, finding the ring piercing my nipple and squeezing.

"Get the fuck *off*." Space in the below-deck bathroom is tight. When I shove him, his back hits the door.

"Are you crazy?" Chase snaps, voice low and his face reddening. "You want people to hear?"

"Touch me one more time and everyone will know 'cause I'll be kicking your pasty ass all up and down the observation deck." I step to the door he's blocking. "Move."

"Tell me what I did," he says, his voice and frown softening. "I know it was good for you, too, so why—"

"Chase, I just want something else right now."

"*Someone* else?"

"If I did want someone else, that'd be my damn business, but I just want myself. I got shit to figure out. *Me* shit. Nothing to do with anybody else, and I don't need attachments, even casual ones, complicating things."

"Casual? Lo, we weren't casual."

"Yes the hell we were, Chase. You could have fucked all of SoHo twice and started on Hell's Kitchen—I wouldn't have cared. We weren't even casual. We were convenient. I wanted some dick. You wanted some pussy. I was willing, and you got lucky, but luck's run out."

"And now I'm no longer convenient?"

I sigh, no patience for some needy boy sniffing around my pants tonight. "Don't act like you haven't had this conversation a hundred times with girls."

"Yeah, but this is different."

"Awwww, is rejection new for you and your dick?" I make a fake sad face. "I feel so bad for the two of you."

"Is this temporary?" he asks.

Is it?

I have no idea. Chase was the domino that dropped and started this *boy*cott...pun intended. That sense of emptiness and dissatisfaction, the ache for something more had been nagging whenever I had sex for a while, but that last time with Chase, fear crept in. He'd held my wrists together over my head, and something had changed.

Snapped.

Broke.

He'd held me that way before. Other guys had, too, and it never bothered me. It actually turned me on, but that time was different. I forced myself not to struggle and claw for Chase to let me go. Rationally, I knew he wouldn't hurt me, but the panic wouldn't listen. When we were done, none the wiser, he lit his usual postcoital joint, but I ran into the bathroom and collapsed on his shower floor, sobbing uncontrollably.

I can't do that again.

"I don't know how long it will take me to sort this stuff in my head," I finally answer Chase, forcing myself out of the troubling memories.

"Like...mental stuff?" he asks, his glance wary, like I may be hiding a butcher knife in my sundress.

"Wow, you make me want to pour my heart out," I say, sarcasm dripping along with my hands. "I need that towel."

He steps aside and watches while I dry the last of the water from my hands. Before he can continue the inquisition, I jerk open the door, only to stop short. Kenan leans against the wall in the small passageway, muscle-corded arms folded over that powerful chest. His long legs are crossed at the ankles.

It's a big boat, and I've been able to avoid him for the most part tonight. He poses a threat and doesn't even know it. It's like he's walking around with a bomb strapped to his chest, completely oblivious that someone's out there with a thumb hovering over the trigger. A six-foot-seven-inch bomb of lean, explosive danger.

There's something regal about his bearing that goes beyond height. Beyond the thick, slashing brows, mahogany skin, and high, sculpted cheekbones. The strong chin and the extravagance of lips so full in a face so lean and spare. It's inside him. An assurance. Confidence. Esteem. I felt the force of it each time we met, and I ignored it. I had to. His posture is indolent, but his eyes—dark, intelligent, alert—fix on Chase over my shoulder.

"Everything okay?" he asks, his voice a warning rumble.

I don't know what he heard or how long he's been here, but I do believe if I say no, he will knock Chase into next week. And as much as I kinda think Chase deserves it, we can't have that.

"We're cool," I answer, glancing over my shoulder at my once-upon-a-fuck buddy. "Right, Chase?"

"Uh, yeah." Chase's nostrils flare, and he shifts like he's grappling with his fight-or-flight instinct. With a man as big as Kenan, fighting really isn't a smart move, so I'm guessing Chase is all flight right now. "We're cool."

He pushes past me quickly and heads back to the party without another word.

"You sure you're okay?" Kenan asks, a frown puckering over probing eyes.

"Positive. Chase and I have an understanding."

"You're dating him?" he asks, his tone neutral but not fooling me. He cares what I say next. I've never experienced such instant chemistry as I did with Kenan, but as vulnerable, as empty as I've been feeling lately, maybe as I've been feeling for a while, he's not what I need. I need simple. Easy. And this man is neither of those things.

"We were never dating."

"Oh, I thought—"

"We were fucking," I correct. "But not anymore."

A muscle twitches along the chiseled line of his jaw. "I see."

He pushes off the wall, stepping closer. Everything in me wants to shrink back. Not because I fear him, but because I fear myself, my response to this man.

I stand my ground, enduring the intoxicating scent of him and the wash of warmth when he's so close his massive body eclipses the world past his shoulders.

"So does that mean the way is clear if someone else wanted to take you out?" he asks, his voice a strong, gentle hand stroking my skin.

"No, that's not what it means." I look up to catch his eyes and refuse to look away even when the cartilage around my knees starts to marshmallow. "It means the opposite. Roadblock ahead."

"A roadblock?" He looks down, so far down at me, one brow quirked, questioning.

"You can't get through, but there are alternate roads. A detour." I nod my head toward the party. "Amanda, for one, seems like she'd enjoy being your alternate route."

"Nah." He shakes his head. "She's not my type."

"Oh, pretty, blue-eyed blonds with big breasts not your type?"

"Used to be." He barks out a short laugh. "I was married to one for a long time."

I'm quiet, choking on something. A woman couldn't be more opposite of me than blue-eyed and blond. I don't even know this man, so it shouldn't sting that he belonged to someone else, that he chose someone so antithetical to me.

"Well, if you change your mind, Amanda's a road I'd call...well traveled," I say, going to step around him. "So wrap it up tight if you ever do ride."

"Like I said, I'm not remotely interested in Amanda," he says. "I'm very interested in you. I'm in New York all summer. Let me take you out."

"Detour," I remind him and follow the path Chase took a few minutes ago.

"There you are," JP says when I reenter the room, but he's looking up and over my shoulder. "We couldn't start without the guest of honor."

When Keir explained Hook Shot, I immediately tensed at the possibility that I might be randomly paired with and asked to kiss Kenan. I would have probably bowed out of the game. I have before at some of these parties, but I overheard Kenan talking with Vale and am almost positive I heard him say "boot." Besides, JP was walking around with the button in his hand, barely trying to hide it. The most JP will give me is one of his famous air kisses.

We reconvene in the main saloon to play. After a few rounds, it's actually fun. That's the thing about these games. We all groan and pretend we hate them, but there's something exhilarating about shaking off the cloak of responsibility, the daily adulting, and playing like kids again if only for a night.

Amanda and Yari both drew a thimble. They knock back their glasses of tequila and then slam them on the table in the center of the room with gusto, both hissing and wiping their mouths with the backs of their hands. When it's time for their kiss, they laughingly make such a show of it to the great enthusiasm of all the guys.

"More!" Chase yells. "Don't stop now. It was getting good."

We go through a few more rounds, sitting on low couches lining the walls, eating and getting drunker by the minute. I try to tune out, to ignore the compelling presence of the man who doesn't quite fit in here, doesn't quite belong with this tribe of crazy creatives but who manages to seem as comfortable floating with us tonight as he would standing at the free-throw line.

I guess there's still a free-throw line. They could have abolished it as far as I know or care. I follow basketball not at all.

I'm aware of Kenan, though. My senses stir and my skin prickles every time something lures his reluctant laughter out of hiding.

"Your turn, Lo," Vale says, cheeks still pink from her kiss and liquor.

I step to the table. A bottle of tequila and two shot glasses are the only things cluttering its surface. With a flourish, I hold up my tiny silk bag to show everyone and then slowly extract the gold button.

"Okay, so who am I kissing?" I search the room until I find JP and wink at him. "Let's do this."

JP winks back, his eyes shining the way they do when a design comes together, but he doesn't move.

JP doesn't move, but to my alarm and horror, Kenan joins me at the table and holds up a button. My eyes dart from him to the button. I could have sworn I heard him say he had the boot, and I could have sworn JP had the button. Right now, I could just swear. Just curse. The very lining of my stomach seems to quiver with Kenan so close.

But I won't back down in front of everyone. And I certainly won't back down in front of him. It's just a kiss. It can be quick and harmless and over in no time.

With deceptively steady hands, I grab the bottle and fill my shot glass to the very top. I slide the bottle his way without once looking at him. My hands may look steady, but I'm vibrating inside. With fury. With frustration. Dammit, I can only admit this to myself, and I swear myself to secrecy—vibrating with anticipation. I can't have this incredible tower of a man, and I will not under any circumstances give myself to him.

Kenan seems too good to be true. Those are the worst men because from my experience they usually *aren't* true. With all I'm sorting through, I don't need that *not true* shit right now. Actually, ever. I've had enough people in my life who I thought I could count on but in the end proved I couldn't.

No, I can't have him, and he can't have me, but we can have this kiss. This one little kiss. The trick is to control it. A little pressure. A little tongue. A tiny taste and then get out.

With my battle plan in place, I meet his eyes over our shot glass rims, and on the crowd's count of three, we knock our drinks back together. The fiery liquid scorches my throat. I give an "ahhhhhh" and slam my glass down. Kenan does the same, and we face each other across the table.

"Let's get this over with." I flash a wide smile and false bravado to my friends. "I'm gonna blow his mind, folks."

They answer with wolf whistles and catcalls, emboldening me. The tiniest quirk of Kenan's mouth is the only clue that he might find this all amusing.

Instead of leaning across the table like everyone else has done so far, he steps *around* the table until he stands directly in front of me. My quips and quick humor wither under the intensity of his stare. He leans down until his lips are only a breath above mine. He slides his hands down my bare arms and grasps my elbows to pull me up, eliminating the last few inches separating our lips.

It starts with the lightest pressure, barely a kiss at all. His lips rest against mine. Him, demanding nothing. Me, determined I won't give him anything, but with a slight shift of his head, the new angle deepens the contact, opens my mouth. It's a petition to enter, to taste, to sample. My lips barely part, but my sigh grants permission, and he doesn't hesitate, cupping my face, tugging gently on my chin, opening me and probing inside slowly and languorously with fiery, liquored licks. When his tongue brushes the roof of my mouth, a thousand fingers, everywhere at once, stroke my arms, my spine, my neck, my legs. Not even the most hidden parts of me remain untouched by sensation. Every inch of me is stimulated. I gasp, and he immediately dives deeper, like he's chasing the secrets tucked under my tongue and sealed in the lining of my mouth.

I don't know if the growl is his, if the whimper is mine, but all the things that would keep this tame—my friends watching, our inhibitions, propriety—melt in the wrath of this heat, like we're kissing under the sun. Rusty cogs inside me, oiled by tequila and passion, start turning in ways long forgotten, if ever known before. Mindlessly, I strain up, push my hands over the width of his shoulders and wrap my fingers around his neck. He's too far, and I want to be close. He splays his hands over my back, completely encompassing as he pulls me into the shelter of his body. He bites my lip, and I lick into the tangy well of his mouth. God, he's delicious. I've never tasted anything like him. Never felt anything like this.

With each second, it intensifies. *We* intensify. Our hands grip tighter. Our mouths grow desperate. The breaths come fast and short through our noses because I won't release his mouth and he won't let mine go. This kiss is a dark corridor, twisting and turning, luring me deeper. I can't find my way out, and if someone opened a door offering escape, I'd slam it in their face.

"Get a room!" someone calls from the crowd. Others laugh.

It startles me. Wrenches me from the false privacy we created with our lips, our tongues, our mouths, our moans. It's like a flashlight shone on us, exposing *me*.

We jerk apart, our ragged breaths intermingled. It's not that I'm self-conscious about what my friends have seen. It's what *he* has seen—that I'm not immune to him.

From above, he searches my face. For what, I don't know, but with the little bit of dignity I have left, I lower my head, hiding from him.

"Well, uh…who's next?" Keir asks, obviously nonplussed but trying to recover.

I take advantage of the attention shifting to the next players. Swiftly and on unsteady legs, I leave the saloon and head up to the observation deck without sparing Kenan a glance.

The vibrant New York skyline never gets old. I let the beauty of the night—the Statue of Liberty, Brooklyn Bridge's trail of lights—comfort me. The evening air calms my racing pulse, and the faint breeze lifts my hair, cools my burning cheeks.

I look up at the stars accusingly, like they've orchestrated this. It's too much of a coincidence, this man surfacing just as I'm starting to deal with tough things from my past. I search the indigo sky for an answer, for confirmation of this cleromancy, but there's no shooting star. No cosmic crisis reflecting the turmoil beneath my skin. Not even a cloud or a strike of lightning.

"Here you are," Yari says, joining me near the rail. "You and Kenan shoulda charged admission for *that*."

"It was a game, Ri," I say, side-eyeing her. "Don't make it a big deal. It wasn't real."

"With that man down there looking like a snack, I'd make it real if I were you."

"Remember this"—I draw an air square around my V zone—"is a no-dick area for the foreseeable future."

"If that man looked at me the way he looks at you, I'd reconsider." She goes quiet for a second. "You like him, don't you?"

What gave it away? I ask silently. *The vacuum cleaner kiss?*

I don't answer. There's a connection between Kenan and me. I knew it the first time I saw him. I felt his eyes on me the whole time in that hospital room when I visited August. I had to force myself not to stare back.

Me crying in Chase's shower, the inexplicable emptiness I've been feeling—they're symptoms of a bigger issue, something I haven't talked about even to Yari. Something I haven't really dealt with. It's been chasing me for years, and it's finally catching up. I can keep running or I can turn around and face it, conquer it. I haven't decided what I'll do yet, but I know I don't need a complication like Kenan while I figure it out.

"Ahem."

The clearing throat draws my attention and Yari's, too. Kenan stands at the top of the stairs leading to the lower deck.

Our eyes collide in the semidarkness. The glittering Manhattan skyline casts a warm glow, adding to the air of intimacy building between us, even with Yari standing watch.

"Um, well, this is awkward," Yari says with a chuckle. "I'm gonna...go. See you down there, Lo."

Kenan steps aside for her to pass but doesn't look away from my face.

"How did you get that button?" I lead with the thing I want to know most. "JP had it. So how did you get it?"

He crosses the deck between us in a few measured steps.

"I told him I'd do the watch campaign if he'd give me the button." There's no apology in his voice nor in the look he gives me.

"Why did you do that?"

"Because I wanted to kiss you."

His admission, frank, honest, snatches my breath, but I disguise it. Look away, down. I turn my back on him and face the night-darkened waters instead.

"You shouldn't have done that," I tell him.

"It was a game, Lotus," he says from far too close. From right beside me, but I lift my eyes to the still-silent sky above. "You didn't have to play."

He touches my arm lightly, but I jerk at the contact—electric and molten. He glances from my arm to my face.

"But you did," he says. "You played because you wanted to kiss me, too."

The truth floats between us on balmy summer air, and I can't draw an easy breath. I bite my lip, debating what I should tell him—how much to reveal.

"That's true." I meet his eyes. "But it doesn't make a difference about what happens next."

"I'd like it to happen again, preferably without a roomful of people watching," he says, wry humor curling the edges of his sensual mouth.

I flash him a rueful smile. "I don't think so."

Disappointment skitters across his face before he tucks it neatly away. He's a man of control, discipline evident in the powerful, sinewy arms JP loves so much. In the flat stomach and the unyielding line of his mouth. His body is a well-conditioned machine—a fire-forged weapon in the battles he fights on court. How would it feel to demolish that control? I bet I could do it, but not without being crushed myself.

"Do I get an explanation?" he asks.

"Maybe I'm just not attracted to you."

He quirks a brow, skepticism etched into the strong planes of his face. "At the risk of sounding arrogant, we both know that's bullshit."

"Okay, then I'll keep it real. I'm off dick right now," I say abruptly, really hoping my crassness scares him away.

"Oh." He nods as if I said I'm giving up dairy instead of dick. "Well, what about the rest of me?"

"What?" I'm at a loss for half a second. I'm supposed to be the one throwing him off. "I don't know about the rest of you."

"My point exactly. You could get to know the rest of me over the summer, and we can discuss my dick later."

In spite of myself, my lips twitch. He twitches back, but the humor slowly drains from his expression. "Look, I won't pretend I'm not attracted to you. I think I've made that abundantly," he says, allowing a self-deprecating smile, "and embarrassingly clear."

I watch, waiting for him to go on.

"But my life's kind of a wreck right now," he says. "I don't know how much you know about me."

He pauses, caution in his unspoken query.

"Very little," I admit. "I don't follow basketball at all."

Something like relief crosses his face before he shutters it. "I'm glad you don't know a lot about me," he says. "That means I can tell you myself. Not tonight, though. Suffice it to say I'm coming off a very messy, very public divorce."

"I'm sorry."

"I'm not." He chuckles, a wry twist to his lips. "I mean, I'm sorry it was messy, but not that I'm divorced. My point is I'm not looking for anything serious—"

"And I'm not looking for anything sexual," I remind him.

"Then I guess that leaves us with a whole summer to be friends. It sounds like neither of us needs complicated. We could keep it simple and see where it goes."

The word "friends" dangles between us like a taunt, a dare. A bluff. That kiss we shared, the heat in his eyes, the spark when we touch make "friendship" an impossible lie. There's something about this man. Simple is the last thing I think when I see him, but he's right. Simple is what we both need.

When I don't answer, he reaches to push the hair behind my ear, tracing my studs, and I shudder.

Simple, my ass.

CHAPTER 4
KENAN

WHEN BRIDGET AND I MET IN COLLEGE, I THOUGHT HER CAPRI-
ciousness, her carefree approach to life would balance me out. Even
then I wasn't exactly the life of the party. Most guys on the team had
two priorities: getting drafted and getting laid.

Okay, so getting laid was high on my list, too.

But even though I was a student athlete there on scholarship,
I never thought I'd end up drafted into the league. My life was
like Google Maps. Rerouting every so often, telling me there was
a quicker or more efficient way, a better path, until my future was
completely unrecognizable. I was nowhere near the law student my
father hoped I would be, and I wasn't destined to be a judge like him.
Things kept changing, and as flighty as Bridget could be, she was a
constant. Maybe I needed that then.

Now I sit across from her in the lobby of our family counsel-
or's office and wonder what the hell I was thinking when I married
her. She was a constant, all right. Constantly testing me. Constantly
making life difficult. Ultimately humiliating me. Betraying me.

"They should be out soon," she says, glancing at her Cartier
watch, a gift from me for our fifth wedding anniversary. The
diamonds, pure and priceless, mock me—mock what I tried to create
with her. She also still wears her wedding ring, which annoys the hell
out of me.

"Yeah." I glance at my watch, too. One JP asked me to try out. Thinking about JP inevitably leads me to thinking about Lotus and our odd, candid conversation under the stars. She'd jokingly told everyone she was going to blow my mind before she kissed me.

She did.

She tasted wild and sweet like some exotic spice. A wildflower. The taste, her scent may have faded, but the memory hasn't, and I want it again.

Blow my mind again, Lotus.

I should be cautious. Maybe once I thought the woman sitting across from me was a wildflower, but she turned out to be a Venus flytrap.

Bridget answers her phone on the first ring, says a few words, and then sends me a triumphant grin.

"My crew is coming up," she says, walking past me toward the elevator.

"Your crew?" I ask, puzzled. "Like, your friends?"

"No, the *Baller Bae* production crew."

"Not here." I rise and cross over to stand in front of her at the elevator. "Bridget, if you even think about—"

The elevator opens, and a group of people carting cameras and cords walks out.

"Where should we set up?" one of them asks Bridget.

"In hell," I snap. "I hear it's freezing over. You can reload your shit and go back to VH1 or BET or wherever you came from."

"You can't do that, Kenan." Bridget gasps. "This is my livelihood."

"Your *livelihood*?" I ask incredulously. "I think you're confusing this narcissistic exhibitionism with actual work. Ironically, it's *my* work that even has them interested in you in the first place. Now tell them to go, or I will."

"You're not going to ruin this for me," she says, her voice pitching higher, her face crinkled into a scowl.

"Who's in charge?" I ignore my ex and raise my voice over

the crew's low hum of laughter and conversation. "Where's the producer?"

No one steps forward right away.

"I said—"

"I heard you, Mr. Ross," a woman says, stepping from behind a tall cameraman. "Is there a problem?"

"What's your name?" I really want to ask her age because she looks about sixteen.

"I'm Lilian James," she says calmly, "but everyone calls me LJ. Is there a problem?"

"There will be if you don't get the hell out of here."

"Sir, we—"

"Don't 'sir' me. Are you aware I have a court order stating my daughter and I are not to be seen on your show?"

"Yes, but Bridget said it would be fine for us to get footage of her entering and leaving counseling."

"Well, Bridget was wrong," I say before she can spout more nonsense Bridget erroneously authorized. "Simone's coming out of her session any minute, and if she is in even one shot, I promise you I will shut your shit down. You understand that?"

Lillian swallows and nods solemnly.

"You're overreacting as usual," Bridget says, sounding bored and long-suffering.

"And you're acting irresponsibly as usual," I fire back. I turn to Lillian, leaving Bridget to find some common sense. "This is our family counseling session. Our daughter's having a hard time with this divorce, and we're doing this to help her," I say. "This is real life. She needs to take it seriously. Coming out to a circus for fake reality TV does not help."

"And where do you suggest we go?" Lillian asks, one brow flicked imperiously. I gotta give it to the kid. She's got balls to be standing up to me when I'm in a mood this foul.

"That, Lillian James, is *your* job." I point a thumb over my shoulder to the closed door of the therapist's office. "My daughter is *my* job. You can park under the Brooklyn Bridge as far as I care, but get the hell out of this lobby before Simone comes out of that office."

"Maybe you can wait in the parking lot across the street," Bridget suggests impatiently. "Get some instant reactions from me after the session."

"I'm sorry, Mr. Ross. I was *told*," she says, shooting a hard, pointed look at my ex-wife, "this had been cleared."

"To be safe," I advise, "anything you're shooting with proximity to me or Simone, you should clear with my team."

"Okay. So I'll contact you if—"

"No, this is the last time you and I speak. If you need anything, you'll go through my agent, Banner Morales. You think I'm an asshole? Wait'll you meet her."

Lillian turns to Bridget. "We'll be in the parking lot when you're done."

I stand by the elevator with arms folded until the last person has left and there's no sign of a camera, cord, or mic.

Bridget watches me in simmering silence, resentment tightening every line of her body. As soon as they're gone, she unleashes all that banked vitriol on me. "What the fuck, Kenan?"

"What the fuck, Bridget? How could you think it was okay to bring a camera crew to our family counseling session?"

"They weren't going in," she says, shifting on her stilettos and glancing away.

"Just the sight of them here could affect Simone's perception of things, of our life."

"You humiliated me."

"Oh, a taste of your own medicine then."

"Is this payback?" she asks, hands on her hips. "Along with leaving me next to nothing to live on?"

"Next to nothing?" I huff a disbelieving breath. "You *do* understand I'm paying you twice what we agreed on in our prenup, right?"

"You wouldn't have to be paying me anything if you had just given me a chance to explain about Cliffton."

God, doesn't she have the self-preservation not to bring him up? "I don't care anymore, Bridget."

And it's true. I hate that this has hurt Simone and disrupted her life so badly, but I don't regret divorcing Bridget and only wish I'd done it sooner.

Before she can challenge that statement, the office door opens and Simone comes out, followed closely by our therapist, Dr. Packer.

"Daddy!" Simone's face lights up, and she rushes over to hug me around my waist.

She's a perfect mix of the two of us, with Bridget's blue eyes and my mouth and cheekbones. Her sandy hair riots all over her head, equal parts curly and coarse. Every time my mother sees Simone's hair, she begs me to let her do it. But Simone is fourteen, too old for me to dictate who touches her hair.

"Hey, Moni." I swipe a hand down my daughter's face. We watched *Face/Off* together last year, and Simone loved how John Travolta brushed his hand down his kids' faces to demonstrate his love. We've been doing it ever since.

"I can't wait to see your new place," Simone says. "I have a room?"

"Of course." I bring her head to my chest and kiss her hair. "You'll have a room anywhere I am. We can grab some food on our way home. This place called Playa Betty's claims to have Cali-style beach food."

"For real?" Simone's expression brightens. Though she's spent most of her life in Houston, she loves California as much as I do. So few things have made Simone happy lately that I notice every one.

"We'll check it out for ourselves," I tell her, "after we're done here."

"Can Mom come, too?" She glances from me to Bridget, a mixture of caution and hope in her eyes.

A smug smile lights Bridget's face.

"Your mom has a commitment after the session," I tell her carefully. "Maybe next time."

"Oh." Simone's expression falls. "Okay."

I'd do almost anything to restore the spark that seems to come and go so quickly in what was once my joyful little girl, but being with her mother isn't one of them. I'll have to find new ways to make her happy.

"Simone, I need to talk to your parents for a few minutes, okay?" Dr. Packer asks, her kind eyes resting on my daughter.

"Okay." Simone sits on the sleek leather couch and pulls her phone out.

The three of us enter the office, and Dr. Packer closes the door behind her, gesturing for us to take the two seats across from her desk.

"Simone is in a very vulnerable place right now," she starts off, no warm-up. "She has a lot of anxiety and is feeling unmoored."

"I was afraid of that," Bridget says, shaking her head. "I told Kenan we should keep trying. I knew the divorce would devastate her."

"Is this a joke?" I demand. "Are you seriously trying to put the divorce on me?"

"I'm just saying I was willing to make certain sacrifices to keep things stable for Simone."

"Well, I'm sure uprooting her life, taking her away from her school and friends in California so you could shoot a reality show helps a lot."

"Actually, it might," Dr. Packer inserts. "Simone says New York feels like a fresh start where everyone at school doesn't know about her family and…what happened."

Fury and shame rage through me. Did the kids at school tease her? Taunt her with all the things TMZ reported about her parents? Welcome to the Shit Show.

"And the school has an excellent ballet program, of course," Dr. Packer adds.

"It does?" I arch a look between Dr. Packer and Bridget.

"Yes, it does, Kenan," Bridget says with a sigh. "If you paid attention to something other than basketball, maybe you'd know your daughter *wanted* to attend this school in New York because of its dance program. That's why I chose to live on the Upper West Side, close enough for her to walk to school."

I look to Dr. Packer for confirmation.

"Don't look at her," Bridget says peevishly. "I'm Simone's mother."

"Oh, now you remember. When did it all come rushing back? When the TV crew you brought to your daughter's counseling session left? Was it right around then?"

"You're not going to make me feel guilty for having something for myself."

"And you won't make me feel guilty for leaving a dead marriage with an unfaithful wife."

"How dare you—"

"Quiet," Dr. Packer says firmly but still not raising her voice. "Both of you. These sessions, this time—none of it is about you. It's about how Simone is processing all of this, and I'm telling you she's not in a good place."

Pain squeezes my chest tight. I never wanted to hurt my daughter, only to protect her. I've shielded her from every outside threat, but the greatest danger was right under her roof.

"She also seems somewhat fixated on the idea that you two might reconcile."

I don't stifle the disdainful bark of laughter in time, and Bridget glowers at me.

"That'll never happen," I inform Dr. Packer. "There are a lot of things we can do to make it better, but that's not one of them. I don't know where she would get that idea. Our divorce only recently became final, but we haven't lived together for a long time."

I had to leave my own house. The one I played eighty-two grueling games a year to buy, I had to vacate. It made sense. I travel so much I wouldn't have been there most of the time, and staying in the house was supposed to give Simone some sense of stability, but then I requested the trade to San Diego. Even though we were estranged, Bridget moved to San Diego because Simone wanted to be close to me, and I wanted that, too. Yeah, she's experienced a lot of upheaval at our hands.

"Well, neither of us has dated anyone since you left the house," Bridget offers.

Anger puckers the smooth surface of my composure.

"No, you did all your dating before our marriage was over," I say, clipping the words.

As soon as I say it, I want to take it back. Not because it's not true, but because it's uncalled for. It's true, but it's not why we're here.

"That's actually not helpful, Mr. Ross," Dr. Packer says, the reproach mild but definitely present in her voice.

"I know. Yeah." I run my hand over my face. "Sorry."

"As I was saying," Bridget says pointedly, "neither of us has dated, and I don't have any prospects right now. Do you, Kenan?"

My memory immediately transports me to that party a week ago. In an instant, I was addicted to the taste of Lotus, more than my mouth could have imagined. Addicted to her sharp sense of humor and the glow that had nothing to do with makeup. The mystery in her eyes that had nothing to do with games. I wanted her lips again as soon as she pulled away.

"Kenan?" Bridget asks, her tone strident. "Is there someone?"

Lotus has told me in no uncertain terms that we're not happening. But I also felt her response to me. I'm not giving up on her. "No, I'm not seeing anyone."

I hate that flare in Bridget's eyes at my admission, some mixture of satisfaction and misguided hope.

"We'll have to be very careful when either of you develops romantic attachments," Dr. Packer says, making a note before looking up at us. "We'll have to take that slowly and one step at a time as a family."

She tosses her pen down, sits back in the chair, and links her hands over her waist.

"You may not be married," she says, "but you're still a family. You have to be, for her. It's the most crucial relationship in her life. You're not man and wife, but you are still mother and father to Simone. You have to figure out how to be that in this new space because she needs it."

Considering all Dr. Packer has said, it's probably good that Lotus and I keep it simple, if we become anything at all. If her situation is anywhere near as complex as mine, a relationship is the last thing we need.

I can tell myself that a million times, but I can't forget how we locked in that kiss—how the world tipped to the side with every tilt of our heads and stroke of our tongues. There's a recognition, an awareness that has crackled between us from the moment we met. So I'll be careful with how I pursue Lotus for Simone's sake, but I can't convince myself we shouldn't see where this goes.

CHAPTER 5
LOTUS

"Join me next week when we explore staying cool in the summer's hottest fashions," I say into the mic. "Till then, it's ya girl Lo. Don't forget, the world might try to get you down, but you gotta glow up."

I pull the headphones off and push the mic away from my mouth, releasing a weary breath. I'm often tempted to stop the fashion podcast I started last year, gLO Up, but it's becoming so popular. I'm gaining new followers every week. I have sponsors now, not only for the podcast but paid partnerships for Instagram. I'm an "influencer." Who knew?

My position with JPL has catapulted my efforts. I'm not under the illusion that all of this would have happened so quickly if I didn't work with one of fashion's darlings.

My first official position with JPL Maison was "intern." Unofficially, glorified grunt. That worked while I was getting my associate's at FIT. Now, with my degree, I've been promoted to assistant design coordinator. Unofficially, whatever JP needs. One day I'm selecting fabrics for him to consider as he's designing, the next I'm organizing pattern-makers. I could be sketching, pressing, steaming, draping. Hell, I'm not above getting in there with the seamstresses and sewing buttons, embroidering, and doing whatever needs to be done. I'm learning fashion from the ground up and at every level. It's the best education I could ask for under the tutelage of a genius.

My eyes drift to the Singer sewing machine in the corner of my bedroom. A gift from MiMi. It blurs through my tears. I don't know how other people grieve, but processing the loss of my great-grandmother will take a lifetime. I can't think of her without aching. She left me so much, though. Not the tiny house Iris and I inherited in the bayou where I spent much of my childhood. Not even the sewing machine she used to teach me how to create an almost invisible seam. Not even the black magic I'm not always sure I completely understand or believe. Those aren't the greatest gifts she left me.

"In the next life, I'll live as a spirit," she'd told me solemnly. *"And God will require my soul, but my heart—that I'll leave to you,* ma petite. *"*

The words poured ice down my spine. I couldn't imagine this world, this life without MiMi's guidance, and it's as hard as I thought it would be.

I can't explain it to Iris or anyone else. They'd have me committed, but I knew the moment MiMi left time and entered eternity. That was how she talked about life. She said most of our existence is before we are born and after we die—that time is a drop in the bucket. The walls of time fall long enough for us to enter this world and then to leave. And after we leave, forever begins.

I know the moment MiMi's forever began.

I was rushing to class, climbing the subway steps to the street, when I felt a prick in my chest like a scalpel making a tiny incision. And then I felt so full, I had to stop right there, morning commuters rushing past me impatiently on the subway stairs like water dumped into the river of the city. Warmth and peace and pain made themselves at home between the slats of my ribs, nestled in the flesh of my heart.

And as it had so often in ways I couldn't explain, the sky, my soothsayer, spoke to me.

Look up.

On a gorgeous autumn day, I looked up and saw a fire rainbow. So rare most people go their entire lives never seeing one—arcs of color blurred, set on fire by the sun and streaking through the clouds.

A rainbow is the bridge from heaven to earth.

And this one was on fire.

"MiMi," I'd whispered. I'd known.

And when my cell rang when Iris called, jarring me from that sacred spot at the top of the subway steps, I knew MiMi was gone.

"Girl, I need a NeNe Leakes GIF for this conversation," Yari says from the next room, pulling me to the present.

Though the voice that answers is low and less distinct than Yari's, it's female. I shuffle on bare feet toward the living room. We share a fourth-floor walk-up in Bushwick. It's a gorgeous old brownstone renovated into four apartments. Yari and I are on the top floor. My steps come to an abrupt halt when a smell invades my senses.

The smell of burning hair.

"Hey, mami," Yari says, smiling at me through a cloud of smoke.

Yari's mother owns a salon in Queens where you can get one of the best Dominican blowouts in the city. As a side hustle, Yari does blowouts here in the apartment from time to time, but she's never used the pressing comb resting innocuously in a small portable stove on the table beside her.

"You're using…" I take a deep breath and try again. "I've never seen you use a pressing comb."

"I know, right?" Yari picks up the iron comb by its wooden handle and drags it through her client's hair. "Usually just the blow-dryer, but Ms. Diva here wanted it extra straight and to last a long time. Even brought her own comb."

The client in question smiles at me from under a fall of newly straight, smoking hair. I try to smile back, but my mouth won't curve. My heartbeat hammers my breastbone, a painful thrumming that shortens my breath. Sweat dampens my palms and under my arms. My body won't pretend—won't cooperate in my charade. A primal scream scratches the sides of my throat, begging to be let loose. I'm afraid I can't contain it for another second, so I turn. I run. Yari calls my name, her voice laced with concern and confusion, but I can't stop. Can't explain. I run past my bed, into my closet, slamming the door, blocking out the world beyond and trapping the smoke and the smell on the other side.

The walk-in closet is a decent size, considering how small the bedroom is. I turn on the light, and my gaze clings to the closet wall. There's an oak tree sketched from corner to corner, its branches stretching, limbs drooping, leaves dangling. I race to it, curling my body into a tight ball around the penciled trunk, taking shelter in its charcoal shadow.

And I wait.

Wait for my heart to slow.

Wait for my breaths to even out.

Wait for the roar of blood in my ears to quiet.

I wait for the room to stop spinning.

I don't know how long I'm there. Long enough for Yari to poke her head in and ask if I'm okay.

"Yeah," I manage to say without croaking. I pull myself up until my back is against the wall, against the tree I drew there. "Sorry. I felt sick. Something I ate."

There's a pause, uncertainty in the look she gives me.

"You sure, Lo?" she asks. "You ran out of there like—"

"Like I was gonna be sick," I conclude for her, forcing a laugh. "Your client probably didn't want vomit at her feet."

"But you're—"

"I had sushi today. Maybe it was bad or something."

"We were gonna go grab some oxtails from that place on Flatbush," she says tentatively. "You wanna come?"

We're never tentative with each other, and I wish I could tell her the truth, tell her everything, but I wouldn't know where to start my story, and it feels like there is no end.

"You go on. I still feel a little queasy," I say, willing myself to sound normal. "And I need to edit the podcast anyway."

"You sure? Because I could—"

"Ri, I'm good." I need her to leave. "See you when you get back."

"Okay, if you're sure." *She* still doesn't sound sure.

"Have fun."

After a few seconds, long seconds where I silently beg her to leave me alone, I hear the steps carrying her back out to the living room. I release a long, calming breath once the front door closes. I flip onto my back, link my hands behind my head, and fix my eyes on the tree. The longer I watch it, the calmer I become. I watch until my body goes silent and still. I watch until the serenity of the room feels like loneliness. And then I call the only person who knows how it all started, even though I've never told her it's not over.

"Hey, Lo," my cousin Iris says from the other end of the line. "What's up, girl?"

I'm silent for a second, letting the voice I've known all my life wash over me. Familiar. Family.

"Lo?" Iris asks again. "You okay?"

"I don't know, Bo," I whisper, abbreviating her childhood nickname Gumbo.

"What's going on?"

"You remember that day?" I ask, my voice hushing over the secret. "The day it happened?"

For a moment, I'm afraid I'll have to explain—that I'll have to say something awkward, something awful to trigger the memory I cannot escape, but she answers. She knows.

"Yeah," she replies softly. "I remember."

"It… I thought I had this shit under control, you know?" One tear at a time rolls from the corners of my eyes and singes the skin on my cheeks. "But it's like…you remember that big hole in MiMi's kitchen?"

"Yeah. She patched that hole all the time," Iris says with a short, rough laugh.

"And nothing ever helped." I bounce the laugh back to my cousin. "She kept patching it up, and every time it rained, water would leak through that ceiling."

"Yeah." Iris's laughter fades, leaving questions and maybe some answers. "Are you leaking, Lo?"

I bite my bottom lip until it hurts, and I love it. It's a hurt I can control. I can turn it on. I can turn it off. If I bite hard enough, I'll see the marks of my teeth. I prefer that to the pain that spreads over my body when I least expect it. That's a pain I can't stop—can't control. And it's invisible. Untraceable, but lately it's hurting me just the same.

I can't see it. I can't find it. I can't fix it.

"Maybe I am." I sit up, pressing my back to the wall, to my tree, and rest my elbows on my knees. "Lately I've been feeling...I don't know. Empty."

"Empty how?"

"Well, you know I'm not one of those people who has trouble with sex," I say, managing a chuckle.

"I'm aware, yeah," Iris says, a grin evident in her voice.

"I always put sex in this box. Sex was to make me feel good, and that was totally fine. I didn't want any strings. I didn't want any emotions. I didn't want..." I hesitate over the word waiting on my tongue. "Intimacy," I whisper. "I didn't want that. Didn't need it."

"And now?" Iris asks.

"It's not enough." I shake my head, shocked at the words I'm saying. "It's not enough anymore, and it feels meaningless. It's not enough, but I can't afford to feel anything other than that. There's this part of me that says it's dangerous to really share yourself with someone. Look at my mother."

Even saying her name makes me want to curl up again under the tree at my back.

"Look what she did for a bad man," I continue. "She was putty for him. Look at your mom. How she chose the wrong men over and over—how she gave herself to them for all the wrong reasons."

"Look at me?" Iris asks. "Am I another cautionary tale?"

I don't answer, but in some ways, she is. I don't want to hurt Iris, but before she found her husband, August, she chose badly, and that man hurt her. He trapped her. He *kept* her, and by the time she escaped, it was almost too late.

"We all make mistakes," Iris finally replies when I don't.

"Is that what you call what Mama did?" I ask, a serrated edge to my voice. "I'm here feeling this, living this because of her 'mistake'? No, thank you."

"So what are you gonna do about it?"

"I've sworn off dick."

Iris makes a choking sound on the other end. "We'll see how long that lasts," she says. "What about that photographer you brought to the Christmas party?"

"Chase?" I suck my teeth. "Just a fuckboi."

I don't want to tell her I cried the last time Chase and I had sex. There are limits to what I can expose.

"You haven't met *anyone*?" Iris asks. "Gorgeous girl like you in New York living the glamorous life. Surely there's a guy."

Glamorous? At this moment, my life is restricted to this closet, and in the life beyond that door, I haven't met many guys worth my time. Definitely not many guys who'd put up with the train wreck I am right now. Except...maybe...

"There's a guy. *Maybe*," I admit reluctantly, unwilling to tell Iris it's Kenan. She's been encouraging me to consider him since that day in the hospital. "But I think he could be the worst option of all because he seems too good to be true. That usually means they are."

"But you like him," Iris says, a smile reentering her tone.

"Yeah, I like him," I admit. "But I won't trust him."

"Well, trust has to be earned. I'm living proof. August took his time getting me to trust him. Proving I could. Maybe if you give this guy some time, time to watch him, to know him, maybe he's the real deal."

"Maybe. He asked if we can keep it simple and get to know each other over the summer."

"Well, you can decide to give him a chance or not, but…" Iris draws and exhales a breath quickly. "But either way you need to talk to someone."

"Huh?" I sit up straighter. "I don't need to talk to anyone."

"So you think you're better than me?"

"What? 'Course not, Bo."

"Well, didn't you tell me I needed to talk to someone? When I was struggling with my past, isn't that what you told *me*?"

Damn, I did tell her that. Advice is so much easier to follow when you're giving it to someone else.

"I'll think about it."

"And what about Mr. Too Good to Be True?" Iris asks, her voice lighter. "You gonna think about him, too?"

I grin and chastise my heart for skipping a beat at the thought of Kenan Ross. "Not if I can help it."

CHAPTER 6
KENAN

"You're going soft, Glad."

No one in the NBA could get away with that lie, but considering my sister plays in the WNBA, she can.

"Oh, yeah?" I ask, adjusting my earpiece and stripping off my sweat-drenched shorts and shirt. "I've been up since four-thirty and worked out for the last two hours. You?"

Kenya's sleep-rusty chuckle comes from the other end of the line, and if I know my sister, she's laughing from the depths of her down comforter.

"Shiiiiiit," she says. "You know I'm still in bed, but I scored thirty points last night, so I should be excused."

"I saw your highlights on ESPN." I lean against the counter, the marble cool against my naked skin while I navigate the apps on my phone. "Not bad for a girl."

Only I could get away with that taunt. Anyone else would be flat on his ass in seconds. My sister is one of the WNBA's most promising athletes and could hold her own with most of the guys I play against.

"You joke about it," Kenya says, her voice losing some of its humor, "but my paycheck says people believe that shit."

"I know, Ken. I wish I could do more."

"Keep speaking out. You and the other leaders in the Players

Association doing that is huge. People need to know it's not just us demanding more money but that you guys believe we deserve it, too."

"It'll take time," I say, pulling up the app to turn on my ice tub. "We'll keep moving forward, but we got a long way to go."

"When our number one draft pick makes fifty thousand a year and your number one makes six million," Kenya says, with a justifiable sharpness in her voice. "Yeah, we have a long way to go. I know we don't bring in the same revenue, but we're not even compensated equitably for what we *do* generate."

I walk to the rear of my spacious, if temporary, bathroom and consider the ice tub with familiar dread.

"Damn, this never gets easier," I mutter, lowering myself into the icy water.

"You icing?" Kenya asks, a wince in her words.

"Yeah, we had an ice tub installed in the New York apartment since I'll be here all summer."

The benefits of cryotherapy—decreased fatigue, quicker muscle recovery, less anxiety, improved performance, and a dozen others—far outweigh how much it sucks to submerge your body in arctic water.

"What are you eating?" Kenya asks. "I know you didn't drag that chef with you to the East Coast."

"He refused to leave Cali," I say with a laugh, breathing easier as my body adjusts to the cold. "But he did recommend someone out here who delivers my meals to keep me on point this summer. I can't show up at training camp with a gut."

"A gut." Kenya's hearty laugh makes me laugh, too. "You never had a gut a day in your life."

"And I don't plan to."

"Man, with the way you live, you could play till you're fifty."

"God, please, no."

"You're not ready to throw in the towel yet, are you?" Surprise colors her voice because with my conditioning, most expect me to play for another four years or so. I'm not so sure.

"It's not my body that's tired. Maybe it's my mind. I don't know, Ken. I've been at this for a long time. I want to do some other things, including spend more time with Simone."

"How is my niece? Still spoiled rotten?"

"She's not spoiled."

Kenya lets her silence speak for her.

"Okay," I concede with a chuckle. "She may be a *little* spoiled, but she's a good kid."

"Still no interest in ball?" There's despair in Kenya's tone. Even in college I still thought I would be a lawyer one day, but my sister has always known she would be a baller. She has high hopes for Simone, too.

"She's sticking with ballet."

"Hey, ballerinas are athletes, too," Kenya says. "I'll take it."

I sink lower into the icy water, letting it reach all the places that will ache from my strenuous workout if I don't. "Her new school has a great program, and she seems committed."

"And how is her mother?" Kenya asks with careful coolness.

"She's…" I sigh, thinking of the scene with the camera crew at our family counseling session. "She's Bridget."

"And that tells me all I need to know."

"Yeah, pretty much. I'm fighting to keep Simone clear of this reality show. I don't want her enamored with fame or what she *thinks* it is. It's not just getting a bunch of Instagram followers. It's having the worst day of your life broadcast for the whole world to see."

"I think she gets that," Kenya says reassuringly. "She saw what you guys went through."

"That's the problem, Ken. She *saw* it all. She knows how dark this can get. That is her life at this age. I hate that our foolishness has even touched her."

"You mean Bridget's foolishness," Kenya returns harshly. "I still wish you'd let me key her car."

"Well, since I paid for the car and the repairs would come out of the alimony I give her each month," I reply wryly, "feels like a no-win."

"She still trying to get back in your pants?" Kenya teases.

"She should know by now that won't ever happen, but she keeps pushing it, yeah. Unfortunately, Simone has it in her head that we might reconcile."

"No way," Kenya says, sounding as disbelieving as I am. "Even knowing her mom cheated?"

"Her therapist says it's a natural response for a kid, even in circumstances where there is known infidelity. Simone sees our marriage, our relationship through a self-centered lens at this stage of her life. Not what makes sense or what's best for us, but what seems best for *her*. And she believes that's for us to be together."

"As long as you don't *actually* go soft and give Bridget another chance."

"The fuck?" My scowl and gritting teeth have nothing to do with the icy water I'm submerged in. "You know better."

"Long as you're sure because I'd never trust that bitch again."

"I'm sure," I say firmly.

"Yeah, but sometimes men think with their dicks. Most times, actually."

"I'm not attracted to Bridget even a little bit anymore." I take a long draw from a nearby water bottle. "I saw the ugliness under all the blond and boobs."

"You gotta fuck somebody, though, right?"

I nearly choke on the water sliding down my throat. I'm surrounded by women worried about my sex life. "We're not going there, Ken."

"I could find you somebody."

Fate already brought a beautiful, fiery woman into my summer.

"I'm doing fine on my own," I drawl, hauling myself out of the ice tub so I can shower and get ready for my day. "Thanks, though."

"That so?" Kenya asks. "Who?"

"No one you know." I don't bother trying to hide it from my sister. Even if I didn't tell her, she'd find her way to the truth.

"Is she fine?"

"As hell," I say, chuckling unabashedly.

"A sister?"

"What's that got to do with anything?" I grimace, irritated by the question I've fielded in some form or fashion many times since I started dating and ultimately married Bridget. "You never objected to Bridget because she was white."

"No, I objected to Bridget because she was a *whore* who cheated on my brother."

I can't argue, and yet I find myself doing just that. "Hey, ease up. She's still Simone's mom, and I never want my daughter to hear me or any of her family talking like that about her mother."

"Okay, I won't say it. Long as you know I'm thinking it."

"Duly noted." I turn on the shower. "And what about you? You seeing anybody?"

"I might have some news, someone for you to meet."

I pause, a grin spreading on my face. I want my sister's happiness more than I want my own. "Now that's what I'm talking about. You coming to New York anytime soon?"

"We have a game there in a few weeks. We'll see how things work out," Kenya replies cagily. "Oh, almost forgot. You talked to Mama?"

Guilt stabs me. I haven't talked to her as much as I should have since my father died.

"I'll call her," I say, releasing a heavy sigh. "She didn't sound too good last time we spoke."

"Same," Kenya replies, her voice uncharacteristically subdued. "They were married forty years. Most of her life was with Dad, and they had one of those epic, forever kind of loves."

"Yeah, if I hadn't seen their marriage with my own eyes, I wouldn't think it was possible."

"Let's both call this week."

"I may do one better," I say. "I need to go to Philly and check on Faded, that barber shop I invested in. I'll swing through to see Mama."

"Take Simone with you. She hasn't seen her grandmother in a while, and Mama would love to see her."

"As long as she doesn't start in on Simone's hair again," I groan.

"Well, Simone *does* need to do something with that head, and Bridget has no idea how to help."

"Give Simone a break. She's figuring it out."

"I offered to help her," Kenya says defensively. "She wouldn't listen to me."

"Yeah, but you just buy hair," I say, laughing because my sister wears extensions year-round.

"And you know this," Kenya says, laughing back. "Hair is trouble, man, especially during the season. I could get Simone's *own* hair tight if she'd let me. Is Lucius still managing Faded?"

"Yeah. I'm thinking of asking if he'd be interested in opening another shop here in New York. Maybe Brooklyn."

"I don't have to ask what you'll be doing when you finally retire. You already have more businesses than I can keep up with."

"More than I can keep up with, too. That's why I pay someone to help me."

"Well, thank you for cutting your little sis in on some of that action since obviously I won't become a millionaire playing for the WNBA."

"Don't even think twice about it. Just introduce me to this potential love interest soon."

"Hey, I'll show you mine if you show me yours."

The thought of Lotus being mine, of her in my life, in my bed, makes my dick hard.

I head back to the ice bath.

CHAPTER 7
LOTUS

THERE'S SOMETHING CALMING ABOUT SEWING. THE HUM OF THE machine. The rhythm. Watching a creation take life and shape under your hands in real time. It's always soothed me in ways few other things do. I was a wild, angry, damaged twelve-year-old when I landed in MiMi's care. She wasn't sure how to occupy my time, how to direct the violent storm churning inside me, so she tried everything. Some things stuck, and some didn't. But from the first time she sat me down at her Singer, sewing made sense.

"You almost done with that?" Yari asks from the doorway leading back to the atelier's workroom.

I like to sew alone. It gives me time to think. Out there on the floor, the seamstresses speak a dozen languages, flying around and distracting. And the gossip is nonstop. I like to see where my thoughts take me. Sewing is meditative and not for the chaos of the workroom.

"Yeah." I hold up the dress for Yari's inspection. "I had to tear the whole seam out and start all over."

"Looks good." She takes the dress, folding it over her arm. "I'll get this to the seamstress so she can start on the buttons. Meanwhile, JP wants you in his office."

"Did he say for what?" I stand and stretch out the muscles locked tight while I concentrated at the sewing machine.

"Nope."

We leave the back room together, but she heads for the workroom. I take the steps up to JP's office. His door is open, so I knock on the doorframe. He glances up from his position on the floor, kneeling in front of a woman easily six feet tall.

"Oh good," he says around a mouthful of pins. "You're here."

I walk over and hold out my hand. He drops the pins from his lips into my palm.

"I meant to ask you something yesterday." Still on his knees, he shifts on the floor from her front to her side, adjusting the fuchsia material he's draping into the shape of a dress for the September show. I rotate with him, handing him a pin without him having to ask. We work well together, read each other well.

"Yesterday?" I frown because JP is notoriously last-minute. "What do you need?"

"Your eye. Your sense of style. Your essence." He bats his lashes through all the BS flattery. "For you to come with me on a shoot today."

"Sure." I nod and hand him another pin. "I didn't know we had one scheduled."

"It's kind of last-minute."

Shocker. "Oh?"

"Yeah, Kenan's going out of town next week, so I asked Chase if he could shoot today instead."

I accidentally prick my finger with a pin at the mention of Kenan's name.

"You know," I say, sucking the sore finger, "maybe I should stay here. We're expecting that shipment of silks today, and I want to be here to receive them. It'll throw off our whole production schedule if anything happens to that delivery."

"Anybody can sign for a package," he says dismissively. "You are the only one Kenan wants to see."

I freeze, glaring at my boss, the matchmaking devil. "Did he ask me to come or something?"

"Not in so many words."

"In how many words?"

"I mean, the man agreed to do the whole campaign for a chance to kiss you," JP says, sparing me a glance away from the material he's draping and pinning over the model's hip. "I'd be a fool not to keep you close."

"You mean use me?"

"Don't think of it that way, Lo." He turns teasingly calculating eyes up to me from the floor. "Or do. Either way, you're coming."

He adjusts one last fold on the dress and pats the model's bottom. "Go on, *cherie*, and ask Yari to take a picture before you disrobe."

The model turns on bare feet and glides gracefully through the office door.

"And watch my pins," JP yells after her. "Be careful taking that dress off. It's worth your weight in gold."

He grabs his man pouch and turns to me. "Ready?"

"Now?" I glance down at my cutoff denim shorts, Spelman tank top, and low-rise Nike Air Force 1s. My hair is in two braids. I have on no makeup. Ordinarily I'd be fine going to a shoot like this. Shoots are hard work, and my appearance is usually the last thing I'm concerned with, but *he'll* be there.

"*Maintenant*," JP confirms, already walking out the door and headed down the stairs. "Lotus, where are you? You're supposed to be the wind at my back. My back feels cold and lonely."

I roll my eyes and mutter, "Suck my dick."

"What was that, *ma petite*?" he calls back, his tone knowing and indulgent.

"I said let me grab my bag *right quick*," I reply louder.

On the drive to the Chelsea loft where they're shooting, I half-listen to JP talk in the back seat about the watch and the prototypes. Mostly, I'm wrestling with my emotions in silence. I'm nervous, yeah, but it's more than that.

Circle of truth and trust.

Members: One.

Member: Me.

I'm excited to see Kenan. It's been more than a week since the party. If he'd wanted to get in touch with me, he could have. Through the office or even JP himself. Hell, through Iris if he'd wanted to, but he hasn't. The prospect of seeing him again has my fingers toying with the frayed denim dripping around my thighs. Maybe he lost interest in a sexless, simple friendship for the summer. Maybe he's decided he needs sex and this *getting to know me* thing won't satisfy him. For someone who *claimed* to want him to leave me alone, my disappointment is ironic. And telling.

"Chaos!" JP declares when we step on set. "See what happens when we aren't here, Lotus?"

It's actually relatively calm, but JP hates tranquility. He once told me he couldn't concentrate in the quiet. I'm sure there's a medication for that, but those aren't the pills JP pops.

Chase looks up from the camera he's setting and walks over to us. He accepts JP's continental air kisses and then pulls me close by my hips.

"I miss you," he whispers in my ear. "Come to my place tonight and I'll eat your pussy for you."

I press my hands to his chest and create space between us. "I already told you no," I say for his ears only. "Friends or nothing, and the next time you grab me, I'm snapping that hand off."

"Don't be a bitch," Chase says with a pleasant smile. "You don't want to cross me."

That dark thing I've learned to tame as I've matured rises and rears inside me. I once asked MiMi if voodoo was bad, if *we* were bad. She said we weren't bad. We're just.

"You don't even understand the power you've been given," she'd say. "Don't abuse it in anger. Gentleness is power under control."

"No, Chase," I answer after a beat to compose myself, to check my lowest impulses. "I'm the one you don't want to cross."

"You gonna put a hex on me, Lo?" he asks snidely.

Once, at my apartment, Chase stumbled upon some of the herbs and potions MiMi sent with me when I left for college. I don't practice voodoo like MiMi did. She devoted her life to the people who needed her help. No, I don't practice, but I've never forgotten the things MiMi taught me about magic, about life. That may not be my path, but I descend from a long line of women who walked that path well. I know my own strength, my own power, and it takes all my restraint not to unleash it on Chase when he's being a jackass.

"You'd do well not to joke about things you don't understand, Chase," I reply, a warning quiet but clear in my voice.

Fear crosses Chase's handsome face.

Good.

"I'm sorry," he says, his Adam's apple bobbing with a deep swallow. "You weren't just an easy fuck to me."

"Whatever we were," I say, gentling my tone a little, hoping to get us back on even ground, "we're just friends now."

He tightens his man bun, his usual cocky grin a little shaky but still there. "You must admit, the sex was incredible."

He's feeling himself a little too much because I've had better, but things have been tense enough between us.

"It was good," I concede with an easy smile. "But our friendship is even better, so let's stay friends."

"If you change your mind…" He cups my face and traces my cheek with his thumb.

"I won't." I step away from his touch. "Let's go make sure JP doesn't ruin your shoot."

Chase watches me for a few extra seconds before yielding a fond smile, the smile of the laid-back boy I met when I first started at JPL, before sex made things complicated. He comes from wealth, from a family who indulged his every whim. That he actually applied himself long enough to become an excellent photographer is a miracle in itself. He's not a bad guy. Just spoiled. And entitled.

And getting on my last damn nerve.

"You've got a point," he finally says. "Letting JP loose on a shoot can be dangerous."

JP's on the phone, yelling and gesticulating, his thickly accented English booming through the industrial space with its rafters, floor-to-ceiling windows, and polished-concrete floors.

"What's wrong?" I whisper to him.

"The silk shipment," he snaps, irritation jerking his thin eyebrows together. "It's been misplaced."

I purse my lips against an *I told you so*, but he knows me too well.

"Don't you dare say it." His plump fingers riffle through his hair. "I'll handle this. You find *him*."

I don't have to ask who *him* is. I know my role here. I'm the carrot JP wants to dangle in front of a giant rabbit with the forearms to launch a thousand watches. I turn to go check on Kenan, JP's French screeching still ringing in my ears. My heart trips over itself at the thought of seeing him again.

When I round the corner, his back is to me. He's towering over Amanda, surrounded by three racks of men's clothes. Amanda's looking up at him like he's an ice cream cone she wants to lick until he drips down her hand. I watch from a distance for a moment, curious to see how he interacts with her.

"We could try this one," Amanda says, handing him a belt from a nearby rack. While he's threading the belt through the loops of his slacks, her hand disappears in front of him.

"Hey." One of his big hands is still on the belt, but the other reaches between them. "Don't do that."

The quiet that falls in the space is tense, filled with the censure of his deep voice. Though I can't see his face, his wide shoulders have tightened, and his posture is stiff.

"If I touched you like that," he says, the words sharp and stern, "it would be a lawsuit, right?"

"I thought—"

"It's obvious what you thought, and I get it. I'm just saying no."

"Am I not… Are you…" Amanda looks at a loss, her pretty face pinched and confused.

"I'm not interested. Touch my dick again, and I won't be this nice about it."

I slip around the corner out of sight, pressing my back to the wall and fighting a smile. Not many men in his position would turn down a chance with Amanda. He said she looked like his ex-wife. Maybe that's why he passed. I don't know, but I *do* know if I had walked up on him accepting Amanda's offer, I wouldn't be smiling.

I start whistling Bruno Mars's "Finesse" to signal that I'm coming. Hopefully it'll give Amanda some time to pick her face up off the floor.

When I round the corner again, her back is to me, and she's flicking through a rack of shirts. Kenan glances over his shoulder.

A smile breaks the scowl on his face. It steals my breath, not just the gorgeous contrast of white teeth against his skin, but the way he looks at me. It's unreservedly pleased, like maybe he was looking forward to seeing me as much as I found myself looking forward to seeing him.

"Hey," he says. "I was hoping you'd be here."

Beyond Kenan's shoulder, Amanda watches us with tight lips and resentful eyes. Her pride is hurt, but I don't give a damn. What she did was highly inappropriate despite the fact I know other men in Kenan's position have been receptive in the past.

"JP dragged me away from the studio." I slide my hands into the shallow pockets of my denim cutoffs, suddenly self-conscious of my dingy appearance under his scrutiny.

"I'm glad." He steps closer, and I have to tip my head back to maintain eye contact.

"Ahem," Amanda interjects pointedly. "We're finishing the first look, Lotus. What do you think?"

I examine the gray-silk shirt and dark slacks that mold the

muscled length of his legs. He's so beautifully made and on such a large scale, he'd be impressive in just about anything, but this shirt isn't my favorite.

"I'm not sure about the shirt." I study the racks to see if there's anything I like better.

"I hate this shirt," Kenan offers.

I glance up and roll my eyes but can't suppress a smirk. I walk over to one of the racks and flip through several pieces.

"I'm the stylist on set, Lotus," Amanda says. "I know what will look best under those lights and how it will translate to print."

"Okay." I don't look away from the rack in front of me. "You go tell JP you refused my help."

Everyone knows JP respects my opinion. If he were a teacher, I'd be his pet.

Amanda huffs and walks past me. "Well, good luck," she says sharply. "I'll meet you out there. See how well you do on your own."

"I'm sure I'll be fine," I answer absently, taking a mint-green shirt from the rack. "What do you think of this one?"

I direct the question to Kenan since Amada has apparently run and left her toys behind.

He steps into the space beside me and leans against a nearby wall, staring at my profile. "I think it's beautiful," he says, laughing when I send him a wry look. "The shirt, I mean, of course."

"Panda" by Desiigner starts thumping through the room's sound system.

"Is that for the shoot?" Kenan asks.

"Yeah, the photographer puts on music to make the model more comfortable," I reply, setting the shirt aside. "To feel more relaxed so we get better shots."

"This is not the music to make me feel more relaxed," he says. "And I doubt it'll get you better shots since I'll be rolling my eyes the whole time."

"You don't like this song?"

"You're using 'song' loosely to describe what this is." Disdain scrunches his handsome face. "I mean, what's he even saying?"

"Panda," I reply immediately.

"What else?" Kenan asks. "Mumble, mumble, mumble."

"Oh my God." I laugh. "You sound like somebody's granddaddy."

He stills and lifts one imperious brow. "And you sound like a millennial."

"I *am* a millennial," I fire back, thoroughly enjoying myself. "Aren't you?"

"Uh…barely. Technically, yes, but my mom calls me an old soul. I identify older, I think." He tilts his head, considering me through a veil of long, thick lashes. "How old do you think I am?"

"I don't know." I shrug. "Twenty-eight? Twenty-nine? A little older than August?"

He nods, assessing me. I know without makeup and with my hair in these two braids, I look about fifteen.

"And how old are you?" he asks.

"Twenty-five."

"Shit." He slips his hands into his pockets and frowns, biting one corner of his mouth. "I'm thirty-six."

"Oh."

"Yeah, oh," he says. "Eleven years."

"Does it really matter?" I grin and bite my thumbnail. "I mean, we *are* just friends."

After a few moments, he relinquishes an answering smile. "Right," he replies. "And friends don't let friends listen to crap music."

"Here we go." I put my hands on my hips and throw my head back. "Hit me with all your oldies but goodies."

"You little…" He chuckles and shakes his head. "Mumble rap is not music, Lotus."

"It totally is." I defend on principle more than because I actually like mumble rap. I just enjoy a good debate. "It's an emerging subgenre."

"Did you read that in *Vibe* magazine?"

"Who in hip-hop do you consider great?"

"I grew up during the renaissance of hip-hop. Take your pick. Biggie and Pac are given, so we won't even go there. Nas. Jay-Z, Rakim. I'll even give props to millennial rappers."

"From *my generation*, you mean?" I mock.

"You're having too much fun with this. Sure. From *your* generation. Kendrick. Lil Wayne. Drake."

"Do *not* say Kanye," I interject. "He's in the sunken place."

"I did see that on Twitter."

"Twitter?" I scratch my chin. "Hmmmm. I *think* I remember Twitter. The little blue bird?"

"So you're strictly Instagram, I assume? Thousands of people who have no idea who you are but who follow your perfectly filtered life? Little Snapchat birds flying around your head and shit?"

"Oh, you *are* old," I say with a pitying shake of my head. "And cynical with it, but Twitter *has* made a comeback."

"Don't get me started on social media."

"We'll save that for another day. Finish schooling me—or should I say *old schooling* me—on my ratchet music choices and how millennials are ruining the whole world."

"Not the whole world," he says, patting my head condescendingly. "Just most of it. Definitely music."

"We probably like some of the same music," I counter. "What's your favorite song to listen to when you want to unwind?"

"It never entered my mind."

"Well, let it enter your mind. Think about it and then tell me—"

"Lotus, stop," he says, squeezing his eyes closed. "Say you're joking."

"What? I'm asking which song you like to—"

"And I told you." He laughs and tugs on one of my braids. "'It Never Entered My Mind' by Miles Davis. It's my favorite song of all time."

"Wait." I run through my mental playlist. "Miles Davis the trumpet player?"

"So you *have* heard of him."

"Does that song even have words?"

"None you can hear, no."

"None that you can *hear*?" I cock a dubious brow. "Explain, old man."

"I'll let you get away with that just this once," he says with a wide smile. "That man speaks his soul through his trumpet. It's not words. It's emotion. Power. Passion. Pain. You don't have to hear one word to know what he's saying."

"I honestly don't think I've heard it before," I admit.

"That's a travesty," he replies, still holding one of my braids lightly in his grip. "I'll play it for you sometime."

"It's on Spotify, I assume?" I ask, pulling out my phone.

"No way." He grabs the phone and shoves it into my back pocket. His hand lingers at the curve of my ass through the thick denim, and our eyes lock. Hold. Heat.

"Sorry." He withdraws his hand from my pocket, leaving the phone behind and clearing his throat. "I want your first time hearing it to be on vinyl."

"Vinyl? And where am I going to find vinyl just lying around? Much less something to play it on?"

"At my place," he answers, his voice low and deep, his glance caressing my cheeks, dipping to touch my lips.

Any retort dies in my throat. My face is on fire, not from embarrassment but from the heat of his look. Of the answering fire it stokes in me. This man is so dangerous. He's the kind who could fool me into thinking I've had it all wrong. That the cycle I've seen from the women in my family is one I could break. That I could share more than my body and be rewarded with more than his in return.

"Michael Jackson," I blurt, needing to shatter the intimacy swirling between us like sweet smoke.

Kenan blinks once, twice, clearing some of the desire from his gaze. "Excuse me?"

"Michael Jackson's pretty universal," I reply quickly. "Millennials love his music. People your age do, too."

He laughs and shrugs, letting me defuse some of the sexual tension with the King of Pop.

"People my age." He inclines his head and leans back against the wall, arms folded and slightly bulging. "You might be right. What's your favorite Michael Jackson song?"

"There are so many." I bunch my brows, concentrating. "Maybe 'Man in the Mirror.' What about you?"

"I used to think it was 'Off the Wall,'" he says, recapturing the braid hovering at my shoulder and brushing the curled tip over my mouth, leaving my lips throbbing, aching. "But I think I have a new favorite."

"Oh, yeah?" I ask breathlessly. "What is it?"

In a flash of straight teeth and wicked humor, he has me hanging on his next words. Waiting to see what he'll say. How he'll fascinate me next.

"PYT."

Pretty Young Thing.

He dips to catch my eyes with his, just in case I miss the significance of the title. I don't. I get it. I get him. After talking to him for the last few minutes and looking under his hood, so to speak, I've found that he's a classic. They don't make them like him anymore, and if I don't change the subject, change the course of this conversation, I'll fool myself that we don't have to keep things simple and that we could be more than just friends, not just for the summer but for a long time to come. As long as I'd like.

"Okay," I say, switching gears without a clutch and pulling a tie off another of Amanda's racks. "I think that shirt could work really well with this tie."

He doesn't look at the tie I'm holding up but keeps his eyes fastened on me. He's not playing along. I've boxed myself into a corner with him. And the quarters are too tight. His scent. His warmth. His intelligence. His thoughtfulness. *He* is pressing in on me, overtaking my good intentions in all the ways I never thought a man could.

"Try this on," I say, blindly shoving the mint-green shirt at him.

When I look at him, he's already peeled one shirt off and is reaching for the one I chose. I didn't think this through. Didn't forecast that Kenan changing from one shirt into another would mean his naked chest. I lose my train of thought and all my chill. Besides my mouth dropping open at the sight of the sculpted terrain of his chest and abs, I give no other indication that he affects me. Taut, bronze skin stretches across his broad shoulders like supple canvas pulled over a frame, the foundation of a masterpiece. He's a big man. Not bulky, but instead chiseled to the specifications of a master sculptor: arms roped with muscles, biceps like rocks under skin glowing with health. The forearms Chase raved about are lined with veins and sinew. And I die for a great chest. I've never seen one more spectacular than Kenan's.

Two words.

Male. Nipples.

Jesus, my mouth is literally watering at the thought of tasting them, sucking them, licking them. And if that pectoral perfection weren't enough, the two columns of muscles, four each, are stacked over his lean stomach arrowing down to a narrow waist and hips. I can't look away. I lick my lips, imagining how he would feel under my mouth. How I'd lick around his nipples and drag my tongue down that shallow path bisecting his abdominal muscles. I'd slip that belt off and sink to my knees. Unzip those pants and take him out. God, hold him in my hands and then take him all the way to the back of my throat. I'd choke on him. A man this big... I'd be so tight around him.

"Lotus," Kenan says, jarring me from my torso trance. "Should I go ahead and put this shirt on? Or did you need a little more time?"

I snap a glance up to his face, embarrassed to find him laughing at me. Oh, God. I'm as bad as Amanda. I turn to leave, but he catches my elbow with a gentle hand and turns me back around, walking us behind two of the racks. He bends until he's almost eye level with me.

"Don't be embarrassed," he says, searching my face intently. "I'm glad you like my body."

"I didn't say I…" My words trail off at his knowing grin. "Okay. So you have a nice body. I work in fashion. Do you have any idea how many great bodies I see on a daily basis?"

"I'm sure many," he says, his smile still firmly in place. "I can't speak for any of them, only for the way you looked at me."

"And how do you think I looked at you?" I ask defensively, forcing myself not to look away.

In the quiet that follows, his smile fades, and heat replaces the humor in his eyes. "You looked at me the way I bet I've looked at you every time you walk into a room," he says, the timbre of his voice rolling over my sensitive skin like a caress. "Like I would eat you if I could. Head to toe, everything in between."

"Kenan," I protest, closing my eyes on a groan. "We said friends. We said simple. This is not how you start a simple friendship."

His large hand cups my jaw and lifts my chin. I open my eyes, blinking dazedly at him. I wasn't prepared for how his touch makes me feel. How I instantly crave more of it, want to lean into the warmth, to turn and trace his lifeline with my tongue. Tell him all the things I could discover just from reading his palm and looking into his eyes.

How can such a large hand feel so gentle, like it's capable of treasuring, cherishing?

"Okay, Lotus," he says, regret and reluctance woven around my name. "Simple. Friendship."

He withdraws his hand, and I want to seek it out again immediately. When I open my eyes, he's pulling on the shirt I chose, buttoning it with quick, deft movements. I'm frozen to the spot, unable to look away from the intensity of his stare. He grabs the tie and extends it to me.

"What's that for?" I ask dumbly.

"I suck at ties," he says, his full lips quirking at the corners, some of his humor returning.

"Oh."

I strain up to loop the tie behind his neck, and he bends so I can reach him more easily. He's so much taller, and I feel like a flower growing along a great wall. Dwarfed. Sheltered. By sheer will, I keep my hands steady while I finish tying the tie. When I'm almost done, he leans forward until his nose aligns with mine and he breathes in.

"From one friend to another," he says, his voice rough and husky, "you smell incredible."

When he pulls back to look into my eyes again, we get hung up—caught in a net of longing. I don't know this man, and he doesn't know me, but our bodies know. Our bodies already know, and it's taking everything in me not to lean up and forward so our lips meet—so I can taste him again. Our breaths mingle. My fingers curl into my palms with the effort required not to grab his jaw and take his mouth, make it mine. My heart clamors behind my ribs. The moment simmers with possibility.

"I could kiss you, Lo," he rasps. "But I won't."

His words snap whatever thread linked us, and I step back, clearing my throat and fixing my face.

"Good," I say, rolling up his shirtsleeves. "Because we did say a simple friendship, and that would complicate matters too much."

"I'll make you a deal," he says.

"I don't make deals with men I don't know." I even my voice out until it's almost normal.

He pauses, a slight smile hitting his lips before he goes on. "Okay, I'll make you a promise."

"Promises mean nothing from men I don't trust," I say with a shrug. "And men I don't know, I don't trust."

"Okay, I'll make a prediction." He lifts both brows and waits for my objection.

"Go on," I say with a nod.

"I predict we will kiss again," he says, and my wide eyes zip to his face. "But only when you want it. The next time we kiss, you'll make it happen."

"Don't hold your breath," I retort with borrowed confidence.

"Mark my words, little millennial."

"Lotus, you back here?" Chase calls from around the corner. He stops as soon as he sees me with Kenan, frowns, and runs a hand over the back of his neck. "JP's looking for you."

"Yeah, okay," I say hastily, speed walking around him.

"I'm ready for you," I hear Chase tell Kenan.

I'm glad one of us is.

JP has averted the crisis with the silk shipment and looks like a pleasant, reasonable man again. We're talking through a few things we'll probably work on when we get back to the office when Kenan walks in.

I chose well. The cool green pops against his skin. He's the portrait of rugged, beautiful masculinity, but once the shoot actually starts, it looks like we caught him in the middle of a root canal. None of the coaxing, coaching, and cajoling Chase typically uses to get the best out of a subject is working on Kenan.

I roll my hips to the heavy beat pouring through the speakers and wonder if this will be a waste of time because the compelling force of Kenan's personality doesn't translate.

The beat.

It's "Bad and Boujee" by Migos.

Mumble, mumble, mumble.

"Hey, JP," I whisper. "What do you think?"

"It's not…working," he says, panic in his voice. "And I need to know we have someone locked down for this. He's much stiffer than I thought he would be, but I still love those arms."

"Mind if I try something that might help him relax a little?"

"Is it sex?" He widens his eyes and squeezes my hand reassuringly. "I'll make everyone leave the room if you need privacy."

"No, it's not sex," I say, trying to sound appropriately outraged instead of hella turned on. "Let me try something."

"It can't hurt," JP says, watching as Kenan looks pained going through the poses and expressions Chase requests. I tiptoe over to the sound system and flip through what's available until I find a song that might work.

At the first notes of "PYT," the tension leaves Kenan's shoulders. The longer the song goes, the better he looks, the easier it seems to come to him.

"You're a miracle worker," JP says, delight all over his face as he watches Kenan. "He looks great, doesn't he?"

I hazard a glance at our subject, only to find him already watching me and smiling. I don't read lips, so it takes me a little bit to decipher the message he mouths to me, but I finally get it.

"Thanks, PYT."

CHAPTER 8
KENAN

So *THIS* IS AN ATELIER.

I step off the elevator and into the small entrance of JPL Maison. Just past the lobby, I enter a beehive. Women—a dozen shapes, sizes, colors—swarm through an open space stuffed with sewing machines and tables sporting large blades. Some cut fabric with surgical precision. The space, with its sterile white walls and neutral floors, is punctuated with vibrant pops of color from fabric in all kinds of patterns and textures. A forest of those headless, armless mannequin things huddles at the far end of the room. Tall bolts of fabric are propped up against the walls and fill the corners. Shelves suspended overhead are crammed with containers of buttons, zippers, hooks, and all kinds of things I've never needed to know the names for.

It's a beehive, and I'm looking for the queen.

"Kenan!" JP calls down from the floor above. "Up here!"

Found him.

The seamstresses' stares make me feel like the last male on the planet, but I ignore the curious looks and take the stairs to the next floor, where JP waits with a welcoming smile. His lips are coming at me, but I put up a hand.

"I don't do air kisses, JP."

"*Oui, oui.*" He laughs and waves me into a glass-walled conference room. "Come see the watches I have for you."

Another man, I think the CEO, if I remember correctly, sits at the long slate table. He and the redhead from the party, Billie, have their heads together and are deep in what looks to be an intense conversation.

"Paul," JP says, his eyes speculative on the couple. I assume they're a couple. There's something intimate about their interaction, but when Paul puts his hand forth to shake mine, I notice his wedding band. Billie's not wearing one. He and Bridget might have a lot in common. A flush rises on Billie's cheeks, and I remember seeing her with Lotus. They seemed friendly that night.

Lotus.

I promised myself if I didn't run into her, I wouldn't go looking, but once JP has shown me the prototypes he'd like me to wear during press conferences and other appearances, I know I'll at least try to find her before I go.

When we're done, JP and Paul remain in the conference room for their next meeting and ask Billie to walk me out.

"It's Billie, right?" I ask, addressing her directly for the first time as we descend the iron stairwell.

"Uh, yeah." She glances at me, her green eyes friendly but guarded.

"We met at the yacht party."

"I remember." Her gaze narrows, sharpens. "That was some kiss."

"It was," I agree with a stiff smile. I swallow my pride and ask the question burning a hole in my tongue. "So is Lotus in today?"

"She's working." With twitching lips, she presses the iPad to her chest. "But I think she had some errands to run."

Dammit. "I see."

I feel like a teenage boy standing at a locker asking some girl's friend if she likes me. I hadn't thought about Lotus's age until our conversation at the shoot. At twenty-five, I hadn't even been in the league five years. I was a new dad, a new husband. I don't even recognize that kid in myself anymore. I can't find him. To think of all I experienced in eleven years—Lotus still has all of that ahead of her.

Something about the way Billie's looking at me makes me wonder if Lotus has talked about us with her friends. Not that there's much of an "us" to discuss yet, but I still feel a certain protectiveness of the friendship we're cultivating. I don't get a gossip vibe from Lotus. I can't imagine her running to TMZ or selling her story to the tabloids, and there's really nothing to tell yet, but Dr. Packer warned us to be careful how Simone finds out about romantic interests.

"I could tell her you stopped by," Billie says, her voice almost conspiratorial, like we have a secret.

"Nah, but thanks." I smooth my expression over and walk ahead of her. By necessity, I got really good at masking my emotions and shutting everyone out. Every day, some reporter was digging in my trash, literally and figuratively. I can't have my life exposed that way again. I don't think Lotus would share my personal details, but look how badly I misjudged Bridget.

I'm almost at the door when I run into Lotus's other friend from the party, Yari.

"Hi," she says. "How ya doing?"

"Fine." I keep my voice curt. Not friendly.

"Were you looking for Lotus?" Her smile teases me, and again I wonder if I'm the butt of some joke everyone knows but me.

"No, I had a meeting with JP." I allow my irritation to show in my frown. "Gotta go."

I stalk off to the lobby, but the damn elevator is taking forever. It's one floor. There's no way I'm standing here for another minute when I could have been down the steps and gone by now. I take the stairs, and I'm rounding the second curve of the staircase leading to the first floor when something heavy pounds me in the chest and knocks me back into the stairwell wall.

"Shit," says a female voice, muffled behind a huge bolt of red fabric. "I'm so sorry."

When she props the fabric up against the wall, I see the woman behind the voice.

"Lotus?" I ask, thrown not just by the blow to my midsection but by the sight of her.

It's boiling hot outside today, and the faintest sheen of sweat coats her top lip and the curves at her temples. Her T-shirt is cut to fall just below her breasts. White-linen shorts sit low on her hips, exposing the firm plane of her stomach and the feminine muscles etched under her skin. A lotus flower tattoo blossoms around her belly button. The shorts are so tiny, they barely hit the tops of her thighs. Ink peeks out from beneath the cuffs, but it's mostly covered and I can't make out what it is.

Desire hits me harder than that bolt of fabric to my belly. I wish I could figure out how to stop wanting her. She's twenty-five years old. Too young for me. Too complicated. We said just friends, but I don't know if I can do that. I want to fuck her every time we're in the same room, and when we're not together, I'm thinking about it. I know we need to keep this simple. That's the smart thing to do, but I find myself not wanting to do the smart thing. I've been blind and stupid before. I can't afford to do that again.

"Sorry about that," she says, her smile open, sweet. "The elevator was taking too long, and I wanted to get this fabric up to the studio. I wasn't looking where I was going."

I wonder what's behind the pretty face. I don't want to question her honesty, her forthrightness, but I've been duped before. I gave a woman my trust, and she turned it on me like a loaded gun.

I don't return Lotus's smile, unsure if I should take steps back or move forward because either way, there may be something to lose. Her infectious grin disintegrates. Her mouth flattens into the line I saw before we started getting to know each other.

"I gotta go," I say abruptly, pushing off the wall and past her, determined to leave it at this and to leave her alone. I'm on my way down the stairs but can't resist one look back. Lotus still stands in the same spot, facing away from me, her back a stiff line, one arm around the bolt of cloth and a hand on her hip.

I'm a jackass.

I rush back to the landing above and stand behind her, looping an arm around her waist. She jerks against my hold, but I don't let go.

"Hey." I expel a long breath, stirring the curls arrowing wildly into my face. "I'm sorry."

She whirls around to face me, shaking my arm from her waist.

"For what? Acting like we don't know each other?" Anger snaps in her voice, but I hear the hurt. I put it there. "I don't think we've fucked yet, so it's a little odd that you're already treating me like yesterday's trash."

"I was abrupt. It's my fault, not yours."

"Oh, I know that," she says, her words as hot as the summer outside these air-conditioned walls. "But it's okay. You do you and I'll do me. Is that *simple* enough for you, *friend*?"

"Can I please explain?"

"No." She hugs the cloth and marches toward the next landing of stairs.

I take the bolt from under her arm and toss it against the wall. Grasping her wrists gently, conscious of the fine bones in my big hands, I lean against the wall and pull her to stand between my legs.

"I'm sorry." I push a clump of curls back, exposing the gold studs running along the whorl of her ear. "May I please explain that I'm a dumbass?"

She stills but doesn't pull away.

"I didn't have to come to the office today," I admit, my voice quiet in the privacy of the stairwell.

She flicks a look up at me from under her lashes, curious and cautious.

"JP mentioned prototypes of the watches, and I offered to come see them in person." I laugh at myself and shake my head. "I jumped at the chance to see you."

She fixes her stare on the floor between our feet. Her shoulders, held tight and high, slowly drop. She's listening. She's hearing me.

"Go on," she says, full lips pinching at the corners. "Dumbass."

Her spirit, her boldness make me smile. I don't like seeing her hurt, especially by me. If we don't have this conversation, these same doubts will resurface, and I'll inevitably hurt her again. She won't even know why. She deserves to know why.

"Tell me what you know about me, Lotus."

Both of her thick brows stretch up, and she blinks a few times.

"I know you're the center for the San Diego Waves," she says, her voice slightly uncertain.

"Power forward," I correct.

"Huh?" She tosses up a confused glance.

"You said I'm the center for the Waves, but I'm the power forward."

"Oh." She shrugs like it's all the same to her...which it probably is. "And I know you have the musical taste of a sixty-year-old man."

I laugh and fake a glare. "That's actually not too far off," I tell her, stroking the silky skin of her wrist. "My father loved jazz, and he passed that on to me."

"Is he a basketball player, too?"

"No." I shake my head and let out a harsh laugh. "He was a judge and wanted me to follow in his footsteps. He was disappointed when I was drafted."

"No way. Most fathers would be proud."

"Yeah, my dad wasn't exactly most fathers." I smile, reminiscing about the man who shaped me more than any other. "When I told him I was planning to enter the draft instead of going to law school, he said, 'A tall black man playing basketball. Wow, didn't see that coming.'"

She doesn't laugh like I expected her to. Instead she searches my face, looking for something. "Did that hurt?" she asks.

"Hurt? Hell no. My father and I were best friends. I may

have taken a different path than he expected, but he recognized that not many get the chance to play at this level—to make this kind of money. He came around and supported me. I don't have childhood trauma. No daddy issues, or mommy issues for that matter. My parents were married forty years. We were well off, well adjusted."

"Must be nice," she says, her expression, her voice wistful. "Especially the closeness you have with your dad."

"It *was* nice." Our eyes meet, hers filling with sympathy even before I clarify. "He passed away last year."

"I'm sorry, Kenan." She flips the wrists I'm holding so that her hands are holding mine and squeezes. I nod and squeeze back.

"He, uh…advised me against marrying my ex-wife, Bridget," I say, feeling out the best way to approach this subject. "Do you know much about my marriage? What have you heard?"

"Just that it's over. You told me that. Remember? I don't really follow basketball." She frowns. "Is there something I should know?"

When Bridget cheated with my teammate Cliff, it felt like the whole world knew, and yet I'm dreading telling this one woman the ugly facts.

"A simple Google search could tell you all the dirty details," I say, unable to keep the bitterness from my voice. "The shit I hate most would come up first."

"I haven't done a Google search on you," she says. "It didn't feel right." She looks embarrassed but has no idea how much she just pleased me.

"Don't google me. Anything you want to know, ask. I'll tell you everything. I'll tell you the truth."

"Okay." She pulls her hands free of mine and looks up at me boldly. "Then tell me why you acted that way when I bumped into you."

"Yeah, that's what I was getting around to," I say wryly.

She folds slim arms under her breasts and waits.

"My ex-wife cheated on me with one of my friends. With a teammate."

Shock rounds her full lips into an *O*, and her arms fall limply to her sides. "With your teammate," she repeats faintly.

"Yes, they were caught in a hotel. Turns out a reporter had been following them, so he had photographic evidence. All of which he released to the highest bidder. It was on TMZ, ESPN, all the blogs. Everyone knew."

"How could she?" Lotus asks, her brows drawn into an angry dip. "What'd she do when it came out?"

"Well, there was no denying it. The photographs were all the evidence needed." Displeasure twists my lips. "Not to mention the gracious friends and distant relatives who gave interviews and shared information."

"Oh, Kenan. I'm so sorry."

"It's okay. It's behind me now, but I…" I take her hands in mine again. "I told myself I'd never be made a fool of that way again. When I was in your office today, I felt foolish—like I was the butt of some joke. Like everyone knew how much I…"

My words fade, but we look at each other and know, even though we don't say it. We both know how much I like her. How much I want her.

"Anyway," I continue, "I started wondering. Has she been talking about us? Would she talk to the press, too?"

"What?" She releases an affronted gasp. "I would never do that."

"I believe you. I do," I reassure her. "It's just I have to be so careful who I let into my life because that affects my daughter. And she heard and knew too much too soon because our shit was every-where. She's my whole life, and I have to protect her."

If anything, the look on her face is intent, understanding. "She's very lucky to have someone who puts her first," Lotus says.

One side of my mouth kicks into a grin that mocks me. "I felt like a national joke, and today…I don't know. I let my thoughts run and started drawing parallels that weren't there. I took it out on you."

"I'm sorry, Kenan," she says, her expression pained, angry. "I hate that she did that to you. That people didn't support you like you deserve."

"No, I'm sorry. I guess I have some lingering trust issues. I judged you today by what's happened before."

I reach up and pull one springy curl, watching it snap back into place. "I'm sorry. You deserved to at least know why I was such a *dumbass.*"

She's quiet for a few moments, and I wonder if what I've told her either has scared her away or doesn't sufficiently excuse my asshole behavior earlier.

"There are things you should know, too," she finally says. "But I'm not ready to share them with you."

She looks up at me, and her eyes are filled with so much pain, I want to demand she tell me right fucking now who hurt her. I haven't known her long enough to feel this way—to feel like I should be the one shielding her—but I do. I admit only to myself that I already do.

"What *can* you tell me?" I ask.

"My mother wasn't like you. She never put me first." She meets my eyes, but they don't give away much. "I guess on some level I never got over it. I told you that I'm not doing sex right now. I don't have a problem with sex. I love it actually. Very much."

"That's good to know." We share a brief smile before hers disappears.

"It's not sharing my body with someone that's hard," she says ruefully. "It's trusting anyone with more than that. I've *never* done that. My problem is intimacy, and sex without it started to feel…bad. I can't describe it except to say it felt empty."

I'm quiet, hoping she'll continue if I stay out of her way—if I don't interrupt.

"You say you don't have childhood trauma." Her glance slides away to the side. "I do. I have a lot of that shit, and I'm realizing that never dealing with it is starting to haunt me. It's affecting me in ways I didn't think it would."

I know better than to press for specifics when she's already told me she's not ready to share, so I ask her the more important question. "So what are you going to do about it?"

She shrugs, and for maybe the first time since I've met her, Lotus looks truly helpless. I'm used to the unassailable confidence, the cocksure attitude. I don't hate seeing her unsure as much as I want her to know she can be unsure with me.

"I know it sounds clichéd," I tell her, "but talking to someone might help. We're seeing a therapist because my daughter's having a hard time accepting the divorce. It's for her, yes, but also for me."

My short, cynical laugh echoes in the stairwell. "Bridget and I never made it to counseling, but I'll be damned if I'm going to screw things up even more for my daughter than I have already."

"You didn't do anything wrong," Lotus protests.

"It doesn't matter that I didn't cheat. I'm Simone's father. I'm responsible for her. It's not about blame, right, or wrong. It's about making sure she's okay. If I'm not healthy, I can't be the best parent possible to her, so every week we're at counseling. And I hate every minute of it, having to hear my ex talk about her stupid choices and pretend she wants to put our daughter first when it's obvious she doesn't."

I shake my head and run a hand down my face. "I'm sorry. This is about you talking to someone, not why I have to."

"Iris has been telling me the same thing," she says with a grimace. "Lately I've been…well, I've been thinking maybe she's right."

I sense that if I press on this any more, I could push her away. I've said my piece. She has to make that choice for herself. I have a different choice to present to her.

"So, full disclosure, I admitted I wanted to see you today, but I didn't tell you I wanted to extend an invitation."

"An invitation?" One brow shoots up. "What kind of invitation?"

"I'm judging this dunking contest at Rucker Park Saturday, and I wondered if you'd like to come."

"Rucker Park? All the way in Harlem?"

"Um…you say it like it's Antarctica."

"I could pack lighter for Antarctica than for Harlem."

I laugh outright and take her hands again, pulling her closer and leaning down until our noses touch.

"Come on," I whisper. "We could have lunch after the contest and hang out."

The air grows viscous between us, and second by second the humor drains away, leaving whatever magnetic thing that has drawn me to her since the moment I saw her. Her lips part, and her breasts rise and fall with shallow breaths. The same desire that rises inside me at the sight of her, at the scent of her, at the promise of tasting her again, I see it in the look she angles up at me. Does she want to kiss me as badly as I want to kiss her?

"Remember what I told you," I say, so close the words brush our lips together for just a second. "The next time we kiss, you have to make it happen."

She steps back, putting some space between us, but it's only distance. Those few inches can't dispel the way we're connected, and soon I think we'll both have to stop ignoring it.

"I don't kiss my friends," she says, only half joking, her eyes sober.

"Good," I say with a smile. "Then when you kiss me, I'll know you want to be more than just my friend."

CHAPTER 9
LOTUS

I'M IN THE BACK ROOM WITH MY LAPTOP WORKING ON SPEC SHEETS when the Spanish Inquisition shows up.

Or rather the Dominican Inquisition.

"So have you talked to Kenan Ross?" Yari asks from the doorway, chewing on a stick of beef jerky. She loves that stuff.

I glance up, slightly exasperated. I'm sandwiched between two sewing machines to avoid the socialness in the office that sometimes distracts me.

Also because I don't want to talk to her about Kenan. Especially after my conversation with him in the stairwell. I haven't talked to Billie or Yari about Kenan because there wasn't much to report. Not anything concrete other than an attraction stronger than I've ever felt before. Otherwise, nothing to see here.

"Uh, we ran into each other on my way back from Mood Fabrics," I say, eyes never straying from my laptop screen.

"He was here looking for you," Billie says, appearing from behind Yari.

Great. Both of 'em.

"Was he?" I ask, all super casual.

"Yeah, girl," Yari says, coming all the way in and hopping up onto one of the dusty sewing tables. "But he was trying to play it off."

"Not with me, he wasn't," Billie chimes in, taking the table opposite Yari's. "Came right out and asked me where she was."

I split an irritated glance between the two of them. "Have you asked yourselves why someone who has a perfectly good office up on the *second* floor is working in a back room on the first?"

"Of course we asked ourselves that," Billie says sweetly. "And we deduced you wanted us to have some privacy so you could spill the tea."

"What tea?" I elevate one brow.

"Yeah, like, have you kissed him again?" Yari asks, gnawing on that damn jerky.

"Of course she hasn't," Billie chides. "She would have told us."

"No, *she* wouldn't," I reply, giving up on productivity and closing my laptop.

"Well, at least tell us how you're doing with the sex strike," Yari says. "We live together, and I don't even know what's going on with you."

"I've been busy." I rub tired eyes. "There's a little thing called Fashion Week coming, and we have a collection to produce, a show to plan. So, ya know, there's that."

"We have work, too," Billie says defensively. "But we wouldn't let that get in the way of the details."

"What details?" I ask cautiously.

"The dick ones," Yari says, looking at me like *why do I have to explain this?* "I mean, we know Chase has been trying again. Did he wear you down?"

"Or wear you out?" Billie flashes a wanton grin and pulls out a cigarette. "You girls don't mind if I smoke, do you?"

"Yes," Yari and I answer in unison.

"Whuh?" Billie asks, the word distorted by the cigarette dangling between her lips. "Where am I supposed to smoke? It's like the whole world has turned on nicotine."

"Because the whole world *has* turned on nicotine," I say. "Around the time we found out it kills you."

"But it's not fair." Billie pouts, still managing to suck on her cigarette like she'll get some of the effect even with it unlit. "I'm sure it's a violation of our civil rights."

"Please don't tell two women of color that not being able to freely smoke your cigarette is part of the struggle," Yari says.

"But the struggle *is* real," Billie insists. "And we smokers do have rights."

"Excuse me, White Girl Magic, but with all the shit wrong in the world," I say, having to suppress my laughter, "you're standing up for lung cancer? That's your soapbox?"

"We all have vices," Billie says, trying to sound earnest, but her lips are starting to twitch, too.

"Just don't blow your vice in my face." Yari chuckles. "But we're getting distracted from the matter at hand. Lo, how is celibacy treating you?"

"It's only been a few weeks."

"Yeah, but you can't go cold jerky," Yari says, chewing on her meat stick.

"I think you mean *cold turkey*," Billie corrects.

"I mean cold"—Yari mimes pushing the meat stick in and out of her mouth—"jerky."

"That's so bad," I say with distaste. "I've gone weeks without sex before, so I'm fine."

I don't mention that the only time I think about sex is around Kenan. They'd run with that, and justifiably so.

"Just promise that if you break your vow with Kenan Ross," Yari says, eyes closed and hands pressed together as if in prayer, "you'll tell us how big his dick is."

Billie snorts, and I roll my eyes.

"Not gonna happen," I mutter, opening my laptop again in the hope that they'll drop it.

"What won't happen? You and Kenan or you telling us about his dick?" Billie asks. "I mean, he's such a big man. Can you imagine if he had a little dick? That would be like a cosmic joke. A curse."

I'm totally silent. They don't even realize how badly they're trampling my nerves.

"And you know how much I love a big dick," Yari says.

"Yeah, remember that guy you slept with when you thought he *might* have an STD?" Billie asks, her face scrunched with disgust.

"One," Yari enumerates on her finger, "he wrapped it up really tight."

I snicker, because only Yari.

"And two," she says, a salacious grin painted on her lips, "he came back clean."

"You got lucky!" Billie says, pointing at her and giggling.

"I *sure* did. He was so fine," Yari agrees half-dreamily. "Now you know a man is fine when he has a gimpy dick and he can *still* get it. Okurrrr."

"Don't invoke Cardi B," I say with a grin.

"And remember that guy you messed around with that time, Lo?" Billie's peal of laugher sails from her mouth and fills the back room. "The seminary student?"

I comb my memory, and as soon as I recall the guy she means, I laugh too. Hard.

"Oh my God," I gasp, covering my mouth. "The one who said if I didn't go down on him, I was gonna miss my blessings!"

The three of us lose it, and my laptop, the spec sheets, the show—all of it is forgotten for a few minutes of cutting up with my girls. I didn't realize how much this residual hurt from my past has been weighing me down. Laughing with them, being silly even for just a few minutes, feels good.

When we sober, I glance at my phone, see the time, and grimace.

"Okay, for real," I tell them, opening my laptop again, "I need to finish this for JP."

"All right, it was good catching up," Billie says, standing. "But you're right. I have a report due to Paul by tomorrow morning."

Yari and I raise our brows to the same level of *don't get us started* but remain silent.

"Don't, you guys," Billie says, all humor evaporating from her expression. "Just leave it alone. I know you think he's not worth it."

"No," I counter, my voice quiet and sober. "I want you to see that *you* are worth it. Worth more than being some sidepiece for a man who would disrespect his wife, his kids, *and* you."

"Yeah, Bill," Yari says, shooting her a chiding glance. "You're on the wrong side of the 'Lemonade.' Do you *really* wanna be Becky with the good hair?"

"Don't look at me like that," Billie says.

"What?" Yari asks with a frown. "This is my resting Bey face."

Even Billie can't resist that, and we laugh again before they go. Once it's just me and the sewing machines for company, I replay the conversation with my girls and hear it as Kenan probably would. Frivolous. He said I am young. He's right. I've always felt mature for my age, like an old soul, but the things he's navigating—divorce, his daughter's well-being during the transition, family counseling— make me feel every year that separates us. All eleven of them. I need to be careful. I never want him to feel I've betrayed his trust. I don't want to talk about him with my friends, with the press, with anyone. And I hate what his wife did to him. How do you choose someone else over a man like Kenan?

We aren't in a relationship, but we're in a *something*, even if it's just a tug-of-war, resisting the pull of each other every time we're together. I know I'm not ready for intimacy, which is what I could have with Kenan. I think I knew that from the beginning, and that was why I ignored or rebuffed him each time we met. The rapport we have developed even in such a short time speaks of a connection I'm not sure I'm ready for. I'm not ready to see it manifested between our bodies—to see how deep it would be and what it would require.

The studio has gone quiet, the workroom emptied out, and there are just a few lights on upstairs when I finish the things I needed to accomplish today. It's dark, and I'm dreading my commute. I wish I could click my heels together and be home. I'm on the J train, head against the window, when my phone lights up with a text.

> Unknown: This is Kenan. I hate texting.
> Me: Um...Kenan who? And how did you get this number? Also, again, you sound like somebody's granddaddy.
> Unknown: Don't change the subject.
> Me: There's a subject?
> Unknown: SUBJECT: Saturday
> Me: Oh. You mean the trip to "Antarctica"?
> Unknown: Harlem's not that far. Come. It'll be fun.
> Me: Send me the deets and I'll see what I can do.
> Unknown: I also hate the word "deets" and all text talk abbreviations.
> Me: I'm sry. IDK. It's NBD. I'll BRB with more deets l8tr.
> Unknown: Real mature.
> Me: Such a grumpy old man!

Text bubbles appear and disappear. The J train keeps moving, depositing a few passengers at their stops while I wait, smile on my face, breath stalled, for Kenan's reply.

> Unknown: I am kind of grumpy with most people, but not with you.

Now it's my turn to let the digital bubbles float, to let my heart float, as I start and stop a few messages before hitting send.

> Me: Why aren't you grumpy with me?
> Unknown: For a million reasons I haven't figured out yet.

My heart performs a triplet in my chest, turning over once, twice, and again, the beat irregular as I read and reread what he wrote.

Me: Do you want to figure it out?
Unknown: I think yeah, very much...TBH. ;-)

My grin grows so wide, I'm probably displaying all my teeth. If this were a game, I'd be showing all my cards, but it's not a game. It's butterflies and emoticons and heart eyes. It's risk and emotion and *intimacy* and all the things a girl like me dreads. I've sworn off Prince Charmings, and the unresolved issues of my past keep intruding on the fairy tale. It's not a fairy tale.

It's real life.

Me: SUBJECT: Saturday. We'll see.

CHAPTER 10
LOTUS

"I'm so proud of you, Lo."

Iris's encouragement has me clutching the phone tight like it's my lifeline. Like she's my lifeline, which she has been to me and I have been to her since we were kids.

"I haven't done anything yet." My short laugh is as shaky as my insides.

"You're the strongest chick I know," Iris says. "And taking this step to get help doesn't make you weaker. It makes you stronger."

Would Iris still think I was strong if she knew I'd been standing in front of this Presbyterian church in Brooklyn for the last forty-five minutes? That the Thursday night meeting ends soon and I haven't worked up the nerve to go inside?

"Thanks," I reply faintly. I glance up the flight of concrete steps leading to the church entrance.

"Call me later to tell me how it went," Iris says. "I have a doctor's appointment, but I'll be available other than that."

I welcome discussing something besides my crazy. I've been genuinely concerned about Iris's pregnancy.

"Everything okay, Bo?" I ask, keeping my voice deliberately even and *un*concerned.

"Yeah, completely. The doctor says my pregnancy is boringly normal. This is a routine visit."

"September will be here before you know it."

"And I can't wait. August is obsessed with the baby."

"Of course he is." August is one of the good ones. One of the few men I would trust with my cousin and her daughter Sarai.

"He told me Kenan asked for your number." Iris lets the comment hang suspended.

"Hmmmm," I reply, finding a small smile despite the anxiety whirring in my belly. "So that's how he got it."

"Well, did he call?" Iris demands, excitement and hope all up in her voice.

"You and August are such matchmakers," I say, avoiding her question. One question will lead to another, and eventually she'll realize I've seen Kenan a few times and we've been…conversant. Hell, we've been kiss-versant.

"Did. He. Call?" Iris persists.

"Text," I reply, giving her just the tip of what she wants. "He invited me to the Rucker on Saturday."

"Rucker Park is like the mecca of playground basketball." I'm not impressed by the awe in Iris's voice. Unlike me, she loves the game.

"Uh-huh. Whatever. We'll see. I haven't decided to go yet."

There's silence on the other end for a few seconds, followed by Iris's big gasp. "Oh my gosh! He's the guy!"

"What?" I'm silently begging her not to put things together.

"The guy you told me about before! The one you said you like. Kenan's in New York for the summer. You and he—"

"Ooooh, girl, you're breaking up," I reply hastily. "Gotta go."

"Lo, I *will* need the details."

"Bye, Bo. Kiss Sarai for me," I say and disconnect.

Whatever is happening between Kenan and me is best left alone and not poked at or simpered over by well-meaning friends. It's our business. Not Iris's. Not Billie's or Yari's. Not JP's. That conviction goes beyond the concerns Kenan expressed to me today. It's me just wanting whatever happens with us to be…different from the conquests I've bragged about in the past. I'm not ready to be more than friends with Kenan at this stage, but it's already starting to feel special. None of the other guys felt special to me. Maybe because I've never let them.

Hearing Kenan talk about therapy yesterday, what it's meant to him and to his family—how he endures the sessions for his daughter and how much he loves her—nudged me over the edge to do this. I've never had the kind of protection and commitment I heard from him for her. I had the opposite. A "parts unknown" father and a mother who never put me first the way Kenan does Simone.

I climb the stairs.

Inside, the church is modest and filled with empty pews. A makeshift paper sign on the wall reads SUPPORT GROUP and sports a red arrow pointing down. I follow a string of arrows leading to the basement, my heart clamoring with every step. When I reach the basement, two women walk past me, headed upstairs. One is sniffling, and the other is wiping the corners of red-rimmed eyes.

Dammit.

I finally work up the nerve to come in, and it looks like I'm too late. Maybe subconsciously that's what I wanted.

"Can I help you?" a woman, maybe mid-thirties with brown hair and kind eyes, asks.

"Uh, no. I'm…"

I'm what? A coward?

"I'm just, uh, lost," I say, lying in church. "I thought the blood drive was down here."

"It's not until Saturday," she points out with a slight smile.

"Yeah. I realize that now. I'm gonna—"

"I thought you might be here for the support group," she interrupts while packing paper plates and cups, putting away cookies.

She pauses in cleaning when I don't respond immediately.

"I'm, well…like I said, I'm lost."

We stare at each other, exchanging truth with a look even as we skirt around it with our words.

"They were, too, when they first started coming." She points up the steps where the two ladies exited. "Lost, I mean. It really can help to talk about it, even to strangers who have their own stuff—stuff like yours. To pull it all apart—find the pieces that don't fit, toss them out, and get new and improved parts. Healthy parts."

"Yeah, okay." I turn to head back up the steps. "Well, good luck."

"Maybe it's good that you were late," she goes on as if I haven't already brushed her off and lied to her. "We could talk one-on-one your first time here."

"Maybe another time," I say, not even bothering to tell her she's mistaken. "Have a good night."

"You could tell me a little about yourself. A little bit of your story?" She pauses. "Or I could tell you a little of mine. It took me a long time to speak out, but now I do all the time. At first it was to help myself. Now it's to help other people."

"I'm happy for you, but I gotta get going." I point vaguely north, the direction of my apartment, one foot on the first step leading back up and away from this conversation. "I live just a few blocks away."

"For me it was my father," she says softly.

I glance over my shoulder and meet her eyes. It's not pain I see there but the strength Iris mistakenly attributed to me earlier. This woman has it.

"It was my father who hurt me," she says, and even though it's not much above a whisper, it reverberates in the basement like a gong. "Do you have any idea how long it took me to say that? To admit it?"

I turn from the steps and stare at her, waiting for more. Needing to know someone got past this and could maybe give me a blueprint to do the same.

"It has taken my whole life," she says, and I see some of the weariness in her eyes behind the strength. "For a long time, I didn't even remember. They say God doesn't put more on you than you can bear. Sometimes, neither does your mind. That's self-preservation. The mind says, oh, she's not ready for this and hides it from us."

She stacks the food and paper products neatly to the side on the table and sits in one of the chairs pulled into a small circle.

"But we can only hide or run for so long before the shit starts to show." She laughs lightly. "Pardon my French in church, but somehow I think God will excuse me. The things our minds do to protect us from unspeakable trauma may work for a long time, for years in some cases, and then one day they just stop working. We deal or don't. And if we don't…"

Her words carry a warning—an urging to choose *deal* instead of *don't*.

I remember huddling in Chase's shower sobbing after perfectly good sex. I see my body curled into a ball, fetal, at the base of a hand-drawn tree in my closet. I smell the hair burning, the smoke curling around my memories. My peace of mind, up in flames.

Are you leaking, Lo?

Drip. Drip. Drip.

"I don't know why now," I say, sudden and without any context, but she seems to understand. "I've been fine. For years, I've been fine."

"I was fine, too," she says. "I'm Marsha, by the way."

"Lotus," I offer.

"Nice to meet you, Lotus. I'm a survivor but also a licensed therapist. I run this support group for survivors of childhood sexual abuse," she says. "So what brought you here tonight?"

"I've been having some, uh…issues with sex. Things I've never dealt with before."

"That's not surprising. It's where the injury took place, so for many of us, for most of us, our sexuality is affected. It is the thing that was deeply violated."

"I thought I'd escaped all that. I've had sex for years and been okay. I mean, I put sex in a category, but I enjoyed it."

"What was this category?" she asks, eyeing me closely. "Articulate it for me."

"Sex was for my pleasure," I say, swallowing hard, my mouth suddenly dry. "Do you mind if I…" I wave my hand at a line of water bottles on the table.

"Sure." Marsha nods to one of the chairs in the small circle. "Have a seat, too."

I hesitate. We're talking, but I still feel like I could make my escape if I need to. Sitting down indicates we might be here for a while. And I'm not sure I want to be here much longer, but I grab a water and sit down. When I take the seat, Marsha smiles but does a decent job of hiding her satisfaction.

"So sex was for your pleasure," Marsha says, picking up where I left off. "Sounds good so far."

"It was." I laugh, but it holds no real humor. "I know a lot of survivors have trouble with sex, but I've always enjoyed it."

"Good for you, and yes, you're right. I, for example, didn't have my first orgasm until I was thirty-three."

My mouth is hanging open, and I know it's rude and insensitive, but damn. I can't imagine. "Not even…touching yourself?"

"Masturbation was a big part of my recovery," she says, her eyes never wavering while she shares such sensitive information. "I couldn't experience pleasure with someone else's hand. I had to feel safe with my own first."

She tilts her head and winks. "Don't worry. With a lot of therapy, hard work, and a very patient partner, things are much better in that department now," she says. "A lot of relationships don't survive the recovery process because we need so much control and our partners can't take it. Control related to our triggers, to the effects of our trauma. Sex requires a lot of trust. We forget how much sometimes— forget the magnitude of sharing ourselves that way."

"I never had trouble trusting someone else with my body," I say, frowning, wondering if something is wrong with me, with the way

I processed everything. "But I could never trust them with anything else. No real…intimacy, I guess. I made sure they knew it was just sex. I've never allowed myself to feel anything else, but lately that hasn't been satisfying."

"Part of healthy sexuality is knowing you are lovable and worthy even if you *don't* offer yourself sexually," Marsha says. "There can't be real intimacy without some love or affection. If you blocked those completely, sex may have started to feel…transactional or purely a physical release."

Marsha offers a one-sided grin. "If we have some time together, I'm sure we can dig around and figure out what you've done to survive. That's all any of us do. We find ways to regain or at least to *feel* that we regain the control that was taken from us. We were helpless and are constantly looking for ways to make sure we're not in that position again. Some people become hypersexual. Some can't have sex at all."

"I decided to take a break from sex," I say, "and I haven't really missed it." Kenan's face, his voice, his scent all invade my imagination, my memory.

"That's common, too," Marsha says, nodding. "It's not unusual at all to have a season of celibacy while you sort things out. It sounds like you've been listening to yourself closely and your instincts are guiding you well."

I am more self-aware than many. I know that is a result of how MiMi raised me—how she taught me to tune in to things I can't see with my natural eyes. Even my own pain.

"It's fine if sex is sometimes just a release," Marsha continues. "Many survivors have sex but detach emotionally because such an early sexual experience was associated with abandonment or some trauma. Detaching emotionally is a protective measure. It could be a defense mechanism because you're afraid to trust someone with much else, especially if you've been betrayed by someone you should have been able to trust, like a family member or…whomever."

I weigh my next words. They're queued up on my tongue and sit there so long I'm not sure I'll ever be able to push them out.

"It was my mom's boyfriend," I force myself to say.

"I'm sorry, Lotus," she says so kindly.

"Yeah. Um, thanks."

That's all I want to say for now. I think I'm hitting a wall, and having said it out loud, I don't want to be in the same room as those words. I stand and toss my half-full water bottle in the recycle bin.

"I'm gonna go," I say in a rush. "I need to…to go."

"Of course." Marsha stands and reaches for her purse, extracting a business card and offering it to me. "We meet every Thursday evening. Same Bat-time, same Bat-place, and my information is there if you ever want to talk some more."

I stare at the card for a few seconds before accepting it and looking up to find her eyes still on me. "Thanks."

I start back toward the steps and pause when a thought strikes me. "Marsha, can I ask you a question?"

"Anything," she says, and I can tell she means it.

"I guess when you're in a season like this, it's a bad time to start a relationship, huh?"

I can't even believe I asked, but what's happening between Kenan and me is becoming irresistible. When I finally do give in, I want to know how to cause as little damage as possible.

"It depends," Marsha says. "Sometimes we hold so tightly to the hurt from the past that we miss the happiness ahead, and if there is one thing we deserve, Lotus, it's happiness wherever we can find it."

I nod, letting that sink in.

"It would require a patient partner," she goes on, her tone gentle, instructive. "Someone who doesn't mind if you lay down some rules, some guidelines, if those would help. Who won't force you to do anything you aren't ready for and who is fine with you controlling the pace."

"I see." I smile at Marsha and turn to go. "Thank you."

"I'd love to see you next Thursday if you want to come," Marsha says. "Or we could talk again, just the two of us."

I take the steps that will lead me back upstairs. I tell her the same thing I told Kenan.

"We'll see."

CHAPTER 11
KENAN

THE SUMMER OF MY ROOKIE SEASON, I CAME TO HARLEM FOR THE pro league tournament at Rucker Park, the most famous basketball court in the world. If you want street cred, you earn it here. It's your pilgrimage to Mecca.

On the surface, it's unassuming. There's no glamour to the outdoor court with two hoops and five rows of bleachers, but legends were made here. Dr. J got his *name* here before anyone really even knew who he was. The summer he played, people crowded the rooftop of the school across the street, climbed and watched from trees, and pressed their noses to the fence for a glimpse of this kid who flew through the air with unparalleled grace and rocked the rim with more force than they'd ever seen. It was the crowds at the Rucker who first chanted "Dr. J." They christened him, and it stuck. He played for Philadelphia, my hometown, and he changed the game. So every time I come to the Rucker, it's special, but today I feel the excitement even more.

And it has nothing to do with the dunking contest I'm here to judge for charity.

With the contest over, the other celebrity judges and I have taken photos with the winners, and now the autographs have begun. The whole time I'm signing hats, slips of paper, shoes, and whatever else people have, I'm scanning the crowd for one woman. Lotus never texted me back, so I don't even know if she's coming. Chances are she's not, but that doesn't stop me from checking compulsively every few minutes.

"How you liking New York, Glad?" Ben Mason, a point guard who came into the NBA the same year I did, asks. We're signing autographs back-to-back, encircled by a crowd of kids.

"It's okay." I smile at a little girl who hands me a T-shirt to sign. "My kid lives here now, so I'm glad to have some of the off-season with her."

"I did hear Bridget was moving to New York," Ben says. "She's on that new basketball wives' reality show, right?"

Ben, like everyone else in the sports world, knows my business almost before I do.

"Yeah, she's here," I mutter.

"Did your divorce finally come through?"

"Yeah, it's quits. Thank God."

"Man, she did you dirty."

Really, Ben? Sure, why not chat about my most painful, humiliating experiences while signing autographs for a hundred eager kids? Perfect timing.

"It's behind us now," I say aloud instead. "We're just trying to figure out how to co-parent my daughter well."

"You're a better man than me," Ben continues. "If that had been me—"

"But it wasn't." I turn around to face him, not even trying to hide my irritation anymore.

"Sorry, Glad," Ben rushes to say. "Man, I'm tripping. I know that was a tough time. I didn't mean to bring it up."

"And yet you're *still* talking." I turn back around and resume signing items and taking photos with fans.

My frustration isn't actually about him, though. I'm disappointed Lotus didn't show. I hadn't admitted to myself how much I'd hoped she would. I did act like an asshole in the stairwell. I thought I fixed it, but maybe not.

"Over here, Glad!" a kid yells, holding up his phone to take a picture. When I look in his direction, a flash of color catches my eye. A small gap in the crowd reveals silk the color of butter spread on sun-toasted skin. A woman wears a backless yellow jumper that clings to her ass. What looks like an intricate zipper with tiny flowers instead of teeth is tattooed up her naked spine. A huge cloud of golden-brown hair with curls and waves on the loose fans out and around her neck and the curve of her shoulders.

"Lotus?"

It comes out as a question, but I know it's her. I'm not the only one noticing every detail of her appearance. The crowd parts like the Red Sea and heads turn as she walks through. She seems oblivious to the lust she's inspiring as she makes her way out of the dense crowd.

Away from me.

There are too many people separating us, and I'd have to rudely push through a lot of teenage bodies fast to catch her at this point, but there's no way she's getting out of here without seeing me.

"Hey, PYT!" I yell through cupped hands in the direction I saw her take. She's so short, I can't even find the top of her head anymore.

For a second I think I've lost her, but that ray of sunshine she's wearing flaunts her presence again several yards away. She's turned to face me now, one hand on her hip and amusement on her face. I grin, fully prepared to be railed for calling her out.

"Where do you think you're going?" I ask loudly enough for her and anyone between us to hear.

"I'm *for sure* not standing around all day waiting for *you*," she yells back, her lips fighting the smile in her eyes.

"Well, you heard her, guys." I sign another hat and sigh. "I gotta shut it down. She's leaving me."

"I'd shut shit down, too, for *that*," a guy standing halfway between Lotus and me says, eyes crawling over every inch of her exposed skin. I want to get her out of here.

"Excuse me," I say, pushing through the crowd after I sign one last autograph. She could meet me halfway, but does she? No, just stands still in the crowd like a daffodil planted in the middle of a traffic jam, waiting for me to reach her. Once I do, I step as close as I possibly can without touching her so she has to tip her head all the way back to meet my eyes. Our gazes lock and don't let go. The steam rising between us has nothing to do with the ninety-five-degree weather. I draw a shallow, Lotus-scented breath.

"You're smelling me again?" she asks, a smile tilting the corners of her eyes like a sly cat.

I allow a twitch of my lips. "Where were you going? You were leaving without seeing me?"

"No." Our eyes hold for a second while I wait for her next words. "It's a lot of people. I was just gonna sit on the side."

"Oh, thanks for waiting."

I push her hair back from her face and trace the gold studs following the curve of her ear with my index finger. She shivers.

"You cold?" I ask, suppressing a smile.

She drops her lashes and hides her eyes. "Freezing."

One skinny strap of her jumper droops from the curve of her shoulder, baring her collarbone so I can read the script I couldn't make out the night of the yacht party.

"*You are altogether beautiful*," I read and pass my thumb along the script marking the fragile bone. "A little reminder in case we all forgot how pretty you are?"

Her smile flickers off and then back on. "My great-grandmother used to say it to me when I was a little girl. It's from the Song of Solomon."

I have twenty follow-up questions for everything I learn about this woman, and I can't ask any of them in this crowd. I reach for her hand and interlock our fingers, checking her expression for any objection. There is none.

"Let's get out of here," I say.

She nods and tightens her small fingers around mine. "Let's do it."

"You hungry?" I ask, and we walk in the direction of the lot where I left my car.

"I am."

"It'd be a shame if we came to Harlem and didn't eat at Sylvia's. Have you eaten there before?"

"You know, I haven't." She tosses me a grin. "But I'd like to."

The organizers kept our cars under watch during the event, so I retrieve my keys, and we walk over to the vehicle I bought last week.

"What *is* this?" Lotus asks, walking slowly around the shiny silver-gray chrome beast.

"It's Lamborghini's SUV, the Urus," I say, opening the passenger door for her. "You like it?"

"I guess." She shrugs like she rides in two-hundred-thousand-dollar vehicles every day. "I'm not really a car person. I take the train everywhere."

"A true New Yorker then." I check for traffic and pull out into the street.

"No, definitely not." She laughs. "But I've adapted."

"You're from New Orleans like Iris, right?"

She's quiet for a moment, and I glance over at her. Where she's from seems like an innocuous enough question, but a shadow passes over her face. "The first part of my childhood was in New Orleans. In the Ninth Ward, yeah," she confirms. "But then I went to live with MiMi on the bayou in this little parish where they spoke French more than English."

"You learned it?"

"Yeah, MiMi spoke French a lot, so I kinda had to pick it up. Came in handy with JP."

"You like working for him?"

"I do, but I know I'll do something else someday."

"Like what?"

"I'm not sure." She leans back into the luxurious leather seat. "I love my job, but I also have this podcast called gLO Up that's starting to get sponsors and gain a following. Or I might branch out with some specialty like lingerie or accessories. Who knows? I don't have to know everything about where I'm going tomorrow to enjoy today, so I just take it as it comes."

"I'm a planner," I tell her, negotiating the Harlem streets. "I always have things mapped out, and I usually follow that course meticulously."

"Sounds like you don't leave much room for the unexpected," she says, turning slightly in her seat to study me while I'm driving.

"That might be true, but when I do, I know it's the right thing. That it's worth going off-road for. I told you I knew I was going to law school and one day hoped to be a judge like my father. The NBA was the biggest reroute of my life, but I don't regret it."

Lotus is one of the most unexpected things I've encountered. The day she walked into that hospital room, I wasn't looking for anything with another woman. I was standing up to my neck in the mess Bridget had made of our lives and was ready to put every woman in the booty-call category indefinitely. It took the space of a heartbeat, a look, and I knew there was something different about Lotus. Off-road? Shit, I was rubbernecking to get another look at her. I was turning the wheel to circle back before I even realized it.

"I think I have what I like to call informed spontaneity," she says, pulling a knee to her chest.

"Okay, I'll bite. What the hell is that?"

"I have a great gut for the risks I should take. Like when I met JP. I was attending Spelman and was planning to finish my business degree and maybe one day do something with fashion. It was safer, but when JP asked me to come work for him in New York, I just knew it was right. I jumped."

She laughs and glances out the window to take in Harlem, history and hip spliced together, the iconic Apollo Theater sandwiched between Red Lobster and Banana Republic.

"Iris thought I was crazy," she continues, her words losing their levity. "We fought and didn't speak for a while. Not just because of that, but…"

She rubs the band on the ring finger of her left hand.

"Anyway." She shakes her head like she's casting off unpleasant memories. "It wasn't for very long. Nothing comes between us for long, not even each other."

"You and Iris have always been close?"

"Yeah," she says. "She's about a year older, and we're cousins but have always been more like sisters. I think of Sarai as my niece."

That reminds me of something odd and awkward I need to ask her. I can't *not* ask her about this, but I'll wait until we've parked and are settled in the restaurant.

"Mr. Ross," the Sylvia's hostess greets me warmly. "Welcome."

It used to disconcert me when people I didn't know already knew me.

"Hi." I smile, polite and to the point. "Got a table for two?"

"Of course." She bites her lip and glances up at me almost bashfully. I know this look. The *I reaaaaally want to ask for an autograph, but I won't* look.

She seats us in an out-of-the-way booth, for which I'm appreciative. I'm not one of those guys who can't leave the house without being mobbed, but my height makes people look twice. And on that second look, many of them recognize me. I don't want a lot of attention on my first date with Lotus.

Is this a date?

Are we still just friends?

Was it ever simple?

I decide not to define it but to just enjoy it. To enjoy her.

I stick to water, and Lotus orders one of Sylvia's signature Bloody Marys with Ketel One and triple-strength hot sauce. She takes a sip and hisses. "Ahhh. That's got a kick."

"What are you getting?" I ask, scanning the menu for anything that fits my regimen. My options are pretty limited.

"I thought about the chicken and waffles, but I think I'll get shrimp and grits." She sets the menu down, her smile a little wistful. "Maybe I'm missing home."

"You ate that a lot in Louisiana?"

"Yeah. I've never tasted it better than MiMi's. And her étouffée was delicious, too. Really everything she cooked was the best."

"New Orleans is a fascinating place," I say, thinking this might be a good segue into the awkward question I need to ask.

"There's no place like it." She gives me a sudden grin. "You'd love all the jazz. Have you ever seen the second line?"

"Second line?"

"Like the funeral marches with the jazz bands?"

"On television or whatever. Not in real life."

"In voodoo, they celebrate after death to please the spirits who protect the dead." She stares at me as if waiting for something, and for a moment I wonder if she already knows what I want to ask.

"Can I ask you something that might be a little"—I search for the right word, but for what I want to ask, I'm not sure there is one—"awkward?"

"More awkward than kissing me for the first time in front of all my friends at a party?"

An unrepentant grin kicks up one side of my mouth. "About the same level of awkward."

"Oh, okay. Then go for it."

I reach across the table and take her hand. Her glance bounces from our linked hands to my face and back again.

"I get these, I think." I touch the three fingers adorned with tattoos of the moon in various phases and then caress the band on her ring finger. "But I wanted to ask about this."

Her fingers clench in my hand, and the look she slants up at me is sharp, alert. She doesn't voice permission but nods for me to go on.

"You remember when we saw each other a few months ago at

that Christmas party?" I ask. "You were with Iris and August and brought Chase with you."

I hate even mentioning that guy's name, but he said something that leads to my question.

"I remember," she replies, her eyes steady on my face.

"You gave Sarai a ring you made that resembled this one and the one Iris wears. What's their significance?"

She watches me for a few seconds without speaking, probably suspecting that my follow-up question is even more awkward. "My great-grandmother MiMi," she says. "She made one for me and one for Iris. It's a gris-gris ring, like a talisman for protection. I never take it off."

"Okay, and that night Chase said it was somehow connected to voodoo?" I leave the question open-ended for her to explain as much as she's willing to share.

"Chase always runs his mouth about things he needs to be quiet on," she replies, stirring a straw in her Bloody Mary. "Gris-gris is a voodoo practice. Amulets and jewelry that invoke protection for the people who wear them. MiMi made them, along with potions and herbs and other things to help people when they had problems."

I frown, trying to assimilate the information into something that makes sense. "So she was…" I clear my throat, not sure if I want to hear her answer. "What did she do? What was she?"

"She was a voodoo priestess, Kenan."

Lotus may as well have said her great-grandmother was an alien who immigrated from Neptune. I wait for her to say she's joking. *Gotcha. Psych.*

"Lotus, what does that even mean?"

She looks at me unblinkingly. "Many of the women in my family practiced voodoo."

"You mean like during slavery or—"

"MiMi was the last one who practiced, and she only passed away two years ago. That was her livelihood."

My smile dies off. I'm not sure how to approach this. Lotus looks perfectly serious. "Do *you* practice voodoo?"

"*Practice* is a strong word."

"Uh, no. *Voodoo* is a strong word. I mean, do you actually believe in it?"

She doesn't answer for a few moments but twirls a stalk of celery in her drink.

"I decided that wasn't my path," she says. "I am who I am, Kenan. I can't change my blood. There will always be things in my life I can't explain to other people."

Her lashes raise to reveal the pride in her eyes. "I feel no need to explain them. I don't hurt anyone, and I help when I can."

The server comes to take our orders, but that interruption doesn't dispel the tension my question introduced, and as soon as she leaves, we resume our fascinating, if slightly odd, discussion.

I search her expression for some clue to this lovely enigma. "So do you believe in spells and potions and stick-pin dolls and—"

"I believe we don't know everything," she cuts in. "And I believe there are forces at work bigger than me."

"Forces at work? Lotus, I know you grew up with these…superstitions, but—"

"These superstitions, as you call them, have roots going back to Africa, to Haiti, to people who had nothing to depend on but their faith, whatever form that assumed. That was part of how they survived."

"Exactly," I say. "Religion is a cultural coping mechanism. They had nothing to depend on, so they made these constructs to give them something they believed could save them—could improve their lives or guarantee something better when they died."

Her full lips tighten and then loosen into a tiny smile.

"You don't believe in an afterlife?" she asks.

"I believe in now. It's the only thing I can see and prove. It's rational."

"One man's rational is another man's cowardice."

"You think I'm a coward because I'm not religious?"

"No, but I think faith, real faith, requires bravery. With every prayer, we risk heartbreak."

"So prayer *and* voodoo?" I ask. "How's that work?"

"People would come see MiMi with their Bibles in one hand and leave with one of her potions in the other. Voodoo and religion grew up together in Louisiana like kissing cousins, whether it was the Baptists or the Catholics." She laughs, resting her chin in her hand. "MiMi started and ended every session with prayer."

"Session?" I rub the back of my neck, not even sure I want to know but asking anyway. "What happened in those sessions?"

Her expression shutters.

"MiMi was the most important person in my life," she says, her voice stiff and starched. "I won't expose her to mockery. I want to keep liking you, and I'm not sure I could if you thought of her as foolish or said the wrong thing."

"Hey." I put my hand over hers. "I don't mean to insult your great-grandmother or your mother or—"

"MiMi was the last. My mother didn't practice." She looks away and toward the door. "Neither did her sister, Iris's mother. Neither did our grandmother." Her lips thin and twist with cynicism. "Now *they* were the ones who really knew how to cast a spell on a man."

I want to ask, to probe, but Lotus said before there were things she didn't want to share yet.

"I just need to know you're not making dolls of me and sticking needles in them or something," I say to lighten the atmosphere.

A smile dispels her sober expression. "I save the dolls for the really bad guys."

"I'm not sure if I should laugh, feel reassured, or run for the hills."

"There's the door." She tilts her head toward the entrance. "If you want to run."

I drag a glance over her wild hair and sultry eyes, the high, full breasts straining against the sunshine silk, and the lips that beg to be kissed.

"I'll take my chances," I finally reply.

She doesn't answer, but the knowing look she gives me all but says *that's what I thought.* The server brings our food, giving me the chance to shift the topic to less dangerous ground.

"That looks good." I point my fork at her shrimp and grits.

"So does yours."

I ordered a veggie plate of black-eyed peas, collard greens, and macaroni and cheese.

"You don't eat meat?" she asks, scooping the shrimp and grits into her mouth.

"I don't eat fried meat generally," I clarify. "And that seems to be their favorite thing here."

"Well, it *is* soul food," she says with a laugh. "What'd you expect? Why'd we come here if you don't eat this stuff?"

"I thought you'd like it, and Sylvia's is one of those things you should do when you're in Harlem."

"I'll have to take you around Brooklyn some time. You can never do everything in New York. And summers here are my favorite."

"I'd love to see Brooklyn. I have to go to Philly next week to check on some business interests. Maybe when I get back?"

"Maybe. I wouldn't want you to think I'm trying to change the conditions of our"—the look she sends me is half-teasing, half-earnest—"friendship."

"Friends do things together."

"Mmmm" is her only answer, accompanied by a smile. "So what's so special about the Rucker?"

I go with *her* change to a safer subject.

"It's a proving ground," I answer. "All the greats go there at some point, some of them playing against local guys who never made it to the NBA but are as talented as the professionals. If making it was purely based on talent, I certainly wouldn't be in the NBA. It's hard work. Staying out of trouble. Understanding the system and working inside it."

"Who are some of your favorite players?"

"The Big O, for sure."

"I'm a fan of the Big O myself," she says with a straight face and teasing eyes.

It takes me a second to put that together, and visions of Lotus mid-orgasm make me choke on my black-eyed peas.

"Very funny," I say, coughing and sipping my water. "But I meant the *other* Big O, as in Oscar Robertson, the first NBA player to average a triple-double."

"I'm sure he's great, too." She shrugs, and that damn strap falls away from her shoulder.

"Why the Song of Solomon?" I ask, nodding to the script tattoo on her collarbone.

"It was MiMi's favorite. She was a romantic at heart, and the Song of Solomon is one of the most romantic pieces ever written, in the Bible or otherwise."

"I never think of voodoo and conventional religion coexisting, but seems like MiMi figured it out."

"She wasn't religious, but she cobbled together her own faith in a way." Lotus takes a sip of her drink before going on. "I make the distinction because I think religion, when abused, has been one of the most destructive forces in this world. Religion killed Jesus. Religion led to the Spanish Inquisition and the Salem witch trials. People conveniently organize their beliefs around their agendas. Taking money, starting wars, segregating, lynching—all of it had some scripture, some tenet twisted around to fit hate. *True* faith is about relationship."

I push aside an empty bowl. "How do you figure?"

"First of all, relationship between you and God. Higher power, whatever you call it. Something bigger than you," she says. "And second, relationship between people. The Bible says *true* religion is taking care of widows and those who can't care for themselves—the most vulnerable."

"I get that."

"But religion, as it's tossed around now, has so little compassion. So little humanity, and faith is first human."

She pushes the last of the grits aside and rests her elbows on the table, her chin in her hands.

"It's us admitting to the universe we don't have all the answers. Too often religion says yes, I *do* have all the answers, and if you don't like them, you can't sit at my table. So we have all these tables. Too many tables and not enough love."

"You sound like you've experienced this firsthand," I say.

"I did, growing up." She nods, sadness, memories, *something* darkening her eyes. "Faith should give hope, not take it away. Church people wouldn't allow MiMi to worship with them. They called her a witch."

"Was she?"

"She was an old woman who wanted to celebrate her faith with her community." Lotus shrugs philosophically. "She couldn't sit at their table, so she made her own. Every Sunday morning, we'd sing hymns on the back porch. She'd pull out her little Bible and read to me. That thing was falling apart, pages hanging out. She kept it by her bed and read it every night."

"And that's how you got into the Song of Solomon?"

"It became my favorite, yeah. You ever read it?"

"We weren't exactly religious. My father was a judge. Elected official, so we went to church whenever he was running for office. I know some Sunday school basics, but beyond that, no."

"I think a lot of people just want to feel like there's something else. Something beyond what life seems to be," she says, running a fingertip around the rim of her glass.

"And you believe there is more than what life seems to be?"

"You know how scientists say we only use, like, 10 percent of our brains?" she asks.

"Scientists don't say that," I correct. "It's a myth, and it's been debunked."

"Are you always this much fun?"

My own quick laugh takes me by surprise. "You were about to make a point using your fake news. Don't let me spoil all your fun with, you know, actual facts."

"Well, the point I was *trying* to make before you butted in with all your facts and shit," she says, rolling her eyes and then grinning, "is I think we only use a portion of this world—that we miss a lot of the things that are right in front of us and we miss a lot of things we can't see but never sit still long enough to recognize."

"Are you sure you're only twenty-five? Now it doesn't even feel right to call you PYT."

Our chuckles and laughing eyes meet over the table. I block out the other diners, the clang of dishes, and the murmur of conversation. I focus on any bread crumbs she might drop that could help me understand what shaped her.

"So should I call you Glad?" she asks cheekily.

"What? Hell no."

"But I heard people calling you that today at the park."

"Yeah, but it's just teammates, media." I shake my head. "Some sports reporter said I was a warrior in the paint and that evolved to Gladiator, and a lot of people shorten it to Glad."

"Everyone calls me Lo."

"I think I'll call you Button," I say teasingly. "I mean, considering that's what lead to our first kiss."

I can't know if a blush lurks under her copper-tinted cheeks, but her lashes sweep down, and her pretty mouth curls at the corners.

"As in cute as a button?" she asks. "I'm already height challenged."

"In the real world, we call that short."

"At least I can walk into a restaurant without squatting."

"You got me there," I concede, chuckling. "Okay. How about if I only call you Button when it's just the two of us? It'll be our thing."

"Do friends have 'things'?" The look she levels over the rim of her glass asks a dozen other questions I want to answer.

"I think we're the kind of friends who do what we want."

Her brows arch, speculation in the mysterious dark eyes. "Oh, are we?"

This conversation has only deepened my attraction to Lotus, and I have no intention of turning back now.

"We will be," I affirm, holding her stare.

If we're two friends who do what we want, I know what I want. And the more I discover about Lotus, the less simple it seems.

CHAPTER 12
KENAN

THERE'S NO PLACE LIKE HOME.

Being here in Philly brings back so many memories, most of them connected to my dad. His markings on the wall for Kenya and me as we shot past our father and mother in height. Him reading his Sunday paper in the bright kitchen of our Society Hill townhouse. His sigh, half weariness, half relief, when he'd walk through the front door after a long day in court. I feel his presence and hear his voice in every room.

Simone and I are unloading the groceries we bought from Whole Foods. Since my mother had sprained her ankle and stayed home while we shopped, it was good to have time alone with my daughter. Simone opens the cabinet to the left of the stove to put away salt, pepper, and oregano.

"Spices to the right, Moni," Mama says, glancing up from her crossword puzzle.

"Sorry, Grandma." Simone smiles at my mom and moves to the other side. "Daddy, can we go to Geno's?"

Her eyes brighten with rare excitement and possibly hunger for the famous cheesesteaks.

"Sure. We'll swing by after we check on Faded with Uncle Lucius. Sound good?"

She nods and presses in to me, batting the longest lashes

known to man, or at least known to this man. "And Federal Donuts, too?"

"Cheesesteaks *and* Federal?" *My arteries just wept.*

"Where else can I get fried chicken *and* donuts together?" she asks, like that's a logical rationale. "We have to hit Federal while we're here."

"Kenan, now you know you did Federal for breakfast and Geno's for lunch growing up," Mama says, her smile wider than I've seen it in a long time. "He might eat all strict and vegan now, Moni, but believe me when I tell you he didn't always."

She's right. Lucius and I ate and screwed our way through the city back in the day. Neither of my favorite ladies needs to know about the trail of condoms I left behind.

"Mama, I told you I'm not vegan." To my mother, you're either eating cheesesteaks and donuts or you're vegan. Apparently, there's no middle ground. "Moni, let's do cheesesteaks today and Federal tomorrow," I suggest. "Sound good?"

"Yes." She nods, and an eager light enters her blue eyes. "And maybe some shopping."

My gut clenches. I gulp.

"Shopping?" I ask, trying disguise my trepidation.

"Daddy, please." Simone presses her hands together and pushes her bottom lip out. "Maybe Forever 21 and Gap, and I think there's a J.Crew at the—"

"Okay." I massage the subtle throb that has started in my temple. "*Some* shopping. And I thought we could catch the outdoor movie at the Oval."

"Eeeeek!" She throws her arms around my neck. "I'm gonna go change clothes."

She practically skips toward the kitchen door.

"Erin Simone Ross," Mama says, using my daughter's full name and never lifting her eyes from the crossword puzzle. "Get back in here and finish putting those groceries away."

Simone stops in her tracks and turns toward us with a sheepish grin.

"Yes, ma'am," she says.

She chatters about shopping and donuts and dance class for the next few minutes while we put away the last of the groceries. I'm glad I brought her to Philly with me. Not only because we needed time alone out from under Bridget's shadow, but because I think it's done my mother good seeing her. And Simone has seemed happier, too.

How different would things have been if I hadn't traveled so much, hadn't spent so much time away from my daughter? There's never been a time since she was born when I wasn't playing ball nine months of every year.

"Done," Simone announces triumphantly. "Now can I go change?"

"Yeah." I love-swipe her face. "Your uncle Lucius will be here soon, so hurry up."

She's gone in a flash of coltish legs and a mop of wild hair.

"Thanks for bringing Simone to see me," Mama says once we're alone in the kitchen.

"Sorry it's been a while. It was hard to get away." I join her at the table. "And it's tough for me to be here sometimes because it makes me miss Dad. You thought any more about selling?"

"Why would I? Him being gone is what makes me miss him," she says, turning the ink pen in her hands. "Doesn't matter where I sleep at night. What matters is he's not beside me when I wake up."

Her mouth turns down at the corners, and she blinks several times. I hate that I said anything. It's been more than a year, and Kenya and I keep trying to help her work through the grief, but sometimes I think she wants it. Like if all she has left of my father is grief, she'll take it.

She's a small woman in a family of giants. My father was six five.

My sister, six three. Me, six seven, almost six eight. My mother is five five in her socks. And she still has about an inch on Lotus.

Thinking of Lotus challenging me in the middle of Rucker Park makes me smile. *She* makes me smile.

"So how's Bridget?" My mother's tone cools noticeably. She didn't see through Bridget like my father did. She embraced her as a daughter and loved her from the beginning. In spite of Dad's years of behooving, Mom was shocked and hurt when news of Bridget's infidelity broke.

"Bridget is Bridget." I sigh, wrapping my hands around the tiny teacup Mama set in front of me. She loves her tea even when it's ninety degrees outside. "This new reality show she's doing… I don't even want to talk about it."

"She still thinks the two of you will get back together?"

I laugh, the sound hard and humorless in the kitchen. "If she does, she'll be sorely disappointed."

"She should find someone who will love her the way she's looking for," Mama says decisively.

"Are you saying I didn't?"

Mama tilts her head in a way I recognize in myself, assessing and weighing her words. "I think she had a harder road than she expected, being married to you."

"Wow, thanks. It almost sounds like you think she was justified in cheating on me."

"No," Mama says firmly. "Never."

"But you do think I didn't love her enough?" I ask with a frown.

"I think your father saw something I didn't see. You and he are so much alike." She twists her lips into a bitter smile. "*Were* so much alike. He was like you before we met."

"How do you mean?"

"Hard to know. Not prone to open up. Men like you have to be pried open slowly, and Bridget tried to crack you like a nut. For the woman you love, though, really love, it's not hard work. I didn't have to crack your father. Didn't have to pry. He spilled himself with me." She shrugs and shakes her head. "I don't know why, really. I didn't do anything special."

"No, but you *were* someone special. It wasn't what you did. It's who you are."

I get that. I feel that with Lotus. It's too early to think that way, but it's hard not to draw the comparison.

"It's not too late for you to find that, Son." Mama reaches across the table and squeezes my hand. "You or Kenya, if she would sit herself down long enough."

I grin at that and walk my cup over to the sink to dump the untouched tea. "She said she has someone for me to meet when she comes to New York, so all's not lost on that front."

"I might get grandbabies yet!" She claps her hands and cackles.

"Excuse me, what's Simone? Chopped liver?"

"One?" she demands, eyes wide but sparkling with humor I haven't seen much lately. "I need at least a spare, since you don't have any prospects."

"Who said I don't have any prospects?" I mutter, grinning and braced for her third degree.

"Kenan Admiral Ross, what are you not telling me?"

"I'm not holding out...not really." I lean against the sink and cross my arms over my chest. "There is this...uh, girl I like talking to."

"*You* like *talking?*" Incredulity lifts Mama's brows. "Go on."

"She's so different from me. She's outgoing and vivacious and the life of the party." I laugh and shove my hands into the pockets of my jeans. "But she's also thoughtful and sensitive. Superstitious."

"Where are her people from?" Mama asks semi-haughtily.

"Her people, as you call them, are from New Orleans, but she went to Spelman and lived in Atlanta before she moved to New York."

"Excellent school."

I don't bother telling her Lotus dropped out to pursue fashion. Despite the huge risks she took, it's all turned out well, and she landed on her feet. Lotus is a cat with nine lives.

"And does Bridget know you're interested in someone new?" Mama shoots me a meaningful look. "She knows she lost a good thing."

"She didn't lose too much. I'm paying her enough every month."

"You know that's not what I mean, and watch that one. I didn't see her before for what she was, but I have since. She's got a vindictive streak."

"Maybe I do, too."

"No, you don't. You can make a person feel like they don't have the common sense of a sheep with one look, but that's not vindictive. It's just your personality. Your father was the same way."

The doorbell rings before I can comment.

"That'll be Lucius," I say.

"So the shop's doing well?"

"Great, actually." I head for the front door. "At least that's what Lucius tells me. I need to see for myself."

Lucius stands on the stoop, sporting a big grin and a white kufi cap fitted tightly to his skull.

"*As-salamu alaykum*," he says, reaching up to hug me.

"*Wa alaykumu s-salam*," I reply, pulling back to give him a once-over. "You leaner, bruh."

"Cutting out that pork." He grins sheepishly, still looking like that guy I played JV basketball with in high school. That is, before I got bumped up to varsity, of course. "And that workout you turned me on to didn't hurt."

"Didn't hurt?" He swore up and down he didn't need my "fancy" diets and workouts to lose weight. "Okay. I'll let you have that. Come see my mom before we go to the shop."

"Your mom still fine?" he asks with a teenage boy's irrepressible smirk. "You know she always had that Claire Huxtable vibe."

I roll my eyes and lead him back toward the kitchen.

"Damn shame we can't even watch *The Cosby Show* anymore. Lisa Bonet was fine as hell," he complains. "We lost Cosby *and* Kanye."

I laugh, thinking of my conversation with Lotus.

"Yeah, I did see on Twitter that Kanye's in the sunken place," I joke.

"Twitter?" he asks, giving me a scrunchy face. "You still using Twitter?"

I wish Lotus was here to appreciate this.

CHAPTER 13
LOTUS

"Happy birthday!"

Billie blows out all twenty-seven candles on the huge chocolate-espresso cake. With laughing eyes and her hair even redder than usual from the glow of candles, she looks ironically younger as she celebrates another year.

"I hope you made a wish," Yari says, aiming her phone at the cake and the birthday girl for a photo.

Billie's smile slips so quickly, I doubt the camera caught it, but I did. We all cheer, and I'm glad the people who care about her most are here celebrating. Paul wouldn't be here with us peons.

Makes me sick.

How an otherwise bright, ambitious, honest-to-a-fault woman like Billie can let Paul have her birthday cake and eat it, too, astounds and depresses me. She has ceded everything to him—all the control, all the leverage. She thinks Yari and I don't understand, that we're too hard on her, but I've seen firsthand and more than once how dangerous it is to trust someone unworthy with your heart. It's why everything I've ever shared with a man was below the belt.

Lately, I haven't even shared that.

Right on cue, Chase leans over and blows in my ear. *Is that shit supposed to be sexy?*

I swat at him like he's an annoying fly.

"Chase, when you gonna give up?" Yari shakes her head and passes around plates with slices of cake.

"I'm not." He squeezes my thigh under the table. "We're on a break, but she'll be back."

"No, *she* won't." I force a smile and push his hand away. "You are firmly in the former fuck category, and there you shall remain."

Amanda, who is still in my personal doghouse for feeling Kenan up on the low, leans forward, affording us a glimpse of her plastic surgeon's handiwork overflowing the dress's plunging neckline.

"I hope you're not holding out for our watch model," she says, her eyes bright with spite and liquor.

"I think you were the one trying to *hold* him, last I checked." I blink at her, all innocence and *don't test me, bitch*. "That didn't work out exactly as you hoped, though, did it?"

Her smile vaporizes, her mouth falling into a thin, flat line.

"Who are you guys talking about?" Chase asks, a frown hanging between his dirty-blond brows.

"No one," I say as Amanda says, "Kenan Ross."

Chase sneers and takes a deep gulp of his beer. "You're both out of luck since I heard he and his wife might be getting back together."

I know it's a lie, and I know I shouldn't care, but my hand freezes midway to my mouth, and my Negroni feels too heavy. I set it down on the table, keeping my movements smooth and my face blank.

"Free to do what he wants to do," I say and shrug.

"So it wouldn't bother you if he went back to his wife?" Chase asks.

"Not one little bit," I lie.

When did it become a lie? When did I lower my guard long enough for Kenan Ross to become a possibility? For him to become an exception to the rules that govern my life and keep my heart intact?

I'm not mentioning my heart in the same sentence as Kenan Ross.

Even as I assure myself of that fact, I remember watching

him at the Rucker last week, admiring his confidence and ease with the crowd. He doesn't try to command every space he's in. It just happens. And it's not just his height. There were other ballers there that day—taller, broader—but he stood out. All eyes were drawn to him.

At least mine were.

And I've mentally replayed our fascinating and disconcerting conversation at Sylvia's so many times. He came right out and asked me about voodoo, and I spoke more freely with him about my heritage and MiMi than I ever do.

"Good thing you aren't hung up on Ross," Chase drawls, slicing his fork into a gargantuan helping of cake. "Your feelings might be hurt seeing him with his wife at that table over there."

Chase nods his head across the room, and before I can stop myself (*dammit!*), I turn in that direction. My eyes collide with Kenan's, and my breath stutters.

The man is fine. There's no getting around that.

Obviously, he's back from Philly. It's okay that he hasn't called. I've been telling myself that it's for the best so we can keep things in a little box marked "friendship." It's only now, when our eyes meet and cling, that I admit I was lying to myself. I missed him and hoped he'd call even while telling myself otherwise. My gaze drifts to the beautiful blond woman at his side.

"Oh, pretty blue-eyed blonds with big breasts not your type?"

"Used to be. I was married to one for a long time."

He said "used to be," but it looks like they still are. I jerk my head back around, and Chase's cruel scrutiny is waiting for me.

"Like I said," Chase says with a stiff little smile, "it's a good thing."

"I heard she's on that new reality show," Amanda interjects, *"Baller Bae,* and that Kenan moved to New York to be closer to her since it's taping here."

That's not how Kenan told it, but I've taken a vow of silence on the subject of Kenan Ross, and I'm certainly not breaking it for these two loose-lipped fools.

"Open your presents, Bill," I lean past Chase to tell my friend. "If you don't love what I gave you, I want it for myself."

Billie doesn't need much persuading and squeals and coos over every gift. The whole time, I stubbornly refuse to look back in the direction of Kenan and his ex-wife, even though I feel his eyes on me more than once.

"Lo!" Billie squeaks and holds up the gift I made for her. "This is gorgeous. One of your designs?"

I smile and nod, swelling with quiet pride when Billie puts on the little bolero jacket. It's sequined, and the stitching is so subtle it's practically invisible. The embroidery on the elbows and at the collar is intricate and vibrant.

"I love it so much." Billie stands for her hug. I take the few steps to reach the head of the table.

"I love *you* so much." I hold her close and whisper in her ear, "Be careful what you wish for, Bill."

She jerks back and peers into my face, startled green eyes searching mine for a knowledge she can't be sure I have. *I* don't even really know, but I get these urges. Promptings. Strong feelings. I don't always know what they mean, and most of them I ignore, but every once in a while I say what I see, and I see Billie wishing for something she shouldn't have.

"Okay, enough of the love fest," Chase says. "Either you two start making out or break it up and open my present, Billie."

Billie stumbles back to sit down, sending a dazed look at me before starting back in on her pile of presents. I return to my seat and, feeling eyes on me from *that* direction, finally give in and glance over to Kenan's table. I'm ready to cross my eyes or stick out my tongue—do something that throws him off his game—but it's not Kenan staring at me.

It's her.

Bridget Ross's eyes are like chilled blue curacao in a frosted glass. I look away quickly, wondering why she's staring at me. I've felt something connecting Kenan and me ever since the first time we met. Is she astute enough to discern the invisible ribbon tying us together across the room?

"You ready for this train?" Yari asks me once we've all paid our bills and boxed up what's left of the cake and are preparing to go our separate ways. "Girl, we gotta make this hump back to Brooklyn."

"Yeah." I snap myself out of any thoughts about Bridget and Kenan. "I'm gonna use the restroom before we start home."

I rush off to the bathroom, hoping no one from our table follows. I need a minute to compose myself—to regain the resolve I had at the beginning of this journey to keep things simple. To be just friends. Because somewhere along the way, things changed, and I'm not sure I'm ready for that. If there's one thing I have to be, it's sure.

I'm walking down the dimly lit passage, almost at the women's restroom, when one word from behind steals all the things I'm sure of and dares me to take a chance.

"Button."

CHAPTER 14
KENAN

She stops mid-stride but doesn't turn.

She's arresting enough from the back. While I was in Philly, she reinstated the braids. Bright and platinum in the half-light of the hall, they are gathered high at the crown of her head and held tight by chopsticks. She's slight and curvy. Her emerald-green dress with its high mandarin collar and printed with pink cherry blossoms fits lovingly to the sinuous lines of her body.

She turns slowly, giving me plenty of time to brace for her, but I'm still not ready.

When she faces me, my mind scrambles a little. I reach for something to say, but my tongue feels heavy, clumsy. She always has this effect on me. I used to resent it, but now it just confirms that we're meant to be special, not simple. If Lotus with her trust issues and her temporary celibacy weren't complex enough, my ex-wife waiting out in the dining room ensures that things will not be simple.

Makeup and false lashes exaggerate the already-dramatic tilt of her eyes. Tiny jade tassels dangle from her ears. Her mouth is scarlet and pouty and, if memory serves me correctly, sweet.

"I thought I told you not to call me Button," she says by way of greeting.

"I thought we agreed I would when we're alone."

And we are alone in this narrow space, but there's an elephant in the hall, and I address it right away.

"I'm here with my ex-wife," I say, leaning against the wall. "And daughter. We had family counseling tonight. Simone's been asking if we could all do dinner after the sessions. Our counselor thought it was a good idea."

"That's nice," she says, lowering her lashes instead of looking at me. "I did see your...ex."

"We were alone because my daughter noticed a friend from school and left the table to say hi."

"You don't owe me an explanation, Kenan," she replies, winged brows drawn in. "We're not dating or a couple or...anything but friends."

"Funny." I reach for her wrist and gently tug her the few inches separating us to stand in front of me. "I didn't think about my other friends every day while I was away."

I tug a little more until the silk of her dress licks between my denim-covered thighs. She tilts her head down so all I see is a coronet of braids.

"And I certainly wasn't tempted to text *them* every day," I add. "My friends, I mean."

"But you didn't text," she says softly, lifting her lashes to stare at me. "Me, I mean."

"I wasn't sure if I should." I pause. "I'm not sure what we're doing or which lines to cross. We have two absolutes. No sex because you're 'off dick.'"

She snort-laughs like I hoped she would.

"And no kisses until you make them happen," I continue, "but those are lines drawn for our bodies, not for our feelings."

"And what do you think you're feeling, Mr. Ross?"

The miniscule moment of silence following her question is a fork, two diverging paths. One is paved with self-preservation. I tell her I'm feeling nothing—protect myself from the wiles of a woman I don't know well enough to trust. The other road is cobblestoned with hope—it's uneven, maybe a little bumpy, but gives her the truth in the hope that she'll return the favor.

"I'm feeling…more," I say, sliding my hand down her wrist to link my fingers with hers. "More than I planned to feel. More than, if I was smart, I'd let myself feel."

"If you were smart?" she asks, her eyes trained on our fingers meshed together between us.

"Yeah. The last woman I trusted ruined my life."

I've never said it that way, but it's true. When the news leaked about Bridget's affair, I was living the dream. I'd won two rings with a team on its way to another championship season. I had a beautiful wife, a daughter I adored, success, and wealth. But it was just that—a dream. A frail illusion shattered by one choice and many lies.

"I'm not her, Kenan."

"And I'm not whoever makes it hard for you to trust either."

She traps her bottom lip between her teeth and nods.

"I'm not saying that to rush you, Lotus. I'm saying we both have reason to be cautious. I told you at the beginning, I don't need complications. My family is a wreck. My ex is a circus. My daughter isn't sure if she hates or loves me from one day to the next half the time. More than any time in my life, I need simple."

I lift her chin, and when she looks at me, eyes shadowed with mystery, I answer her question of what I'm feeling.

"I *need* simple," I repeat. "But I *want* you."

She closes her eyes and squeezes my fingers as if she's holding on to this moment—sealing it in her hands and searing it in her memory. I'm hoping after I've taken the risk of trusting her that she'll trust me, too.

"Daddy?"

Simone's voice startles me. It must startle Lotus, too, because she jerks her hand from mine and steps back. When I look up the hall, Simone stands there with a curious expression on her face. Bridget stands behind her, her eyes condemning.

Like she has a fucking right.

"Moni, hey, baby," I say, keeping my voice even. "How was your friend? Camilla, was that her name?"

Simone stays silent for a moment, eyeing Lotus before looking back to me with a slight frown. "Camille. She's fine. Invited me to a sleepover next week."

"We'll have to see about that," Bridget says. "We're ready to go home, Kenan, if it's not too much of an inconvenience."

Bridget's love language is passive aggression.

"Of course not. I'll get the car." I turn to Lotus. "I want you to meet someone first. Moni, this is Lotus. Lotus, my daughter, Simone."

Simone doesn't move but watches from a safe distance a few feet away. After a brief hesitation, Lotus steps forward and extends her hand.

My daughter is tall for her age. She has no choice considering her parents' height. At fourteen years old and five feet seven inches, she's already taller than Lotus, who barely looks her in the eye wearing heels.

"Hi, Simone," she says, her voice low and husky, strong. "Nice to meet you."

Simone takes and quickly drops Lotus's hand.

"And this is Bridget," I say. "Simone's mother."

Bridget's mouth tightens, and her nostrils flare. Based on Dr. Packer's advice, I should focus on Bridget's role as Simone's mother, not on her former role as my wife. She should be happy to be introduced at all.

"Nice to meet you," Lotus says, extending her hand to Bridget, who takes it with only the tips of her fingers, as if she's afraid Lotus might contaminate her somehow.

"Mmmm," Bridget responds with the rude syllable.

"Lotus is—"

"From JPL Maison," Lotus cuts in, her smile impersonal and

serene. "I work for Jean Pierre Louis, and Kenan's the new spokes-person for our watches."

That's fine for now, but my hope is that at some point Lotus and I will have some explaining to do. At least to Simone. Who the hell cares what Bridget thinks about my personal life?

"The car, Kenan?" Bridget asks sharply. "Simone needs to get home. She has an early-morning dance rehearsal."

"Well, it was nice meeting you," Lotus says. "Good night."

She turns back toward the bathroom and walks in like nothing ever stopped her. Like I didn't stop her.

The three of us are silent while I pay the bill. I collect the car and take Simone and Bridget back to the apartment Bridget is leasing on the Upper West Side. I've done nothing wrong and have no inten-tion of apologizing for talking to a friend in the hall. Still, there's a chill in the air despite the humidity of the July evening. Neither Bridget nor Simone voices her thoughts, but I know they're specu-lating. If things develop with Lotus as I hope, there will be a time and place to orient Simone to her. If things stall—if Lotus decides this is as far as we go—we've disrupted nothing.

I've walked them up to the apartment and come back down to my car parked out front when my phone lights up with a text.

Lotus: This is Button...if you're alone.

Wearing a face-splitting grin, I prop my elbows on the steering wheel and reply.

Me: I'm alone. I didn't get to say that you looked beautiful tonight.
Lotus: Don't change the subject.

I chuckle when I realize she's echoing our first text exchange, so I follow suit.

Me: There's a subject?

Lotus: Subject: SATURDAY

Now we're talking.

Me: What's happening Saturday?

Lotus: Brooklyn, if you want.

Me: Oh, I definitely want.

Lotus: I'll send deets. I know how much you love those. ;-)

CHAPTER 15
LOTUS

"This is not a date," I tell the girl in the mirror.

I've tamed my braids into a topknot and kept my makeup light, natural. I'm wearing a lilac strapless top and tiny denim shorts that barely cover the tattoos ringing the very tops of my thighs. My eyes are sparkling.

Dammit, why are my eyes *sparkling*?

What is this *boom-crash-thump* my heart does while I'm waiting for Kenan's knock at the door?

Why is my belly flip-flopping at the thought of spending the entire day with him?

"This is not a date," I grimly remind my reflection.

"If it looks like a date and quacks like a date," Yari says from the door to my bedroom, "it's a date."

"What do you know?" I ask, turning around to grin at her. She's still in her pajamas, and her hair is a half-curly, half-straight mess all over her head. "Also, what bush did you sleep in?"

"Girl, there wasn't much sleeping," she says, her smile a dirty, satisfied smear on her pretty face. "Pedro spent the night."

"Oh, well, look at you, getting some." I laugh and put on oversize hoop earrings. "Haven't you known him, like, forever?"

"One of those guys from the neighborhood who's been sniffing around since high school, yeah. I never gave him the time of day, and after all these years, I finally did." She tips her head down and slants me a meaningful look. "Lo, dude showed me what he was working with last night. It's a lot."

I smooth sunscreen on my arms and legs. It's a myth that brown doesn't burn. "That good, huh?"

"Yeah." She pauses to look me over, head to toe. "You say you don't want to catch a fish, but you're baiting that hook mighty hard. You look good, Lo. You might have to remind Kenan it's not a date, too."

"He knows," I say and grab my small leather crossbody bag.

The teasing leaves Yari's face. "What's really going on with you two?"

I pause, making sure I have lip balm and cash for the day. "What do you mean?"

"Look, I know you claim not to be into Kenan like that, and I know you're in this *legs closed* phase, but you don't fool me. I know you, Lo," Yari says. "You like him, and I don't want to see you get hurt."

"I don't know, Ri. I'm attracted to him. He seems too good to be true. We haven't kissed again since that party, but…"

I recall the firm, soft press of his mouth into mine. Remember him handling me like I was precious.

"But…" Yari prompts, smiling.

"He says the next time we kiss, I'll have to make it happen." I release a breathy laugh. "I want to make it happen. I do, but I got some real shit to sort through."

I fiddle with the strap of my purse.

"I always thought the issue would be falling for a bad man, like my mother did, but falling for a good man could be worse."

"How do you figure?"

"With those other guys, it was just sex. We knew what it was. They could have my body but nothing else. Kenan won't settle for that, and I don't know if I'm ready to trust him, to trust anyone, with more. I never have."

"Well, maybe you could—"

A knock at the door cuts into whatever sage advice Yari was about to hand down.

"Oh!" I touch my pockets. "I need to grab my phone and get myself together."

"I'll get the door."

"Looking like that?" I ask dubiously.

"Why the hell not?" she asks over her shoulder as she leaves my bedroom. "He's not *my* date."

"It's not a date!"

I find my phone and hurry to the living room before Yari says or does something outrageous, which is her default. By the time I get in there, Kenan is already overpowering our small couch.

Gladiator.

He does look like a warrior in repose. Massive. Powerful. Intimidating. Towering even when sitting down, his face set in austere lines while he listens to whatever crazy thing Yari is saying. He's dressed casually in shorts and a white polo shirt.

Damn. He should never be allowed to wear white. The contrast with his skin… It's too much. It should be outlawed. I'm already mentally drafting my letter to Congress.

When he catches sight of me over Yari's shoulder, his expression softens, and he smiles. It's a slow build, taking its time moving from the dark, deep-set eyes to his beautiful mouth. Have I ever thought of a man's mouth as beautiful? Kenan's is, a precise, wide bow at the top and a full, sensuous curve at the bottom. I remember how those lips felt on mine. How his tongue dove into my mouth, aggressive, seeking. I remember how he tasted.

Yari glances back at me and grins.

"Well, I have some chilling to do," she says. "You kids have fun getting blisters walking all over Brooklyn."

Once Yari's gone, Kenan and I stare at each other for a few seconds, a warm, wordless greeting.

"Blisters, huh?" he finally says. "You said we'd be exploring Brooklyn, but you didn't say anything about blisters."

I chuckle and step closer to inspect his black-and-silver athletic shoes that look like there should be a dashboard under the laces. "I think you'll be fine. I like those kicks."

"Thanks. Designed them myself."

I peer closer and notice *Gladiator* sketched along the side. "Oh, it's *your* shoe."

"Well, they let me help."

"And I see you're wearing our watch," I tell him, walking to the door.

"Yeah, trying it out, but JP did *not* let me help."

"JP doesn't let anyone help. Believe me."

We start down the four flights of stairs instead of waiting for the elevator the owners recently added to the brownstone.

"He seems to have a soft spot for you, though," Kenan says. "He lets you help?"

"Collaborate some, but my job is mostly details and grunt work and the occasional opinion. JP trusts my instincts and my style."

"You always look great, so I guess he's smart for that."

His words warm me. I don't tell him but keep walking toward our first destination.

"You didn't drive, right?" I ask. "I will not be held responsible if that tank of yours gets stolen while we're gone."

"No, I took Uber Black."

"Oh, I've heard of that." I grin up at him as he walks beside me. "Rich people's Uber."

"If you say so." He chuckles and glances around my neighborhood. "This is nice."

"Yeah, they say Brooklyn's the new Manhattan. I didn't know the old Manhattan. I'm a transplant, so it's always been like this to me. Ri and I love Bushwick."

"It's a cool-ass vibe for sure."

"Oh, just wait." I rub my hands together. "We'll go to Williamsburg. We can go to Prospect Park. Maybe we should see the carousel. It's so historic. We can take the train and—"

"You mentioned food?" he cuts in.

We laugh together, and I shake my head.

"I take it you're hungry?"

"Yeah, my regimen requires me to eat a lot and all day," he says.

"I got you. There's this place called Sally Roots on Wycoff Ave. We'll be there soon. Their brunch is off the chain."

"Healthy options?"

"Some, yes, but you are eating ice cream today."

"It's not a cheat day for me," he says with a grin.

"Oh, yes, it is. You can afford one day off." I poke his stomach, but my finger goes nowhere. It doesn't sink but presses into steely abdominal muscle. "Shit, you can afford a week off, a month."

He grabs my finger and curls his around mine, smiling down at me and not letting go. "I haven't taken a month off in a long time. It's a way of life for me. I can't imagine being that undisciplined for that long."

"Not even in the off-season?" I hope I sound normal, but he has moved from holding my finger to stroking that sensitive strip of skin between my thumb and index finger, and I'm straight up breathless.

"What off-season?" His laugh comes short and quick. "At my age, I can't afford to let up. And no old man jokes, PYT." He grins and then frowns. "Shit, I'm sorry, Lotus. I got you practically running and out of breath."

"It's okay." I pull my hand away and slow my steps, both things helping to steady my heartbeat some. "You walk a little slower, and I'll walk a little faster. We'll meet in the middle."

I'm grateful when we reach the restaurant. Despite my talk of walking all day, it *is* Brooklyn in July. And it's hot as a mofo. Sally Roots is blessedly cool, with an island vibe that transports us from the urban jungle to a tropical paradise in a matter of steps. Island knickknacks and antiques are crammed on the shelves of the bar, and the walls, painted blue like the Caribbean Ocean that inspired the menu, cool the space like a breeze.

We forego the crowded dining room and ask the server if we can sit in the backyard, which is shaded by umbrellas and overhanging trees.

"This is nice," Kenan says, looking around the near-empty space. "Laid-back. I like it."

"Me, too. Ri and I love their brunch on the weekends." I look at the menu through his eyes. "So anything here work for your super-strict diet?"

"It's not super strict. It's strategic and not a diet." He narrows his eyes on the menu. "I like to limit sugars, especially during the season and playoffs because they slow down recovery after games. I can indulge a little since it's summer." He catches my eyes over the menu. "Since it's you."

I look back to the menu right away. I can't do this all day—have a fluttering heart and stuttering pulse every time he turns those intense eyes on me.

"So what are we having?" the young man who's serving us asks after bringing Kenan water and me a mimosa.

"Ladies first," Kenan says, still studying the menu.

"I'll have your akee and saltfish," I tell him.

"Dumplings and sweet plantain okay with that?" the server asks.

"Perfect."

"And you, Mr. Ross?"

It would jar me to have people know who I am when I first meet them and know nothing about them, but Kenan seems used to it, and his expression remains unchanged.

"I'm looking at your omelet." He glances up from the menu. "Can I get it with egg whites? Eight of them? And with just the veggies, skip the bacon?"

"For sure." The server nods and scribbles on his pad. "Fries and salad okay?"

"Nah. Let's skip the fries." He turns a blinding-white smile on me. "Apparently I need to save room for ice cream later, but I'll take the kale-and-arugula salad."

"We'll get that right out."

When the server leaves, silence falls on the backyard. We're the only ones out here now, and intimacy thickens the air. I truly wonder how long I can hold out. A month ago, I would have been crawling across this table to kiss him, dragging him into the bathroom and scratching this itch so hard I'd break the skin.

But that was before I found myself crying in Chase's shower. That was before I found myself huddled in my closet with a bass drum where my heart should be. I don't want that with Kenan. I want to sort my shit out. Not just for him. For me. But there's no denying I want him.

And based on the way his eyes keep probing the edge of my strapless top and sneaking glances at my legs in these itty-bitties I'm wearing, he wants me, too.

"We should talk about what happened at the restaurant," he says, concern momentarily dousing the lust in his eyes.

I would prefer feeling the pull of him in the balmy air and silently wondering how long I'll be able to stop myself from humping him, but if we must...

"You mean how your ex-wife wants to deport me so she'll never have to see me again?"

A shout of laughter crinkles his eyes at the corners, and his chest moves subtly with the force of it. When he throws his head back, the strong length of his throat is exposed. I could watch this man laugh all day.

"Bridget's like this kid who had a toy she got tired of," he says, looking at me from beneath a thick sweep of lashes. "Unfortunately, I'm the old toy in this scenario, and she found a shiny new one. Now she wants the old one back and doesn't want anyone else to play with it."

"I have no interest in playing with you," I tell him, the words sneaking out before I think better of it.

We watch each other for long moments, the muted sounds of the city and the muffled laughter and clinking glasses from inside a soundtrack for the story our eyes keep building, adding another line, another chapter with every second.

"Well, that's disappointing," he replies straight-faced.

I laugh, and he joins me, not breaking the tension but bookmarking it until our eyes meet again.

"I've been as honest with her as I can be," he goes on. "I don't want her. I don't want a life with her. I wouldn't even be in the same city if she didn't have my daughter."

"So you don't share custody?"

"We do, but it's complicated." He grimaces. "Basketball has an eighty-two-game regular season, one of the longest in sports. It's September to July from camp to playoffs, if you make them. And during the season, you're constantly on the road. Away from home. I can't provide any real stability for Simone with that schedule. Bridget wasn't wife of the year, but she's a good mother. She and Simone are close. There wasn't even a question of Simone staying with me in San Diego when Bridget decided to move to New York. Maybe for the summer, but there's this dance program here that Simone's excited about."

There's an openness to his features when he talks about his daughter. Usually so guarded, he doesn't try to hide his love for her.

"She's dealt with a lot of crap because of us the last couple of years," Kenan continues. "Leaving Houston when I requested a trade to San Diego. Now moving from there to New York. She hasn't been into anything like she's into dance for a while. I couldn't deny her this chance by demanding she live with me in Cali over the summer."

"You could have denied her," I correct. "But you're a good father and chose to put her first."

"Of course." He frowns like that's a given.

It's not a given. I know what it's like for it *not* to be given. To be withheld. I envy Simone, having two parents who love her this way.

Even if one of them is a shine-grabbing cheater who shook my hand like I might have crabs. "Your ex seemed suspicious of me or something."

He's about to speak when the server arrives with our food. Kenan attacks the mammoth omelet of egg whites, and I'm not shy about my meal, either.

"Suspicious?" Kenan finally speaks, wiping his mouth with a napkin. "Maybe. I'm not sure why she thinks she wants me back."

"Really?" I ask disbelievingly. "You don't know why she wants a handsome, intelligent, handsome man who—"

"You said handsome twice," he interjects, grinning.

"Don't interrupt. A handsome man who's obviously a good guy? She's probably kicking herself from here to the moon for being so careless. For losing you."

"Well, if she is, she can keep kicking because there's no chance."

"None?" I ask. "What she did killed your love?"

He looks down at his plate and sets his fork aside.

"I'm going to be completely honest with you for some reason." He shakes his head like he can't believe he's telling me this. "I think there was something broken in our marriage long before Bridget cheated on me."

His look is sad and holds regret.

"I'm not an easy guy to know," he says with a one-sided grin that goes straight to my heart. "You might not believe that by how I've talked your ear off, but I'm not usually this talkative. I'm an introvert. I like to be home. I love my music and to read and to relax. I love my business interests and pour a lot of time into making them successful."

He takes a long sip of his water before speaking again, and I don't try to fill the space with words or questions. He needs to tell me these things, and I want to hear them.

"We married straight out of college right after I was drafted into the league," he says. "My family was well-off growing up, but getting drafted meant money like I'd never seen. Millions and millions of dollars on day one. Maybe Bridget thought we'd have this rock-star lifestyle. That I would suddenly become this guy who wanted the limelight—that I wouldn't be able to resist the lure of fame—but I don't care about it."

"And she does?"

"She does now." He shrugs. "The saddest part is that I'm not sure she ever really knew me, and I'm pretty sure I never really knew her. Not if *Baller Bae* is what she's after."

His sardonic laugh comes and goes quickly. "We had Simone, but we didn't have much else in common. My dad tried to tell me. He's gone now, and I see what a hole it's left in my mother's life. They were deeply satisfied with each other. I never had that with Bridget."

"I'm sorry," I say, feeling bad for them both, but especially her being married to a man like Kenan and never really knowing him.

"Well, I wouldn't be sitting here if things hadn't gone how they did," he says, sobering when he looks back to me. "And I'm really glad to be here with you."

"This is not a date," I blurt.

His sinfully full lips compress against a smile, but he manages not to laugh. "That was a very timely reminder," he says with false sobriety. "Thank you."

The server brings our check, and I'm seriously wondering if the whole day will feel like this—like we're in a pressure cooker. Like I'm boiling under my skin every time he looks at me for more than two seconds.

We stand to leave, and the server comes back to the table. He's already collected the bill, so I'm not sure what else he needs. His smile, hesitant and sheepish, clues me in.

"Mr. Ross," he says, scrunching his face. "Could I get a selfie? It'll only take a second."

I imagine it requires some patience for Kenan, a self-confessed introvert, to deal with this on a regular basis.

"Sure," he says with a gracious, if somewhat reserved, smile.

I consult the list on my phone for all the things we're doing today while they take their photo.

"You ready?" Kenan asks once they're done.

"I think the question is are *you* ready, Mr. Ross, for all that I've got planned?"

While we walk, he puts his hand to my back. I try to ignore the heat of it—ignore the electric storm brewing in the air around us every time we brush against each other on purpose or by mistake. With us, there's no such thing as a casual touch.

"No," he says, shaking his head and not smiling. "I don't think either of us is ready for this, but damned if I'm not doing it anyway."

For a few seconds I'm thrown, lured deeper into his unbreakable stare, but I try to lighten the moment, break the tension, and *stick to the plan.*

"Well, I hope the old man can keep up with the millennial."

After a second, he yields a grin. "I can't believe I'm gonna be that cliché, the older rich guy dating a younger woman."

"Don't get ahead of yourself," I scoff, forcing myself to maintain eye contact. "Oh, no, you're not."

He stops us on the sidewalk, bending until our faces align and our lips almost touch in the meager space separating us.

"Oh, yes, I am."

CHAPTER 16
KENAN

"So you weren't kidding when you said blisters, huh?" I ask the question jokingly, but I wouldn't be surprised if I've walked a hole in my Glads. Except for one Uber ride, we've been hoofing it all day.

Lotus laughs, walking backward and a little ahead of me.

"Technically, Yari mentioned blisters, not me," she says, giving her ice-cream cone a long lick. "Now I know a man in such superior shape is not complaining about a little bit of walking."

"A little bit?" I stop in the middle of the sidewalk and wait for her to do the same. She finally rolls her eyes and walks back to me. "You've dragged my ass from Bushwick to kingdom come—"

"Did you or did you not enjoy the Botanical Gardens?" she demands, one hand on her hip, the other clutching her ice-cream cone.

"I mean, I—"

"Yes or no?"

I look down at her tiny self with narrowed eyes. "Yes, but—"

"And did you or did you not love riding Jane's Carousel?"

"A six-foot-seven-inch grown-ass man on a—"

"Yes. Or. No?" She lifts sleek brows and tilts her head for the answer she already knows I'm going to give her.

"Okay. Yes. It was fun because it was ridiculous. There were four-year-olds riding with us."

She flings her head back and laughs with such gusto it shakes her whole body. She doesn't care that people are strolling past us, staring at the loud woman busting up in the middle of the sidewalk with her dripping ice-cream cone. I love that about her.

"And was Roberta's not the best pizza you've ever had?" she asks.

"It was all right." I shrug and understate about the best pizza I've ever had.

"You lying..." She slits her already-tilted eyes and twists her full, pouty, lipstick-long-gone lips. "It was bomb, and you know it. And what can we say about this ice cream?" She licks the vanilla dome. "Hmmmm. You probably can't remember the last time you had something this sweet."

Her tongue circuits the ice cream, and my mouth waters remembering that tongue in my mouth, licking inside, sparring with mine, both of us gasping for air.

"Nope," I say, hoping my voice doesn't sound too hoarse. "It's been a while since I had something that sweet. You're right about that."

Her licks slow to occasional swipes while we stand on the sidewalk eye-fucking each other, which we've been doing intermittently all day. To my great frustration and delight.

Frustration because I've never wanted anyone the way I want Lotus. Her breasts in that strapless shirt and smooth, lean legs in those miniature shorts? I'd trade one of my championship rings to have her. I mean, I've got two rings. There's only one Lotus, as far as I can tell.

And delight because it is so obvious she wants me, too. I'm not a conceited guy. I've been a baller half my life—high school, college, pro. I could never be sure if women wanted me for my prospects and earning potential or for me.

Lotus wants me for me. There's no artifice to her—no tricks. No game she's running. No agenda. When she looks at me and her eyes burn hot and her breath comes short, it's for me. The pure way she wants me back and the hard time she has fighting it may be one of the most alluring things about her.

"Well, we're almost done," she finally says, and starts walking again. "You survived."

I match my stride to her shorter one, and for a few minutes we're quiet while she finishes her ice cream.

"I feel like today I've used all my words for the next month," I tell her with a chuckle.

She turns her face slightly up toward me. Her profile scallops delicate curves into the shadows falling with the approaching sunset.

"What do you mean?" she asks.

"I just…don't talk much usually."

"I think we can safely say that has not been the case today," she says, her laugh low and sarcastic. "I couldn't get a word in edgewise."

"Okay, now you're exaggerating."

"Well, at least I found a nickname for *you*."

"What is it? I'm not gonna like this."

"Big Mouth."

"Not creative *or* accurate." I tug on one of her braids that has fallen down to her shoulder. "Back to the drawing board."

"You keep telling me you're an introvert, but I don't see it."

I slow my steps a little as we approach the long stretch of the Brooklyn Promenade's railing. I weigh the words, wondering if I should say them. They're true, but they may tell her too much too soon.

"I'm not this way with anyone else," I say softly. "I know it sounds crazy since we don't know each other that well and haven't known each other long, but I'm only this way with you."

CHAPTER 17
LOTUS

I BITE MY LIP, NOT SURE HOW TO RESPOND TO KENAN'S WORDS.

I talk to everyone all the time, and I'm hyper-social, but I know what he means. I think the point isn't that he actually talks to me when he doesn't talk to other people much. I think the point is that he *wants* to talk to me, and that I get because even though I talk to everyone, there's something unique about my time with him. Something I wish I could replicate with other people but at the same time love that I've only experienced with him. I haven't even shared my deepest, darkest secrets yet—the things that chase me into my dreams and arrest me in the middle of the night.

But I think I will.

Soon I will share those things with him, and he's right. It makes no sense. But I, unlike Kenan, am used to things that don't add up. I'm accustomed to things that defy explanation. I was raised on hope and weaned on miracles, so the exceptional feels familiar to me.

Even so, this is different.

I stand on the base of the rail, placing my feet between the rungs, and face the New York skyline and the water lapping at the city's edge.

"Nothing to say to that?" Kenan asks softly.

"Oh, I have a lot to say to that, but right now I just want to watch the sunset," I whisper, not because there are other people around who might hear—tourists and natives alike lining the rail to catch the last of the day like us. I whisper because there's something sacred in the sky. Every time the sky speaks to me, I'm reverent, whether it heralds good news or bad.

"Cotton-candy clouds," I say, turning to smile at Kenan.

"What?" He blinks in that way he does when someone says something unexpected. He blinked like that when Chase said he had great forearms. I chuckle, recalling how Kenan looked at him at the Christmas party. Like Chase was gum he'd stepped in. "What's so funny?" Kenan asks.

"Nothing." I shake my head because saying Chase's name, saying any name that isn't Kenan's or mine right now feels wrong.

He leans his elbows on the rail, so close the heat from his body reaches out to stroke my skin. I feel his eyes on my profile as tactile as a caress. Like his touch over the verse on my collarbone, soft and curious and savoring. He looks away from my face to the horizon. The Statue of Liberty. The Brooklyn Bridge. Bulky buildings hugging the river's edge. And the pointy tip of one skyscraper that seems to pierce right through a pink cloud.

"I was saying the clouds are pink," I go on with a smile. "Pink clouds mean happy days."

"Huh?" he asks.

I climb down, turn my back to the view, and climb back up, propping my elbows on the rail. I'm facing him now and can see his response as he watches the sunset.

"I looked it up once," I say. "I used to love watching the sunset from a tree in MiMi's backyard."

"This tree is magic, child. When you're feeling blue, climb this tree."

I swallow emotion. Still, after two years, it hurts that I can't ask her advice. Can't hop on a plane and see her when I want.

"What'd you find out about pink clouds?" he asks, tracing the shell of my ear, running a finger over the studs, leaving a trail of shivers in his wake.

"Well, they say—"

"'They' being...?"

"Scientists, I guess." I laugh and shrug. "Whoever *they* are, they say when the sun sits low, sunlight passes through more air than during the day when it's higher. More air means more molecules to make the violet and blue in the sky seem more distant. It literally chases the blues away."

I catch his eyes when he turns from contemplating the pink clouds and contemplates me.

"So happy clouds because no more blues." I smile, and I wonder if he can tell it's ironically tinged with sadness. I long for that tree. Even on days when the sky tells me through pink clouds to be happy, it doesn't feel the same as it did from my perch in MiMi's backyard.

"Cotton-candy clouds?" he asks, watching me closely.

"Yeah, they're like cotton candy. I had to design a dress for my final project at FIT. It was cotton-candy pink and absolutely perfect."

"Did you make it for a model-sized person or a you-sized person?" he asks, chuckling low and deep.

"Oh, I made it for me. Exactly to my measurements."

"I'd love to see it on you."

"I've never worn it."

"What are you saving it for? Why not wear it?"

"I'll know when. It'll be a special occasion," I tell him, fake-defensive. "Get outta my closet."

We laugh just as his phone rings. He pulls it out of his pocket and scowls at the screen but answers. "Hey, Bridget. What's up?"

His scowl deepens. If Bridget could see his face right now, she'd hang up. He looks pissed. Beyond pissed. Disgusted. I'd shudder if he ever looked at me that way, and she has no idea. Or maybe she's gotten used to it.

"If you're lying, Bridget—"

I hear her whining voice cutting into his comment. He squeezes the bridge of his nose and shakes his head. "Tell her to be ready in an hour, and I'll come get her."

My heart sinks. Our day is almost done, but I was hoping we could ride home together on the train and then he could take his Uber...excuse me, Uber Black...back to the Upper West Side.

"I'm sorry, Lotus," he breathes out in frustration. "I was supposed to have Simone tomorrow, but Bridget says she has some commitment and needs me to get her tonight instead. I know Bridget's probably playing games and manipulating, but I don't ever want Simone to feel like I choose not to have her with me. You know? I'm already playing catch-up with her."

My heart contracts. He has no idea how much I know. I know how it feels for your mother to choose a lover over you. How it feels for her to choose not to have you with her. Not just for a night but for years. To forfeit an entire childhood for an unworthy man.

"I get it," I say simply, inadequately conveying my understanding. "Simone should be first. I'll never begrudge you that."

His eyes, usually so guarded, aren't that way now with me. His face is as intimidating as the rest of him. Handsome but composed of sharp lines and blunt bones—austere. But when he looks at me, the hard lines soften, and it's like watching rock melt. I'm the sun.

I feel that power for a moment—the power to make someone as hard as Kenan look tender. That power surges, and then it converts into responsibility.

Gentleness is power under control.

And I feel the urge—despite him being so much bigger, a hundred and fifty pounds heavier, and ten times stronger—to be gentle with Kenan. To be careful with the power he vests in me every time he shows me more, tells me more.

I feel a sense of responsibility that a man like him, who has been betrayed by someone who should have been faithful, might just choose to trust again. To risk trusting with me again. We're not so different, he and I. I was betrayed by the one who should have protected me, too. Not a wife but a mother—by a family's complicit silence. We're not so different, and maybe that's what my cotton-candy clouds are trying to tell me. It's a good day. A good day to trust again.

Standing on the rail makes me tall enough to reach him. I touch his face, caress the strong rise of bone beneath the mahogany skin, and turn him toward me until our lips brush together. He pulls back the slightest bit with a stare that doesn't waver.

"Remember what I said." His voice is husky and heavy, maybe with the weight of this no-turning-back moment. "When we kiss again, you have to make it happen, and it means you want to be more than friends."

I close the space he inserted between our lips and lick into the seam. He gasps, and his eyes close immediately.

"I want to be more than friends," I whisper over his lips. "Open your eyes and don't look away."

When he opens his eyes, they lock with mine, and I suck his lower lip and lick into the corners. He angles his head to capture my top lip between his, never dropping his glance. His hand, huge and encompassing, curves at the back of my head, his fingers curling at my nape. He deepens the kiss, tasting me with surging, hungry licks that make me whimper and moan. Now it's my turn to gasp and close my eyes because the contact is so charged it sends a current down my spine and through my toes.

"Don't look away," he echoes back to me.

We set a frantic rhythm of bobbing heads as the kiss grows more urgent. I'm turning my head and he's angling his, both trying to delve deeper without breaking the electric thread of our gaze. While our tongues mate and our lips beg and our bodies strain to learn the shape of each other, we never look away. And it's more intense than fucking.

This kiss wipes away every man who came before him in a

baptism of greedy lips and searching tongues, dipping me, dousing me, saving me.

Changing me.

I'm new. Different.

Even when it ends, our lips still cling, loath to let go of this revival that purifies even the air we breathe. And here, trapped between our lips, each breath is holy. Here between our chests, our hearts bang like ancient drums. Here between our eyes, his and mine, a searing glance sees everything.

It's the best kiss of my life. It's my first glimpse of real intimacy.

And it's almost more than I can bear.

CHAPTER 18
KENAN

I HAD SIMONE ALL DAY YESTERDAY, AND SHE SPENT THE NIGHT. Now it's Monday, and I haven't been able to see Lotus again. I want to badly after our "not date." It may not have been a date, but it was definitely a kiss. I want a repeat as soon as possible. I'm getting off the elevator to Dr. Packer's office when my phone flashes with an incoming notification from a local florist.

Your package has been delivered.

That August is good for something. My San Diego Waves teammate, married to Lotus's cousin Iris, has been bugging me ever since I asked for Lotus's number.

"So how'd the date go?" he'd called to ask yesterday.

"What date?" I'd replied, deliberately obtuse.

"Brooklyn." There'd been barely checked eagerness and frustration in his voice. "If you play this right, we could practically be brothers."

"As appealing as permanently chaining myself to a wet-behind-the-ears rookie is," I had said, letting the barb I always use with him sink in, "I think I'll handle this myself."

"You don't think Lotus told Iris every detail?"

That had given me pause.

"She did?" I'd kept my voice neutral. They're close. It wouldn't have been unheard of. It's just so new, and I haven't told anyone yet.

"No," August had grudgingly admitted. "Iris couldn't get anything out of her. We're both on pins and needles here."

"Why don't you and your little wife worry more about having that baby and less about what grown folks are doing here in New York."

"You're grown, but Lotus isn't," he'd countered and laughed. "Good ol' Glad. Robbing the cradle."

If we'd been together, I would have body-slammed him. Or at least given him a good headlock.

"Even though you aren't sharing shit with me," he'd said, "I'll give you some free advice. Something I did for Iris, and you see where it got me."

"Like I need your advice," I'd scoffed.

The phone had gone silent for a few dead-air seconds, and I'd huffed an exasperated sigh. "I mean, you may as well tell me now."

He'd taunted me with his laughter before sharing his advice. She'd better like the flowers I sent.

"If you steered me wrong, August," I mutter under my breath as I cross the lobby, "I'm shaving all those damn curls off next time you fall asleep on the plane."

Simone and Bridget are already seated in the waiting area. I know I'm not late. I usually beat them here.

"Hey, Moni." I swipe my hand over her face to greet her and reach up to tug her ponytail.

"No, Daddy," she says, blocking my touch with both hands. "Don't touch it. I need it neat for the recital tomorrow."

"There's a recital tomorrow?" I frown, glancing between them. "It's not on my calendar."

"Well, guess Davis made a mistake," Bridget says waspishly.

My assistant, Davis, back in San Diego, doesn't make mistakes with my schedule or any aspect of my life. I'd be lost without him.

The door opens and Dr. Packer walks out with a warm smile for all three of us.

"Good to see you," she says, gesturing for us to precede her into the office.

"Wait out here for a few minutes, Simone," Bridget says, cutting her eyes at me. "We need a few minutes alone with Dr. Packer first."

"We do?" I ask, frowning. First I've heard of it.

"We do," she confirms, sailing past me and into the office.

What now?

"Is there a problem, Bridget?" Dr. Packer asks from behind her desk. "I know we chatted a few weeks ago without Simone, but I like to limit impromptu meetings like this and instead schedule our time without her. Seeing this could make her feel like we're talking about her."

"Well, we kind of are," Bridget says, "thanks to Kenan's reckless behavior."

"Me?" I point a thumb at my chest. "Reckless? How so?"

"This is how so." She pulls her phone out and shoves it at me.

When I see the photo on Instagram, I want to roar at Bridget for being in my business. At the same time, I want to kick myself for not being more careful. The server at Sally Roots posted the selfie with me. Just beyond the shot, almost like a photo bomb, Lotus is looking at her phone. Her head is down, but those platinum-colored braids are distinct. Bridget saw them that night at the restaurant. I asked the server not to tag me, and he didn't, but he used #KenanRoss.

"You object to me taking a photo with a fan?" She's going to have to say it—be petty enough to make a big deal out of something that isn't.

"What I object to," Bridget spits out, "is this woman you're running all over New York with."

"Running all over New York? Hardly."

"What do you call this then?" She shoves her phone at me again.

This photo shows Lotus and me on Jane's Carousel. We're laughing in the shot, and I almost smile again at me looking so big and ridiculous on that carousel despite the awkward situation I'm in now. The poster's caption: "Don't see this every day. #KenanRoss"

Bridget must have been trolling me and searching by that hashtag on Instagram. I want to hurl her phone into the nearest wall.

"May I see?" Dr. Packer asks and accepts Bridget's phone. "What's the problem?"

"You said we shouldn't get involved with other people," Bridget says testily.

"No," Dr. Packer replies. "I said you should be careful how it's introduced to Simone. I admit Instagram isn't the best way, especially given the past...drama that came through social media."

Bridget clears her throat at the mention of all our trash strewn in the streets via her antics.

"But these photos could be interpreted as mere friendship, too," Dr. Packer says. She turns her attention to me. "Is this just a friend, or is she someone we'll need to introduce to Simone eventually?"

Here's the moment of truth. I could deny it and get Bridget off my back. I could delay this and see Lotus discreetly—avoid this altogether for another few weeks.

Except I don't want to.

I want to be more than friends.

Lotus's sweet, husky words have haunted me since Saturday.

Don't look away.

"We're seeing each other." My voice is strong and sure like my feelings for Lotus, and I'll be damned if I'll lie about them, about her, to satisfy Bridget's misplaced, too-late possessiveness.

"I knew it," Bridget says hotly on an expelled breath. "At the restaurant. You and her in the hall. I saw the way you looked at that little—"

"You will not talk shit about her," I say with quiet fierceness.

Bridget blinks, her blue eyes startled. It's silent for a moment while she and I assess each other, neither backing down.

"I think we take this one step at a time," Dr. Packer says, snapping our stare-down. "Do we want to introduce...what's her name?"

"Lotus," I say.

"We have several things slated for today's session," Dr. Packer says, glancing at her notes and then back to us. "Do you want to add introducing Lotus?"

"Simone has a big recital," Bridget says sharply. "Let her get through that before we give her unpleasant news like this."

"It's not unpleasant news. I'm not doing anything wrong."

"Are you fucking her?" she demands, eyes icy.

Dr. Packer's gasp is the only sound in the room.

"That's none of your business," I reply, controlled in spite of the fury clawing at my belly. "And not appropriate for you to ask me here or anywhere for that matter."

I stand and head for the door.

"I'll bring Simone in," I say. "Since we're obviously done here."

Simone joins us and starts talking about dance and her new friends and all the things that seem to be going better in her life. It puts me somewhat at ease. It's only when I feel Bridget's baleful gaze on me every few minutes that I wonder if maybe we aren't done here at all. Maybe the drama with Bridget is just beginning.

CHAPTER 19
LOTUS

"We have guests coming," JP says, his tone distracted as he squints at the color swatches splayed across his large glass desk, an anachronistic concession to the modern era in an office peppered with French antique furnishings.

"Guests?" I flip through the fabric samples I brought for him to consider. "Who?"

"I think some of those housewives? Paul coordinated it. They're coming under the guise of looking at dresses for an event. They're always searching for pretty places to have their fights and keep it interesting." He pulls a set of green-rimmed glasses from his shirt pocket and slips them on. "Where's this one from?"

"There should be a tag." I lean forward and flip the sample over. "Here ya go. B&J Fabrics."

"It's close but a bit too yellow, *non*?" He levels a look over the fashionable spectacles and shudders. "You know how I feel about chartreuse."

"Of course." I pluck the offending fabric from his fingers. "Want me to mix a few colors and take something to our guy over on Thirty-seventh? He may be our best shot at a custom match."

"Good idea." He looks past me and smiles. "Ah, I wondered when you would descend, Vale."

His assistant strides in, a study of Icelandic sophistication and cool efficiency.

"We are behind," she reminds us unnecessarily. "The show is less than two months away."

"*Mon Dieu!*" JP presses a plump hand to his chest. "I had no idea! Did you know Fashion Week is so soon, *ma petite*?"

I return the twinkle-eyed grin he aims at me with a wry smile. Angels are already upholstering a seat in the VIP section of heaven for what Vale endures with JP.

"I'd heard something about it, yeah." I gather the fabric samples and kiss Vale's powdered cheek. "I'll go work on that production schedule due yesterday."

"That was my next item of business." Her expression softens, and she nods to the vibrantly colored fabrics in my arms. "Chartreuse may be the color JP can't stand. Red is Paul's. We better be in the black after this show. Much work to do."

That's my cue to scurry into my own cubicle. Each show is a massive undertaking, and the closer we get, the less time we'll all have for anything beyond these walls. The week before the show, we've been known to camp out here, sleeping and neglecting everything personal, including hygiene, to get it done.

Two heads poke around the sleek divider providing a flimsy semblance of privacy to work.

"What do you two tricks want?" I glance from my laptop to Yari and Billie hovering at the edge of my partition.

"Um…we come bearing gifts," Yari says, glee threading her words.

I hope it's one of the matcha lattes I love from up the street.

"Not from us," Billie all but squeals and pulls a bouquet from its hiding place behind her back. "But we're dying to know who sent these!"

Billie's holding a small vase with a few lotus flowers in vivid hues of pink and purple and blue. I know how hard lotus flowers are to come by locally, and they're nearly impossible to transplant. They're a lot of trouble to get and only last a few hours. I consider the small vase with a ribbon tied at its neck and a sealed envelope attached. My friends stand with tongues practically hanging from their mouths. Obviously they're not planning to give me much, if any, privacy.

Billie holds the flowers while I tug the envelope free and open the card inside. The barely legible words look like someone flung them on the page.

Button,

I told you I hate texting.

Unfortunately, lotus flowers don't live long cut off from the soil they're planted in. This loses some impact knowing they'll be wilted by the time you come to my place for dinner tonight. Oh. Would you come to my place for dinner tonight? I'd like to see you. I can pick you up from work. You can just text yes…or no…and what time I should come get you.

"Let me see your face.

Let me hear your voice for your voice is sweet and your face is lovely."

—Song of Solomon 2:14

—Kenan

Oh, this is bad.

The breath being syphoned from my lungs. The involuntary grin kissing my lips. The fluttering under my ribs. All signs that Kenan, when he sets his mind to it, has major game.

"Who're they from?" Yari demands, patience nowhere in her voice. "Are they from who we think they're from?"

With one hand, I take my vase of doomed petals. With the other, I press the card to my chest.

"They're from a secret admirer," I say, turning my back on them to place the vase on the edge of my desk.

"You don't know who they're from?" Billie asks.

"No, *you* don't know who they're from," I reply with a grin to rub it in. "That's the secret."

They both look like they want to strangle me. I sit back down and slip the envelope into my desk drawer.

"We know they're from Kenan," Yari says.

"No, you don't know." I return to my laptop. "You're fishing."

"Well, we *think* it's Kenan Ross," Billie says, hands on her slim hips.

"Well, you *might* be right." I shoo them away with one hand. "We'll talk about it later. If I tell you now, you'll have a million questions I don't have time for. I need to focus."

"Good luck," Yari says. "We have guests coming."

"I heard." My eyes snap to her face. "I can't afford disruptions today."

"I heard Paul talking about it." Billie shrugs. "They think it'll be good exposure for the brand."

Most large fashion houses are barely profitable, if at all, because the sheer cost of production at this level is exorbitant.

"As long as the exposure doesn't come this way," I say. "And I can't imagine why it should."

"You leaving on time tonight?" Yari asks, already turned to walk away and studying me over her shoulder. "You on the J with me at five?"

The vibrant spray of color in the vase coaxes a small smile from me, and I shake my head. "Nah. I got plans."

As soon as they've both gone back to their desks, I grab the phone from my purse and text Kenan.

Me: Yes. Six o'clock.

Kenan: See you then.

Me: Am I allowed to text my thanks?

Kenan: No. Thank me later. ;-)

At the start of the day, it seemed to be flying by and too short to get everything done. With six o'clock and Kenan as my finish line, the day is officially taking for-freaking-ever to end. It's only three o'clock when I check the time on my laptop and stand to stretch. I grab one of the flowers and press it to my nose, drawing in the sweet scent.

"Some of our team works over here," I hear JP saying. "But all the sewing happens downstairs, and we keep the clothes for you to view down there, too. Follow me."

That must be the reality TV cast. Thank God they didn't make it to my area.

"Oh, here you are."

I look up, stunned to find Bridget Ross standing at my cubicle.

"Can I help you?" It's a question embedded with *what the hell?*

"I wondered if your office was up here," Bridget says casually, strolling closer. She stares at the flowers on my desk before turning frosty-blue eyes on me.

"Are you here with the crew?" I ask. "It's *Baller Bae* looking at the collection?"

"Yes. I wanted to see what all the fuss was about." She pauses significantly, running her eyes over my skinny jeans, ribbed tank top, and sheer cardigan. "I don't get it."

My patience is fraying.

Lord, grant me the serenity not to kick her ass.

With God on my side, maybe Bridget will make it out of here in one skinny blond piece.

"What can I do for you, Bridget?" I ask. "It was Bridget, right? We met the other night at the restaurant, I believe."

"You know damn well who I am," she drawls with deceptive indifference. "Or at least you should since you're fucking my husband."

Lord, don't fail me now.

"I think you should probably go before you make yourself look even more desperate," I tell her, I hope with some kindness and not the middle finger I want to shove up her nose.

"Sure you don't want me to stick around?" She sits on the edge of the desk and caresses one lotus petal. "I could give you some pointers on how Kenan likes his dick sucked. We were together over a decade. Maybe save you a lot of time."

I step close until I'm standing right in front of her. I carefully slide my flowers away from her touch.

"Why would I want advice from the woman who lost him?" I ask, my voice hushed. I don't need a scene. I'm sure her cameras are within striking distance. I'm giving her as little ammunition as possible.

"You won't be able to keep him," she sneers.

"Well, at least we'll have something in common and maybe enjoy each other better next time, but for now, I repeat: Leave."

"You have no idea who you're dealing with," she says, chin up, hair flung back.

"Oh, no, you don't know who *you're* dealing with," I say, my tone soft with danger she doesn't, couldn't understand. "You should pray to God my kindness and patience don't run out or you *will* know."

"Just remember I offered to help you get it right," she says spitefully, standing to her feet.

"You can best believe when I *am* fucking your *ex*-husband," I tell her, "you'll be the last thing on our minds. Now get the hell out of my face, out of my office, and stay out of my way."

"I won't let you ruin things for us," she says, her voice vehement.

"You already ruined it," I say pityingly.

And I do pity her. I'd hate myself if I lost a man like Kenan, lost a life with him. Desperation clings to her, and I wonder if she cheated on him and then woke as if from a dream to realize what she had done. What she had lost and squandered.

She stares at me and then at the flowers one more time. Something gives in her eyes, and the facade slips. She blinks overly bright blue eyes, turns, and leaves.

CHAPTER 20
KENAN

I'M LEANING AGAINST "THE TANK," AS LOTUS CALLS MY SUV, WHEN she comes out of the building. All the skinny individual braids are gathered and braided into two thick ones. She looks like a little girl, except for that ass and those breasts and her lips and every other part of her.

So just the hair, pretty much.

I open the passenger side, but when she steps past me to get in, I grasp her elbow gently and turn her so her back is to the open door. I prop my arms against the car frame overhead and lean down.

"Hi." I pitch the word low and dip to kiss the line of her jaw.

"Hi, yourself," she says with a tiny smile. I mold my hand to her waist, my thumb barely brushing the underside of her breast.

"Kenan," she says breathlessly. "I can't think when you touch me like that."

I slide my hands into my pockets.

"Look." I lean forward, hovering over her lips. "No hands."

With the kiss, our lips are the only point of contact, our mouths linked by a single strand of lust. Our moans meet in the middle and syncopate. Inches separate us. My arms aren't wrapped around her, but the passion of just our lips and tongues burns away the space between us, and I feel every inch of her.

"Not out here," she says softly, ruefully, after a few seconds and pulls back.

She's right. I already have Bridget hashtag hunting on Instagram. I don't need some photo to pop up and make things more complicated with Simone before they have to be. I'm dreading talking to Lotus about it, but she needs a heads-up about what happened in the counseling session with Bridget. I don't anticipate drama, but you never know with my ex.

I press my forehead to hers for the briefest of moments but can't resist sneaking another quick press of our lips together. I've been thinking about this all day. Shit, I've been thinking about kissing Lotus again since our last kiss ended.

She returns the press. Our mouths don't open. Our tongues don't tangle, but just that simple pressure feels incredible, like there's something we exchange even through a touch this chaste.

I close the passenger door once she's in and climb into the driver's seat.

"My chef delivered dinner to my place," I tell her, pulling out into the side street bordering the atelier. "I wouldn't subject you to my cooking."

She bends her head, biting into the curve of her bottom lip. "Kenan, there's something I need to tell you."

I stiffen and my hands tighten on the steering wheel at the sober note in her voice. "That's never good," I murmur. Sitting at a light, I turn to study her profile. "What's up?"

"Bridget came to the studio today."

"Bridget? As in my ex-wife?" Shock and fury wrangle inside me. "Came to your job? What the hell?"

"Exactly. We got word that a reality show wanted to come through. That's not unusual. Producers are always scoping cool settings for the drama the casts get into. Fortunately, my drama with Bridget was just between us. She didn't bring any cameras to my cubicle."

A hundred scenarios run through my head, none of them making any sense. With each second, the flame under my anger turns up until I'm boiling mad.

"Green," Lotus says.

"Huh?" I turn unseeing eyes to her. "What?"

"The light turned green."

A honk from behind jars me out of my enraged stupor.

"Damn." I plow forward, struggling not to take my anger out on the car. I want to slam the accelerator and gun the engine, channel all the power I won't let myself expend on Bridget. "I'm sorry, Lotus. What did she say?"

"She accused me of fucking her husband and offered to teach me how you like your dick sucked."

A growl rumbles in my throat. "What else?" I ask with a calm I'm far from feeling. "And what did you say?"

Lotus opens her mouth, slams it shut, and looks out the window.

"Lotus? What else? I need to know."

"Okay, damn," she says grudgingly. "I told her that when I do fuck her *ex*-husband, she'll be the last thing on our minds."

Her words land like a hand on my cock. How could they not? I'm silent, marinating in the thoughts, the images her words evoke.

"Kenan, did you hear what—"

"Yeah, I did." I slant a look, part lust, part laughter, over to her in the passenger seat. "Heard you loud and clear. When we fuck. Got it."

"I'm sorry if I said the wrong thing."

"Uh, no." I tap my fingers restlessly on the steering wheel. "I think it was...fine. What you said."

"I couldn't let her—"

"Of course not."

"I let her think we're already...you know. Active."

"You make it sound like a checkup at the health clinic," I say with a grin. "So, tell me, Ms. DuPree, are you and Mr. Ross *active?*"

"Well, I didn't tell her we won't have sex for a long, long, long—"

"Really?" I squeeze the bridge of my nose. "That many longs, huh?"

She tosses her head back and cackles.

"You're evil." I laugh, shaking my head and pulling into my building's parking garage.

"Funny. Your note today sounded like you like me a lot."

Her small hand curves around mine on the console between us. "Thank you for the flowers and the note. It made my day."

"You mean after my ex-wife destroyed it."

"Oh, no." Lotus shakes her head. "She doesn't have that much power over me."

We're pretty quiet once inside the building and keep our distance until we board the private elevator that leads to my apartment. When the doors close, I pull her in to me.

"Hi again." I lean down, tease her lips open, and then slip in to taste her. God, so sweet. She goes up on her toes, and I grab her ass and lift her.

"Kenan," she laughs into the kiss. "Put me down."

"Why? I bench-press more than you every day."

"Show-off," she says, her mouth curled into a happy smile.

"I have to find *some* way to impress you."

She rests her elbows on my shoulders and caresses the back of my neck. She's suspended in the air. "You've impressed me from the beginning," she says.

"Oh yeah?" I set her on her feet when the doors open for my floor, take her hand, and walk to my apartment. "Is that why you were always so eager to kick it when we saw each other the last couple of years?"

Her smile slips and then disappears. "I suspected this could happen." She waves a hand between us. "And didn't think it was a good idea."

"Why?" I let us into my place and immediately bring her close. She snuggles into my shoulder like she missed me as much as I irrationally missed her. All out of proportion to how long we've known each other. Beyond the few kisses we've shared.

"Why didn't you think it was a good idea?" I ask again.

She wraps her arms around my waist and lays her head to my chest.

"The women of my family make fools of themselves over men," she says, her voice a confession. "They let men influence them. Ruin them. I don't want that."

I kiss the top of her head and draw her a few inches closer. "I don't want to ruin you or make a fool of you. I know how that feels."

"I know you do." She glances up at me, her eyes as guarded as they are vulnerable. "That's why I decided to kiss you in Brooklyn."

"Why?"

"You have as much to lose as I do—as much of a leap to trust again." She shrugs. "Maybe I'm kidding myself because I was tired of resisting the attraction, but that's what I told myself before I kissed you."

I nod, thinking this may be the one time all the crap Bridget put me through has worked to my advantage. I take Lotus's hand and lay it against my chest, cover it, completely eclipsing hers. She's so small but not fragile. If I'm using one of MiMi's Bible stories that even *I* know, Lotus is the pebble David slung to take down Goliath. Maybe I'm not the gladiator after all but Goliath. Am I falling? Falling from a little pebble right between the eyes?

"Let's eat," I say after a few moments like that.

We walk into the dining room where the chef left the food in warmers.

"Nice place," she says, surveying the open-plan apartment and settling into the dining-room chair.

"I can't really take credit. It came furnished. The only thing I've really added of my own is the ice bath."

"Ice bath?"

"I take ice baths after every game and really hard workouts. Helps with recovery. I had one installed for while I'm here."

I press a few buttons on the wall and music, "In a Sentimental Mood," seeps into the room. Some of the tension I've carried in my shoulders ever since Lotus told me about Bridget drains away. Each note from John Coltrane's saxophone seeks out the knots in my neck and rolls over them with precisely the right amount of pressure.

"I actually think I recognize this one," Lotus says, propping her chin in her hand.

"Is that so?" I serve a portion of the grilled chicken and vegetables for her plate and a larger portion for mine. I set them both on the table and nod for her to start. "Dig in."

"Yeah. It's from the soundtrack for *Love Jones*," she says and slides a forkful of mushrooms and asparagus into her mouth.

I almost spit out my water mid-sip. "One of the greatest songs of the last century, by John Coltrane, a genius, and your context for it is a movie?"

She laughs and shrugs, teasing me with her eyes and taking another bite.

"Wait," I say. "Are you messing with me?"

She squints one eye and squeezes her thumb and index finger together, leaving a small space. "Maybe just a little."

That is the pointy tip of Lotus's sharp humor.

She shows me a lot of it over the next hour. We talk so much during dinner my food gets cold, neglected because I'm absorbed in how she thinks, the way she voices her opinions. The entire night is a stream flowing easily from one topic into the next. Our conversation drifts effortlessly from movies to music to politics. We don't align on every point, but hearing how she arrives at her opinions is as satisfying as sharing them. Coltrane yields to Chet Baker and his funny Valentine. By the time we make our way to the couch, Miles Davis takes center stage, and we fall quiet, me sitting in the corner of the couch and her snuggled against me, knees tucked beneath her.

"It's this one," I tell her when "It Never Entered My Mind" begins.

"Your favorite song?" she whispers as if afraid she'll interfere with the dialogue between the man and his instrument.

I nod, hearing it not in this room now but in the book-lined walls of my father's study for the first time, sitting with him, listening while he reviewed material for his court cases and I did my homework. "It was my dad's favorite, too."

She turns eyes filled with compassion up to me.

"You miss him."

I swallow, surprised by the burn in my throat. It must be remembering him with this song playing, reminding me of his contemplative nature and appreciation for beautiful things. How he passed both on to me.

"Yeah. I do," I answer after a few seconds. "You think you're fine and then…"

She nods against my shoulder, biting her lip and knotting a handful of my shirt in her fist.

"I think about MiMi almost every day," she says. "Not always sad. Good, too. Something she told me, taught me. A recipe. A sewing pattern. I used to fight memories of her because it hurt, but I realized it was like her knocking at my door and me not letting her in."

She shrugs, a sheen of tears over her dark eyes. "She always let me in. Not thinking of her would be like forgetting parts of me exist. The best parts."

"I never thought of it like that." I kiss the top of her head and draw her a little closer. "I want you to meet my mom. She's not dealing with it well. I think she'll like you."

It only occurs to me after I say it that it might be too much. That she might think I'm already wanting her to meet my family and it's too fast.

She smiles, blinking the last of her tears away. "That'd be nice."

I return her smile, glad it didn't feel like a big deal to her. "And you can meet my sister Kenya next week. She can't wait."

"You told her about me?" Surprise colors her voice and the look she angles up at me.

"Only that there was someone I liked."

"I tried that with Iris, but now she knows it's you," Lotus says, her laugh rumbling into my chest. "She's been hounding me."

"God, August is the same."

"Why are they so obsessed with us?"

"I know, right? Did you tell her about our first kiss?" I ask, hoping to disconcert her. She blinks a few times but doesn't otherwise seem surprised or affected.

"No," she replies with a little pull of her lips.

"And our second one?" I ask, smiling wider. "Did you tell her about Brooklyn?"

"No, I've been kind of protective of this—of all of it—and not wanting a lot of input, I guess. Testing my instincts and limits. Does that sound weird?"

"No, but it has me wondering." I shift so I can reach her lips when I'm ready to. "Will you tell her about this kiss?"

"Which kiss?" she whispers, her eyes fastened to my mouth.

I press my mouth to hers, tease her tongue out to play with mine, and her sigh, her moan, the sounds she makes rocket through my blood. I sit up, pulling her onto my lap, and one lean denim-clad thigh and then the other falls on either side of my hips. She comes back, opening my mouth with hers, thrusting her tongue in aggressively. I slide my hands under the thin tank top and explore the silk of her back. She rocks her hips over me, and we both gasp.

"Do that again," I command hoarsely.

She obliges, grinding into me and drawing a groan from my throat. She wraps her arms around my neck and dusts kisses over my jaw, my cheekbones, my nose. It's tender and sweet and hot as fuck.

I don't even realize my hands have drifted to her ass and are coaxing her hips into a steady ride that has her panting and my dick hard in my jeans. Her whimpers grow louder, her cries harmonizing with the notes falling from Davis's trumpet. She's close. God, she's gonna come. I pull back enough to see her face, riveted on the play of emotions, the hunger, her mouth dropped open, her head hung back.

And then she stops.

"Kenan," she breathes, eyes squeezed tightly shut. "I'm still off dick."

I sit perfectly still and will my cock to shrink to its normal size. Will my breathing to steady.

We sit like kids waiting for a storm to pass, only we're the storm. This feeling between us is a tempest, and I have no desire to take shelter. When she kisses me, I forget everything and want to stand in the rain.

"Obviously, I'm attracted to you." She breathes a laugh, shakes her head, and lowers her lashes. "But there are some things I'm still working out."

She glances up to search my face.

"Are you mad at me?" she asks. "For getting you worked up?"

I pass my thumb over her kiss-swollen lips. "I'm not a teenager. If I can't stop when you ask me to without sulking, I shouldn't be kissing you. You're off dick until further notice. That's the deal, and I'm fine."

She drops her forehead to my chin and nods but slips her hand to my nape and brushes her fingers there over and over, as if she's calming a wild animal. The way my emotions and hormones are raging, that's not too far off base.

"Are you ticklish?" I ask, needing a distraction from the way my body still burns and my blood still roars.

Her head pops up, and she bites into a grin. "Not at all."

"Liar."

I flip her onto her back on the couch and tickle her sides. Her squeals drown out the first strains of Sarah Vaughan. After several minutes of wrestling and tickling and almost getting worked up again, she stands, breathing hard.

"I should go. I have a really early morning and late night tomorrow," she says. "We have fittings and a lot of other stuff to do the closer we get to Fashion Week."

I nod, a lot more disappointed that she's leaving than that I'm not getting laid tonight. Am I horny? Oh hell yes. I'll probably be putting the ice tub to extra use for the foreseeable future, but I honestly would be happy just to have her here close against me, Miles on repeat, talking and tickling. I hate that she has to leave.

"I could take the train home, you know," she says in the elevator down to the lobby. "I do it all the time."

I don't justify that with a response but keep my eyes on the flashing numbers.

We don't talk much on the drive, but it's okay. She reaches for my hand, toys with my fingers, stretches to rest her head on my shoulder. When we pull up in front of her place, she insists I not park or come up.

"That means you have to kiss me here then," I tell her.

The kiss heats fast, smoldering, sizzling in the front seat until she climbs over to straddle my lap. Her hips are rolling. I'm thrusting up. We're sharing sharp, hot breaths and clawing at each other's clothes. If we don't stop, I'll be fucking her in the back seat in front of her brownstone.

I jerk my mouth away and bury my head in the arch of her throat.

"Lotus, we gotta stop or I..." I palm her head and turn my face into the sleek line of her jaw, leaving safer kisses there.

"I know." She nods and burrows into my neck.

She crawls awkwardly back to the passenger side, grabs her purse, and gets out, not waiting for me to open the door. She turns to leave and then comes back, leaning her head into the open window.

"What will you do about Bridget?" she asks.

Lotus said Bridget would be the last thing on my mind when

we fuck, but she already is. I hadn't thought about her all night, but I know I have to deal with her.

"I'll take care of it," I say, my voice quiet, my resolve steely. Bridget has ruined things for me so many times. She's not ruining this.

I lean across the console and Lotus meets me halfway, popping her head into the car for one last sweet kiss.

I'll take care of you.

CHAPTER 21
KENAN

"So when do I get to meet her?"

"Meet who?" I ask my sister absently, pausing on the sidewalk to look at a retail space for rent. "This space is great, but Soho's not right for Faded."

"Nah." Kenya presses her face to the window, peering in. "Brooklyn, Queens. Harlem, even. One of those. Now don't avoid the question. I asked when I get to meet this girl you can't stop talking about."

"Who? Lotus?" I shoot her a puzzled look. "I've barely mentioned her."

"Yeah?" Kenya resumes walking beside me. "Then how do I know she works at JPL Maison, she was born in New Orleans, and she sews? Oh, and she likes mumble rap. She has a lotus flower tattoo around her belly button and—"

"Okay. Maybe I shared a few details." I toss a grin to my sister. "And she only pretends to like mumble rap to push my buttons."

"Well, I'm in town until tomorrow, so I need to meet this woman who's turned you out."

"She has not turned me out," I scoff. "And you'll meet her at dinner tonight."

"And where do things stand with Bridget since she rolled up in there, guns blazing?" Kenya smirks. "That is some basic bitch stuff, showing up at homegirl's job like that."

"We aren't exactly on the best terms." I grimace. "It wasn't pretty when I confronted her, and she tried to lie, say it was a coincidence. I've told her if she keeps meddling in my life, there will be consequences."

"Money?"

"It's my only leverage with her right now," I say. "I pay her twice what our agreement stipulates, plus alimony. Simone's needs are more than taken care of. Everything else is gravy, but it's gravy Bridget likes. We'll see if it works."

"I hope it does." Kenya looks down at her phone. "Hey, we're here."

We cross the street and enter the gallery. The Gilded Bean boasts an airy space filled with paintings, photographs, and sculptures.

"Nice, huh?" Kenya asks. "My coach swears by this place. She got all her artwork here. And they'll deliver out of state."

"Let's see if there's anything you like."

I'd love to buy a few things for her, but she's as proud as I am. Maybe prouder. She makes decent money, but I make more for one game than she does the whole season. I really do need to bring up the women's salary increase at the next Players Association meeting here in New York. I was elected to the executive committee three years ago, and it's been one of my favorite things I've gotten to do in the league. Many of my heroes who came before me served in the same capacity. It was Oscar Robertson who negotiated free agency for players when the NBA and the ABA merged. We're still benefitting from his work.

I'm a fan of the Big O myself.

Lotus's joke from our day in Harlem replays in my mind, making me grin and shake my head. I find that happening a lot. We haven't gotten to spend much actual time together. She had to accompany JP to Milan unexpectedly, which sucks. She got home last night, and we're trying to arrange for her to meet Kenya tonight.

"Your girl into hip-hop?" Kenya asks, texting and not lifting her eyes from her phone.

"Yeah. Why?"

"There's this concert. Maybe we could go after dinner." She looks up at me, but something over my shoulder captures her attention. "Man, that would look good on my wall. Shit, that would look good on anybody's wall."

I glance over my shoulder to see what's so great and stop, the blood freezing and then boiling in my veins. I cross the gallery with quick strides to join a small group clustered at the base of a photo that must be blown up to six feet tall, mounted on the wall.

It's a woman.

The slim figure is tucked into the corner of a window seat. Her lean legs, smooth and sun-kissed copper, are slightly parted. Her head, haloed by a caramel and butterscotch mane of wild curls and coils, is flung back, exposing the sleek muscles of her throat and a wisp of bone, her clavicle, inked with scripted words. She's wearing a man's white shirt, unbuttoned, opened, the tails hanging on either side of her toned thighs. One breast is partially covered by the shirt, but the other is exposed, the shirt dripping off her shoulder and running down her arm. A tiny gold bar pierces a plump berry-colored nipple dangling like heavy fruit from a vine. The beginnings of a tattoo ringing the tops of her thighs peek out from beneath the shirt tail.

Her pussy is in shadow, but it's obvious she's not wearing panties, and the lightly muscled plane of her stomach rises above her lap, decorated with a flower blooming around her belly button. Her hand, limp at her side, is adorned with one silver ring and tattoos of the moon on three fingers. My eyes follow the line from her knee, past her calf, to the well-crafted bones of her ankle. The black polish on her toenails is slightly chipped, an intimate, candid detail, like all the other intimate, candid details no one in this fucking gallery should be gawking at.

I squeeze my eyes shut, at once blocking the image and also trapping it behind my eyelids for later. Forever. I want to rip it from the wall and burn it. I want to take it home and wake up seeing it every day. My jaw aches with the pain of clenched teeth. My hand opens and closes, making and releasing a fist.

"Nice tits, huh?" A guy with a receding hairline nudges me in the ribs and shares a roguish grin.

I grab his arm and squeeze. He yelps, and Kenya pries my fingers from his elbow.

"Kenan, what the hell?" Kenya asks, turning apologetic eyes to the man who is rubbing his elbow, fury and fear on his face. "My brother has, uh…PTSD. Sorry about that."

"Sorry," I mumble. "I didn't mean to—"

"No problem," he says hastily, walking away and flinging parting words over his shoulder. "Thank you for your service."

"My service?" I ask, bewildered. "What's he—"

"You're welcome," Kenya snaps. "Better a troubled vet than the NBA player he could sue the pants off for mauling him. Dude, what's wrong with you?"

I look back to the photo.

"This?" She points her thumb at the wall. "The Lo thing?"

"It's not a *thing*," I grit out. "It's her."

"Huh?" Her brow wrinkles into a frown and then stretches wide with realization. She looks back to the wall. "Lo? That's Lotus?"

A guy beside us snaps a picture of the photo with his phone. Before I can snatch and crush it, a woman in glasses walks up to address him.

"No photos." She points to a sign a few feet away. "Please show me your phone. I need to see you delete the photo you took."

I watch in anger and frustration, holding my tongue until she's done.

"How much?" I ask as soon as the guy walks off.

"Excuse me?" She turns to me with a polite smile, but her eyes gleam avariciously behind her rimless glasses. "For Lo, you mean?"

"For the *photo*, yeah."

"It's only been in the gallery two days," she says. "And we've had so many inquiries about it already. It fetches quite a price. It's—"

"Not for sale," a man's voice, semi-familiar, says from behind me.

When I turn and Chase is standing there, I almost lunge for his neck. He and I stare at each other, dislike shimmering in the air like heat waves rising off asphalt.

"How much is that one?" I point to the photo to the left of Lo.

"Six thousand," he replies with a smirk.

"And that one?" I point to the photo on the right.

"Oh, that one's a steal at fifty-five hundred," he says.

"And that one?" I point to the wall behind me, not even looking at what's back there.

"Whichever one you mean," he says, his eyes gleaming with malice, "they all have price tags, except this one."

"Seven thousand," I offer, leveling my tone, controlling my anger.

"No," he says, his jaw set at an obstinate angle.

"Ten thousand."

"I said no."

"Fifteen thousand," I snap, the little patience I've ever had for this motherfucker completely gone.

"Kenan," my sister whispers. "Let's go."

"Twenty thousand dollars," I offer, my eyes trained on Chase.

"I told you, she's mine." His smile taunts. "You can see why I wouldn't want to give her up."

"Ahem." The gallery attendant clears her throat. "Mr. Montclair, surely we could—"

"Nope," he cuts her off, not looking away from me. "Mine."

I don't even realize I've taken the three steps that separate us until I'm right in his face, looming over him, and Kenya pulls me back by my shoulder.

"We understand," she says with a stiff smile. "My brother is a… collector and has been looking for something like this. Goodbye."

She drags me out of the gallery, and I draw in a huge lungful of fresh air, clearing some of the red haze from my vision.

"Have you lost your fucking mind?" Kenya demands once we're a few feet beyond the gallery.

"That's…" I flounder, fury pumping through my blood. "He has her up there for everyone to see. He shouldn't… He has no right."

"She must have signed off on it, Kenan," she says. "She must want it to be seen. It wasn't that bad. You only see her breast."

She doesn't get it. No one gets it. I hate people seeing her like that. I hate that *he* has seen her like that. She told me they used to fuck. I know that with my rational mind, but that photo flaunts an intimacy he never deserved with a woman he's not worthy of.

"Ken, I need to, uh… I got something to do," I tell her, dropping a kiss on her forehead. "That all right?"

"Yeah," she says, concern on her face. "But get your shit under control before you talk to her."

Kenya's right. If I see Lotus now, like this, I'll screw something up. But seeing her displayed like that, hearing Chase gloat over her, having him *deny* me like that…how can I not?

CHAPTER 22
LOTUS

"OH, SO YOU JUST OUT HERE LIVING YOUR BEST LIFE AND SHIT, HUH?"

Yari's joking question draws my attention away from the sample I'm consulting on with one of our seamstresses.

"Gimme a sec," I tell her, grinning and turning back to the seamstress. "So the embroidery will go all along here." I run my fingernail around the waistband of the skirt.

"But won't see?" she asks, her English broken and her face puzzled.

"Short shirt." I draw an imaginary line under my breasts. "You'll see the embroidery on the skirt because the shirt will be so short."

"Ahhh." She offers a beatific smile of understanding and walks back over to the JUKI sewing machines that are standard issue in this studio. I prefer my old Singer at home.

"What are you talking about, Ri?" I ask, propping my butt against one of the sewing tables.

"Jet-setting off to Milan." She waves her hand in front of me. "Fly outfit. Face beat."

"The makeup and dress were for a CFDA luncheon JP asked me to attend with him." I tug the clingy silk away from my body and let it pop back. "Believe me, I'm about to slip into something more comfortable so I can get my work done."

"Ooooh, love that dress," Billie says, crossing the work room toward us. "Last year spring?"

I nod. It was one of my favorites. Burnt-orange silk, strapless, A-line, it streams over my body from breast to knee, flaring out at the hem. We finished the look with gold rhinestone-studded ankle-strap stilettos, which are killing me.

"And the hair, too," Yari chimes in. "I haven't seen you wear it platinum without the braids."

I touch the huge cloud of curls the humidity will only make huger. I took the braids out but kept the color. "JP's brilliant idea," I say dryly. "Experimenting, he calls it."

"So now that you're back," Yari says, "Billie and I are thinking we need some BFF time. What do you say to movie night at our place? I'm thinking we're long overdue for *Black Panther*."

"Again?" Billie asks faintly.

"Wakanda forever," Yari says, crossing her chest in the *Black Panther* salute.

I repeat the salute and laugh. "But Wakanda will have to wait because I have plans."

With Kenan, I singsong in my head.

I don't mean to smile, but even thinking his name has me all up in my feelings. When I got home from the airport last night, I had mail. No return address, but I knew immediately who had sent it. I recognized that nearly unreadable scrawl, and my heartbeat quick-ened when I slid it open.

> *"There is no one else but you, my friend, my equal."*
> —*Song of Solomon 5:2*

I stowed the card in the clutch I carried today and have probably read it twenty times.

"What plans?" Billie leans one hip on a sewing table. "These plans wouldn't happen to be with Kenan Ross?"

My smile slips, and I look from one friend to the other, wondering how much to tell them. I haven't exactly been purposely keeping things from them, but I haven't talked about how the relationship has progressed. I haven't told them I kissed Kenan…a few times. I haven't told them we are now more than friends.

Okay. Maybe I have been purposely keeping things from them.

"If you don't want Kenan Ross," Yari says with a shrug, "I'll assume he's free game and go for it. He looks like he might welcome some Latina loving."

"Bitch, do not even," I say with a knife of a smile.

"Now we're getting somewhere." Yari laughs. "Come on. Tell us."

I draw a deep breath, exhale, and glance around at the seamstresses with their heads down, seemingly absorbed in their tasks.

"Okay, so we're seeing each other," I say low enough for only us to hear.

"Yes!" Yari fist pumps. "Bill, you owe me five bucks."

"We bet on how long it would take," Billie admits, digging into her pocket and handing Yari a five. "She said before Fashion Week. I said after. Dammit. I thought you'd hold out for the summer."

My mouth hangs open, and I swing a surprised look between them.

"You guys are obviously into each other," Yari says, pocketing the money. "It was only a matter of time."

"Yeah, well, *please* don't talk to anyone about this, guys," I say, pressing my hands together under my chin. "We're not exactly hiding it, but we're being really discreet. His ex is tripping and could make things complicated, especially for his daughter. They're planning to tell her he's seeing someone in their next family counseling session on Monday."

"Lips sealed," Billie says, running an imaginary zipper over her mouth.

"Locked down," Yari agrees. "But you'll keep us posted? We just want to make sure you're happy, Lo."

"I am." I fiddle with the slim gold chain around my neck. "He's pretty great and fine with me needing to take things slowly."

"You mean still being off the dick?" Billie asks.

"Pretty much." I twist my lips. "I'm just working through some things."

"We're crazy," Billie says, watching me intently. "But you know we're here if you need us, right?"

"I know."

Besides MiMi and Iris, I've only talked to Marsha about what happened to me all those years ago. Maybe telling my friends is the next step.

"I, um, I've been attending a support group for childhood sexual abuse survivors." My voice, though soft, goes off with the report of a bullet in the quiet room.

"Shit," Billie mutters and takes my hand. "Lo, I am so sorry."

"It's okay. I'm okay, or at least getting there," I say wryly. "So far, I've just listened to the other women, but I've talked to the group leader. I think it's helping."

"So the whole sex break thing…" Yari frowns and takes my other hand.

"Yeah, it's complicated." I exhale a quick breath. "But I'm working through my shit."

"Whenever you want to talk," Billie says, "we're here."

"I know." I nod, grateful for them. "Just be patient with me. I'll get there, but for now, at least you know."

I look between my two best friends, deep affection momentarily crowding out the ache in my heart. "I love you, guys."

"And we love you, too," Yari says, looping an arm around my shoulders. "Bring it in for the real thing."

We huddle together in a quick three-way squeeze that has me holding back tears.

My phone rings in the clutch behind me on the table. I disentangle from my girls to grab it. When Kenan's name flashes onscreen, I can't suppress a grin.

"Hey." I turn my back to my friends, facing the lobby and lowering my voice. "I was gonna call you to confirm things for tonight."

"I'm outside," he says abruptly, not acknowledging my words. "Can I come up?"

"Okay. That should be"—I spot him walking off the elevator with the cell pressed to his ear—"fine."

As soon as he comes in, heads pop up, and he's the center of attention. He glances around the room, his thick brows knitted. He spots me, and the frown doesn't lift as he comes over.

"Hey," he says, dividing a terse greeting between the three of us before settling his gaze on me. "Can we talk?"

"Uh, sure. Later, bitches," I tell them with a wink, hoping to dispel the *duh duh duuuuuhh* vibe Kenan ushered in. "We can talk back here."

We walk past the curious seamstresses, who inspect every foot and inch of Kenan as we pass. I open the door of the back room, my usual haven. He walks past me, and I lock the door in case someone gets curious or wander-y.

"Welcome home, Lotus," I say, clutching the knob in my hands behind me, my back pressed to the door. "Glad to see you, Lotus. How was Milan? Did you—"

"You have a nipple piercing."

He says it almost like an accusation. I'm mystified because we've had a few deep, shivery, drawn-out kisses, yes, but he hasn't seen the girls yet, so far as I can recall.

"I do," I agree quietly, frowning. "How do you know that?"

"Anyone in Soho could know that," he says, walking in tight circles. "Step into the Gilded Bean and bam. It's right there."

Something pricks my memory. The Gilded Bean. Where have I heard…

"Chase," I blurt. "He has some photos showing there."

"Bingo." He props his big body against an unsuspecting table I'm not sure can hold him. He's not exactly sitting but not quite standing. I worry for them both.

"Is there a photo of me in the collection or something?" I ask. "You think you saw something that—"

"I don't *think* I saw shit, Lotus," he snaps. "I would recognize my girlfriend in a photo that's as tall as I am."

His girlfriend.

It's the first time he's called me that, and I can't even appreciate it because of this interrogation.

"No, it can't be." I shake my head, unable to compute the data. "You saw my face?"

"I didn't need to."

"Then you *could* be mistaken."

"The tattoo on your collar bone, the moons on your fingers, your gris-gris ring, the lotus flower around your belly button. Do I sound mistaken?"

"That doesn't make sense. I didn't sign a release for any nudity. I saw the photos he took. I'd remember that. I don't have a problem with nudity in art, for the record, but I didn't want to do it personally."

"But you did pose for him?" Another accusation. One he isn't entitled to, and it's starting to irk me.

"Yes, I did," I answer stiffly. "I was finishing up at FIT and was basically an intern here making no real money. Chase paid me to sit for him. It's not a secret, and it's none of your business."

He runs a hand over the back of his neck. "I know. You're right. I just…" His head drops back, his eyes on the ceiling. "I hate people seeing you like that."

"I don't belong to you, Kenan," I tell him. "You don't get to criticize me for posing for photos, even if there isn't supposed to be any nudity. I'll deal with Chase, believe that, but you don't get to come up in here growling with some caveman shit over things that happened before we were…anything. It doesn't work that way, and if you think you can tell me what to do, let me set you straight. I am *not* that chick."

"I know you don't belong to me, Lotus," he growls. "Why do you think I'm acting like an asshole? It makes me crazy that you don't. If I'm honest—"

"Yes, please, let's try that."

"If I'm honest," he repeats, both brows raised meaningfully, "it makes me crazy that Chase had something with you that I haven't yet. He knows you in ways I don't."

"You mean because we fucked?" I cross my arms over my chest. "In this little game where you and Chase keep score, it bothers you that you're behind? We can fuck right now and your problem will be solved, right? You'll be even? You want to fuck me, Kenan?"

"Of course I do, but not just that." His frown softens. His voice softens. "You know not just that, Lotus."

I push off the door and walk over until I'm standing in front of him. "Then what is this about?" I ask, my voice softening, too. "Chase and I had sex, yeah, but I thought you wanted more."

"I do." He cups my hips with huge hands and pulls me to stand between his legs. "You know I do."

"Then don't ruin it," I whisper. I press closer, and with him sitting and me in my stilettos, I can more easily link my arms behind his neck. "Don't let him ruin it."

His hands shift from my hips to rubbing my back through the silk.

"I haven't been jealous of him before," he says. "I mean, I didn't like that you'd been with him, but you're a grown woman with a normal sex life, so I get it."

"Things haven't been exactly typical for me in the sex department lately." I laugh dryly. "But go on."

"The photo is so gorgeous, and he wouldn't sell it to me." He tucks my unruly hair back, tracking the shell of my ear like he does often. "You're fantastic in it, so uninhibited. It's decadent, and you look like you're…"

"Like I'm what?"

"Coming."

The word caresses my lips.

"I realized he's seen your face, how you look when you come, and I haven't. He knows things about your body that I don't. For instance, I have no idea what the ink is at the top of your thighs.

I've seen flashes of it, but I don't know. He does. I guess what I'm saying is he knows you intimately."

"No, he knows me sexually. I draw a line between those two things, and no one has ever crossed it."

I lift a little higher to kiss his jaw.

"But you could," I whisper. "I think you could cross that line, Kenan, and it has scared me since the moment I met you."

I draw back a few inches to peer into his face. "That, what I just told you, is intimacy. It's truth that I'm trusting you with. Chase never had that."

He nods and slides his fingers into my hair, angling my head closer and taking my bottom lip between his. His hand slides down my back, drawing me even closer until our chests touch, and I'm on fire from the brush of our bodies together. As much as I told him he had no right, his possessiveness turns me on, and I'm deepening the kiss, desperate for as much of him as I can have.

"I missed you," he confesses into the kiss.

The words fist my heart, squeeze. I nod my agreement, needing to be close. Wanting more intimacy. Craving more trust between us. I hop up onto the table beside him. Curiosity is clear in his eyes. It turns to lust when I slowly work the silk dress up my thighs.

"Chantilly lace," I say, tracing the intricate pattern of the tattoos ringing the tops of my thighs. "There were these stockings in a little shop in Paris. At the top was the most exquisite lace I'd ever seen. No way I could afford it, so I took a picture and had it inked here."

I study the scrolls mimicking the lace pattern. The bands aren't very wide. "I kept them really high in case I ended up hating them so no one would be able to see."

"They're beautiful." He traces the intricate pattern with one finger. His knuckle brushes against my panties, and I lose my breath. He glances up at me sharply. "I'm sorry." He clears his throat. "I should probably go."

I grab his finger, staring at the contrast of the ink against my skin. "Do you want to see?" I ask, my voice raspy, husky, low.

"See what?" he asks, a perplexed frown pinching between his brows.

Am I really taking this step? Stepping off a building and believing I can fly? Do I have faith in the man I'm getting to know and care about? Can I trust him? Can I trust what's happening between us?

Real faith requires bravery.

Provoked by my own words, I step off.

"Do you want to see me come?"

CHAPTER 23
KENAN

THE BRAZEN QUESTION FALLS FROM HER LIPS WITH THE IMPACT OF a landslide, pelting me with a hundred responses and questions at once. She licks her bottom lip, flicking a glance at me through long, thick lashes.

"I thought you weren't ready for—"

"I'm not, but last I checked you can come without having sex." Her laugh is hollow. "I do it all the time."

A deep breath expands my chest. Even the thought of seeing Lotus touch herself—of seeing her unravel that way under *my* hands…I'm seized by lust, in its grip. And I don't need anything from her. I want her to take and take and take and not even think about what would make me feel good. I've never wanted someone's pleasure this way. To see it. To taste it. To make it.

"Are you sure, Lotus?"

"I'm sure I'd like to try," she says softly. "The bleakness I've felt the last few times I had sex, the emptiness and meaninglessness, I don't ever want to associate that with you." She frames my face between her hands. She presses her lips to mine in a barely there caress. "Touch me, Kenan."

We open our mouths to each other at the same time, inviting each other in, prompted by an invisible harmony of need. I'm drawn into the heat and sweetness of her mouth—how she gasps and moans for me. She pulls back, holds my gaze, and tugs the top of her strapless dress down.

I swallow deeply at my first sight of her. The photo is gorgeous, but it can't compare to this closeness—to the potential of touching and watching her body respond. Her warm, naked flesh stuns me, distended nipples begging for my touch and my kisses. Watching her face, making sure she's fine, I brush my thumbs over her nipples. The breath whooshes from her, sharp and startled.

I flatten my palms against her breasts, rotating in circles that slowly build, faster until her nipples furl tight and round. Her head drops back, her hair a spill of platinum curls around copper shoulders. I caress her back, my hands meeting, overlapping at her spine. She feels so fragile. Not just the delicate bones, but the dark eyes aglow with trust as she waits for me to do what I'm longing to do. I take the pierced nipple into my mouth tenderly. Reverently.

"Yes." Lotus's hands at my head urge me forward. "Please, Kenan."

I don't need any more encouragement. I suck, softly at first, but the taste of her, the feel of her budding and tightening in my mouth, overwhelms my good intentions. I pull her breast deeper in. I want her closer. I pull her up until she's off the table and I'm holding her suspended in my hands while I feed, running my tongue along the bar piercing her nipple. The texture of her in my mouth—the cool metal of the bar, the warm, turgid nipple, the silky surrounding skin—it's almost too much. I take the other in my mouth and groan. It's just as sweet. Just as round and responsive between my lips. Her cries grow more urgent—her hands at my head, tighter.

I set her back on the table and caress her thigh, my hand venturing up to the inked lace. She takes my hand and twines our fingers. I look up, and her eyes burn bright. Never looking away, she pushes our linked hands into her panties.

"Fuck," I mutter. She's warm, wet silk under my fingers. Under *our* fingers. The two of us together explore and stroke until her hips jerk and she bites her lip, her eyes drifting closed. She takes her hand from her panties and reaches up, running her fingers over my mouth. I lap at the wetness she's gifted me and groan at her flavor, addicted from one taste. I drop my head until our temples touch, my fingers still working her and her hips still rocking a desperate, reaching rhythm.

"Let me taste," I whisper into her ear. "Can I taste you?"

Her nod is quick. She's quiet except for little muffled cries she swallows every time they threaten to escape.

I drop to my knees and pull the black silk down and over her legs. I press her legs wide and then open my mouth over her, wanting it all at once, greedy. She goes still for a second and lets out a sharp cry before she rocks harder into me. I drag her to the edge of the table and slip my finger inside, still sucking the mound of nerves. She's so tight and my finger is so large, she contracts around me.

"Another," she groans. "Add a finger, Kenan."

I don't want to hurt her, but I want her even tighter around me, so I slip another finger in and pump slower, building to match the rolling cadence of her hips.

"Shit. Yes. Oh my God, yes, Kenan. That's it. I'm...oh."

She palms her breasts, squeezing and pinching them roughly, her face twisting as she bucks against me, her leg lifting and landing against my back. Her heel digs into my shoulder.

"I'm coming," she breathes. "Watch. If you want to see, watch."

And I do. While steadily caressing and touching and licking and laving her pussy, I pin my gaze to her face. Her head is angled slightly to the side, and her lip is caught between her teeth. Her brows are knitted, and long lashes kiss the tops of her cheeks. Her mouth drops open, and she unburdens herself, a wail of pleasure coming as she does. I'm obsessed with her wet heat, working my fingers between her legs. I stand, never losing touch, but I need to see.

Her head tips back. Tears roll over her cheeks and down her chin.

I dip to lick them. I drink them like a queen's cupbearer, taking the first taste. I rain kisses over her face and down her throat, over her breasts. She curls into me, riding the final waves, her hand fisted in my shirt, her eyes opening wide, showing me the desire, the desperation, and, finally, the satisfaction in her gaze.

I did that. We did that together, her showing me how she likes it and me giving her exactly what she wanted. An exchange of passion and patience and longing and trust. She's the one trembling, whimpering, but my knees are weak. She says she's never known true intimacy. If this is what it's like between us—this undiscovered passion like nothing I thought possible—then I have to admit it at least to myself.

Neither have I.

As her body quiets and stills, I shift to sit on the table and pull her onto my lap.

"This table cannot hold us both, Kenan," she says, her words lispy and lazy. She buries her head in my shoulder and curls into a ball like a little cat in my lap.

"What you're really saying is it can't hold *me*." Her punishment is a squeeze and a kiss in her hair.

"Hey, you said it." She chuckles and slides her hand under my shirt, running her palm over my abs. My muscles jerk at the contact. "This doesn't even feel real."

"What doesn't feel real?"

She lays her head back on my shoulder and catches my eyes. "Can I look?"

"Look at what?"

In answer, she runs her hand over my stomach again and lifts both brows. A surprised laugh rolls out of me. "Baby, of course. It's just abs. You've seen them before."

She slides off my lap, a wicked grin painted on her pretty lips. When she lifts my shirt, her mouth drops open.

"Just like I remembered them." She pushes the shirt up a few more inches, and her eyes widen. "You have the most beautiful chest. God, these nipples."

While I'm searching my memory for any time someone's complimented my nipples and coming up empty, she dips and takes one into her mouth.

She's completely absorbed, eyes squeezed shut and her cheeks hollowing out. She takes one nipple between her teeth, flicks her eyes up at me, and bites. Hard.

"Shit." My hand slams the table. "Lotus, fuck."

Her tongue darts out to soothe the sting, and just as I'm sure I'm going to come in my pants, she bites the other one and grins up at me.

I laugh, turned on in spite of the pain or possibly because of it. "You little witch."

"Won't be the first time someone's called me that," she says dryly and runs a palm over the muscles of my abdomen, laughing when they clench involuntarily. "Someone's sensitive."

"Or horny." I laugh. Her smile falls away, and she palms my dick.

"I'm so selfish," she says, distress written on her face. "I didn't even—"

"No. That was for you. I wanted it to be just you."

She opens her mouth, I'm sure about to argue, but my phone rings. I can't resist kissing her still-open mouth, smiling against her lips, before answering my phone.

"Hey, Ken," I say, not looking away from Lotus, and she doesn't look away from me.

"We still on for tonight?" Kenya asks.

"Lemme check." I hold the phone away and ask Lotus. "You still down to meet my sister for dinner?"

"Sure." She winks. "I can ask for all the embarrassing stories of your childhood and awkward puberty."

"I was never awkward," I tell her. "Yeah, Ken, we're good. Gimme the details."

I pantomime writing, and Lotus dashes over to a table in the corner and grabs a pen and some kind of sewing pattern that has a dress on it. I scribble the details for dinner and the concert afterward. My handwriting is even less legible than usual, but I can make out most of the letters when I read it after we hang up.

"So dinner at six." I look up from my chicken scratch. "And then the concert."

"Who's the artist?" She wrinkles her nose. "I don't want to sit through somebody I don't like for two hours."

"Yeah. That would be whack. This is actually a surprise concert in Central Park," I say, faking a frown. "I'm not sure you've even heard of this guy."

"Who is it?" she asks, suspicion and skepticism mingling in one glance.

"Grip?" I ask innocently.

By the way her mouth drops open and her eyes stretch like saucers, I'm guessing she has.

CHAPTER 24
LOTUS

I'M STILL FREAKING OUT THAT I GET TO SEE GRIP IN CONCERT. When he came to New York last year, the tickets sold out in hours, and I missed it.

I almost cried.

He's one of the most woke hip-hop artists out there right now. His lyrics are conscious and thought-provoking. His flow, ridiculous. I can't wait for tonight, but first I have something to take care of.

When I enter the Gilded Bean, it doesn't take long to spot myself on the wall. I stare dumbly at the life-size—no, bigger-than-life-size, since it's about a foot taller than I am—photo. I know I've never seen this shot, much less signed a release for it.

I dip my head so my hair falls forward to cover my face. I stand right in the middle of the group, and no one connects the abandoned girl on the wall with the one huddling into her hair.

"I wondered when you'd come," Chase says from right beside me. "Beautiful, isn't she?"

"I need to speak to you alone," I say, not looking away from my likeness on the wall.

"I'm pretty busy, obviously," he drawls. "This being the first week of my exhibit."

I turn to face him, every muscle in my body drawn tight. The struggle is so real right now. I want to pounce on him and pull that man bun through his ass.

"Fine," I snap, loud enough for those around us to hear. "We can talk right now, right here, about how I'll sue your ass for using this photo without my permission. How my lawyers will be—"

He cuts me off by grabbing my arm and dragging me out of the showroom and into a small office.

"Are you crazy?" he demands immediately. "Saying shit like that? You could ruin my exhibit."

"I can *still* ruin your exhibit." I shake my head, furious. "When did you take that photo? You know I never saw it, Chase."

He watches me for a few seconds in silence, probably weighing if he can get away with some lie or if he'll have to tell me the truth. Finally, he blows out an exasperated sigh and swipes a hand over his handsome face.

"You fell asleep at one of the shoots." His laugh is short and his eyes almost affectionate. "You had a project for school, I think. I went to get a piece of equipment, and when I came back…"

He gestures behind him, in the direction of the showroom on the other side of the office door.

"When I came back you were like that," he says, crossing the room to stand in front of me. "I *had* to, Lo. You see how beautiful that shot is? How beautiful you are? How could I not take it?"

"You violated my privacy," I reply. Quiet. Vehement. "Not only did you have no right to take it, but to show it? Without a release from me?"

"But I—"

"Stop." I hold up a hand. "I didn't come to hear your side of it or how you've rationalized this to be okay. It's not. I could ruin not just your show but your career. You know that, right?"

"Wow." He shakes his head, and a malicious smile contorts his lips. "You have a very high opinion of yourself, huh? To think you have that much power. That anyone would pay attention to a glorified fashion flunky."

"I could remind you that this 'fashion flunky' is, for all intents and purposes, the right hand of one of the most powerful voices in fashion," I say, barely controlling my anger. "Or I could remind you of, you know, the law and how a lawsuit at this stage in your career would be devastating."

I step so close our bodies almost touch. His breath comes heavy, and he swallows. I tip up on my toes to whisper.

"We both know what this is really about, Chase," I say, making sure my lips graze his ear. He groans. "Pussy. Mine. And you being a spoiled little boy because you can't have it anymore."

I glance down to see his fingers twitching at his sides.

"You can barely breathe and are trembling to touch me," I tell him. "You tell me who has the power here."

"Lo, I can't stop thinking about you," he says hoarsely. "Maybe it started casual, convenient, but at some point it became more."

"Not for me." I step back. "I'm not trying to be cruel or heartless, but you crossed a line. Was this supposed to get my attention?"

"You wouldn't take me seriously," he says, sulky, petulant. "I want you, Lo."

"Where do men like you get off thinking you can have anything you want? I want the photo down, or this becomes a legal issue. Also I want any digital copies and the print hanging out there. I'll leave delivery instructions."

I'm done and ready for my night out. I head for the door, but Chase stops me, not turning me around but grabbing both my arms so tightly I wince.

"That's it?" he asks from behind me, grinding himself into my ass. "You think you can walk out and act like we never happened?"

He presses himself into me hard, flattening me against the door. My heart kicks me in the ribs. Sweat springs from my pores. A long-lost but familiar dread unfurls in my belly. I draw a deep breath.

"Let me go, Chase," I say calmly, hoping he doesn't smell my fear. "Or this gets worse for you."

"Worse for me?" he asks with a heartless laugh. "You said you had things to figure out, but you're giving it to him, aren't you? You're fucking that ballplayer."

I force myself not to squirm or try to free myself from his iron hold. Trying and failing to get free will only reiterate that I'm helpless. That he's stronger. That I'm vulnerable...like before. Like that day. Dark spots appear before my eyes, and I blink in hopes of clearing them. Of refocusing.

"You've asked me before about the voodoo," I rasp, hoping I've kept the panic from my voice.

He goes still behind me.

"Yeah, now I have your attention, you dickless bastard," I spit. "Let me go, or I promise you pain. You think you can hurt me because you're bigger and stronger?" I bark a humorless laugh. "That's not power. I can make your life miserable for years to come in ways you cannot even imagine. One curse would do it."

I turn my head and glare at him over my shoulder. "I swear it. Test me, Chase."

In the silence, I can almost hear his thoughts churning, his fear rising to match and soar above mine as he remembers the herbs and amulets and stones in my apartment. Wondering what they're for and what I'm capable of.

"Let me go," I repeat, infusing my voice with returning confidence. "And I'll leave instructions for you to deliver *my* photograph."

His fingers loosen enough for me to wrench away and turn. I raise my knee and aim straight for his balls. They're for show anyway. He crumples, his hands between his legs and his face wreathed in agony. I shove his shoulder so he falls on his back. He rolls over, his face all red and spotty. I stand over him.

"I want my photo," I tell him, my voice hard. "And to answer your question about the ballplayer, you're right."

I squat down and find his pain-squinted eyes.

"He can get it."

Kenan and I stand in front of the restaurant a few minutes earlier than we told his sister, Kenya, we'd meet her and her friend. The day is cooling some but is still very warm. Too warm for the elbow-length sleeves of my top, but Chase's rough handling left bruises on my upper arms. I don't feel like answering questions or talking Kenan out of beating Chase to a pulp. I have better things to do. Like see freaking Grip in concert!

I think the shirt looks fine, though. It's black-and-white-striped, tightly molded to my torso and cropped above my belly button. I paired it with a black tulle skirt, flaring out and kind of flirty, and some comfortable red flats because…walking.

"You look so beautiful," Kenan whispers, his cool breath fanning the hair at my ear.

"So do you."

And I ain't ever lied. He is…magnificent is my favorite way to describe him, and it still doesn't properly convey the effect this man has on me. The towering height and the breadth of his chest and shoulders. The legendary arms that don't bulge but are roped with muscles and veins. And as tall as he is, he's the *slightest* bit bowlegged.

I die.

Like, really, God? You had to put *that* cherry on top?

The mahogany skin. That striking face with jutting bones and onyx brows and piercing eyes, so dark and like a one-way mirror, seeing out but not letting you see in.

But he lets me see in. That's probably the sexiest thing about him, and that is saying something. My man is fine.

I just called Kenan *my man*. After telling him today that I don't belong to him, I just claimed him in my head. And I think I would cut a bitch if she tried to take him from me. Exes included.

"Babe?" Kenan peers down at me, frowning. "You okay?"

No, I'm not okay, I scream in my head. *I'm falling for you, and this is not part of the plan. Shiiiiiiiiit. And double shit.*

"Uh, yeah." I fan one hand. "It's a little hot."

"Let's wait for them inside." He thumbs over his shoulder to the restaurant. I glance up at the mustard-yellow awning emblazoned with SERAFINA. It's one of my favorite spots for Italian. The girls and I have hit it a few times after the Met, but it's close to Central Park, too.

I nod, and Kenan takes my elbow to guide me in. He's also, unlike Chase and most of the douches I've been with, a gentleman. I need to start my list of reasons to *stop* falling. Not reasons why I *should.*

We take the stone stairs to the top level where there's balcony seating. It's always crowded and the restaurant doesn't have a ton of space, but the food is great, and we can get to the park pretty quickly from here.

We've ordered drinks and an appetizer when his sister arrives. She's tall, which shouldn't surprise me considering she is Kenan's sister and plays in the WNBA. Her features also echo Kenan's in subtle ways. He stands, his smile wide and natural, as he reaches to hug her.

"Kenya," he says, turning to me, "this is Lotus DuPree. Lotus, my sister, Kenya."

"What's up?" Kenya studies me carefully, cautiously. I sense the protectiveness for her brother, and I like her right away. He's been through a lot, and she *should* vet anyone who enters his life and has such intimate access to him.

"Hi." I stand and reach for her hand. "Nice to meet you."

"Yeah, you, too." She slants a teasing look at Kenan. "I've heard so much about you. Like, sooooo much."

"Shut up, Ken," Kenan says, shooting her a quick frown, and they seem so much like a typical brother and sister it makes me smile. "Introduce me to *your* friend."

A slim woman steps into view from behind Kenya, holding her hand. She's pretty with smooth skin the color of rich mocha. No makeup that I can detect. Long, curly lashes frame her big brown eyes. She wears baggy jeans, Chucks, and a white Public Enemy T-shirt. Cornrows peek out from the edges of an Oakland Raiders cap.

"This is Jade," Kenya says. "Jade, my brother, Kenan, and his…" She looks between the two of us as if she's waiting for confirmation on how she should refer to me.

"This is my *girlfriend,* Lotus," Kenan answers dryly. "Nice to meet you, Jade. I haven't heard as much about you. Kenya's been keeping secrets."

"That's all right," Jade says with a chuckle. "Nobody's been talking about her ass either."

We all laugh, sit, and settle into easy conversation over my Chardonnay, Kenan's water, and the beers the two girls order.

"So you work in fashion?" Kenya asks.

I'm mid-bite of my orecchiette pasta when she asks, so I gulp it down and wipe my mouth with a napkin before answering. "I do. For Jean Pierre Louis."

"Never heard of her," Kenya says, picking up a slice of her pizza.

"Him," I correct with a smile. "He's the founding designer for JPL Maison."

"Fancy." Jade chuckles. "If it's not Converse, Nike, or Gap, you have to school me."

"Kenya, your brother already told me you play ball." I turn the question back around to them. "And what do you do, Jade?"

"I write music," Jade says and shrugs. "Been doing it all my life, but kinda new at getting paid for it. So far, so good."

"Speaking of which," Kenya says, glancing at her watch, "should we be heading to the park? The show starts soon, right, babe?"

Jade nods and glances at her phone, lit up with a text message. "Oh, this is Grip. Lemme see what he's talking about."

My mouth is hanging open. Kenan gently presses my chin up to close my lips and whispers, "You surprised or just catching flies?"

"She *knows* Grip?" I whisper back, hoping I'm being discreet, but I'm low-key about to lose my shit.

"Yeah. Kenya says they're cousins. I didn't tell you? We have front-row seats. We'll go backstage to meet him after."

"Um, nope," I say. "You skipped right over that part."

"I'll have to communicate better now that you're my girlfriend," he says. His smile fades. "I just said it and didn't even ask you if it was okay or if—"

I don't consider his sister or his sister's girlfriend sitting right there but lean forward to cut off his explanation with a kiss. It's quick, but it's enough. He cups my face, and he kisses me again, longer and with such tenderness it soothes the soreness from my confrontation with Chase. Not the bruises on my arms, but the other ways Chase hurt me today. Violating my privacy. His attempts to objectify me. Every way he tried to make me feel less fades in the shadow of this kiss.

"For real, though?" Kenya's amused voice butts in. "Y'all just going for it at the table?"

Kenan's fingers tighten on my face so I don't pull away. "Yup," he says against my lips with a smile. "Can you blame me?"

When I pull away, Jade is texting her famous cousin, I presume, but Kenya is looking at me, and her eyes brim with as much concern as humor.

"I'm gonna run to the restroom before we go," Kenan says. "Be right back."

When he's gone, I look at Kenya, waiting for whatever comes next.

"So here's the deal," she says slowly. "I need to know what's up with you."

I lift my chin and take the last sip of my wine before setting the glass back down.

"What's up with me?" I ask. "In what way? What do you mean?"

"You know the deal with Bridget's drama," she says. "I heard she rolled up in your job."

"Damn," Jade mutters, flicking a glance at me before turning her attention back to her phone.

"When all that shit came out, if Kenan hadn't stopped me, I would have kicked Bridget's ass," Kenya says, her face serious. "And that's the truth. I just wanna know if I'm gonna have to kick yours at some point for doing my brother wrong."

I always did admire the direct approach.

"Don't be fooled by my size," I start by telling her. "My ass doesn't get kicked."

"Guess she told you," Jade mumbles, still typing on her phone.

"Is that right?" Kenya asks, a grin starting on her lips.

"That *is* right." I tap the stem of the wineglass. "And I have no intention of hurting Kenan. I care about him a lot."

"He cares about you a lot, too." She chuckles and shakes her head. "I thought he was gonna get himself arrested when he saw that photo. I had to hold *him* back, and he never loses control."

Her mouth slowly straightens from the smile into a line, so like Kenan's. "If I hadn't been there, he would have kicked that guy's ass for sure."

I rub my arms, wincing at the lingering tenderness from the bruises hidden beneath my sleeves. I'm even more determined that Kenan won't see them.

"That situation is handled," I assure her. "I've dealt with Chase."

"Does Kenan know that?"

"Does Kenan know what?" he asks, frowning between the two of us.

"Hey," Jade says, standing. "We gotta roll. The car's outside to take us."

"It's only a few minutes away," I say. "We could walk."

Kenya and Kenan look at each other and say together, "New Yorkers."

"Y'all want to walk everywhere." Kenya laughs and follows Jade to the exit. Kenan and I are right behind.

"What did Kenya mean?" he asks. "Do I know what?"

I draw a shallow breath and release it quickly. "She asked me about the photo in the gallery."

"Dammit." Kenan grimaces. "I'm sorry. I have no idea why she even mentioned it."

"I know why. She loves you and was afraid you would get into some trouble going after Chase."

"She might be right," he says, a rough chuckle rolling out of him. "But it was all good. If you didn't sit for it or sign a release, we need to figure out how to handle it, though."

"Yeah, I, um…did. I already handled it."

We reach the sidewalk, and Kenya and Jade climb into the waiting black SUV.

"How did you handle it?" He stops before we reach the car.

"Kenan." I glance around him and see impatience gathering on both girls' faces. "Let's talk about it later. They're waiting."

"Let them wait."

"Kenan, come on," Kenya says.

"You can wait one minute," he tells her sharply, "or go the fuck on. Up to you, Ken."

She rolls her eyes and huffs a heavy breath. "Well, hurry up."

"Okay," he says, turning back to me. "Now that you've got everybody waiting…"

"*I* have everyone waiting…" I laugh at the tiniest gleam of humor in his dark eyes. "I can't believe you, Kenan Ross."

"Tell me. What'd you do? How'd you handle it?"

"I went to see Chase."

The spare lines of his face tighten. "And how'd that go? Did he give you any trouble?"

"No trouble. It's been removed from the exhibit."

It's a long summer day, and the sun hasn't quite set. In the near dark, he searches my face before nodding.

"Okay. You handled it. Good." He flicks a grin to his sister. "Coming. Doesn't hurt you to wait sometimes."

On the very short ride to Central Park, I tell myself I didn't lie. I omitted parts of the truth to protect him, and I'm still fully realizing how important that is to me.

CHAPTER 25
KENAN

"He's good," I say as Grip leaves the stage on Central Park's Great Lawn.

"Good?" Lotus asks, her face scrunched up. "Frozen yogurt is good. Boiled eggs are good."

"I prefer scrambled."

"The new James Patterson is good."

"Is it really?"

"It's all right." She shrugs and gives her head a quick shake. "My point is, Grip is *great*. Amazing. Gifted."

"So he's in your top five?"

"For sure."

I glance over to where Jade and Kenya are talking to some big guys I assume are security guards. "Looks like you'll get to meet him soon."

"I'm going to try really hard not to embarrass you and your sister," she says, her face completely serious.

"Damn, Lotus. I've never seen you this excited about anything. Should I be jealous?"

"Absolutely not," she says. "Never."

But we both know I was jealous earlier and acted like an idiot. "About today," I say, clearing my throat. "I'm sorry I showed up at your office with my...how did you put it? Caveman shit?"

"Glad!" someone yells from behind us.

I brace myself to be nice and patient when all I really want to be is with Lotus. We've had almost no time truly alone since she got back from Milan. I've kept a respectable distance most of the night to make sure nothing suspicious shows up on social media before we can talk to Simone in Monday's session. "Gimme a sec," I tell Lotus and nod toward the approaching fan.

This is the job.

One autograph turns into two and then more. I don't think of myself as famous most of the time. Nights like this remind me, but this isn't really my life.

"If you're finished being all *the champ is here,*" Kenya drawls from nearby, "we want to go see Grip. He has to leave soon."

I laugh at her joke. And it is a joke. My sister knows me better than anyone and realizes I would be perfectly fine if no one ever recognized or approached me. I'd prefer it.

When they lead us backstage, Lotus grabs my hand and squeezes. Hard.

"Oh my God," she squeals, her eyes bright. "It's happening."

"Um, remember that whole trying-not-to-embarrass-me thing?"

"Yeah, sorry. That's out the window. Brace yourself for fangirling. Major fangirling."

I'm loving this. My little always-cool-and-self-possessed badass is going to lose her shit.

We're taken to a small room with a few couches and a table stocked with bottled water. I recognize Grip right away, of course. He's taller than I thought, maybe five inches shorter than I am. He's still wearing what he performed in, jeans and a black T-shirt with DOPE written in white. His shoes, though, give me sole envy. The original 1985 Air Jordans.

"What's up, cuz?" he addresses Jade with a wide smile. He crosses the room and hooks an elbow around her neck, steals her Raiders cap, and kisses her forehead.

"What'd I tell you about the hat?" Jade grumbles, but she belies it with an affectionate smile. "I want you to meet somebody. Be on your best behavior."

"Only behavior I got," he jokes.

"Uh-huh. This is me you're talking to." Jade twists her lips and rolls her eyes. "I know your ass."

She motions Kenya forward and takes her hand. "This is Kenya," Jade says. She's a hard chick, but her eyes soften when she looks at my sister.

"Heard a lot about you, Kenya," Grip says. "I'll pray for you trying to put up with this one."

"Much needed and much appreciated." Kenya laughs and gestures toward Lotus and me. "This is my brother—"

"Glad!" Grip says. "I didn't make the connection. What's up, dude?" He walks over and daps me up. "I'm keeping my eye on the Waves." He points a warning finger at me. "Don't come for my Lakers."

"Oh, the purple and gold, huh?" I ask.

"For life, bruh," Grip replies with an apologetic shrug. "I'm an LA kid. I got no choice."

"You get a pass then," I tell him, reaching for Lotus's hand. "This is my girlfriend, Lotus."

Grip shifts his look to Lotus and then looks back at me, brows raised approvingly. Everyone knows he's notoriously in love with his wife, Bristol, so I know he means no disrespect. The opposite, actually.

"Hi, Lotus," Grip says with a smile. "Nice to meet you."

"Yeah, uh… Well, I'm…" She draws a deep breath. "Sorry. I'm such a fan. The show was fantastic."

"See?" Grip stretches his arm toward Lotus, his palm open. "That's what I'm talking about. None of you busters gonna even tell a brother he did good."

He gives Lotus an exaggerated nod and bow. "Thank you, Lotus. Glad *someone* noticed."

"Someone needs his ego stroked again?"

The question comes from a woman at the door, with dark hair and silvery-gray eyes. She's not in the public eye much, but I know it's Grip's wife, Bristol.

He walks over, drops a quick kiss on her lips, and pulls her in front of him, crossing his arms over her waist. "Don't come in here talking about *stroking* if you're not willing to deal with the consequences, Bris." He peers down at her, focusing a wicked look and grin on his wife.

"Ewww." Jade grimaces, walking over to give Bristol a quick hug. "'Sup, Bris. Grip, don't start with that shit. You got a room around here somewhere. Use it. Where's the kids? That's who I really came to see."

"With Mama James," Bristol says, settling back against her husband's chest. "Back at the hotel."

"I thought they'd be here," Jade says.

"Just because Grip dragged us on tour with him," she says, giving him a gentle elbow to the stomach and a grin, "doesn't mean my children have no structure whatsoever. They're not rock stars and are in bed the same time every night."

"The hotel's around the corner," Grip says. "Come back with us. We're rolling out soon. Another show. Another city tomorrow." He runs a hand over his face. "I'm exhausted and wanna crash."

He smiles at us. "You guys are welcome to come with us and have some dinner. My mom smuggles a hot plate into our hotels because she refuses to eat room service. It's kinda ghetto, but you'd be amazed what she can pull off with such limited resources."

"That's Aunt Mittie." Jade laughs. "Yeah, I need to see her before you roll out."

She looks up at Kenya. "You down? You gotta meet her."

Kenya looks to us, a question on her face. As cool as Grip seems and as much as I'm sure Aunt Mittie can make miracles with only Crisco and a hot plate, I really just want to be alone with Lotus. She's a Grip fan, though, and I won't deny her the experience.

"Totally up to you," I tell Lotus, keeping my expression neutral.

"It sounds like so much fun," she says.

I swallow my disappointment and start convincing myself that we'll have time together tomorrow or another day. The closer she gets to Fashion Week, the less time she has. And my time will be nonexistent soon because I'll have to show up for training camp. Then preseason games, then regular season. Hopefully playoffs.

"But I better not," Lotus continues. "I have an early morning." She looks up at me. "I think I should get home and rest," she says. "That okay with you, Kenan?"

Our eyes cling, and the same banked desire I've suppressed all night, fought every time our hands brushed or our legs accidentally connected under the table, burns in the look Lotus gives me.

"Yeah," I reply, keeping my voice even. "Early morning here, too."

"Early morning, my ass," Kenya says, giving me a knowing look. "Well, all right. You still coming to my game tomorrow?"

I reach for a hug and kiss her cheek. She makes a disgusted face in response, and everyone laughs.

"I wouldn't miss it, baby sister." I give Jade a quick hug, too. "Great finally meeting you. You'll be at the game tomorrow?"

"Yeah," Jade replies. "I heard I might get to meet your daughter."

"Probably not," I tell her ruefully. "She thought she could make it, but her mom texted me that she has a dance commitment. Maybe next time."

I turn my attention to Grip and his wife. "Really great meeting you," I tell them, extending my hand for fist pounds.

He grins, tucking Bristol, who looks like she's about to fall over from fatigue, in closer to him.

"I love that skirt, Lotus," Bristol says. "Jean Pierre Louis?"

"Yeah, it is." Lotus lifts a frothy layer of her black skirt. "And thanks."

"I love his stuff," Bristol adds.

"Lotus works with JP." I toot her horn, since she obviously doesn't plan to.

"No way!" Bristol's eyes widen and sharpen with new respect. "It's the one show I want to attend during Fashion Week."

"I can get you a ticket if you like," Lotus says easily.

"Seriously?" Bristol walks over and pulls her cell from her pocket. "Let me get your number."

"I was invited to play in the celebrity game at the All-Stars next year," Grip tells me. "You know ballers want to rap and rappers want to ball."

"Not this baller," Lotus offers. "Kenan's more of a jazz guy."

"For real?" Grip's brows arch. "I love Miles, Monk, Coltrane, Ella. Who you into?"

"All of the above and then some," I reply, pleased to find someone my age with a real appreciation for another era. "You'll have to come see my vinyls."

"Oh, you'll have to see his, too," Bristol says with a grin. "He's obsessed. Vinyl and sneakers."

"Yeah, I noticed the eighty-fives," I tell him, nodding to his Jordans.

"Well, you know," he preens, "just a lil' something for New York."

We all laugh and start the final round of hugs and goodbyes.

"I'm back on the West Coast in a few weeks," I tell Grip. I don't look at her, but Lotus stiffens beside me. Her hand clenches mine. "Let's try to get together before All-Star weekend."

"Sounds like a plan."

Once we've gone our separate ways, Lotus and I walk back to the Great Lawn and into the park. I broach something I've been thinking about all night.

"Lotus, we haven't had much time together since we became"—I hesitate over what to call us—"more than friends."

"True," she says, linking her elbow with mine. "And it's only gonna get harder. I'd almost forgotten you have to go back to San Diego soon."

"Yeah, I've got about a month left. Training camp starts in September." I guide us over to a bench to sit for a second. "I want to make the most of the time we have before I go."

"And the show is only three weeks away," she replies. "It's about to get crazy. No sleep and barely time for anything besides JPL."

"Yeah, I know." I bring her fingers to my lips. "Come stay with me tonight. We don't have to—"

"Yes." Moonlight softens the angles, the bones of her face. "We don't have to fuck, you were gonna say."

I laugh and pull her in to me, wishing I could drag her onto my lap right now. "Basically, but I want tonight with you. I want to wake up and have breakfast."

"French toast and bacon and eggs?" she asks tauntingly.

"Uh, egg whites and fruit for me," I reply with a smile. "But go for yours."

She shifts until our eyes meet.

"Oh, I'm definitely going for mine."

CHAPTER 26
LOTUS

ON THE RIDE TO KENAN'S APARTMENT, WE SIT IN THE BACK OF THE Uber holding hands, that one point of contact reverberating through every cell of my body. We speak very little, but there's no need. The air grows heavy with unspoken want and smothered desire. My head spins with fantasies of how he will please me tonight. How I might please him. I'm not planning for this to be *the* night, but I'm more open to him than I've ever been to anyone. It's not just sex I want, which is all I've ever had. It's that elusive intimacy—the sharing and exchange.

He doesn't release my hand on our brisk walk through the lobby. As soon as we step onto the elevator, he turns my back to the wall and takes up the seduction his silence began on the long ride home. He nips at my lips and kisses down my chin and over my breasts, suckling my nipple through my blouse.

"Kenan," I breathe, my head flung back against the elevator paneling. "I want this."

He kisses the curve of my neck and shoulder. The elevator dings and opens, and he tugs me by the hand to the door. His long strides make it hard to keep up, but my eagerness has me stumbling to try. Once inside, he turns my back to the wall and goes down on his knees in front of me, a supplicant king. He brushes his tongue repeatedly over the flower blooming around my belly button. I moan, digging my fingers into the dense, ungiving muscles of his shoulders. He drops lower, kissing my pussy through the sheer, fluffy layers of tulle and silk panties, a growl jerked from his throat when he inhales.

"Fuck, you smell…" He glances up, his eyes dark and feral. "You smell like you want me."

"I do." My voice is as ragged as my resistance—as frayed as my control. I frantically pull my skirt above my thighs and expose my panties and myself. "So much."

Groaning, he runs his nose up and down the front of my pussy and mouths me through the panties, greedily seeking, finding, sucking my clit through silk and lace. I scratch the wall at my back, looking for purchase, for strength to stand. I can't bear another minute without his mouth on me. Brazen, desperate, I pull the panties aside. His mouth seizes me, feasting, licking in the slit, taking my lips hostage between his. He reaches up, his huge hand grazing my stomach and sliding under my cropped shirt to squeeze the pierced nipple.

I don't know how I'll get what I need without fucking him. I need to be filled with him. I need every inch of this empty space inside me occupied, taken over by his body, by his patience and care. By *him*.

I pull away and go down in front of him, heedless of the marble floor, cold and hard under my knees. I grab his neck, pull him toward me, take his mouth with mine, and taste myself on his tongue, an erotic recognition that tightens my nipples and leaks down my thighs. My hands fumble with his belt—I'm trembling with the need to have him. He doesn't stop or help me but thrusts one hand into my hair and rubs between my legs with the other, sneaking under the panties to insert two fingers inside me.

I go still against his chest, my breath stilted, my hands useless on his zipper, my hips rolling in time with the fingers invading and retreating. His thumb rubs my clit while he fingers me with dogged certainty, his eyes locked with mine.

"Oh, God." My head drops to his chest as a tingle begins in my toes and flutters through my calves, my knees, my legs, and converges to the spot he is still ruthlessly, methodically possessing. And then I can't fight it. With one hand on his zipper, the other clenched around his bicep, I come. The orgasm runs rampant over my body, leaving no part of me untouched. A scream rips through me—rips through the apartment. Dry sobs tear at my throat, and wracked with pleasure, I bury my face in his neck, open my mouth over the muscled curve, and bite down. He tenses, growls, his muscles tight under my hands.

We go still. I draw back enough to look into his eyes, and our labored breaths collide between our mouths. Not releasing his gaze, I lower his zipper, slip my hand into his jeans, and pull on him through his briefs.

"Lotus," he mutters, his eyelids hanging heavy, his pupils blown wide with lust.

I don't wait for whatever he'll say next but push on his shoulder, coaxing him to his back, to the marble floor. I urge his shirt up and lick my lips at the sight of his torso, a slab of sculpted muscles. And those nipples.

My weakness.

I straddle his belly and bend to take one into my mouth. I moan at the taste of him—the smooth and rough texture on my tongue. I reach down and pull his dick out, rubbing up and down in rhythm with my head bobbing over his chest, sucking his nipples. He emits gruff, strangled sounds and plunges his hand into my hair, urging my head downward. I yield, leaving kisses as I descend. I whisper "yes" over his pecs, the sturdy cage of his ribs, the contraction of his abs.

His belt is already undone. His zipper, down. I glance up, ensnaring his eyes when my mouth reaches the most vulnerable part of him. I gulp. Kenan is a big man. I assumed he'd be no different here, and I was right.

"God, you're beautiful," I tell him, not even trying to keep the reverence from my voice. He's perfectly formed, chiseled, massive.

Mine. For tonight, for as long as I can keep him, *mine.*

I take his dick down my throat and swallow, relishing the wild sounds he gives me as a reward. I lick up and down, from root to crown, not overlooking an inch. I dip lower, taking his balls into my mouth one at a time, laving them until they're shiny, wet, slick.

"Fuck, Lotus," he moans, both hands fisted in my hair so tightly it stings. I don't care. I just want to feel with him. I slip my tongue into the slit at his tip, and at the first taste of the salty milkiness, I lose control. I'm a starved beast, gripping his powerful thighs with my hands, the rough hairs abrading my palms. I'm manipulating his balls and taking him so far down my throat I choke, saliva pooling in my mouth and running from the corners.

"Baby, I'm coming."

I nod jerkily, holding his hips in place and taking him down farther. My throat contracts around him with every hard-won gulp.

"Jesus, Lotus." His handsome features twisting with agonizing pleasure, he caresses my jaw as it works around him.

The first warm spurt coats my tongue and the roof of my mouth and rushes down my throat. I moan at the taste of him. Voracious, I hollow my cheeks to milk him of every drop. When the stream finally stops, I lick from the base to the tip, gathering all of him that I can. Savoring the taste, savoring him. When I've licked him clean, I crawl up his chest and tuck myself into the crook of his arm, my ear pressed to his heart seeking its reassuring thump. His fingers sift through my hair, and one large finger traces the blossoming zipper tattooed up my spine.

We lie there for a long time, heedless of the fact that the marble floor of his foyer is cold and hard. Heedless of the messy stickiness we coaxed from each other's bodies. It's quiet except for our slow, calming breaths filling the air. Our bodies are teaching us the scope of true intimacy. It's another's pleasure over yours. It's hunger unique to one other person—satisfied only by him. Only by her.

"That was…" Kenan's words fail, trail away, but I don't need them.

I touch his ridged torso and sprinkle kisses over his chest.

"I know," I whisper, my eyes wet with emotion. "I know."

CHAPTER 27
KENAN

The events of last night, after we gorged on each other in the foyer, are murky. We were both exhausted. I picked Lotus up in her skirt and top, leaving her purse, panties, and shoes and my jeans right at the door. We barely made it to the bed, collapsing in the center and falling asleep almost right away. I wake with her back spooned to my chest, and her soft roundness hardens my cock even beyond the typical morning wood.

"Someone's happy to see me this morning," Lotus says, her voice husky with sleep and, I hope, arousal. She turns to face me and slides one slim, toned thigh between my legs. My arms tighten around her, and I wish we could wake this way every morning. Is it too soon to think like this? To start exploring scenarios where we can *be* like this, together, all the time?

"I *am* very happy to see you," I murmur into the velvety sweep of her neck. "I want to see you all day. Is that possible?"

"All day?" She lifts her head and props herself on her elbow to peer down at me. "It's a Sunday, but JP still may need something this close to the show. Can I check with him before we make plans?"

"Sure." I'm distracted, dotting her jaw with kisses and rubbing her thigh beneath the tulle skirt. I roam higher and find the firm, naked curve of her ass. We look into each other's eyes, and last night's memories, the fiery moments, resurge between us.

"I didn't get to really see you," I tell her, my voice deep, scraping bottom with desire. I find the tiny button at the back of her skirt. "Let me look at you. We don't have to do anything you don't want to."

She shifts to make it easier for me to get the skirt off. With her panties in the foyer, I have an uninterrupted view of shapely, copper-toned legs, subtly curved hips, and a plump, bare pussy.

Grooming goes a long way.

I tug at the hem of her shirt, wanting to see her breasts, the bar that pierces one of her nipples. The shirt is almost over her head when she starts to struggle, to pull away.

"Kenan, no," she says, her voice pitched high.

"Baby, it's okay. I'll stop," I start reassuring her but lose track of my thoughts when I see dark bruises on her upper arms.

"Kenan," she whispers, completely naked in my bed, her eyes wide and worried. "I can ex—"

"Who?" I cut in, slamming my teeth together to contain my fury. "Who did this? How did you get these?"

"It's noth… It's nothing," she says. "Let it go."

"Tell me right now who put their hands on you," I grind out. "Do not lie to me."

"Kenan, you're making a big deal out of—"

"Dammit, Lotus."

"Okay. It was Chase," she says in a rush. "Geez. It was Chase, but he didn't mean to. He just grabbed me rougher than he—"

"Chase grabbed you when you went to confront him? You said you handled it and that he didn't give you any trouble."

"I did and he didn't," she says, sounding slightly defensive. "I was fine on my own."

"These," I say, lightly touching the dark marks on her arms, "say otherwise."

"Please don't blow this up into a thing." She rubs her eyes and releases a frustrated breath. "I can take care of myself. I kneed him in the balls and threatened legal action. It's done."

"Why'd you have to knee him in the balls?" I ask, my voice low and my frustration high. "What'd he do?"

She blinks at me, her gaze opaque, giving nothing away.

"Look," she finally says. "Kenya told me you overreacted at the gallery."

"No, I didn't."

She levels a wry look at me. "If it was anything like how you acted when you came to the studio…"

She leaves the rest unsaid, leaves me to replay it all in my head. Kenya *did* have to say I had PTSD to keep me from getting sued or arrested.

"Okay, I may have overreacted a little," I admit. "But these bruises? I can't let this go."

"I told you I handled it. I already talked to him."

I watch her in grim silence. I'm not going to talk to Chase. I'm going to punch him in the face. I don't make any promises, don't say a word, which seems to worry her even more.

"Kenan." She drops her head, crazy curls all over the place, into her hands. "Please leave it alone."

Impossible. First he takes a photo of her partially nude without permission. Then he has the balls to display it without a release. Then he leaves bruises on my girl?

My girl.

God, that feels right. I called her my girlfriend last night without even thinking about it. It rolled right out of me and felt as natural as breathing. As right as anything good I've ever had.

"I don't want you to get in trouble." Her brows pinch, and her lips press together. "You have a lot to lose, Kenan. I don't want drama in my life putting you in the news for anything other than how amazing you are. You said Bridget ruined your life. I don't want to do that."

"Don't even put yourself in the same hemisphere as Bridget," I say impatiently. "What she did is nothing like this. She betrayed me and got me caught up in a media circus."

"Here's a headline," Lotus says sardonically. "NBA PLAYER ARRESTED FOR ASSAULT AND BATTERY. Would that be circus enough for you?"

"You're right about one thing." I frame her face, tracing the delicate bones with my hands. "I have a lot to lose." I kiss her forehead, her temple, her chin. "I have you to lose, Lotus," I say, pulling back to hold her troubled stare. "No one will hurt you and get away with it."

Something flickers in her eyes, and she glances down at her hands. "Only two people in my whole life have ever protected me," she says, her voice wobbling. "Iris and MiMi. I haven't trusted anyone else to."

I know someone hurt her badly in the past. Her childhood trauma. I can't think too much about how it connects to the struggle she's been having with sex. If it's anything like what I've imagined, I'm going to lose my shit when she finally tells me. Even the thought of someone harming Lotus, my tough, tiny girl, sets bloodhounds loose inside me.

"You trust this ring to protect you," I say, taking her hand and stroking the ring she never takes off, "because MiMi gave it to you."

She nods, her head lowered, linking her hand with mine.

"What if she gave *me* to you?" I bend to whisper over her lips. "What if I'm your gris-gris now?"

Her head jerks up, and her eyes, darkened with emotion, fill with tears.

"I don't believe in spells or potions or voodoo." I put my hand over her heart, between her bare breasts. It covers most of her torso. "But I believe in this. I believe something special is happening between us, Lotus, and yeah, I've been hurt before. Lied to. Cheated on. But I'm not running away from this, from you, because of it. I won't let what happened in the past keep me from giving us a chance."

I kiss her nose, and she shifts so our lips meet and cling briefly, sweetly.

"Let me protect you," I whisper into our kiss, my hand still covering her heart.

She nods and scatters kisses over my jaw, my neck. While we were disagreeing, I didn't pay attention to her nudity, but it pierces my consciousness now until I can't focus on anything else. I want to explore all her body's secrets. To inspect the gift I've been given.

"I wanna look at you," I breathe across her pierced nipple, a dusky delicacy, and walk my fingers down to the lotus flower blooming around her navel. I glance up to find her studying me studying her, her grin indulgent. I trace the French lace filigreed at the tops of her thighs. My knuckle brushes her pussy, and her breath catches. Her throat moves with a deep swallow. My cock was so far down that pretty little throat last night. "You sucked my dick, and I almost lost my mind."

"You ain't seen nothing yet," she promises with a lascivious laugh.

I grin and slide my hand between her legs. "You're wet," I pant, my mouth watering.

"You have that effect on me."

I tongue the smooth skin of her belly and lavish kisses between her breasts and suck the bar in her nipple between my teeth. I look down, and she's dropped her legs open and is rubbing her clit. Her eyes are closed. Her neck arches.

"Don't stop," she gasps.

Hell no I won't stop.

We work together—her between her legs, me at her breasts, conspiring to bring her pleasure. She's writhing under her own hands, under my lips. I want her to come all over my sheets. The scent of her hair, the sweetness of her body—I want them to linger in this bed for days after she's gone.

"Fuck," she says on an expelled breath, her mouth falling open and her head pressing deep into my pillow while her body quakes and shudders.

When she quiets, I turn her over gently to feather kisses down the zipper decorating her spine and the small flowers running along the sides.

Damn, her ass is perfect. I squeeze both round, firm globes, and she gasps. I slide my finger between her cheeks and down to her pussy, spreading the juices she just poured out over the lips and then over her asshole, not daring to stick my finger in. We haven't even had sex yet, much less anal. Lotus may not even be into that, though judging by the way she pushes her ass against the pressure of my finger and moans, she may be open-minded.

"You eat ass?" she asks suddenly, and I know she's trying to throw me off.

"I'd eat yours," I reply truthfully. Because there is no part of her that would not be good to me.

We both seem to find that really funny and crack up laughing. I flip her back over and pull her in to me so I can feel the vibration of her happiness. I'm tickling her sides when a noise catches my attention.

"Did you hear that?" I ask, pausing, my fingers poised over her stomach.

"Yeah. Like a door?" She sits up. "Sounds like someone came into the apartment."

"Nobody has a key, but..." I hop off the bed. "That has to be Simone. She's the only one with a key."

"Crap," Lotus says under her breath, scrambling to get her top and skirt back on. Horror dawns on her face. "Kenan, my shoes and panties are still at the door."

"And my pants," I groan. "Dammit."

I slip on sweatpants and a T-shirt and make my way quickly to the front room. Dr. Packer had a family emergency and canceled our last session, so we still haven't talked to Simone about Lotus. I'd almost rather find a burglar than my daughter in the apartment right now, but it's Bridget and Simone standing beside the pile of clothes we discarded in the foyer. Simone stares at Lotus's panties, purse, and shoes. Bridget looks smug and furious.

"I don't remember you being quite this sloppy, Kenan," Bridget says, kicking our things out of their path. "Or having feet quite this small."

"Hey," I say, trying to keep my own anger out of my voice in front of Simone. "I wasn't expecting you."

I walk over and kiss Simone's forehead.

"Morning, Moni," I say "I thought you had dance."

She nods, her eyes still on Lotus's things. "I skipped because I wanted to see Aunt Ken play."

"I called," Bridget says with a note of defensiveness, "but it rolled to voicemail."

"When?" I frown at her. "I didn't get any message. When did you call?"

"Earlier," she says vaguely.

I'm sure she's playing games again. I'm so sick of it.

"Whose things are those, Daddy?" Simone asks, her voice subdued, her eyes downcast.

I'm kicking myself. Yes, Bridget shouldn't have barged into my place, but the weight of Simone's sadness presses on me. I wish I'd pushed to have the conversation with Dr. Packer sooner or waited to move forward with Lotus, though that's hard to imagine given how badly I want her. My daughter is once again caught in her parents' crosshairs—Bridget's spitefulness and my carelessness, my lack of control. However we got to this juncture, we're here now, and I can't lie to her. She's fourteen, not four. I need to respect her intelligence and the fact that she's been exposed to a lot more than I had at her age.

"Do you remember the woman I introduced you to at the restaurant?" I ask, watching her face for signs of recognition.

"Lotus," she says, meeting my eyes and nodding.

"Yeah. She and I are dating, Moni. She's my girlfriend."

Bridget gasps, and her frustration and anger grip me like a hand at my throat.

"She's here." I reach down to grab Lotus's belongings. Scoop up my jeans. "I'll be right back."

When I walk into my bedroom, Lotus sits on the bed, the tulle skirt flared out around her, an anxious look on her pretty face.

"Is everything okay?" she asks. "Is the coast clear?"

"Yours, I believe," I say, offering her the panties.

She grimaces, slipping them on and her feet into the red shoes.

"The coast is not clear." I reach for her hand and walk toward the door. "There was a, let's call it a mix-up to give Bridget the benefit of the doubt, and Simone is going to the game today after all."

Lotus stops, tugging on her hand. "What are you doing?"

"Babe, she was standing beside your purse, panties, and size-six shoes, which obviously weren't mine. She's not stupid, and I didn't want to lie to her. I told her you're here and that we're dating."

"Is she okay?"

That's the question I ask myself every day. I wonder what goes on in my daughter's quick mind—how she's processing the changes in her life. Huge sea changes that have come in waves and thrown her world into chaos.

"She'll *be* okay," I say with more confidence than I sometimes feel. "Lying to her won't help. Come on."

After a brief hesitation, Lotus nods and follows me.

When we reach the living room, my daughter sits on the couch, typing on her phone. With the open floor plan, I can see Bridget in my kitchen, poking around in my refrigerator.

"Do you not have any mineral water?" she yells.

I ignore her.

"Moni, you remember Lotus, right?"

She scrutinizes every detail of Lotus's appearance, starting at her red shoes and inspecting every inch to the wild platinum curls.

"How do you get your hair to do that?" Simone asks, her brows pinched, eyes curious.

"Um, to do what?" Lotus touches her hair uncertainly.

"Curl and stuff," Simone answers grudgingly, like even this small interest in Lotus is being dragged from her.

"Well, it wouldn't always." Lotus laughs dryly. "When I first tried, it wouldn't curl at all. It's taken me a long time to figure out the products that work for me."

Lotus eyes Simone's hair, scraped back into a ponytail.

"I'd guess you're a 3C, like me," Lotus says.

"What's a 3C?" Simone asks.

"It's just a hair type. There's a system to determine hair texture. It helps you figure out the best products." Lotus hesitates, biting her lip before speaking. "I could help you if—"

"That won't be necessary," Bridget snaps from the kitchen. "Kenan, I wanted to talk about tomorrow if we can."

"About what?" I ask with deliberate calm. I have no desire to speak privately with her. We'll just fight, and I'd rather do that under Dr. Packer's unbiased third-party watch.

Bridget slides a meaningful look to Lotus and then back to me. I want to tell her to leave my apartment and go ruin someone else's Sunday, but Lotus clears her throat, drawing my attention. She shakes her head subtly.

"I need to get going. I'm catching an Uber," she says, making her way to the door. She smiles at my daughter. "It was nice seeing you again, Simone."

Simone pretends to be occupied with her phone and flicks a long-suffering look my way, like she's wondering why she has to endure my new girlfriend.

"Let me at least walk you out," I tell Lotus, my hand at her back.

"No, that's okay," she says quickly. "I'll talk to you later."

I follow her out into the hall and close the door behind me.

"Kenan, go back inside," she whispers. "Your daughter needs you. I don't think she's taking this well."

"No, but we'll work on it tomorrow in our session, when she was *supposed* to find out about you. I know Bridget did this on purpose trying to catch me off guard." I run a frustrated hand over my head. "This isn't how I saw us spending our morning."

"How'd you see it?" Lotus asks, walking backward to the elevator, her eyes never leaving mine.

I take a few steps in her direction, closer, so I won't have to be loud.

"Like last night," I say softly, and glance at the closed door. "Spending time getting to know my new girlfriend."

The elevator opens with a ding, and she steps in, holding the doors for a second and meeting my eyes, no humor in sight.

"I love the sound of that," she says, letting the doors close.

I could ask if she likes the sound of me getting to know her better or the sound of me calling her my girlfriend. I think, I *hope,* it's both.

———————

"Tell us what you're feeling, Simone."

Dr. Packer's calm tone doesn't soothe the turbulence in my daughter's eyes. It's Monday, and Simone barely spoke to me yesterday when I returned from the elevator. She gave me the cold shoulder on the ride to Barclays, where Kenya's team played. She was borderline rude when she met Jade, giving us all sullen silences and rolling eyes. If there's such a thing as the terrible teens, we're smack dab in the middle of it.

With her lips parted to speak, Simone flicks an uncertain look between Bridget and me, only to clamp her mouth into a stubborn line and trace the hole at the knee of her jeans with one slim finger.

"You can tell us, Simone," Dr. Packer prods gently. "Your parents won't get upset, and we need to all be honest if we want to make this work."

"Daddy wasn't honest," she says, not looking at me.

"Simone, I didn't mean for you to find out about Lotus that way," I say. "But I didn't lie to you."

Accusation flares in the eyes Simone finally turns on me. "You said she was a friend when we saw her at the restaurant."

"She *was* a friend then," I return evenly. "We decided we…like each other more not long after that. I planned to tell you about her in our session today."

I hope the look I flash to Bridget, seated on the other side of Simone, isn't as irritated as I feel.

"But when your mom brought you to the apartment yesterday," I say, "it took me by surprise. I thought I'd have time to tell you. I promise I had every intention of discussing it."

"It's true, Simone," Dr. Packer confirms. "It was on today's agenda."

"So you knew, Mommy?" Simone demands.

"Yes." Bridget clears her throat. "I didn't mention it because we were planning to tell you today."

But you showing up unannounced ruined that plan, huh, Bridge?

God, I wish I could say it out loud, but I bite back the comment.

"With that said," Dr. Packer says, "can you tell us how your father's new relationship makes you feel?"

Simone swallows and rapidly blinks long lashes. "Sad."

I open my mouth, ready to dive in, not even sure what I'll say but needing to make her feel better. Dr. Packer catches my eyes, offering a subtle shake of her head.

"Why sad?" she probes.

"Everything keeps changing," Simone whispers, a frown gathering over her troubled eyes. "And I just want it to be how it used to be when my mom and dad were together."

When I meet Bridget's eyes, they hold the hint of the smugness I expect, but there's also helplessness. Hurt. Guilt. I want to scream *"You did this!"* But the more distance I have between our marriage and our current situation, the more I gain perspective. I know Bridget isn't to blame for everything. I wasn't the best husband. Hell, on the road three-quarters of every year, I wasn't always the best father. I share that guilt in Bridget's eyes.

"Marriages don't always last," Dr. Packer says. "But family does."

Simone's bottom lip quivers. "How long was Grandpa married to Grandma, Daddy?"

The question is a foul ball, errant, flying over the fence and landing in the middle of the conversation. All the emotions I've carefully suppressed bob to the surface at the mention of my father. I look to Dr. Packer for guidance, and her quick nod encourages me to answer.

"Uh, they were married forty years," I reply.

"Did you think you'd be married to Mommy that long?" Simone asks, her eyes intense, bright, scouring my face like a searchlight.

"I thought I'd be married to your mom the rest of my life, Moni." I slant a look at Bridget's increasingly strained expression. "I took my wedding vows very seriously."

"So did I," Bridget says, her words curt. "Just because I made a mistake doesn't mean I didn't value our vows."

I don't answer because this isn't the time to rehash my past with Bridget but to acclimate Simone to my future with Lotus.

"You were gone so much," Bridget mutters.

God, if that woman burps, she finds a way to blame me for it.

"That still doesn't excuse…" I smother the words and my anger before continuing. "It's behind us now. We both made mistakes, and it's time we move on."

"Are you gonna leave me if I make a mistake, too?" Simone twists her fingers into an anxious knot in her lap.

"Never." I reach over and gently tilt her face until she looks at me. "I won't ever leave you, Moni."

"What's the difference?" she whispers, glaring. The daggers in her eyes stab my heart, and I struggle to keep my voice even while I'm bleeding inside.

"I can't undo my blood in your veins," I tell her. "You're part of me, and nothing can make me *not* your father."

"But the divorce made Mommy not your wife," she says, her eyes shiny and the same exact shade of begging blue as her mother's. "You can't forgive her?"

I look past Simone to catch Bridget's alert stare and then to Dr. Packer.

"Tell her, Kenan," Dr. Packer says.

"I don't know, honey," I reply honestly, shrugging. "I'm sure I'll forgive her one day, but we won't ever be married again. It's not going to happen."

"Because of *her*," Simone says, her voice carrying a bitter edge. "You're so busy with Lotus that—"

"Simone, don't," I warn, as close to sharp as I'll be, keeping my voice gentle but not having it. "You know your mother and I were apart long before I met Lotus."

"So you're already in love with her or what?" Simone scoffs, but her bravado doesn't hide the hurt and fear.

"I care about her a lot. We're in a relationship. I think you'd really like—"

"Are we done?" she cuts me off, jerking her glance to Dr. Packer.

"We actually have a few more minutes." Dr. Packer glances at her watch. "But we're almost finished and—"

"*I'm* done." Simone stands abruptly and strides to the door. "I'll be in the car, Mommy."

The door slams behind her and I release a heavy breath, lean forward, and rest my elbows on my knees. My head feels so heavy in my hands. My heart, like lead in my chest.

"Well, that went well," Bridget drawls dryly.

The tenuous hold on my frustration snaps. I swivel my head to scowl at her.

"Why the *hell* did you show up at my apartment unannounced yesterday, Bridget?" I grit out. "We could have avoided all this if you'd just—"

"If *you'd* just kept your dick in your pants?"

"Don't you worry about my dick. Stay out of my personal life and away from my relationship."

"Your relationship." Bridget twists her lips into a disdainful curve. "With a girl barely out of college you've known for, what? A couple of months? Spare me. It won't last. I don't even know why we bothered telling Simone."

"We bothered because Lotus is important to me," I tell Bridget, seeing through her bravado the same way I saw through my daughter's. I force myself to soften my tone despite my irritation. "Simone's not the only one who has to accept that, Bridget."

She stares back at me, the ire flickering and fading until she bites her lip and lowers her lashes.

"I agree this wasn't an ideal way to introduce this subject," Dr. Packer says, "but at least you've been honest with Simone. She's hurt and confused and still getting used to her new life. Her foundations have been shaken, and any hope she had of restoring things seems farther away than ever now."

Dr. Packer leans back in her seat and eyes us both.

"I think Simone may benefit from a few one-on-one sessions with each of you," Dr. Packer says. "There could be some things she's reluctant to say in front of one or the other."

Bridget and I nod our agreement.

"Give her time, watch her closely, and put her first," Dr. Packer says. "That means setting aside all this acrimony."

She splits her gaze between the two of us, her brows lifted. "Think you can do that?"

Bridget and I exchange a look charged with all the things that infect our every interaction—resentment, anger, fear, regret—before both nodding curtly. Bridget stands as abruptly as Simone did, and she, too, walks away.

CHAPTER 28
KENAN

I'VE RETURNED TO THE SCENE OF THE ALMOST-CRIME.

And Kenya's not with me this time when I enter the Gilded Bean, so I need to check myself.

"Oh." The woman with the glasses from the other day looks up from her writing pad. "You're back."

"Yeah. I'm sorry if I…came on too strong the other day," I say, pulling from my very limited supply of charm. "I was disappointed the photo wasn't for sale."

"Yes. I picked up on that, Mr. Ross."

"You know who I am?"

"When a man offers twenty thousand dollars for a photo in my gallery," she says wryly, "I make it my business to know who he is."

"The offer still stands. I want that photo very badly."

"It's not for sale. Actually, as you can see," she says, gesturing to the wall where the photo of Lotus hung before, "it's no longer in the exhibit."

I study a picture of the High Line where the Lo photo hung. So Lotus was right. It has been removed.

"May I ask why you were so interested?" she asks "I mean, besides the obvious. She's a beautiful girl."

"She's *my* girl. My girlfriend, and that punk ass didn't have her permission to display that photo."

"That's a serious allegation." She glances at the new photo and frowns.

"I'm not here to make allegations. It's up to Lotus how she wants to move forward. I just want to speak to Chase. Is he here?"

It's a tiny lie. I want to do more than speak to him, but I school my expression into something harmless and only mildly interested.

After a pause and a searching glance, she points down a hall to the left. "He's in one of the rooms working with a few photos."

"Thanks."

I follow the direction she pointed, and sure enough, Chase is up on a ladder, adjusting the mounting for one of the displays. I kick the ladder lightly, and it wobbles for a few seconds, almost toppling. Chase lets out a high-pitched curse, and I grab the ladder to stabilize it at the last moment.

"What the hell are you doing here?" Chase frowns at me from his perch.

"Get down," I say in as calm a voice as I can. He's not nearly as big as I am, but he's much bigger than Lotus, and he put his hands on her. I keep seeing the dark marks on her arms, and I'm getting madder by the minute.

"Excuse me?" he asks, one brow lifted, the picture of arrogance.

"You can climb down and we can talk face-to-face, or you can stay up there and I kick this ladder so you fall. Either way, you're coming down."

He runs a hand through his hair, left loose to his shoulders today, and expels an exasperated breath. He climbs down and, once he's on the ground, folds his arms over his chest.

"Look, Lo came and we sorted it out," he says. "So you and I have nothing to discuss, as far as I can see."

"That's the problem. You don't seem to see very far."

"I don't know what you mean."

"If you'd had any foresight," I say, stepping closer to him, "you wouldn't have grabbed her. You wouldn't have bruised her arms because then you might have forecast that you'd have to deal with me."

He swallows, his eyes shifting nervously to the door behind me. "She had bruises?"

"She actually tried to hide them because she was afraid I'd come and punch you in the face or something."

I bend slightly until our eyes line up. "Because I *am* going to punch you in the face."

"You can't just go around hitting people," he says, but he doesn't sound completely sure.

"Why not?" I frown and tilt my head, as if I'm really contemplating this. "You go around taking naked pictures of women without their permission and displaying them in your exhibit."

"You may not realize this, but Lotus and I have a history," he says, his expression self-satisfied. "She and I used to—"

"Fuck. I'm aware."

He pauses, his eyes narrowed.

"But we're getting off topic," I say with deceptive calm. "I'm here to punch you in the face."

"Why? I took the photo down."

I step even closer to make him feel every one of the inches I tower over him. Let him see how it feels being threatened by someone bigger.

"You left marks on her," I say, "so I leave marks on you, and you won't press charges because you broke the law and she could prosecute you and your career could be over. Yadda, yadda, yadda."

"And I'm supposed to just let you hit me?" he asks, expression outraged.

"Do I look like I need you to *let* me hit you? I just hit you. I'm explaining to *you* why I get to do it without any consequences."

"Dude," he says, swallowing anxiously. "You don't have to do this."

"*Dude*," I mock with malice. "You should have thought about that before you put your hands on my girl."

"Your girl?"

I won't repeat myself. I squint one eye and survey his pretty-boy features.

"So chin, nose, eye, cheek? You get to pick." I touch my balled fist to his face. "You're welcome."

CHAPTER 29
LOTUS

I DON'T HAVE TIME FOR THIS.

We're only a week away from the show. It's as hectic as it always is, and I've been working closely with Sasha, the show stylist, coordinating as many details as possible. JP designed about a hundred and fifty pieces for the collection, and we've landed on thirty looks to send down the runway. We've booked most of the models, of course, but there were a few girls JP saw in Paris last February who were unbelievably still available. They're doing other shows during Fashion Week, but the scheduling works so they can squeeze us in, too. Which means last-minute fittings and shuffling some of the other look-pairings to adjust. The three of us—JP, Sasha, and I—slept in the atelier last night and probably will again tonight.

Like I said, I don't have time for this.

And yet here I am, standing outside a Presbyterian church on a Thursday night when I should, by all rights, be at the studio. I told JP, though, that I really needed a couple of hours to take care of something personal. He knows I never allow myself to need anything the week before a show, so he knew it must be important.

And this is.

I've been showing up a little earlier each week until I was actually sitting in the circle, nibbling on cookies and sipping coffee. At first, it helped simply to know that I wasn't alone. Childhood sexual abuse is so invisible and prevalent. I'm staggered that one in every four girls is sexually abused before the age of eighteen.

I'm one of them.

So many of us are walking around like I've been, living with secrets—living with resentment that the adults who should have protected us failed us.

Living in the dark.

I've been mostly listening to the other women. There are only four of us and Marsha, who guides the group. I'm thankful for the small size. It builds trust faster. I don't know what these women do from nine to five, but I know who hurt them. I know how far it went. I know how it affects each of them to this day.

Sherrie's uncle started touching her when she was only four years old, and it wasn't discovered until she was eight. He was never allowed to be alone with her again, but no charges were brought against him. He never spent a day in jail. She got no real help, and it wasn't until she was battling depression and had attempted suicide that a therapist unearthed what was really beneath it all.

It was Chloe's cousin.

It was Kyla's aunt.

I may not know where they live or their favorite TV show, but I'm intimate with their pain, and I sit in a circle of light where they expose their darkest secrets.

Kenan doesn't know about my Thursday nights. The last few weeks have been magical in so many ways, with our relationship growing, deepening, at the perfect pace. We've had relatively little time together because of my schedule and his. He's had to travel overseas for a few commitments and appearances, and my life is confined to the atelier. But when we are together, it's like nothing I've ever felt before and more fun than I've ever had. Exploring the Brooklyn Museum, Coney Island fireworks on Fridays, Saturdays at Smorgasburg, Brooklyn's food flea market in Prospect Park, ferry rides, music festivals, and Shakespeare in the Park. He's seeing New

York through my eyes. I'm seeing life through his. We're stretching each other, absorbing each other.

We're falling in love.

We haven't said the word, but I'm sure I'm falling in love with Kenan Ross, and I'm certain he's falling in love with me.

And, yes, the sexual chemistry between us is combustible. Simply a look, a barely there touch sets us on fire. He knows my body's secrets, and I know his. Sometimes I'm the one who drags us back from that last step. Sometimes it's actually him because he wants me to be sure. He wants me to be ready, even though he doesn't know all the reasons I've held back.

I haven't told him details, but I think he has his suspicions. Marsha said it would require a patient man. Kenan has been that and more. He really must think he's robbing the cradle. We've been dating for a month, and we haven't "gone all the way." Soon I'll ask for his letterman's jacket and a corsage for the prom.

He's in Croatia, of all places. Apparently, basketball has become a big deal there. The letters I receive in the mail every day almost make his absence worthwhile. He must have someone local sending them while he's gone because there's no way they'd get here from overseas in time. I reach into my bag and pull out yesterday's card.

"You have made my heart beat faster."
—*Song of Solomon 4:9*

I slide the card back into my bag, careful not to bend it. When I get home, I'll put it with all the others in this vintage metal lunchbox I used as a sewing kit when I was a teenager. That old lunchbox has been with me through high school home ec, traveled from the bayou to Spelman, and got me through my stint at FIT.

"You coming in?" Sherrie asks from the top of the church steps. Her smile is open and friendly. The look she gives me, compassionate.

She waits while I climb the steep stairs to reach her, and we walk inside and down to the basement together.

I'm the only one in our little group who hasn't shared my story. I've told them a little about the emptiness, how I sobbed the last time I had sex. The sensory-triggered flashbacks and panic attacks. They even know I'm dating someone amazing but I'm afraid to take that final step with him.

"Good evening, ladies," Marsha says, taking a sip of her coffee and looking into the eyes of each woman in the circle. "How's the week going?"

"I finally told my family about what my cousin did to me," Chloe says, blinking rapidly at the tears crystallizing over her eyes. "They didn't believe me. Not even my own mother."

The silence that follows should be filled with astonishment, but it's not. We've all been betrayed by someone close to us—all been let down or disbelieved.

"My mother had the nerve to bring up 'my past,' as she likes to call it," Chloe says, biting one of her already-nubby fingernails. "She says a girl can't be as promiscuous as I was and expect people to believe her when she makes accusations. I was seven when it happened. She made me feel like a whore. Like I was some slut crying wolf."

Tears course down her cheeks unchecked.

"I tried to explain." She sniffs and looks helplessly at Marsha. "I used the language you helped me with. I told her some of us may have a lot of sex, or some of us may not be able to have sex at all, but we're all trying to gain mastery of the original abuse. She didn't get it, though, and said I was making excuses."

"Tell me your truth, Chloe," Marsha says, her voice pitched low and soothing but firm. "Your mother made you feel dirty, but tell me what is true about you. What you've discovered about yourself."

"My self-worth was connected to sex," Chloe says haltingly, casting quick looks around the circle. "I believed I had to be sexually desirable to be worth anything to anyone, but that's not true."

Kyla went on a second date with a man she met online.

"He's so sweet," Kyla says, her smile coming and then going. "He tried to kiss me, and I froze. It wasn't as bad as it's been before when I...fought, but I still froze."

A single tear skids over her cheek, and she swipes at it impatiently. "I just want to kiss someone nice, someone good, without thinking about what *she* did to me." Kyla swallows and closes her eyes. "I'd forgotten for so long. I wish it had stayed buried and I'd never remembered."

"Our minds don't usually let us get away with that forever," Marsha says. "And even if we don't remember, it will find a way to manifest. At least when we remember, we know what we're dealing with. We know *how* to deal with it."

"He was really sweet about it," Kyla adds with a smile. "We're going out again."

"That's amazing, Kyla," Marsha says, real affection evident in the look she gives the other woman. "Keep us posted."

Marsha glances at her watch and then around the circle. "Anyone else want to share before we close out?"

Chloe sniffs and accepts a tissue from Marsha with a smile. They're all so brave, so vulnerable, and have never pressured me to share much at all. Each week they allow me to sit here and absorb. The trust it takes to share such difficult things with strangers—to trust them with your deepest hurts—is remarkable.

"I want to share something," I say, my voice so low I barely hear it myself.

"Sure, Lotus," Marsha says, not overly eager and with exactly the right amount of encouragement. "Go on."

"I told you that I'm on a..." How do I say this without sounding ridiculous? "A sexual hiatus, for want of a better word."

We exchange smiles around the circle.

"Sex was always completely devoid of intimacy," I say with a shrug. "I wasn't hyper-sexed, and I wasn't afraid to have it. I just detached, and that started to feel really shitty, so I've stopped having sex for a while." My laugh emerges, harsh and humorless. "Leave it to me to meet a great guy right as I swear off the dick."

The other women laugh, and we seem to collectively relax for a moment.

"So he's been patient?" Marsha queries. "Understanding?"

"He has, one hundred percent," I confirm. "And I haven't even told him what happened, but I think he suspects."

My throat burns when I approach the next words, and I swallow several times, stopping and starting before getting them out. "I've learned so much about intimacy with him, even though we haven't had sex." I laugh dryly. "I mean, we make out long and hard and do everything possible except the kitchen sink."

Their laughter comes again, and it makes me feel a little lighter, but that fades with the next words I want to say.

"But I didn't cry before until after sex," I say. "And it's an awful, lonely feeling. I'm afraid it'll happen with him and that'll somehow mean I'm not getting better, and I need to *feel* like I'm getting better. Things are so good for us. I don't want to mess it up—to think I shouldn't have tried. It's like if I can't find intimacy, satisfaction with *him*, who's such a good man and everything I could have asked for, then maybe there's no hope for me."

"Don't put so much pressure on it," Marsha says. "I mean, it's a big deal, yes, but if I'd given up with my husband the first time I had that same negative response I'd had in other situations, we wouldn't be where we are today. Hell, we wouldn't be anywhere. I would have run and assumed it would never get better." She reaches over and squeezes my hand. "It does get better. It can take time, but it can get better."

"Have you considered telling him what happened?" Sherrie, who's been kind of quiet tonight, asks. "So he's prepared for any negative response? So he can know what might be triggers or things he should avoid doing?"

"I've thought about telling him," I say, with ropes knotting in my belly. "But every time, I can't imagine it. Only my family knows what happened, and not even all of them. I've never told my story out loud. I don't even know what it sounds like."

"You could test it on us," Marsha offers softly. "Or not. Whatever you feel like doing."

I glance at my watch. They have to go, I'm sure, and soon so do I.

"I know we're almost at the end of our time," I say, shaking my head. "I don't want to keep you from anything."

Chloe settles back and crosses her arms over her chest. "Frozen dinner is the only thing waiting for me at home."

"My cat'll be fine for a few extra minutes," Kyla murmurs.

We all look at Sherrie, who's typing on her phone. She glances up with a smile. "Telling my roommate to turn off the Crockpot because I'll be a little late."

"See?" Marsha offers a triumphant smile that urges me to spill all my secrets. "We've got all the time in the world."

CHAPTER 30
LOTUS

TWELVE YEARS OLD

"Sit still, Lo! I'm almost done," Mama says, impatience popping in her words. "Hold your ear."

I obediently pull the top of my ear down so it won't get burned while she runs the hot comb through my hair. Smoke rises from the heat and pressure that flatten the crooking coils that bother her so much. I can do it myself sometimes, but I end up with even more burns, and it takes a long time. And we're already running late.

"See?" she says, a smile in her voice even though she stands behind me and I can't see her face. I can't see the glowing red eye of the stove that lends the comb its heat. "In a few minutes, your hair will be straight like Iris's."

I glance at my cousin Iris in the corner, reading the library's copy of *The Lion, the Witch and the Wardrobe*. Iris doesn't need a pressing comb, and her hair isn't exactly straight. It's wavy but as fine as the white girls' hair at school. Her skin is almost as pale, too. Her mother's, my aunt Priscilla's, complexion is a mixture of dark honey and the palest caramel, just like Mama's. Both of them have silky hair hanging to their waists.

I'm the only one who needs the hot comb.

"All done," my mother declares with satisfaction, dividing my hair into sections for ponytails.

"Can you leave some out?" I ask.

So it hangs down my back like Iris's. Like yours and Aunt Priscilla's.

I don't say it aloud, but that's what I want.

Mama's hands pause, but then she parts my hair so a large section in the back is left free of the bands, pulling the rest into two ponytails.

"I'm leaving some out," Mama says, a warning in her voice. "But you can't run all over the place sweating. Your hair will go right back and not be straight anymore."

"You done?" Aunt Priscilla asks, inspecting my hair. "We'll see how long that lasts. I don't know why you bother pressing it in the middle of the summer."

"It'll last today," Mama says. She turns off the stove. "You ready?"

"I got potato salad and fried chicken," Aunt Priscilla answers. "Check on those sweet potato pies. We need to go."

"We gotta wait for Ron anyway." Mama opens the oven to check the two pies.

"Well, he better bring his broke ass on," Aunt Priscilla mutters, not quite under her breath enough that we don't all hear.

"Don't talk about my man." Over her shoulder, Mama gives Aunt Pris an irritated look.

"Honey, what you see in that trifling man I don't know. He can't pay your rent, and neither can you. Far as I can tell, they ain't worth keeping if they can't pay *at least* a bill or two. That's a recipe for a new man if I ever saw one."

"Ron's different," Mama says, her voice softer than usual. I'm used to hearing a sharp edge to Mama's every other word, but not when she talks about Ron. She says Ron is different, but I say *she* is. I've never seen her act the way she does with him. "And he's so good with Lo."

No, he's not. He creeps me out and touches me every chance he gets.

It's nothing unusual. Mama and Aunt Pris keep creepy men around who help pay the bills. Iris and I have gotten really good at avoiding their hands, but Ron has stayed longer and seems to have more hands than the rest.

He finally shows up thirty minutes later.

"You're late," Mama tells him, a frown puckering over her dark eyes.

"I say I'm right on time, baby." He lowers his head to kiss her, shutting her up.

"So nasty when he puts his tongue in her mouth," I whisper to Iris.

"I know." Iris scrunches her expression. "But they seem to like it."

By the time Ron takes his tongue out of Mama's mouth, she doesn't look irritated anymore. She wraps her arms around his neck while he whispers in her ear. Aunt Pris enters the living room, looking like a buttercup in her yellow sundress. She rolls her eyes and twists her bright-red lips.

"Like we ain't late already," she says, popping Ron on the head as she walks by. "Let's go."

Iris, Aunt Priscilla, and I squeeze into the back of Ron's old Cutlass Supreme. Mama rides with him up front.

"No air in here?" Aunt Pris complains.

"You *could* be walking," Ron says, looking at Aunt Pris in the rearview mirror.

"And you *could* be home, since this ain't *your* family reunion," Aunt Pris fires back.

Iris and I giggle, and I catch Ron glaring at me in the mirror, too. I don't care. I like it when Aunt Priscilla says all the mean things to Ron I wish I could say.

"Broke ass," Aunt Pris mutters again under her breath.

"Broke ass" is the worst thing a man can be in Aunt Priscilla's book. Usually Mama's, too, but ever since Ron started "sniffing around," as Aunt Pris calls it, she's changed. For once, Mama doesn't seem to care that Ron can't pay her bills—that sometimes she has to pay his. Aunt Priscilla never hides her irritation that Mama is fine with Ron's wallet being empty as long as her bed isn't. It breaks their code of survival.

I stick my arm out the window and let it wave like water.

"If you don't roll that window up, Lo," Mama snaps. "Long as it took me to press that hair, and you gonna roll down somebody's window?"

"Sorry, Mama," I mumble, rolling the window up but leaving a tiny, rebellious crack at the top to let the breeze in.

"I hope they're playing horseshoes," Iris says.

"I'm not good at horseshoes," I remind her.

"I'll show you. Remember when you couldn't even get hopscotch right?"

I pinch her side playfully, and we both giggle. When we were younger, I could never get hopscotch, so Iris would jump ahead of me and I would follow her lead until I started doing it on my own. I don't know why it was so hard for me, but mimicking her steps was the only way I got it. "Hopscotch" is our code now for when one of us needs help from the other. We've both yelled "Hopscotch!" on the playground when a bully has tried to mess with us. Maybe it's silly, but it's our thing. It's hard in New Orleans' Lower Ninth Ward, and we don't have much, but Iris and I have each other.

"We're here," Mama says. She half-turns in the seat and studies my hair. "Remember. Don't sweat your hair out."

I glance out of Ron's car window doubtfully. It's so hot they already have sprinklers on at the community center where the reunion is being held.

"Go find the kids," Mama says, hands on her hips. "We don't need y'all in grown folks' business today."

We "find the kids" and play horseshoes and kickball while the grown folks play spades, Bid Whist, and dominoes, their laughter and all the things we aren't supposed to hear reaching our ears anyway. When it's time to eat, Iris and I sit at the kids' table with a little bit of everything on our plates.

"What's your favorite?" I ask Iris.

"Fried chicken," she says around a greasy mouthful, pointing to a leg, thigh, and breast on her plate. "Can't you tell?"

"I like this étouffée." I spoon up some of the soup and rice from a Styrofoam bowl.

"I can teach you how to make it," an old lady nearby says.

It's my great-grandma MiMi. We don't see her much since she lives in the bayou out in the middle of nowhere.

"Okay." I shrug. "Maybe someday."

She takes my chin between her fingers and studies my face. "You're growing up, Lotus," she says. "Such a pretty girl."

Does MiMi see Iris sitting beside me with her light skin and long, silky, "good" hair? She's the one people usually notice, not me. We're dressed almost identically, both wearing white tube tops and shorts.

"Uh, thank you." I look away when MiMi keeps staring at me. She has a way of looking right through you. Mama says she practices voodoo like a lot of the women in our family used to do. MiMi's kind of scary, and I'm glad when she lets my chin go and moves on.

We eat and run all day until it's close to getting dark. The sun's about to go down, and I'm playing hand slap with one of our cousins when Aunt Priscilla walks over, frowning and glancing around the pavilion.

"Lo, I don't see Iris anywhere," she says. "Go find your cousin so we can go. I don't want to be in that death trap of Ron's on the road at night."

"Yes, ma'am." I take off toward the field where I last saw Iris playing with one of the dogs someone brought along.

"Bo!" I call. Aunt Priscilla is Creole. Iris's father is German, so Iris is all mixed up and got a little bit of everything in her. That's why I call her Gumbo. Bo for short.

I wander into the old sugarcane field that borders the community center. Looks like no one harvested it last season. All the tall stalks, some of them rotting, make it hard to see.

She wouldn't have come this far in. I turn, ready to retrace my steps and find my way out, but I bump into something solid.

"Oh, Ron," I say, looking up at him cautiously. "Hey."

"Hey, Lo." He addresses the words to the little buds on my chest in my tube top. "You growing up fast."

His smile makes my stomach knot with nerves, but I'm not sure why. I glance around and see nothing but stalks and Ron.

"I better get back." I go to step around him, but he steps with me. When I step right, so does he.

He chuckles and touches my face. "We got a few minutes."

"I–I gotta go. Aunt Pris sent me to find Iris." My voice shakes a little, and my heart is pounding so hard I hear it. "She'll be looking for me."

"Naw. Her new man just got here," he says easily. "She'll be occupied for a while, convincing him to pay next month's rent. We never get to talk, you and me."

"I'm gonna go on back, Ron."

He grabs my wrist and pulls me in to him. "You been running around here half-naked all day," he says, his voice coming deeper, rougher. "Looking all good."

The word *naked* sets off alarms in my head. He shouldn't be talking to me like that. Or looking at me like that. Or sneaking in little touches every chance he gets.

"No, I haven't." I try to pull away, but his fingers tighten. "Let go."

"Just one kiss, Lo," he whispers, leaning forward and pressing his mouth to mine.

"No!" I jerk back, but he holds my head in place with one big hand. I open my mouth to scream, and he shoves his tongue inside. It's wet and thick and muffles my voice. I gag. How can Mama like this? I bite his bottom lip until I taste blood.

"Little bitch," he snarls, letting me go and touching his bleeding mouth.

I run but don't get far before he pushes me from behind. I fall, and my head hits the ground hard. The world darkens, spotted with little pegs of color like the Lite-Brite toy I got from Goodwill last summer.

Then everything goes black.

When I open my eyes, I can't move. Ron has my wrists in one hand over my head. A breeze passes over my legs, and I realize my shorts and panties are gone. I'm trapped beneath his hips and thighs, and something hard pokes at me.

"No!" I scream, turning my head back and forth so hard, one of my ponytails comes loose. I can't see through the thick, dark curtain of pressed hair. "No! Please."

"This'll be just between us," Ron hisses in my ear. "You'll like it. Promise."

"Please," I sob, the smell of my hair and his cheap cologne and rotting sugarcane clogging my nostrils. "Ron, don't."

But he does.

And the pain is everywhere. In my head from the fall. In my wrists from the iron fingers clamped below my hands. Between my legs where it feels like a pipe is on fire and forcing its way inside. He grunts over me like a rooting pig happy in mud, his mouth hanging open and his eyes rolling back in his head. Spots swim in front of me, and I squeeze my eyes shut. Tears scald my cheeks and trickle into my hair.

There's a scream in my head that no one hears but me. I keep screaming, but my mouth is frozen shut, the sound trapped inside. It's a secret cry, so loud in my mind it's all I hear, but it won't come out. Oh, God, the sound won't come out.

Look up.

It's the faintest whisper, barely heard through the screeching in my head.

Look up!

That whisper comes again, urging, more urgent, and through the pain and the noise, I look to the sky. Two clouds bunched together slowly pull apart. They look like jaws, and as they stretch open wide to reveal the sun hiding behind them, my mouth opens, too, stretching with the clouds. And finally, my voice floods the rotting field.

"*Hopscoooooooootch!*"

"May, now you know how fast these girls are." Ron stands shifty-eyed and shadowed in the setting sun, belt hanging loose and his zipper undone. "Lo may be young, but she already got a taste somewhere, the way she was coming on to me."

"You lying!" Iris yells, squeezing me protectively.

I huddle deeper into her, shaking so hard it hurts, my teeth chattering in the summer heat. My hair is half-down, half-up, and wild. That private place between my legs is so tender, even the cotton panties burn against my torn flesh.

Mama glares at Ron and then at me, as if she's not sure who she hates most right now.

"Lotus, I told you about being fast," Mama says, but doubt trembles in her voice. She knows. She has to know he's lying—that I wouldn't.

I can't even defend myself. I haven't said a word since I yelled "Hopscotch" and brought Iris running. Mama and Aunt Pris weren't far behind. The five of us stand in the middle of this field, and Ron's lies are as rotten as the sugarcane.

"May," Aunt Pris starts, her lips pressed tight together. "I don't know if—"

"That's right, we don't know," Mama says, her eyes narrowed on her sister. "I just need a minute to think, Pris. Gimme a…"

Her voice breaks like a dish crashing on the floor, and she starts crying, both hands covering her face. Ron reaches for her, and she slaps at his shoulders, at his face and head.

"You no good..." she screams, her light skin going red. "How could you, Ron?"

"Baby, come on now," he says, capturing her flailing limbs, trapping the talons of her fingers in one hand and pulling her against his chest with one thick arm.

"I ain't coming on," she screeches at him. "Not this time."

"Baby, you know me," he coos into her hair, making circles on her narrow back with his hand. "I love you. You know how it is with us."

Sobs shake her against him, and she tosses her head back and forth, denying, but she stops scratching and clawing and starts clinging, burrowing into his neck.

"How could you?" she whispers over and over again, sounding more hurt than angry. Broken, not outraged on my behalf.

"We gotta tell the police," Iris says, as if she's the adult.

"No!" Mama and I say in unison.

"No," I say again. Iris's face blurs through my tears. "I don't want anybody to know."

I turn pleading eyes to my mother. "Mama, please, no cops." I glare at Ron. "Just make him go away."

She stiffens at my words, looking helplessly between me and the man who hurt me, like there's a hard choice to be made.

"Make him go, Mama," I beg again. "Please, we don't have to talk to the cops. Just make him go away."

"But, Lotus, we..." She licks her lips. "We all probably need some space to figure out what happened."

"I know what happened, Mama," I protest. "He ra—"

"Lotus!" Mama cuts in like a blade. "Don't say that."

"But he did," I weep into Iris's hair. "He did."

"Maybe you should stay somewhere else for a while," Mama says, avoiding my eyes. "Until we all feel more comfortable."

"Me?" I bounce my shock between Mama, Aunt Pris, and Ron, whose bloodied lip pulls with a smug smirk. "But, Mama, I—"

"Just for a few weeks, Lo," she says, some of the guilt on her face turning into impatience.

"No," Iris screams, squeezing me tighter. "Don't send *her* away."

"Just for a few weeks," Mama says again, her tone firmer.

"Then I'm going with her." Iris pulls her lips into a flat, determined line.

"You ain't going nowhere, girl," Aunt Pris says. "What I tell you about getting in grown folks' business?"

"But Mama," Iris says, her voice thick and wobbling, "where's she gonna go?"

The stalks shift and part, snapping under someone's feet, startling us all. It's my great-grandmother MiMi. She takes her time looking at each of us but finally fixes wrathful eyes on Ron. He gulps, shivers.

"I'll take her," MiMi says, looking at me with those ancient eyes. "She can come stay with me."

CHAPTER 31
KENAN

IF THERE'S ONE PLACE I NEVER EXPECTED TO BE, IT'S HERE.

New York Fashion Week. Front row of the JPL show. Yet here I sit, anxiously awaiting the first "look," as Lotus calls it. She told me the show JP has been designing and planning for months will be over in less than twenty minutes.

My kind of event.

The waiting audience is seated on a terrace overlooking Lincoln Plaza. I can't fully appreciate the city on the verge of sunset or the excitement electrifying the air because I'm ready for it to be over. I'm happy for JP and his team, whom I've come to know and actually like over the summer. But the sooner the show and the after-party are over, the sooner I can have Lotus to myself. She warned me her schedule would be bruising in the last few weeks leading up to the show, but I wasn't prepared for how little time she'd have for anything else.

How little time she'd have for me.

I've never been involved with someone whose schedule and commitment to their craft rivaled mine. In three weeks, I report for training camp, and the NBA will own almost all my time for the next nine months, at least. Ten if we make playoffs, which August and I are determined to do. Then Lotus will be on the receiving end of my career. It's not easy to live with. *I'm* not easy to live with. I'm even more obsessive about my eating and workout regimen during the season. I watch film constantly. I talk even less because I'm in my head studying plays, scoping other teams' offenses, mentally picking apart their defenses before games.

It's all ball.

I may not have started out thinking I'd be an NBA player, but I've always been driven in every endeavor. I would have been this way about law if I'd fulfilled my father's dream and pursued it. If I'd been a farmer, I would have been this way about fruits and vegetables and soil. It's the way I'm made, and nothing has ever disrupted this pattern in me. I know what Bridget did was wrong, but I also recognize that I'm no picnic, especially once the season starts.

And Bridget lived through a lot of seasons.

She's the last thing I want to consider right now. I've moved on completely. It doesn't matter that Lotus is in fashion, something I never gave a rat's ass about, or that she doesn't know Oscar Robertson from Oscar Meyer. That I'm eleven years older. Or that I live on the West Coast and she's on the East. It doesn't even matter that she may believe in voodoo. Maybe she's a witch. I don't know. I do know one thing for sure.

I'm falling for her.

And if I'm keeping it one hundred, at least with myself, I'm probably already in the past tense on that score. I've *fallen* for her.

You'd think with all the drama *and* trauma I experienced with Bridget, I wouldn't be doing this again. But that's just it. There is no "again" to what I'm feeling. This is uncharted territory. I've never felt this way about anyone. God, it shames me to think it, but Bridget and I met in college. I've known her for sixteen years, been married to her for most of those, and I never felt for her what I feel for Lotus after mere months.

I've always jealously guarded my solitude, so wanting to be with someone all the time is not only foreign but disconcerting. I read the Song of Solomon for notes to send her. That's right. It's in the

Bible. This is some body-snatcher shit. I don't know who has taken up residence in this mind and body I've always been so disciplined with. Who has taken up residence in this heart.

The circular path of my thoughts stalls when the lights drop and music fills the terrace. The song is like Enya screwed a DJ and gave birth to some bastard New Age music possessed by a heavy bass line. A woman, tall, thin, strides with confidence and swagger down the runway. She poses, pops, turns. Before she's out of sight, another has taken her place at the end of the runway.

The next twenty minutes present a parade of women whose beauty is only rivaled by the gorgeous clothes they wear. I may not know much about fashion, but I know these clothes are art, and I feel pride that my girl was such a crucial part of this masterpiece. Celebrities, not just critics and fashion insiders, stuff each row. I spot Bristol James, Grip's wife, a few seats down. We wave briefly, but Bristol returns her attention to the clothes right away.

It's all over in twenty minutes like Lotus promised, and JP emerges from behind the curtain, joined by all the models, and struts to the end of the catwalk, waving and receiving the adulation the collection deserves. The crowd is on its feet. I'm scouring the scene for any sign of Lotus, but she's probably backstage.

As a spokesperson for the line, I have a pass, which I use as soon as the show concludes and people start dispersing. Lotus said the Fashion Week schedule is brutal. Back-to-back shows scheduled in venues all over the city have most critics, editors, fashion bloggers, and attendees doing their damnedest to get from one to the next on time.

Among the Amazons, some of whom almost look me in the eye wearing their high heels, it's hard to find my little Lotus. When I spot her, she's hugging JP and wearing midnight-blue skinny velvet pants that mold to every line of her svelte figure. The shirt, if it can be called that, is ivory-colored silk. It's not much more than a bra with long sleeves clinging to her arms and some kind of crystals pouring from the wrists and over her hands. A hint of dark nipples shows through the fragile shells cupping her breasts, and her stomach is bare, a lotus flower the only interruption of her smooth skin. She turns to answer someone, and I gulp. Her ass in those tiny pants is criminal. God, I want to lick that zipper climbing her spine. I should be used to this—how parts of me go painfully hard and other parts of me go unbelievably soft at the sight of her—but I'm not. I half-hope I'll never get used to it.

Maybe she feels my eyes on her. I wouldn't put it past her. There is something unique, different about Lotus. She senses things, feels things I'm not always in tune to. She searches until she finds me.

"Kenan!" she squeals, and quickly picks her way through the shoulder-to-shoulder crowd to reach me. She's wearing more makeup than usual and a nose ring, a tiny gold hoop encircling the keen curve of her nostril. As soon as she's close enough, I bend my knees, wrap my arms around her, and, with my elbows locked under her ass, pull her up to me.

"I'm so proud of you, Button," I whisper through that cloud of platinum curls.

She stiffens in my arms, pulls back to peer into my face. Her smile is blinding, an amalgamation of joy and fulfillment. "You know it's not my line, right?" she teases, resting an elbow on my shoulder and tracing my eyebrows, my cheekbone, with one neat nail.

"I know everything you've done," I insist. "And I know nothing about fashion, but the show was fantastic." I kiss the warm line of her throat. "You're fantastic."

She dips her head until our eyes meet, and the smile fades from her eyes, from her lips. She lays her forehead against mine. "I want to spend the night with you, Kenan."

My heartbeat trebles behind my breastbone, and I swallow my eagerness.

Calm your cock and lower your expectations.

We haven't had sex, and I'll wait a year, two, however long it takes for her to feel comfortable. She's spent the night several times, and it's always hard to stop, but I do. For her, I always will until she says we don't have to. So when she says she wants to spend the night, my cock and I should know by now it doesn't mean…

"Sure." I set her on the floor. "You mentioned an after-party—"

"I'm not going," she cuts in, her eyes affixed to my face. "I already told JP."

"Oh, okay. Yeah." I clear my throat. "If you want to grab something to eat—"

"I don't." She takes my hand and peers up at me in the dimness of backstage. Models, critics, celebrities, JPL staff all mingle around us, but for me, we're the only two people here. "I want to go to your apartment, and I want to spend the night. Kenan, I'm ready."

"Lotus, baby, you don't have to—"

"Kenan!" JP shouts near my ear.

Lotus and I don't break our stare immediately but linger on each other for a few seconds before we look to her boss. He's practically vibrating with triumph, and I get it. I'm happy for him, but right now I need to figure out what Lotus means. What she's saying—if it's what I think she's saying. If it is, we're out of here as soon as possible.

"Did you enjoy the show, *mon ami*?" he asks me.

"Yeah, it was great." I pull Lotus in to my side, caressing the smooth skin of her back. "Everyone seemed to love it."

"*Oui!*" His obvious pleasure coaxes a smile from me. "And Lotus, you're sure you don't want to come with me to the after-party? Everyone will be there. All the industry giants."

Lotus snuggles more deeply into my side with a husky chuckle. "After all the hours I've put in for the last month," she says, sounding tired but happy, "there's only one giant I want to see."

My smile stretches so damn wide it hurts. I can't even hide it, what she means to me and how I want her. Now that Simone knows, I don't give a damn who sees us together. People aren't generally interested in my life except when Bridget makes a mess of it.

"Well, I like to take some credit for this," JP drawls, his French accent thickening and his eyes gleaming, "since it was *my* button that brought you together."

"I think I would have found a way with or without the button." I bend to kiss the top of Lotus's head. "But thanks for the help."

"*De rien.*" He flicks his head toward a side exit. "Go on and get out of here then, lovebirds."

"You're sure?" Lotus asks, her fingers tightening at my waist.

"We'll start again soon enough," he reminds her. "So go before I remember that I can barely function when you are not with me at these awful parties."

For someone so small, Lotus manages to drag a man twice her size through a crowd with seemingly little difficulty. As soon as the door opens, September sunlight pours into the backstage area. Lotus draws a deep breath before stepping outside a little ahead of me.

"Freedom," she says, releasing an extended breath. "It's over."

A wry chuckle unwinds from her and is quickly gobbled up in the squawk of horns and New York's urban cacophony. She glances back at me over slumping shoulders, the look filled with weariness and anticipation.

"Take me home, Kenan."

CHAPTER 32
LOTUS

THIS IS WHAT I WANTED. *HE* IS WHAT I WANTED.

To be here with the man leaning against his apartment door is what I've wanted for days, weeks. Kenan didn't even notice JP practically salivating over him in the three-piece suit from the JPL Men line, but I did. The perfectly groomed shadow darkening his granite jawline. The impossibly wide horizon of shoulders straining the tailored fabric and narrowing to slim hips and the powerful length of his legs. There's an indolence about him, but it's deceptive. The air pulses with want—a patiently checked desire I'm finally ready to indulge.

I'm so proud of you, Button.

Not *you look beautiful*, which would have been nice, too, but *I'm so proud of you.*

The perfect thing to say to the girl whose one parent spent so much time changing and molding her, pressing out her crinkles and straightening her waves, but was never satisfied.

I'm proud of you.

"I'd like to talk first," I say, sitting on the living-room couch and slipping off my shoes.

"First?" He pushes off the door, stalks to the couch, and sits in the opposite corner, leaving a few feet between us.

"Yeah, first." I smile despite the churning in my stomach. "Before we make love."

"You know I'd wait months, years," he says, eyes fastened to the large hands on his knees. "I want you badly, Lotus. I think you know that, but I'll wait as long as you need. You mean that much to me."

His words, perfectly timed, placed, spoken, settle me, and the story comes pouring out. "I told you before there were things I needed to share with you."

"Yeah." He glances up, and that flick of lashes is the only detectable movement. He's gone completely still, and alertness sharpens his stare.

"I'm ready to"—I swallow the nervousness threatening my words—"to tell you why I needed to wait and what happened."

A muscles twitches in his cheek. "You're going to tell me someone hurt you," he states, not asks.

Remembering his response to Chase, I think this might be nearly as difficult for him as it is for me. I shift on the couch until I'm beside him and take his hand between mine, kissing his knuckle. "Yeah, I need to tell you."

He nods and pulls me closer until my head is on his chest and his chin rests in my hair.

"I don't want to do details tonight," I say softly. "I shared the whole story, detail by painful detail, with my support group last week, and—"

"Support group?" he asks.

"You may not have noticed because it's only for an hour every Thursday, but I've been attending a support group for…for, um, childhood sexual abuse survivors."

His massive chest swells under my cheek with a lengthy inhale. The heartbeat in my ear surges, accelerates, thuds.

"Okay," he says simply.

"My mother was never happy with me." I shake my head against him. "I'm not really dark, but compared to the rest of my family I was. My hair was all wrong."

"Your hair?" He runs a hand over the mass of it, kissing the crown. "What did she think was wrong with your hair?"

"It's not like hers or Iris's or Iris's mom's or any of our family's. It seems like such a small thing now, but growing up, it was a big deal. It made me feel like I wasn't good enough."

I shrug, a dismissive gesture that doesn't come close to telling the story of how my mother rejected me in a million small ways before she rejected me in the greatest way possible. In the worst way possible.

"She had this boyfriend who..." I falter, my throat closing around the secrets, around the dark memories. My body is reluctant to release them, but I have to. I'm not holding on to this trauma. It's holding on to me. It has me in a vise grip. I have to get it out to move on.

"Dammit," I mutter, twisting my fingers in my lap.

"Baby, you don't have to—"

"I want to," I tell him, glancing up. "I need you to know."

He stares down at me and passes a callused thumb over my lips. "Okay. Tell me."

I nod and swallow, forcing myself to keep going. "She had a boyfriend."

"What was his name?" Kenan demands before I can go any further. His hand is clenched into a tight fist on his knee.

"Ron Clemmons," I reply in a hushed voice.

I want it behind me. I want it out in the open and left behind so I can run forward.

"He, um... He raped me when I was twelve."

"He..." Kenan's words get caught up in his throat like a jammed rifle. "Is he in jail? What happened to—"

"He's in hell," I interrupt, the words falling fast, sharp, heavy, like a guillotine, quick to execute judgment. "We made sure."

I meet the questions collecting in Kenan's eyes, but he doesn't ask how one "makes sure" someone goes to hell because I think he knows that is, believe it or not, the least important part of this story.

"When I told my mother what he'd done," I continue, the hardness melting into a sorrow I'm not sure when or if I'll ever be able to shed, "she didn't believe me."

A hollow laugh spills over my lips. "Or she did believe me but didn't care. Not enough to give him up."

"You're saying she stayed with that motherfucker?" Kenan demands, pulling back to stare at me. "After what he did to you, she stayed with him?"

"She chose him and sent me to live with MiMi."

"*That's* how you ended up living with MiMi?" Kenan's voice rises, powered by outrage and fury and scorn. "What kind of woman does that? Baby, what the…"

He stands abruptly, prowling in tight circles like he's caged and doesn't have full use of the expensive apartment, only that tiny portion his feet outline in the carpet. His breathing changes, becoming erratic.

"Kenan," I say gently, standing and approaching him. "It's okay."

"The hell it's okay." The words charge out of him like a battle cry, and murder and bloodlust seethe in the eyes looking down at me. "How could she choose that piece of shit over you? Over her own daughter, knowing that he…"

He slams his eyes shut maybe against images that for me are more than imaginings. They're memories.

He shoves breath through his nostrils like a bull. Just this morsel of the dismay I've eaten all my life nauseates him, turns his stomach and sickens him. His fists open and clench compulsively at his sides. He can barely contain his rage on my behalf, and it makes me love him that much more.

I love him.

There is no more falling. There is no more choice or turning back. It's done. I'm his in every way but one.

"I didn't have trouble with sex," I tell him, calm falling over me like a veil. "I needed to figure out why I'd always been able to have sex and feel nothing, until it made me sick that I felt nothing. I'd been detaching emotionally."

"So you stopped having sex," he says, searching my face.

"Yes, I had to figure it out. My counselor says our minds do that sometimes to protect us. We forget, compartmentalize, detach. Whatever mechanism it takes to survive, we do it, but then when it stops working, you have to deal with the shit you've hidden from yourself."

My laugh is dry and self-mocking. "Mine stopped working this summer. So I decided to stop having sex right when the sexiest man I've ever met started sniffing around."

"You'd better mean me," he says, humor breaking through his scowl for the first time since I started my story.

"Yeah, you," I confirm softly. "I was so afraid to risk myself with you at first, and then I was afraid that the same bleakness I felt with sex before, I'd feel with you."

I walk over to stand in front of him and take his hand, link our fingers. "I was afraid it would happen again."

"What would happen?" he asks, confusion in the glance he gives me.

"I'd have sex and feel nothing but emptiness," I say uneasily. "But the last time I had a flashback and panicked. I was so scared. As soon as it was over, I cried like a baby."

"And you thought that might happen with me, too?"

"I was afraid if it happened with you, there was no hope, considering how I feel about you."

Tension throbs in the beat of silence following my statement.

"And how do you feel about me?" he asks, his eyes alert, intense.

The words lodge in my mouth. Too many confessions in one night. Too many things I've exposed to him. I'm tired of telling. I want to show him how I feel. I don't need words to tug at the tiny crystalline bow holding the shells together that cover my breasts. It loosens easily. Liberated, my breasts fall free. Kenan's eyes drop to my nipples, hard and round, before returning to my face and waiting for my next move.

I shrug one shoulder, letting the sleeve slip down my arm until the shirt dangles from my body. I shrug again and the other sleeve slides away, dragging the insubstantial scraps of silk to the floor.

Still his unblinking stare doesn't stray from my face, searching my eyes.

I slide a finger into the tiny slit holding my velvet pants together at the waist, unbuttoning and pulling them down over my hips and stepping out. They lie with the blouse in a pool of expensive fabric at my feet. His expression is as stony and impenetrable as the face of a cliff, but his fingers twitch, and I know he's dying to touch me. I'm dying to touch him back. I tuck my thumbs under the little strings of my thong and start pushing, but his big hands at my hips stop me.

"No." It's his first word since I started stripping. "Let me."

Our glances tangle. My mouth tingles, trembles. I lick my lips with something approaching nervousness and nod my permission for him to finish undressing me.

Finally, his eyes roam all over my body, from my toes and knees, over my thighs and hips and waist, lingering at my breasts. A lifetime passes before I feel the slightest pressure at my hips, his long fingers pushing at my thong. His palms slide down and under the strings to cup my bare ass. My breath hitches when he squeezes gently. His hands are so large, they cup each cheek completely. He keeps pushing until the thong slides the last few inches past my shins to cuff my ankles.

I stand before him completely nude, but feeling no more exposed than I did when I told him about Ron, about my mom and my struggles. That was true nakedness. This body he's seen before, but one wouldn't know that by the intent way he watches me, as though if he looks away he'll miss a breath.

"Is there anything I should know?" he asks, searching my face. "Anything you don't like or don't want me to do?"

"Don't…" I haul in a breath. "Don't hold my arms over my head."

"Okay," he agrees softly. "Anything else?"

"Everything we've done so far has been amazing, but I'm not completely sure what might, um…trigger me." I shrug and lick my lips. "But I want to try with you. I want *you*."

"You sure?" he asks, and there is a quality to his voice that speaks of restraint at its limit. I know for a fact that if I said right now I couldn't, I didn't want to, he wouldn't, but I also know that as soon as he's sure I want this as much as he does, he will devour me.

And I want to be eaten whole. Don't parcel me up. Don't take me in small bites. Consume me in one starving gulp because that's how I want him.

I tip up on my toes, pushing my breasts into him, relishing the bite of the buttons from his suit vest pressing into my naked flesh.

"I'm ready," I whisper, my voice breathy and nearly broken with suppressed desire.

My words unleash the storm. He sweeps me up and walks us to his bedroom, kicking the door closed. This isn't his first time seeing me this way, but now we both know I won't stop. Tonight, we're taking a step I didn't know when I'd be ready for, and if I'm being honest, I can't be sure how I'll respond to it. I won't know until I try. My mind might play the same tricks on me, on my emotions. My body and my heart are ready, but my mind may not comply. I could end up sobbing alone in Kenan's shower the way I did Chase's.

The tenderness in Kenan's eyes makes my heart pause, skip beats, and then pound. No, I won't sob in the shower alone. If I cry, it'll be in Kenan's arms. If it feels bleak, I'll let him past the walls to comfort me. That's the bond of intimacy we've established—one I never had with anyone else.

Once I'm standing in front of Kenan, I venture under his suit jacket, finding his shoulders to slide the perfectly tailored coat over sleekly muscled arms, like steel inside the expensive cotton. A man in a suit vest has always set me off. Kenan in the vest, the crisp white shirt contrasting, is almost beyond bearing. I deftly begin undoing the buttons, and he doesn't stop me, nor does he offer assistance.

He's a magnificent mountain of a man, every line, sinew, and muscle sculpted with a master's skill and attention to detail. Even his roughest edges appeal to me. The scars and nicks in his flesh from battles on the court. The hands callused from years of ball handling and the rigors of professional sports. I'm in awe of the physical specimen standing in front of me.

Once I've divested him of the shirt and pants, he stands in only briefs.

I've seen his dick. Held it. Choked on it, but he's never been inside me. I don't ask myself any of that silly nonsense about will he fit. Of course he'll fit. It might be tight, and I might feel like I'm going to burst with that big dick stretching me open, but he'll fit. I'll mold my body around him until the fit is so perfect, no woman after me will feel right again. I already suspect that after him, no one else will do.

"Have I told you that you're a beautiful man, Mr. Ross?" I ask, running my eyes over the expertly hewn ridges of his impressive body.

"Maybe." He shrugs one heavily muscled shoulder. "I can't really think straight right now to remember. Not with this in front of me."

He brushes his thumb over my pierced nipple, sending an electric charge from the sensitive tip to a pulsing spot between my legs. I draw a shaky breath. His thumb continues its descent, tracing the quivering muscles in my stomach, outlining the flower inked around my belly button, and gliding between my thighs. With our eyes locked, he pushes his thumb between the folds of my pussy and rubs my clit over and over in a seductive rhythm that literally buckles my knees. He loops an arm around my back to keep me upright, but his thumb never lets up on the sensual torture. When I'm sure I can't take another second, he slides his thumb down and hooks it inside me.

"Shit," I hiss. His thumb is like three of my fingers, and he doesn't hold back, thrusting aggressively. "Kenan."

His name stutters out on a needy breath. He walks me back the few steps to the bed and lays me down, hovering over me, bending to work first my pierced nipple between his lips and teeth and then the other. He shifts, his thumb rubbing my clit again and three huge fingers inside me, stretching me, readying me. Tremors start at my toes, rip over my thighs and back, and explode when his hands bring me to orgasm with tender intent.

I'm sure my eyes roll back in my head. Color splashes across the backs of my eyelids—a kaleidoscope of bright lights with every wave of sensation. I can't see a thing; the pleasure is so overwhelming. I blindly reach between us and take his dick in my hands.

"Lotus," he chokes out. "Baby, wait."

"I'm ready." Lust-dazed, I open my eyes to meet his. "I've waited, we've waited so long. Please, Kenan."

He reaches into the drawer beside his bed. Before he can put it on, I take the condom. The heat we've checked since our first touch melds our glances together. Hell, since the first time we saw each other, my body, my heart has wanted this. I wrest control, hovering over him, and slide the condom on, taking my time, lingering. Anticipation. Hunger. Frustration. I relish every emotion sketched on his handsome features.

"Lotus, come on," he pants.

"Are you sure *you're* ready?" I tease, grinning down at him.

Answering humor darkens his eyes. He pulls me over him, guides my hips into position. Our laughter dissolves, melted by the heat between our bodies. And then he's inside me, an astonishing initiation. A christening. At once a seal is broken, even as we're sealed together.

"Don't move," he rasps, gripping my hips and holding me in place, swallowing and closing his eyes. "Let me feel you for a second."

I know what he means, why he says it. I savor my body's first taste of him—a communion of flesh and bone and heart and soul. I'm perfectly still, but something I've never felt shakes me to my foundation. It's invisible and undeniable. He reaches up and brushes my hair back from my face, a gesture so familiar now, so tender that tears prick my eyes. We haven't exchanged the words. They're the last frontier, but in my heart, I know. And his eyes echo the same.

The first undulation of my hips draws a gasp from us both.

"Jesus, babe," Kenan says, shifting his hands from my hips to my back. "Do that again."

I laugh down at him and move again, a slow, deliberate roll of my hips. I clench my pussy around him.

Mine.

Let another woman even try.

I lift my chin, tighten my thighs at his hips, and roll again. Clench tighter, introducing his cock to its new mistress. I will possess this warrior under me. The man they call Gladiator taken captive by a girl half his size and a decade younger. I'm a girl he could crush, but everything in the way he looks at me says *cherish.* Says *treasure.* Says *protect.*

Says I'm his, too.

Mine, his eyes answer.

That look, this feeling, it's a lasso, slithering over my shoulders, past my arms, squeezing me, keeping me in place. I'm not going anywhere.

I ride him so long, so hard, the muscles of my legs and belly ache and tremble from the torque force twisting us together. And still he demands more, thrusting up hard, his hands reaching for my breasts, squeezing, pinching, rolling the nipples. His is a merciless sensual assault that I can't withstand much longer.

"I want you to come again," he says from beneath me. "Touch yourself."

With his thumbs flicking my nipples to stiff peaks, I reach between us to find my clit. My head falls back, and my pussy clenches like a fist around his cock.

"That's it," he whispers.

I'm on the verge of tears. The pleasure is so thick, so much richer than anything I've known. He slips a finger between my legs, gathering the wetness and then reaching behind me.

"I'm going to put my finger in your ass," he rasps. "Is that okay with you?"

Just the thought...

"Yes, please," I gasp.

He does it. His thumb, slick with my juices, slides inside my tight hole, and it's too much. His hand tweaking my nipple. My finger rubbing my clit. His thumb in my ass. His dick a swollen, rigid column inside me. My hips undertake a jerky, frantic rhythm, riding him like I'm being chased. My mouth opens on a silent scream.

"Fuck," he says, pounding up into me, unrelenting.

We ride it out together, the tempest that sweeps us along. I collapse onto his chest with him still inside me, a sweaty, spent, content mess. He drags his open palms over my back, caressing me, touching me, feeling me. I loop my arms around him and bury my face in his neck. He jerks away, takes my chin, and searches my face.

"You're crying," he says, his frown composed of concern and self-castigation. "Baby, I am so sorry. Dammit, I wanted it to be perfect. I should have—"

"It was," I cut in, only now aware of my tears, but they're not for what he thinks. There's no emptiness. I'm full. There's no bleakness. I feel joy. "Kenan, it was perfect."

His shoulders drop. His eyes close on a sharp exhale before he looks at me.

"I thought I hurt you," he says, pushing his nose into my neck, cupping my head, plunging his fingers into the untamed nest of hair.

"No, you didn't hurt me," I promise, kissing his throat, his shoulder, his face—any part of him I can reach. "You healed me."

I know it was the support group. It was taking a break from sex—dismantling my emotional detachment. It was Marsha and the counsel she gave me every step of the way. It was all those things that brought me to this place, to this point when I was ready to receive the man I've come to love.

But it was Kenan, too. His patience. His kindness. His trust. He fed me my first taste of true intimacy between a man and a woman, not just for the last few minutes but for the last few months. It was first with our hearts, with our souls, with our minds, in the words we exchanged and the notes he sent and the time we shared. This came slowly for us, at the pace of melting ice. What we just did in this bed was a sacrament—an outward sign of a promise we've negotiated, drafted, pledged since our very first kiss. It was spiritual, this act, and the implication of it hums between us like a sacred tune.

He sits up, still inside me, the muscles in his stomach flexing beneath the taut, bronze skin. He repositions me on his lap, shifting my bottom on his powerful thighs. My warrior wearing no armor. Guard gone. Vulnerable to me. The look in his eyes is like nothing I've seen before. It's a balm over every rejection—a shelter from every storm that's ever chased me. A defender from the demons haunting me.

He swallows deeply, staring at me in silence for long seconds and brushing away my tears with his thumbs. And when he speaks, the words he says are as perfect as every moment has been since our bodies joined. The words are from the Song of Solomon, but the truth of them, it's his. It's mine, too.

"I have found the one whom my soul loves," he quotes.

More tears rain over my cheeks, a release years overdue. I weep for every time I've felt unloved, unwanted, unnecessary, and imperfect. It's all there in the look he settles on me. To him, I'm more than enough. I'm all that he wants.

"Kenan," I hiccup through tears and bracket his high cheekbones with trembling hands, pressing our foreheads together. "I said I didn't belong to you."

He nods, his expression braced against the violence of his own emotion, his eyes raking possessively over my face.

"I was wrong." I shake my head against his. "So wrong."

I pull back to look into his eyes and give him the passage I've hoarded in my heart and never thought I would say to a man.

"My beloved is mine, and I am his," I quote the song over a salty trail of tears, brokenly, truthfully. "Kenan, I'm yours."

He swells and hardens inside me at the passionate words I pour over him like oil anointing the head of a king. His hands drift down my back and settle on my hips, gripping in confident possession.

"And I," he says, his words kissing my lips even before he does, "I am yours."

CHAPTER 33
KENAN

"For a man who never wanted to go to New York," August says, dribbling two balls, one with his left hand and one with his right, "you sure seem to be missing it. Moping around practice like somebody stole your bike."

I toss him a look of half-irritation but focus on my own drill. I've only been at training camp for a week, and I miss Lotus even more than I thought I would. We've been apart for a week before, but adding sex to our relationship took it to another level. She stayed at my place until I had to return to San Diego and report to camp. There was a rhythm to us that I got used to.

"Or maybe it's *Lotus* you miss," August continues, "not the city."

"Wouldn't you like to know," I mutter. "Punk ass."

"I would like to know, actually." He stops dribbling and crosses the small space on the court that separates us. "Tell me what's up with you and Lo. Why are you holding out on me?"

Because I'm having too much fun torturing him.

"You know we're dating," I say, disguising my amusement with a blank expression. "Isn't that enough? Next you'll want to go to the bathroom with me and have sleepovers and shit. Why are you in our business so hard?"

"She's like a little sister to Iris, Glad," August says, no sign of levity in the gray eyes under his flop of dark curls. "To me, too, and I just need to be sure she's okay and you won't…"

He shrugs, glancing to the side, looking uncomfortable.

"I won't hurt her," I assure him, trapping the basketball between my hip and my arm. "I care too much about her."

Surprise stretches his eyes before he recovers. "Okay. That's all I wanted to know."

"Lotus hasn't told Iris anything either?" I ask, resuming the cross pattern of dribbling.

"A little." He starts his double dribble again, too. "She says you guys are together but hasn't given much detail. To be honest, Iris is so preoccupied with the baby coming, she hasn't dug as much as she usually would."

"So you're digging for her?" I ask, cocking one brow.

"Something like that." He flashes a grin. "I mean, some dirty old man is after my wife's young cousin. It's my duty to investigate."

"I wondered when the old man jokes would start," I say, laughing and shaking my head.

"Expect more of those," he says with a wink.

"You guys got a secret, or would you like to share with the rest of the class?" our new coach yells from the other end of the court.

He's not exactly new. He's our former assistant coach, Ean Jagger. Coach Kemp, who has led the Waves since we started as an expansion team a few years ago, is battling prostate cancer. Of course, we wish him the best and want him to get better, but it's also exciting to have such a young, brilliant mind at the helm this season. With his reputation as a master strategist and his off-the-charts basketball IQ, Ean could have any job in the league. We're grateful and slightly confused as to why he stayed with an expansion team with no hopes of making the playoffs its first four seasons.

But we'll take it.

"No secret, Coach," I reply. "I'm having the sex talk with Rook here. He wasn't sure how his wife ended up pregnant. I was explaining where everything goes."

The team laughs, and I have to stop dribbling and bend over laughing myself at the look August levels at me.

"Wow," Ean says, taking his time crossing the court to reach us. "I expected more from the team captain."

August is the franchise player and the future of the team, but he's only got a few seasons under his belt. They brought me in because of my reputation for discipline, my on- and off-court leadership, and my two championship rings. I know how to win. All attributes they're hoping I can pass on to my younger teammates, especially August.

"Since you and West seem to have so much to chat about," Ean says once he's standing right in front of us, "let's see if you can climb and talk at the same time."

August groans, and I'm with him. Nobody likes climbing the rope. It's old-school and not one of our standard drills anymore. But that is part of what makes Ean so coveted. He's a great blend of old-school sensibility and cutting-edge innovation.

"I hope you kept in shape over the summer break, old man," August jibes as we head for the two ropes hanging at the far end of the court.

"Summer break?" I ask blithely. "What's a summer break? I think I heard about those. Maybe I'll take one someday."

"Apparently, this *isn't* the best way to shut down the chatter," Ean says dryly, "since both of you are still running your damn mouths. Go at the whistle. Touch top and mat. Touch top and mat again."

"Shit," August mumbles. "Last time I'm talking to you during drills, Glad."

"Well, that's one bright spot." I give him a deadpan face and curl my hands around the rope.

I'm gonna smoke his ass.

The whistle blows.

August is out of the gate like a thoroughbred, racing up and inches above me. I pace myself but never let him get too far ahead. No way I'm letting this kid show me up.

He's still slightly in the lead when we touch the mat and start back up for the second climb. That's when I make my move, digging deep for a burst of speed I keep in reserve. I've also got an inch in height, a few inches in wingspan, and a good fifty pounds of muscle over him. My reach is longer, and I pull myself up higher with less effort. I tap the top and start back down milliseconds before he does. When my feet touch the mat half a breath before his do, I'm relieved I held my ground. I'm the guy with the rings. I'm the team captain, but in this league, you're never done proving yourself.

"Age before beauty today, Rook," I tell him through harsh puffs of air.

"Don't feel too bad," August says, swiping Gatorade from his lips. "I'm sure your girlfriend Lotus thinks you're beautiful."

That sparks the curiosity and jokes I'm sure he knew it would.

"Glad got him a girl?"

"When do we meet her?"

"Bet she's a dime."

I can barely focus for the rest of the practice with all the grown-ass men asking me nosy questions about my girl.

"Bet you wish you'd let me win, huh?" August asks, grinning like a thirteen-year-old while we walk to the parking lot after practice.

"No, but you do."

"Nice whip," he says, whistling and walking around the Urus. "That max contract money is long, huh?"

Banner negotiated a max contract deal for me the year before I left Houston. Lucky for me, since I traded the following year. It gave me a nice paycheck before I left.

"You should talk." I click the door open. "You got that franchise tag money."

"We both know which is longer," he says with no spite and much humor. "You've earned it."

"Get it while you can," I tell him, sobering. "Too many of us live high on the hog, and then when it's time to retire, the butcher is closed. Make your money. Invest your money, and then make more money. Banner told me that from the beginning and is riding me about it at the end."

"The end?" August goes still, leaning against the vehicle and frowning. "You ain't trying to leave now, are you?"

I shrug. "Everybody hangs it up at some point."

"You're in better condition than everybody on the team." August huffs a wry laugh. "Including me. You could play till you're forty if you want."

"The operative word being *want*."

"Why wouldn't you want?"

"There's a lot more to life than ball. You know that, August."

"Yeah, for sure, but I was hoping you'd help me win a ring before you hang up the ol' gym bag."

I chuckle and settle against the SUV beside him. "I don't know about that. I've missed a lot with Simone. This life is hard on families."

"Yeah. I have to be really intentional about being present when I'm home since I'm gone so much." He shakes his head. "Man, we had a great summer. So much time with Iris and Sarai. Iris has had a great pregnancy."

"You ready to be a dad again?" I ask.

"I guess. I've had Sarai since she was so small, she barely remembers anything before Iris and I were married." He laughs. "Why? You got pro tips?"

"Shiiiiiiit." I shake my head and offer a wry chuckle of my own. "I'm the last one handing out advice on fatherhood. I'm not exactly Simone's favorite person right now."

"How'd things go over the summer?"

"Okay. We were in family counseling while I was there. She's still really struggling with the divorce. She thought we might get back together."

"You?" August asks, his eyes wide and his brows up. "And Bridget? Get back together? Why would she think that?"

"She's a kid and wants her life back." I suck my teeth, disgusted with my ex. "And this *Baller Bae* show premiering soon won't help. I've got a bad feeling about it. You know Bridget had the nerve to show up at Lotus's job? Poking around and trying to scare her off."

"Scare *Lotus* off?" August asks, his tone incredulous. "She obviously doesn't know her. Lo doesn't scare easily. I certainly wouldn't cross her. And Simone's not a fan?"

"Nope. Not at all." I shrug and open the door to toss my gym bag in the back seat. "But she'll have to get over that because Lotus isn't going anywhere."

"So details begin to emerge," August says with some satisfaction. "You really *are* into her."

"Like you haven't known that since the day I first saw her in that hospital room."

"True." August's grin is wide and teasing. "Bruh, she walked in and you were *shook*."

I smile despite the ache in my chest. Shook? Over Lotus?

I still am.

CHAPTER 34
LOTUS

"YOU CAN DO IT!"

My throat is raw, but I force the words out one more time, praying that something will end my cousin's agony soon.

"I can't," Iris say, tears running from the corners of her eyes. "I can't, Lo."

"Yes, you can." I mop the sweat from her brow and hand her a cup of ice chips. "You will."

"I want August."

"I know, honey." I glace at the clock on the wall. "He's on his way."

"I hate basketball," she says, her bottom lip quivering.

"I've been trying to tell you," I joke. "Took labor for you to hear your girl."

Her mouth twitches the tiniest bit.

"He's really almost here?" she asks again for the hundredth time.

"He is. The team landed a little while ago, and he called from the airport."

It's preseason, and the Waves had a game in Toronto. Iris wasn't due for another few days.

"First thing I'm gonna do when this little man gets here," I say, giving her a smile, "is tell him to synch his schedule. Got all of us thrown off."

I wasn't supposed to fly out to San Diego until the weekend and was planning to spend a few days in Hawaii with JP. Fortunately, I got the call before we left for the airport and was able to change my flight.

The upside is that I'll get to see my boyfriend before the team leaves for China in two days. When Kenan said his schedule would be brutal, I didn't think he was lying, but even the preseason is intense.

"Ahhhh!" Iris bellows. Rivulets of sweat sluice her forehead, making the fine hairs at her temples curl. "How's Sarai?" she pants once the pain passes.

"Good. I got an update from your friend a few minutes ago. She says Sarai's playing with dolls."

Iris smiles, her eyes shifting past my shoulder. "Dr. Matthews, hi."

"Hi, Mrs. West," Iris's obstetrician, Dr. Matthews, says from the door. Her voice is calm but carries a hint of urgency. "We need to talk. You've been in labor for eight hours and have stalled at five centimeters dilated. I'd like to do a scalp test."

Iris has been given some drugs for pain, though she didn't want an epidural. I know she hasn't been sleeping much for weeks. Dark shadows rest beneath her eyes. Between contractions, her lids droop drowsily. She's exhausted. I need to be alert on her behalf.

"What's a scalp test?" I ask.

The doctor looks at me questioningly and then to Iris, whose head has lolled to the side.

"I asked you a question," I remind the doctor with soft firmness. "What does the test involve, and why do you need to do it?"

"Tell her," Iris whispers. "She's my only family."

Technically not true. We both have mothers alive and well in New Orleans. Neither of us has seen them since MiMi's funeral. I haven't spoken to mine since I was twelve years old.

"And Mr. West?" Dr. Matthews asks, brows up.

"En route," I reply, my stare unwavering. "The test?"

"We place a plastic cone in the vagina and against the baby's scalp," she explains. "We take a small blood sample, which will be analyzed and tell us in minutes if he's getting enough oxygen."

"You okay with that, Bo?" I ask. "Did you hear the doctor?"

Iris nods weakly and licks over the teeth marks on her lips. "Okay," she says. "Do it."

They get Iris in stirrups and conduct the test quickly.

"I was afraid of this," Dr. Matthews says when she comes back a few minutes later. "We need to get that baby out. We should start discussing other options. Possibly a C-section."

"No, I don't want..." Tears course down Iris's cheeks. "We wanted to do it naturally." She looks at me, distress and panic flooding her eyes. "Where is he, Lo?"

My phone rings, and it's August. *Thank God.*

"It's him!" I laugh and hold up the phone before answering. "Dude, how close are you?"

"I'm around the corner," August says, frustration in his voice. "But there's an accident. Hoping this clears soon. How's she doing?"

"Great," I say, smiling reassuringly at my cousin. "She's doing great. They're a little concerned the baby may not be getting enough oxygen and are talking about a C-section."

"No, she doesn't want one," he says.

I walk a few feet away from the bed and turn my back to Iris.

"She may have to, August," I say, pitching my voice lower. "She needs you. I don't care if you have to get out of that car and run, get your ass here."

I look over my shoulder and give Iris another smile. "Wanna speak to him?"

"Yes." She nods, her dark hair fanned out in a tangled mess against the pillow. "Please."

I can't make out August's words, but Iris draws a deep, calming breath and blows it out.

"I know," Iris says, her voice wavering. "I remember. I just want you here. I'll get the C-section if I have to, August. I don't want to do this without you."

Her voice breaks, and fresh tears roll over her flushed cheeks. "I want you. Please don't miss our son's birth."

When they hang up, I take my phone back and sit beside Iris's bed. Just as I'm about to find something to distract her while the doctor goes to make arrangements, another scream tears through Iris.

"Dammit!" she yells, screwing her face into a pained mask. "This shit hurts. It didn't hurt like this before."

With Sarai, Iris had a difficult pregnancy, but the delivery itself was relatively easy. This time the pregnancy was a breeze, but the delivery is being a little bitch.

"I can't do this, Lo," she whispers. "God, I'm so tired."

"Yes, you can." I grab her hand and lose the train of what I was about to say when Iris grips my hand so tightly I fear it might break. *Damn, that hurts.*

Iris grits her teeth and sits up to push as Dr. Matthews walks in with a team to prep for the C-section.

"What's going..." She checks between Iris's legs and peeks back up, beaming. "That's what I like to see. Not sure what you did, Mrs. West, but you're at eight centimeters."

"I am?" Iris asks, a smile breaking across her pretty face like sunshine. "How? I didn't do anything."

"I guess your body just needed a few more minutes to recover and move things along," she says with a wink. "You had a power surge. Now let's push."

Iris is on her second hard push, and the scream is bloodcurdling. I'm not sure how much more I can take. For as long as I can remember, her pain has been my pain, and my pain has been hers. Tears prick my eyes, but I never release her hand, even when my fingers go numb from the pressure. She unleashes another screech when August barrels through the door.

"I'm here, baby," he says, rushing to her side.

I start to move so August can take my place, but Iris won't let go. She shakes her head that I'm not to leave.

"Hopscotch," she whispers tearfully. "Don't leave me, cuz."

We've always been there for each other, done what the other needed, and that word has been our touchstone through the hardest, darkest things life has had in store for us. Emotion scalds my throat, but I manage to nod, determined to withstand the bone-crushing grip for as long as it takes, for as long as she needs. She'll do this for me one day.

Our eyes hold, and our gris-gris rings lock together, like our lives, our destinies, have remained entwined. It could be my imagination, but as she bears down and squeezes my hand for one final agonizing push, I feel that power surge the doctor mentioned. The power in our veins passed between two little girls in the Lower Ninth. We held it in a field of rotting cane, even when we were torn apart. It flows between us now through years of heartache and unconditional love. The power of an unbroken line.

We are the magic.

CHAPTER 35
KENAN

Is it really only the preseason?

I sink into the ice tub I keep at the Waves arena. Even though it was only an exhibition game, I gave it my all.

There are definitely times when we have to ease up and play conservatively. Tonight wasn't one of those. Cliff, my one-time friend and teammate, bounced around the NBA like a rubber ball kicked all over the playground after I left Houston. This is probably his last year, and despite winning one ring with us, he hasn't prepared for retirement as well as I have. He hasn't had the career I had or the success. He doesn't have the money.

But he had my wife right under my nose for weeks, and we played his team tonight. No way I was taking an L from that motherfucker. It's not even about Bridget. It hasn't been for a long time.

The first time I faced Cliff after everything came out, people thought I might fight him on court or erupt in violence. I did the opposite. I froze him out. I froze them all out, encasing myself and my game in a wall of ice. Many in my position would have taken the fine for not being available to the press that night. Not me. Every time a reporter asked a question about Cliff, about Bridget, their affair, I just stared at them in wintry silence until they sat down and the next question came.

Now reporters know better than to ask questions about my

personal life. They haven't for the last two years. Depending on how much of our dirty laundry Bridget decides to air on her reality show, that could change.

The door opens, and I glance over my shoulder to see our president of basketball operations, MacKenzie Decker, stroll in. He recently turned forty. An injury forced him into retirement a few years ago, earlier than he would have liked, but I doubt he misses those last seasons he could have had. He'll be first ballot Hall of Fame, and after just a few years out of the league, he's already a front-office exec poised for partial ownership of the Waves. Not bad.

"'Sup, Deck?" I ask, sinking deeper into the icy water.

"I was coming to ask you that," he says, taking a seat near the tub. His year-round California tan, bourbon-colored eyes, and thick dirty-blond hair make him a treat for the ladies. He's devoted to only one woman, though, his girlfriend, Avery Hughes, a sports anchor based in New York.

"How's your girl?" I lean over to adjust the setting on the ice tub.

"Still mine," he answers with a swashbuckler's grin.

"You gonna make an honest woman of her soon?"

"Oh, she's already honest," Deck returns. "But if you mean am I going to marry her…" He leaves the words hanging in the air, making me wonder as much as the media has about their relationship. Deck and Avery have been pretty private about it until recently.

"Then between you and me," he says, the humor fading from his eyes and something more sober taking its place, "very soon. I can't keep doing this. I need her with me."

Avery is one of the most popular anchors on SportsCo, a large sports channel second only to ESPN.

"Her contract is up for renegotiation this year," Deck confides, leaning back in the chair. "She's requesting the show record in LA instead of New York."

"Bruh, that would be fantastic."

"Yeah. This long-distance shit gets old quick."

You're telling me. I've only been doing it for a few weeks, and I'm sick of it.

"How was it playing Cliff tonight?" he asks, skipping the bullshit and getting right to the heart of the matter. It's one of my favorite things about Decker.

"Another day at the office." I grin and tilt my head. "But it felt good shutting his shit down. We squashed 'em."

"That we did," Decker agrees, chuckling darkly. "I'm glad it's behind you."

He hesitates, flicking a searching glance at me. "But I know you're still dealing with the repercussions. What with Bridget's show starting soon and Simone living on the East Coast now. You know I've navigated this. My ex was a real piece of work when we divorced. She up and moved on me, too."

"Out here, right?"

"Yeah, out to LA when I was living and working in Connecticut." He sucks his teeth and shakes his head. "Man, I was furious with her. I mostly didn't want our daughter to see us fighting and to be dragged all over the place."

"You hit the nail on the head with that one," I mutter, passing a hand through the frigid water, hoping it might cool my rising temper as I think about all the tricks Bridget has pulled that ultimately hurt our daughter more than they hurt me.

"I know you guys were doing counseling and you lived there this summer," he says. "That's good. Keep putting your kid first, man. Even when Bridget takes the low road, which we've all seen is her default, take the high. Show your daughter over and over and in every way you can that she's your priority. They're in such a weird space at this age."

"Tell me about it. Fourteen is hell."

"Everything you're doing now, even though it seems hard and maybe even like it's not working, it'll pay off later when your relationship with Simone remains intact."

"That's exactly what I needed to be reminded of. Thanks, Deck."

He stands and daps me up, chuckling and pointing to the water. "You and the ice tubs. It's a wonder your dick doesn't freeze off."

"Oh, it works great," I assure him.

I still hear him laughing even after the door closes behind him. I drop my head back to the lip of the tub. My dick definitely still works. With this long-distance relationship, it would come in handy if it didn't. I'm sure there's a masturbation joke in there somewhere, but I'm too tired and horny to work it out. At least I should get to see Lotus for a few hours when she's done at the hospital. Speaking of which…where's my damn phone?

In the locker room, I remind myself. She could be trying to call me now with an update on the baby. I'll grab it when I'm done.

I've got another five minutes of recovery in here before I can go.

The door opens behind me again.

"Forget something, Deck?" I ask, eyes still closed, absorbing the healing effects of the glacial water even while it bites my skin.

When there's no answer, I look over my shoulder to the training room door.

Lotus.

"Hi," she says, her voice deep, welcome, husky. Exactly as I remember it, except last time it was hoarse from screaming after a marathon of fucking on my last day in New York.

I haven't been back in Cali long, but it feels like months since I've seen her. Desire, need—fuck it, I'll say it to myself though we haven't said it explicitly yet to one another—*love* intensifies the longing and stretches out the time.

I have found the one whom my soul loves.

My beloved is mine, and I am his. Kenan, I'm yours.

I've replayed those moments and the sentiments we borrowed from King Solomon a hundred times in my head. Turning them over, analyzing them to see if there is any way she *was not* saying she loved me.

"Hi, yourself," I finally reply, unable and unwilling to withhold my shit-eating grin any longer. "How'd you get back here?"

"Oh," she says, leaning against the training-room door, "August owed me a favor."

"Yeah?" I ask, taking her in. The platinum hair is golden-brown again. I can't keep up with her hairstyles and colors. A simple royal-blue sundress ties at one shoulder, leaving the other exposed, and follows the curves of her body faithfully from breast to ankle.

"Yeah," she continues, tilting her head to the side. "I practically delivered his son."

A happy laugh barges past my lips. "Holy shit! So it *is* a boy?"

"Yup, secret's out," she says, joy lifting some of the fatigue from her eyes. "Michael Spencer West."

"Nice. I've got a stick I've been saving for Rook."

"A stick?" One sleek brow lifts, and she turns the lock, the sound echoing in the otherwise-silent room. Even in the frigid water, my cock goes hard. "You mean a cigar?"

"Usually." I don't relinquish her heated stare. "But a stick could mean a lot of things, now that I think about it."

"Hmmmmm." She frowns, takes the few steps that bring her to me beside the ice tub. "What else could a stick be?"

"Well, it could be…"

Words melt in my mouth when Lotus unties the knot at her shoulder and the dress falls to the ground. She's completely nude, and with me sitting in the tub, I'm eye level with one tight pierced nipple.

"You were saying?" she asks, brows brunched like she can't imagine why I stopped talking. "Something about driving stick?"

At her modification, I release a strangled laugh. She leans her elbows on the tub, serving up two dark nipples I can't resist a moment longer. Fuck flirting. I lean forward, taking the pierced one into my mouth, and watch her face. Her eyes drift closed, and a shiver trembles through her body. She grips my head, pressing me harder into her ripe curves.

"I missed you, Button," I mumble against the silky skin between her breasts before shifting my mouth to the other nipple.

"I'm picking up on that," she says, her breath stilted. She pulls back and uses the step against the tub to climb up.

"Lotus, babe, no. It's freezing in here," I warn her.

"Scared you can't get it up in the cold?" she asks, standing on the step and looking down on me for once.

"Oh, it's already up." I spread my legs so she can see the erection in my trunks through the water. "But for real, babe. You don't just jump into this. It takes a long time to acclima…"

I trail off when she tests the water with one small foot before climbing in and sitting on the opposite side, facing me with her breasts bobbing on the water's surface.

"Oh, this is *sooo* cold." She fakes a shiver. "I don't know how you big boys stand it."

"You're not human." I laugh. "Maybe you *are* a witch." I extend my arms toward her, and she takes the two steps through the water to reach me. "*My* witch."

I kiss her, and the first taste of my sweet girl does things to me. Of course, my dick goes even harder despite the freezing water, but everything else melts. There's a wall I erect when the season starts—a firewall of sorts to insulate me from the constant scrutiny, the pressure that never lets up, and all the drama that has nothing to do with ball. It's what allows me to focus so completely, almost to the exclusion of all else.

Against Lotus, that wall doesn't stand a chance.

It's down and she's storming the gates, inside, invading, marauding, destroying all my defenses. My attention, my thoughts are her willing captives.

"God, baby." I can't get enough, pulling her mouth open wider, spearing both hands into her hair to hold her head still so I can eat my fill. "What you do to me."

Her hunger rises to match mine, her small hands gripping my head and her eager tongue delving in aggressively, devouring me back. She spreads her thighs over mine, rubs her breasts into my chest, mewling like a little cat in heat, scalding me in arctic water. She tugs at the string on my trunks. With her hands shaking, she jerks them down over my hips.

Damn, that's cold.

"I don't have a condom," I mutter into the wet, searing heat of our kiss.

"Good," she says, turning her back on me, catching my eyes over her shoulder, positioning herself over me. "You don't need one."

In one swift move, she takes me into her body, offering sanctuary, and we share a gasp. The contrast between the freezing water and the wet heat of her pussy squeezing me, the muscles contracting to keep me, steals my breath and most of my sanity.

"You okay?" I ask into the damp silk of her neck.

"You tell me," she says, laughing as she starts to move.

Fuck. Fuck. Fuck.

She clamps her internal muscles, and they drag on me every time she propels herself up and down. And the view...

The motherfucking view from back here is breathtaking.

She pulls her hair away from her neck. Does she have any idea how she looks? A handful of tattooed stars trickles down her nape. The flowered zipper embroiders the sexy length of her spine and undulates with our every thrust.

And her ass—

Those two round, plump globes riding my dick. She reaches back to spread the cheeks, taking me even deeper. I reach one hand around to cup her breast and slide the other hand down to caress her clit, spreading my whole hand over it, rubbing my palm over her until it's a hard, tight nub.

"Oh my God, Kenan."

We create a rhythm of shared sighs, breaths we draw together, a copulating choreography. The pace turns furious, the vigor of our bodies churning the icy water into a riptide. We ebb and flow like a wave, turbulent waters climbing, rising. Even submerged in the cold, sweat glazes my forehead, her neck. We are wild and hot beneath the frigid water. I lay my hand flat against her heart, which roars in her chest like a beast trapped in a cave. My heartbeat answers, clamoring to get out. To find its other beating half locked inside her.

My beloved is mine, and I am his.

She turns her head, and I bend to take her mouth, slide my hand down the tight plane of her belly, and find her clit, pinching, twisting, rubbing until her lips break free of mine on a whimper, then a moan, and then a scream that yanks an answering cry from me—a call, a response. Our voices and our bodies twist, mating until we're both hoarse and spent.

And finally, we're silent.

CHAPTER 36
LOTUS

"So I guess we have to clean this tub out," I joke a few moments after the storm has died.

The door is locked, but the demands of both our careers wait on the other side. The plane he's taking to China in two days. The one I'll take back to New York.

But right now, it's just us in the quiet split by the rumble of his chuckle.

"It's self-cleaning actually," he replies, kissing my temple. "Low maintenance. Lucky for us."

The reverse cowgirl has flipped around, and I'm sideways on Kenan's lap in the cold water.

"Does this water never get warm?" I ask. Now that the initial rush of passion has died, the cold is getting to me, but I don't want to move. Not until Kenan does. I don't want him to outlast me.

"Never." He lifts my hand with its fingertips, puckered even though I haven't actually been in that long. "You ready to call it? The cold too much for you?"

"Nope," I reply immediately, clenching my rattling teeth. "Feels great in here. I love it."

"I agree." His head drops back, and he spreads his arms out over the lip of the tub, as if he's got all night. "I fall asleep in here sometimes."

Oh, hell no.

I stand abruptly, disrupting the water's smooth surface. I'm climbing out when his mocking laughter makes me turn.

"I win," he says, his white grin a taunt on that damn handsome face.

"Not everything's a contest, Kenan," I say, faking exasperation.

"Oh, yes, it is." A well-muscled arm slinks around my waist, and his lips brand my butt, a kiss on each cheek. "And I win. I won you."

When I glance over my shoulder, he's still seated in the water, and the look on his face is almost reverent. Did King Solomon look at his lover this way? Did her resistance crumble like mine? Did his beloved feel him wrapping around her heart like a vine? Did they have an inkling that centuries later, two people would take the words they passed between each other, destined to be canonized, to heart? That we would take their passion, their words for one another literally *to our hearts*?

But who am I to hide behind their bold declarations of love? To *not* bare my soul, my heart, to a man finally worthy of it?

I turn, sitting on the lip of the tub, and take Kenan's face in my hands. I want to, need to tell him in my *own* words. In my own way.

"I love you, Lotus."

It's an eerie silence that follows his words to me before I could say them to him, the kind that follows a miracle, the kind that chases the supernatural, searching for reason. That's what this is—the synchronicity of our hearts, a shared beat and thump. The miracle is that we've found each other.

"I wanted to say it first," I tell him, tears pricking behind my eyelids. "You beat me to it."

"I told you I always win," he says with a gentle, if slightly cocky, smile. That smile starts in his eyes and spreads over his face, slowly but surely, until it illuminates all the dark passages no one else has ever ventured into. He's a castle with secret tunnels and abandoned dungeons and heavy locked doors.

And I'm his skeleton key.

I dip to kiss him again, wanting as much of his taste as I can keep.

"You're staying, right?" he asks, his hands working the muscles of my naked back. "Until I leave for China in a couple of days, you'll stay?"

"Why not?" I shrug. "Got nothing better to do."

"Why, you little…" He wraps his arms around my waist and hauls me back into the icy water.

Shit!

The frigid shock forces the air from my lungs.

"Kenan!" I slap the water with my hand so it flies in his face.

He laughs, pulling me onto his lap and clamping me to his wide chest with one hand and tickling my sides with the other.

"No!" I yelp. "Stop it!"

I can barely breathe. We're both wheezing with laughter, struggling to catch our breath. When he finally relents, I lie limp against his heaving chest, breathing as hard as he is.

"I love you, Button."

It's even sweeter the second time. I can't hold back my tears. They roll of their own accord over cheeks still aching from laughter. "I love you, too."

His arms tighten around me, and I lean back to kiss him again, but my phone rings, disrupting the moment.

"Leave it," he mutters against my lips. "Don't go."

"First of all, it's freezing in here." I leave one last quick kiss on his lips before scrambling over the side to grab the phone from my dress pocket. "And second, it's Iris's ringtone."

"Nice view," Kenan says from behind me.

"No more reverse cowgirl for you," I warn, glancing over my shoulder and wiggling my naked ass.

"Oh, anything but that." His smile drops. "No, for real. Anything but that."

I smirk and answer the phone. "Hey, Bo. What's up?"

"Lotus, where are you?" The solemn tone of her voice sobers me right away.

"What's wrong?" I reach for a towel hanging on a nearby hook. "Is it Michael? Is he okay? Are you—"

"We're fine," she rushes to reassure me. "I'm sorry. I didn't mean to… We're fine."

There's a hesitation, a pause before she resumes.

"My mom called," she says.

"Aunt Priscilla?" A frown knots my eyebrows. "What'd she want?"

"She didn't have your number."

"Neither of them do. Why would they?"

"She was calling to let us know your mom's in the hospital, Lo," she says. "Mama says you need to go home."

CHAPTER 37
LOTUS

Home is not New Orleans.

And home certainly isn't anywhere near May DuPree, the woman who abandoned me thirteen years ago for a piece of shit named Ron Clemmons.

I haven't called Aunt Priscilla back. I don't know if I will. Iris's relationship with her mother isn't quite as bad as mine, but it's not much better. It was a coincidence Aunt Pris called the day her new grandson was born. Iris hadn't shared any of the details of her pregnancy with her. They have their own drama.

I've chosen to have no contact with my mother and don't see any reason to change that. Iris thinks if it's as serious as Aunt Pris says, I may want to try making some kind of peace before it's too late.

It's taken me years to be as healthy as I am now. What if seeing my mother, revisiting that place and that time, sets me back? What if all the ground I've gained over the summer I lose chasing some idealized peace that seeing a dying woman won't actually give?

My mother gave birth. Whoop-de-do. Cats and dogs give birth to entire litters. There is no miracle to birth, from what I've seen. The miracle is what follows. The miracle of selflessness. The phenomenon of nurturing self-worth and sacrificing for a child—feeding not just their bodies but their souls. Oh, I know what a mother is, and it is not May DuPree. I had a mother. When I was dead inside, a walking, catatonic open wound of a child who refused to even speak, MiMi gave me *life*.

That's a mother, and mine is already dead.

"You have to do what's right for you," Marsha tells me over the phone.

"Yeah, but what should I *do*?" I ask. "How am I supposed to know what's right for me?"

"I think—"

"Yes," I cut in. "Please tell me what you think. I don't need your professional distance, Marsha."

"I'm your friend *and* a professional," she reminds me. "I think if you go, you need to know why you're going and manage your expectations. What would you want from her? For her?"

"I don't want anything for her," I spit, shifting to bring my legs under me on Kenan's couch. "She was basically dead to me anyway. We haven't spoken since the day she gave me away."

"Okay, that's fair. Then what would you want *from* her? For yourself?"

I think about that for a moment and ask honestly what I'd want from her if we were in the same room.

"I'd want the words—for her to tell me," I answer in a rush of indignation and long-corked rage. "Why'd she give me away? How could she choose him over me?"

My chest rises and falls with heaving breaths, like I've been running.

"But what could she say that would make it better, Lotus?" Marsha asks. "What could she possibly say that wouldn't sound like a pitiful excuse?"

Nothing. There's nothing she could say to make it right, and anything she came up with would feel like an insult.

"So why go?" I ask, shrugging, feeling helpless and furious, like something is boiling in my belly with a tight lid. Like I could blow at any moment.

"What if the words you need aren't *from* her," Marsha says, "but *to* her?"

"You want me to forgive her?" I ask, choking on the concept.

"Not necessarily. If you can, great, but if you can't, not forgiving someone else doesn't mean you can't heal. I don't agree when people say a survivor can't really move on until they forgive the people who hurt them. The key, from my perspective, is releasing the hurt. Moving on in your life without the hurt holding you back. Maybe it's not words you need to hear from her but words you need to say to her that will help you in this situation. If you think that could be the case, then that's why you go. Not expecting anything she could ever say to make you feel better about the inexcusable thing she did."

Her words land with the thud of truth in my belly where MiMi used to say your "knower" lives. Your gut.

For a long time after Marsha and I hang up, I sit there on Kenan's couch and wonder what I would say to my mother. Marsha suggested I write it down, but I'm not sure I know where to start.

Kenan comes in from practice and drops his gym bag on the floor, watching me with a concerned frown. He walks over, flops onto the couch, and pulls me onto his lap. I burrow into the clean smell of his neck.

"Aw man. You showered," I say, affecting disappointment. "I was hoping to lick the sweat off your body."

"I could go back and sweat again," he offers hopefully.

"Maybe next time." I kiss his jaw and twine our fingers, enjoying him, his silence, for a few moments. "I'm going to New Orleans."

He stiffens under me, pulling back to peer into my face. "You are?" he asks. "You sure?"

"Yeah."

"Damn the timing," he grumbles. "If I didn't have to go to China for this exhibition game, I'd go with you."

"I'll be fine."

"And with the new baby, Iris can't go," he goes on, like he's turning it over in his head, searching for a solution. "Maybe Billie or Yari?"

"I'll be fine by myself. Really."

"Call me." He presses his lips into my hair. "I want to be there for you however I can."

I nod against his chest and wrap my arms around the broad torso.

"Can I ask you something?" I ask after a moment of us wrapped up in each other.

"Anything."

"Well, you have this reputation for being kind of surly."

He chuckles. "How do you know that? Remember you don't even follow basketball."

"It doesn't take much digging. And I didn't google you. My friends were very quick to tell me all about how intimidating you are. How you don't talk much to the press. How everyone thinks you're all hard and enigmatic."

"Okay, your point?"

"You've never been any of that with me, Kenan." I glance up. "From the start, you were open and curious about me, and you told me things and—"

"I wanted you," he interrupts. "I hadn't ever wanted anything or anyone the way I wanted you almost from the beginning. I saw you in that hospital room, and that was it. I'm not saying I fell in love that day, but you wouldn't leave me alone."

He's quiet for a beat and then glances at me, a flicker of uncertainty foreign on his strong features.

"You didn't feel anything that first day we met?" he asks. "Or at that awards show? At the Christmas party last year? Any of the times we ran into each other?" He gives a quick shake of his head. "It doesn't matter. You feel it now."

I take his chin between my fingers and direct his eyes to meet mine. "You're asking if all the times I fled the room as soon as possible, all the times I pretended you weren't there or was a smartass to put you off, if I was feeling anything?"

He lowers his face until our noses touch.

"I told you before you scared me to death," I confess, licking my lips. "I should still be scared. Love is hard. Trust is hard."

"Well, I have no choice now," he says, kissing one of my cheeks and then the other. "You have something of mine that I'm not sure I'll ever get back."

"Oh, yeah?" I ask huskily. "And what do I have of yours, Mr. Ross?"

He tells me in the way he knows melts me into a puddle—with a song.

"You have stolen my heart with one look of your eyes."

CHAPTER 38
LOTUS

IN THE HOSPITAL ROOM, I SEARCH FOR MY MOTHER THROUGH THE tangle of wires and tubes. She's unconscious, giving me time to study her without the awkwardness of what I should say. Of what she could *possibly* say to me.

"You came."

Aunt Priscilla's voice is a mix of sweet tea and Sazerac, the French Quarter cocktail, an old Haitian family recipe of bitters, Cognac, absinthe, and the peel of a lemon. That's the bitter edge Aunt Pris's voice carries from scratching out her living in the Lower Ninth. With Aunt Pris, you gotta take the bitter with the sweet.

I don't know how she does it, but Aunt Pris never ages. She looks like Iris's slightly older sister, not her mother. A shade darker than Iris and a few shades lighter than I am, she is more beautiful than us both. Her hair hangs in a fluid wave to her waist, and her eyes, still unlined, could make a man jump from a cliff to get to her. I've seen it happen, figuratively at least. Men who left their wives, abandoned their kids, lost their jobs for a taste of Aunt Priscilla. She, however, was wiser than my mother and never developed a taste for *them*. She never got caught up on one particular man—never gave herself so fully to one lover that she would excuse his sins against her own flesh and blood. That she would turn her back on her daughter with no regret. No, she committed different sins, and those are for her and Iris to sort. I'm here to deal with my own demons.

"Yeah. I came," I reply.

"Thank you."

Her voice actually trembles, and when I look at the ageless beauty, I see real vulnerability, real fear. Seeing anything sincere on her face is new to me. She and my mother knew all about armor—about shiny facades to draw a man close enough to pay but to keep him at arm's length so he couldn't inflict pain. They cared less about keeping their daughters safe, apparently.

"She's in a bad way, Lo," Aunt Pris says anxiously, clasping her hands in front of her. "They say it's a stroke."

"A stroke?" I ask. My mother had me when she was seventeen and is barely forty-two years old.

"It's not unheard of," Aunt Pris says. "Unless…you don't have anything to do with this, do you?"

"What?" For a moment I'm completely at a loss. Clueless. "Me? What do you mean?"

Aunt Pris licks her lips and considers me with careful speculation.

"Well, I know MiMi taught you things," she says, and then rushes to clean it up. "Not that I'm accusing you of doing this. I just wondered if, considering how young she is, this might be some black magic. If it might be a root, a spell, something you could maybe break?"

God, I'm such a fool.

Here I thought Aunt Pris wanted me to come make some kind of peace—to see Mama before she passes on—but she believes I can save her.

I swallow my anger, my resentment, and decide to play along.

"I'm not sure what I can do," I say with appropriate solemnity. "I need to see what we're dealing with here."

Aunt Priscilla's eyes brighten, and she nods eagerly. "Yes. See what we're dealing with. It could be anybody behind the spell. You know she's got a...a mess of wives who hate her—husbands, too, truth be told. Is there anything I can do to help? Anything you need?"

"Yes." I frown, pretending to think long and hard. "Go to the house."

"Uh-huh," she says, nodding.

"And bring to me..."

"Yes, what do you need?" she asks, breathless with hope.

"A piece of her jewelry," I finish, meeting her eyes for a second and then looking away.

"Jewelry?" Aunt Pris's brows draw together. "Just any jewelry?"

"Something she loves, preferably, and would want to take on her...her journey."

"To the afterlife?" Aunt Pris whispers, blinking back tears.

I feel bad for a moment, but that passes. If I'm to have any kind of time alone with my mother, Aunt Pris has to go.

"If it comes to that, yeah," I say in a rush before my guilt stops me. "But I may be able to use that before it does."

"It won't take long." She heads toward the door, pauses, and looks back at me. "Thank you for coming. I didn't think you would."

"Neither did I," I mumble. "You better go on so you can get back with the jewelry."

I haven't allowed myself to look at my mother lying prone in the hospital bed, not really. Once Aunt Pris is gone, I do.

I've seen her twice in thirteen years, both times when death was near. Once at Ron's gravesite and the other at MiMi's. And the last word she ever spoke to me was goodbye. Now, when it feels like the only thing that will make this right is her words, she can't speak. The beep of the machines, the only sound in the room, may be the bell tolling. Death may be with us again.

If Aunt Pris looks like Iris's sister, my mother looks like Aunt Pris's aunt. Yet Mama is the younger. Life has been harder on her, or maybe she just never figured out how to shed the years like Aunt Pris did. We look more alike than I realized. I get the tilt of my eyes from her, the shape of my mouth. People used to say I looked like her, and she would tilt her head, studying me like I was a stranger, and say, "Really? I don't see it."

"How do you think that made me feel, Mama?" I ask the silent woman. "You didn't want to look like me. You didn't want to see the resemblance, but there is one."

A bitter twist masquerades as a grin on my mouth. "I work in fashion now, and I wear beautiful clothes, and sometimes people actually want to take pictures of *me* and hang them in galleries because they think I'm pretty. You never saw that, though, did you?" I ask her. "Is that why you did it? Is that why you chose him over me? I wasn't light enough. Pretty enough. Did you always wish you could send me back, and first chance you got, you did?"

Tears flood my throat, floating the inevitable question to my tongue.

"Why did you let him hurt me, Mama?"

I sniff, impatient with my own tears. "Why did you choose him, knowing he was rotten? Knowing he had hurt your baby girl? Why didn't you ever come for me?"

The question is harsh and raw in the sterility of the hospital room. "Did you never miss me? Did you ever go back to that day and reconsider giving me away?"

The line of futile questions stacks up around me, going nowhere, bouncing off the walls. Aunt Pris will be back soon with whatever jewelry she thinks I can use in a spell to save my mother.

I didn't come here to save May DuPree.

I came to save myself.

Maybe not "once and for all" because trauma doesn't work that way. There may not ever be a "for all" to my healing. It may always be that the smell of pressed hair sets me off. There may always be days here and there when I can't shake the sadness, the uncertainty that comes from being abandoned and betrayed. I may see trace amounts of this in my life forever, like a bloodstain on the floor that shows pale pink but is never again spotless.

Oh, the blood of Jesus that washed us white as snow.

The line from one of MiMi's hymns we used to sing on Sundays when no church would have us rises up to meet my pain. *She* rises up to meet my pain, like she always did. Head-on. Fearlessly. With wisdom. Compassion. Unconditional love. The things she taught me got me this far. She was the first to lay bandages on my wounds. Today, I close them.

"I thought I needed your words, Mama," I say, my voice hushed. "But my friend says the words that help me more may be the ones I say to *you*, so here goes."

I reach in my purse for the journal I used to write the trauma narrative Marsha guided me through. The last page I flip to is where I begin.

"You had your chance," I read the first line in a strong voice that doesn't waver. "You had your chance to love me unconditionally, but you chose to change me. You had your chance to protect me as a mother should, but you chose to betray me for the man who split me in two. I was a little girl before Ron raped me, and after that day, I knew things I shouldn't know. Had questions it wasn't time for me to ask. He stole my innocence."

The shock of that pain fills the room like floodwaters, rising all around me and over my head. I hold my breath. I gasp for air. The panic batters me in waves, but I draw air into my lungs by little sips at a time until I can take deep breaths. Like it has so many times before, this pain tries to drown me.

But it can't. I won't let it.

"He stole my innocence," I say, picking up where I left off, my voice trembling and fainter but still loud enough for me to hear—for her to hear if she can. "And instead of punishing him, instead of seeking justice for me, you chose him. And I've asked why almost every day since. Oh, I may not have said it aloud, but every time I doubted myself, thought I wasn't pretty enough, light enough, needed to be different, needed to be more, I was asking why you did it. Trying to get to the bottom of what was so wrong with me."

My spine straightens, and I push against the weight of old pain and faded nightmares. I square my shoulders, finding the strength to toss them off like a cloak. "But you know what?" I ask rhetorically because I already know the answer. "There ain't a damn thing wrong with me. The problem was with you. The sin was his, and the shame, the guilt, the dirt I carried around for years, those were his, too. I refuse to keep them."

I shake my head, tears streaming over my cheeks, into the corners of my mouth, collecting at the base of my throat.

"The only good thing you ever did for me was give me away," I say, stroking my gris-gris ring. "I didn't come here to see my mother before she dies because my mother is already gone. MiMi was the best mother I could have asked for. Anything good about me finds its way back to her, and anything that's not, she taught me how to accept or change."

I close the journal because I've memorized the last line. It is the truth that I came into this room knowing, and I'll leave this room having said my piece.

"I came here not to blame you for giving me to her," I tell May DuPree, "but to thank you for giving her to me."

The hospital room door opens, and Aunt Pris rushes in with a jewelry box.

"I just brought the whole thing," she says, handing it to me. "In case you get a…a vibe from one piece instead of another."

"A vibe?" I ask, lifting one brow.

"I don't know." She shrugs elegant shoulders. "Whatever you and MiMi do, just do it. Just save her."

"I can't." I shake my head and pass the box back. "I don't know how to save anyone."

"No, you can." She clutches my hands between hers, desperation making her grip painful. "You have to. MiMi said you were the strongest."

"What? When?"

"Always," Aunt Pris says impatiently. "Even when you were a

little girl, five, six years old, she said you were the strongest of us all. She said all the power we didn't want passed on to you."

"What? I…" I falter and process that. "Well, I can't save a dying woman."

"You have to," Aunt Pris says, tears turning her dark eyes even more luminous. "They say she may not have much time."

And as though her words were an invitation, death comes. It's not some cloaked figure that only I see holding a scythe. Not a dark angel or a creature with horns and a tail. It's the sudden cold and the goose bumps that spring up on my arms.

MiMi said we miss most of what's happening in the world because we can't see it—that we miss the important things by relying only on the evidence of our eyes.

Like when death enters the room.

"I can't save her," I tell Aunt Pris. "But there's one thing I can do for her."

"What?" Fear twists her ever-pretty face. "Anything. What can you do?"

I take Aunt Pris's hand, grasping it tightly, and look to my mother dying right in front of me.

"You know who I am," I say, my voice, in spite of the bold words, shaky. "I'm here to make my judgment known."

"What are you doing?" Aunt Pris tugs on her hand, but I don't let go. "I don't want to be part of no spell. What is this?"

"It's the power of an unbroken line," I tell her, keeping my voice calm since her fear is evident. "Two women from our lineage have more power than one."

She stops pulling her hand away. "And we can save her?"

"No, but I think we can help her along the way."

"No." Tears spill over her smooth cheeks. "She can't… You have to…"

I slowly shake my head, grip her hand more firmly, and turn back to the bed.

"You know who I am," I say again. "I'm here to make my judgment known. This woman's soul hangs in the balance."

I replay all the things I read to Mama, all the things she never said to me, all the questions I'll never have answers for. Even if she could answer me, it wouldn't be enough.

I remember all the pain her actions caused me. I live with the legacy of it still.

I honestly don't know if I have any influence over this woman's afterlife. She's practically a stranger to me. So maybe this is just a show for my aunt to ease her coming grief. Maybe in death, I'm giving May DuPree something she never had in life. Or maybe this is a selfish act and the words I whisper are not for her in the afterlife but for me in this one.

"I lay a stone on the side of…"

I hesitate over the final word like it really will reverberate in eternity, and then I drop it like a stone in water whose ripples are infinite.

"Peace."

CHAPTER 39
KENAN

I REALLY WANT TO REACH MY DESTINATION BEFORE THE SUN GOES down. These backroads and swamps are creepy as fuck. Any minute now, I fully expect Google Maps to say, *"Really, dude?"*

If it fails, I also have the directions Iris sent me. She said the last few miles can get tricky.

"Tricky?" I ask aloud, even though I'm the only one in the rental car. "Feels more like Middle Earth than Louisiana."

The closer I get to MiMi's house, or I guess it actually belongs to Iris and Lotus now, the more uncertain I feel. It's not the backwoods or the alligators or the trees that seem animated with arms reaching for me as I drive by. I'm uncertain because I don't know what state I'll find Lotus in. No one's heard from her. The last time we spoke, she was heading to New Orleans to visit her mother in the hospital. I was in China, wishing like hell I was back in the States and could go with her. That was a week ago. The team is still in Shanghai, but the game is over. It's all goodwill stuff and appearances, so I told them I had a family emergency and needed to return early. It's still preseason, so things are looser.

It does feel like an emergency. Iris hasn't spoken to Lotus in three days, not since she got word that May DuPree had passed away. Lotus told Iris she was going home and hasn't been heard from since. Every call rolls into voicemail, and I'm going out of my mind.

This could be a fool's errand, me coming all the way to the middle of nowhere. What if she isn't even here?

It's a chance I'll take. If she's hurting, I want to be with her. I would want her with me.

The little house is squat, with a trail of stones leading to the porch and a blue door. I can't tell if the yard is overgrown or if it always looks like this—like an extension of the swamp but with no water. Hopefully no gators.

I park, leaving my overnight bag in the car in case I won't be staying because she's not here. I knock and wait, but there's no answer. When I try the knob, it doesn't turn. There's no car here besides the one I'm driving, so I'm not sure how she would have gotten here or would plan to get home. More and more, it feels like I've wasted my time.

She's talked about this place so much. I don't know what I expected, but I have trouble imagining my vibrant, beautiful girl growing up here, so isolated and removed from everything. But she spoke of it lovingly, even longingly. Maybe it was the woman who lived here who made her love it—the world MiMi made for Lotus that she loved. A world where pink clouds chase the blues away and magic trees make you feel safe. To Lotus, it's not a swamp but a wonderland of sorts, exactly what she needed after the hell she went through.

People had nothing to depend on but their faith, whatever form that assumed. That was part of how they survived.

Lotus said that to me at Sylvia's when we discussed religion and voodoo. Is that what she found here with MiMi and her gris-gris and potions and spells? Maybe Lotus found faith, in whatever form it assumed, so she, too, could survive.

I used to love watching the sunset from a tree in MiMi's backyard.

Her words from our day in Brooklyn come back to me, and I glance at a path worn in the grass leading behind the house.

Worth a try.

I follow the path with no real hope of finding much, but there's a whole other world I wouldn't have known existed. A canopy of trees shades the path down to the water. Flowers bloom everywhere, not well kept but wild, beautiful. And then I see what must be Lotus's tree. It's huge, and I can imagine a little girl thinking she could see the whole world from up there. I search the line of limbs and branches until I catch sight of something bright, something gold.

There's a rustle of leaves and a shifting of branches. I walk a few feet to the left and have a clear view of Lotus on a limb maybe twenty feet off the ground.

"Lotus!" I yell up at her.

She turns her head, unstartled, and looks right in my face, but there's no response. Her eyes, even from here, seem vacant, distant, as if the girl I know, the one I love and who loves me, has gone into hiding somewhere.

"Baby, come down," I coax. "It's too high. I don't like you up there."

No answer, but a frown that draws her fine brows together. She shakes her head.

"Dammit, Lotus," I mutter under my breath and walk to the tree, glancing at my sneakers. "Guess we'll see if these Glads are made for climbing."

I can't say I've ever actually climbed a tree. I grew up in Philly. I'm a city boy through and through and never saw the value in climbing anybody's damn tree, but if I can beat August climbing a rope, I can climb a tree.

There aren't many limbs between her and me, but there's a lot of space between each one, and I'm not sure how she made it up here when I'm struggling. I'm one branch below her, close enough to look into her eyes, when she speaks.

"Why are you here?" she whispers.

I'm not sure how to answer that. Obviously I'm here for her, but grief has a way of making things less obvious.

"I came for you," I say simply. "I've been worried about you. I've been calling you, Lotus. I've been…"

Losing my mind, I finish silently, tightening my fingers on the limb.

"I'm sorry," she says, swallowing, blinking rapidly. "I should have called. My phone died, and I didn't bother—"

"It's okay."

And it is. Face-to-face with her pain, it doesn't matter that I flew here, drove to some tiny parish in the bayou on the mere hope that she would be here. I'm just glad she is.

"I'm coming up to you." I reach for the last branch that will take me to her.

"I'm not sure it'll hold us both," she says.

I pause, my hand on the branch, my eyes on her.

"Then you could come down," I suggest.

She looks at me for a long moment before shaking her head no. "I'm not ready to come down yet."

"Then I'm coming to you, and you better hope this tree holds us both."

Not waiting for permission, I grab the last limb, glad to find it sturdy and steady even when I pull on it, and hoist myself up to the thick limb where she sits. I carefully slide behind her, let my legs fall on either side like she has, and pray to God I won't die falling from this tree.

I slowly push my back to the bark, find my center for stability, and then put my arms around her. She stiffens at first, resisting, but I tighten my hands at her waist. I let her feel me, hoping I feel as right to her as she always feels to me.

By degrees, her shoulders relax and she sinks into me, until her full, slight weight all belongs to me, leans on me. I pull her closer so her curls tickle my nose and caress my lips. "God, I missed you, Button."

She turns her head to look at me, and for the first time, she smiles. "I missed you, too."

Those are the last words we say for a few minutes, but I've got my girl back. She's safe, and she'll be okay. Whatever hell seeing her mother took her to, she'll come back to me.

And if she doesn't, I'll go get her.

"I always felt safe here," she finally says. "MiMi called this my magic tree. When I was sad, I'd climb this tree and somehow feel better."

"Then it's good you came." I link our hands at her waist and tuck my chin into the curve of her shoulder and neck.

"Mama never woke up," Lotus says, shaking her head. "I always thought it would be me asking her questions, getting answers that would make the pain go away, but it doesn't."

"The pain doesn't go away?" It's killing me to hear that because it kills me to see her hurting—to know I can't make it stop.

"Not all at once, no," she says softly, but turns to smile at me, her face radiant despite the hurt, the tears lingering in her eyes. "But I'm getting there."

"And I'll be right here, baby," I whisper.

Her fingers tighten on mine, and she nods. "I love you, Kenan."

My throat is on fire. I have no idea what it is about this place, about this woman that turns me inside out, exposes my raw spots, but when she tells me that, I could cry. Me, the Gladiator. Known as one of the toughest guys in the NBA, broken down by one tiny woman telling me she loves me.

"I love you so much, Lotus."

"And you'll always come for me, won't you?" she asks, a smile in her voice.

"Yes," I promise. "Always."

"I'll always come for you, too, Kenan," she says, and then points to the sky. "Look."

I follow the line of her finger and almost want to thank the sky for its perfect timing.

"Pink cotton-candy clouds," she whispers. "Chasing the blues away."

CHAPTER 40
LOTUS

ANGEL'S WINGS.

White sheets are pinned to the clothesline, flapping in the wind. MiMi used to call them angel's wings. I glance around the backyard, opening the door to all the memories the two of us made here.

It rained my first week living with MiMi, and something about the fierceness of the storm, the ominous sky streaked with silver lightning, had called to me. I'd gone to the back porch, not caring when the rain whipped at my clothes and stung my face. The drops had run through my hair, still pressed from the family reunion, until it returned to its natural state of waves and crinkles.

"Some people are afraid of the storm," MiMi had said, walking up beside me.

"I'm not," I'd said defensively, still resentful of her. Of this boondocks place. Of being separated from Iris. Of being exiled from all that was familiar to a place and with a woman I didn't know.

"Of course you aren't afraid of the storm," MiMi had said with a smile. "You *are* the storm."

I'd had no idea what that meant and frowned at her, not asking the question.

"Lotus." She had looked from the dark clouds overhead to my face. "We haven't really talked about Ron."

My stomach had clenched, knotted at his name. Fear had risen in my throat, and my nostrils had once again filled with the rot of a forgotten sugarcane field.

"I know you said you didn't want to talk to the police, but—"

"No," I'd protested hastily, panic gripping me. "Just…no, please don't make me."

She'd watched me unblinkingly for a moment, her eyes filling with a dark promise.

"No police," she'd finally agreed. "But there are other ways."

I hadn't thought about what that meant but just felt relief that I wouldn't have to tell anyone or see Ron again.

"Now your hair's a mess," she'd said briskly, her smile and eyes bright again. "Let's wash it."

She'd washed it and let it dry on its own. That night, she'd laid the comb on the red, livid eye of the stove.

"No," I'd said, my voice hushed. "I don't want my hair pressed."

She'd looked at me, looked *through* me, and seen things I hadn't even known.

"Let's braid it," she'd said, sitting on the couch and pointing to a spot on the floor between her knees. I'd sat down, and her fingers, still nimble for a woman her age, had worked steadily through my hair for an hour, maybe more. When she was done, she'd held up a mirror for me to see.

"This is…" I'd touched the swirls and patterns she'd created. "It's pretty."

"You're pretty," she'd said like she was reminding me. "And now, your hair reflects who you are."

I'd looked in the mirror again. "What do you mean?"

She'd traced the patterns, telling me what each represented. "This is your courage," she'd said, touching the pattern on the right. "And this is your kindness."

She'd run her fingers over the whorls in my hair on the left. "And this is your discernment." She'd touched the pattern in the back. "The eyes in the back of your head to see what others miss."

"And what about this one?" I'd asked, touching the pattern on top.

"That, my beautiful girl," she'd said, smiling, "is your crown. Your pride. Your self-esteem. The glory of knowing who you are and that it's enough. No one has to tell a queen to wear her crown."

Her words, all the things she told me in this backyard, whisper through the oak trees. Her wisdom flaps in the white sheets pinned to the line and blown by the wind.

Angel's wings.

I washed the sheets so Kenan and I will have something to sleep on tonight. Last night, we ate from the snacks and sandwiches I brought with me. We talked and laughed.

I cried.

Telling him about the hospital and my mama, I cried, and he held me until we fell asleep on the couch. We'll leave tomorrow, but we have one more night here alone, and I'm determined we'll sleep in a bed on clean linens. I'm pulling the last of the sheets from the line and into the laundry basket when strong arms scoop me up from behind and whirl me around.

"Kenan!" I screech and laugh. "Put me down right now."

He keeps one arm around my waist and uses the other to grab a sheet from the basket, tossing it to the ground.

"I just washed that," I protest, frowning at him over my shoulder.

"Good." He lays me down on the soft cotton, looking down at me. "I like clean sheets."

I reach up to trace the bold planes of his face, the sensuous curve of his mouth, the thick feathering of lashes against his hard cheeks.

"You're magnificent," I whisper. "I think in another life you ruled a planet. You were the king of your own galaxy."

"And in this other life," he says, the laughter fading from his eyes, "were you my queen?"

In this place where I learned about all the things our eyes ignore, the dimensions teeming with life just beyond the evidence of what we see, I could conjure up our existence together before or the one to come, if that's a thing. I'm not sure what's true sometimes.

"I'll be your queen in this one."

We stare at one another across centuries, across continents, across time and space, and I actually believe that I would have found him anywhere. There is no place, no spot on the continuum of time that could have hidden this man from me.

He smiles, lifting some of the weight from the moment, and coaxes the hem of my dress up past my knees and over my thighs.

"What are you doing?" I ask, my breath snatched when his fingers caress the inside of my thigh.

"Fucking my queen out in the open," he breathes in my ear. "How often will I get to do that?"

Dirty things on angel's wings.

I should resist, but who am I kidding? He presses into the cove between my thighs, and our gasps mingle. Even through my panties and his sweatpants, he's hot, hard. I'm wet. Ready. He lowers his head, his chin nudging aside the neckline of my dress to worship my nipple with his lips. He slides sure fingers into my panties, and I stretch my neck in unmitigated pleasure. I come in seconds. My eyes drift closed, and I bite down on my lip, but my whimpers escape into the air. I fill the backyard with the sounds of my ecstasy.

When I open my eyes, he's watching me. "I never get tired of seeing you like that."

His kisses start gentle, soft as clouds on my cheeks, drizzled like raindrops over the bridge of my nose. But then our mouths, our bodies collide like two bolts of lightning in the sky.

You are *the storm.*

He pushes the dress above my waist, and I urge the pants down past his ass. He slots his lean hips between my thighs and slides my panties aside, entering me in one powerful thrust.

"Home," he rasps.

He's big. There's no denying that, and I have to spread my legs wide to accommodate his body. His cock is thick and hard and, even soaked and stretched, that first thrust knocks the wind from me. Then he eases in deeper until he hits that spot only he seems to have ever found inside me, and I moan. I rock into him, answering the rough, quick motions with the roll of my hips, the tightening of my thighs. My most intimate places put a demand on him.

Deeper. Harder. Faster. More.

Deeper. Harder. Faster. More.

Deeper. Harder. Faster. More.

It's an imperative rhythm. In the shadow of the tree I always thought was magic, we make our own. An alchemy that's uniquely ours. In the shadow of the place I thought was safe, I realize it's not a tree, a city, or a particular place where I find safety. It's in Kenan's arms, in the harbor of his love. That's the safest place I've ever known.

I wake with a start.

I don't know what wrenched me from sleep, but I jerk up like someone's dumped a bucket of water over my head. My heart clamors behind my ribs, and a thin layer of sweat slathers my skin. The moon illuminates a swathe of the bed, showing me Kenan asleep—peaceful, still. He's too big for the bed, but there isn't one in this house large enough to hold him. His feet hang off the edge, and his massive shoulders and chest leave only a sliver of mattress for me. I didn't mind. I laid on top of him and fell asleep. It was the best rest I've had in weeks, until now.

Even though it's almost October, it's still warm in the bayou, and we slept with only a sheet covering us. A violent shiver reminds me of my nakedness. There's a quilt I used to love in MiMi's old room, so I trip down the hall and open her closet to search for it while the warm night air caresses my skin.

The warm night air.

I check the kitchen, the living room, the bathroom—all warm.

It's only cold where we slept.

My thoughts riot, an unreasonable panic sending me down the hall at a gallop and stumbling into the bedroom. It's so abruptly cold, the marked difference in temperature stops me at the threshold. An unnatural chill sprinkles goose bumps over my arms and shoulders, pebbling the sensitive skin around my breasts. I approach the bed slowly, afraid to see if Kenan is still breathing.

He draws in long, even pulls of air that lift and lower his bare chest at regular intervals.

But I know what I feel. I know what this is. I've felt it before.

A dozen things MiMi told me, all the things she ever taught me crowd my mind. I mentally sift through the information, discarding the useless, grabbing hold of what I need with desperate hands. I rush through the house, collecting the necessary items. Salt. Candles. I dig around in boxes, searching until I have everything I need.

I watch Kenan for hours, I think. I'm not sure. Seated naked at the foot of the bed, I watch over him, willing to call in every cosmic favor, to invoke any saint, to utter any prayer. I'll beg God not to take him and do whatever is necessary.

My shoulders have grown stiff and my feet are numb by the time he wakes. It's still dark in the room, but I'm not sure of the time. He reaches for me, sliding his hand across the cotton sheets, blindly searching.

I'm right here.

I don't say it. Fear locks my jaws and ties my tongue in a knot.

"Lotus," he mutters, squinting and pulling himself up to sit, his shoulders almost as wide as the headboard of the narrow bed I slept in as a girl. He's a king, a pharaoh, the ruler of my heart. And I'll fight anything, anyone who tries to take him from me.

I'll fight death itself.

"Lotus, what the hell is going on?" He sweeps the room with a confused look, taking in the four lit candles strategically placed around the bed at the north, south, east, and west. At the salt encircling us.

"What's all this?" He looks at me, naked and completely still, sitting cross-legged with my hands pressed together between my breasts. "What were you saying?"

"Psalm 35," I croak, my voice raw from repeating the psalm the protection spell required for so long.

"Why?" He walks on his knees toward me, naked, magnificent. Mine.

Tears sneak past my lashes, and jagged breaths fight their way out of my lungs.

"Okay," Kenan says, his voice hardening. "You tell me right the fuck now what's going on. Why you're crying. What's—"

"It's death," I cut in over his building tirade. "It's here. In this room. I can't lose you."

Confusion gives way to frustration as he realizes what I'm saying.

"Lotus, this shit isn't real," he says, his words heated. "I hate seeing you upset over superstition and hocus-pocus bullshit people use to control others, to make money off them."

"No." I shake my head adamantly. "Yes, there is some of that. I know what you mean, but this isn't that, Kenan. I know what I feel. I felt it when MiMi died. I felt it when my mother died. I know how death feels, and it's here."

I close my eyes because I know he won't believe what I say next and I need him to believe me. "It's here for you."

He sits on his heels and runs a hand over his face, dropping his head back and contemplating the ceiling before returning his gaze to me. The moon reveals the stark masculine beauty of his features. It reveals his disbelief.

"I'm gonna blow these candles out before you burn down the damn house."

He jumps out of the bed and runs his foot through the salt, disrupting, destroying the circle. All four candles snuff out at once.

Dread starts as a knot in my chest and blooms over every limb.

"What the…?" He looks from the extinguished candles to my face and back again. "These trick candles don't fool me, so—"

"They're not trick candles, Kenan," I tell him solemnly. "I know you don't believe me, but—"

"Of course I don't, Lotus." He sighs. "Baby, what do you expect me to think when I wake up in the middle of the night surrounded by some candles and salt and you chanting? I… It's too much. Tell me you know this isn't real."

We watch each other in mutual obstinacy, the silence an impasse hanging like a broken bridge between us. I won't say it's not real. I don't know everything. I don't always know what's true, and I can't always interpret what I sense, but I know there is more beyond the limits of the three dimensions we see—that the walls between one dimension and another aren't as thick as we might believe. Beyond this life lies eternity, infinity, time that's not measured by minutes, hours, days, or years.

"I can't lose you, too," I finally whisper. My hands tremble around Saint Expedite, the little statue I found at the bottom of MiMi's chest. "If anything happened to you, I…"

The stiff lines of his shoulders, the inscrutable expression softens. One strong arm scoops me from the end of the bed and into his arms, into his lap. He rocks me like a baby and kisses my hair.

"Nothing's gonna happen to me," he says in what I'm sure is supposed to be a reassuring voice. "We fly out tomorrow. Let's get some rest."

I bury my face in his neck and swallow my tears, letting him think he's comforting me, but long after he falls asleep, his heartbeat evening out under my ear, I lie awake. In this house, I learned to peel the film from my eyes—to discern beyond what's right in front of me. I may not be able to see the threat, but the threat sees me. I show it my rabid heart, prowling in a fiery, salted circle, my teeth bared. Vigilant. A psalm on my lips and the little saint who guards the grave clenched in my hand.

CHAPTER 41
KENAN

Lotus and I are exiting the airport, headed for the car my assistant, Davis, arranged for us when the first reporter approaches.

"Kenan," he says, the phone aimed at me to record, audio or video, I'm not sure. "How'd you feel about tonight's episode?"

With the fast trip back from China, going down to Louisiana, and our idyll in the bayou, I'd forgotten the first episode of *Baller Bae* aired tonight.

Dammit.

"No comment," I mutter, lowering my head and pulling Lotus closer.

"Lotus, is it true what Bridget said?" another tosses out. "About you and Chase Montclair?"

Lotus's head jerks around in the direction of the question the reporter hurled at her. "What are they talking about?" she asks, looking up at me with wide, angry eyes.

"Ignore it, babe."

"Yeah, but—"

"Don't give them anything." I spot the car service ahead. "Banner's blowing my phone up. I'll call her in a second. Let's get out of here."

I settle Lotus in the back seat and hand our bags to the driver so I can escape the glare of any cameras as soon as possible. It's not the chaos that followed the scandal, with a hundred cameras and questions catapulted at my head every time I stepped outside, but if we don't get this shit under control now, it could be.

I call Banner back as soon as we pull off.

"B, what the hell is going on?"

"Where are you?" Banner asks with that forced calm I've learned to see through over the years.

"Just landed in New York, but heading back to Cali day after tomorrow." I frown and lean forward. "Tell me what's wrong."

"Nothing's wrong, per se."

"The hell, Banner. You don't call me four times for some 'per se' shit, and reporters harassed me as soon as I stepped outside the airport doors. *What's going on?*"

"You checked any TV, social media? That kind of thing?"

I stiffen. "No," I say, dragging the word out. "Why?"

"I'm sending you a link. Don't lose your temper. It's nothing, but I wanted you prepared." Banner hesitates. "Is Lotus with you?"

I told Banner about Lotus soon after we officially became "more than friends." She represents me best when she knows what's going on in my life and what's important to me, so she definitely needed to know about my girl.

"Yeah, she's here. They had questions for her, too."

Lotus glances up at me, something that is concern but not quite worry in her expression. We're both exhausted. Waking up in the middle of the night to some *Angel Heart* shit didn't exactly make for a good night's sleep. We haven't discussed it further, thank God. Things have been relatively normal all day. Until all this *not normal* hit us.

"Watch the clip," Banner says. "And let me know if you need anything."

"Bye." I hang up and grab the link from her text.

The preview of the video already has me gritting my teeth before I've even pressed play. It's the *Baller Bae* logo and a still of Bridget at lunch with two other cast members in the sequence.

"I tried to make it work." Bridget shakes her head, apparent sadness and regret on her face. "I know it wasn't right, what I did, but Kenan abandoned me in the marriage. I was so [BEEP] lonely, and he didn't care about anything but ball."

A sheet of ice forms over my anger. I want to stop the video and not listen to the two minutes and forty-one seconds remaining, but I need to hear what else she has to say. Banner wouldn't have asked about Lotus if she wasn't involved in this nonsense somehow.

"And now he's dating this *child*." Bridget rolls her eyes, touching the hand of one castmate who murmurs something to commiserate. "She's, like, fresh out of college. Not much older than our *daughter*. Can you believe that?"

"Girl, that's how they do," says a woman I recognize as the girlfriend of some guy in the league, but I can't remember who. "He married you right out of college. You raised his baby, kept his house, stood by him while he built his career, and now he wants some fresh snatch."

"That's why we gotta revaginate, honey," the other cast member says. "Keep it tight or they stray like that."

Stray? As in *I* strayed? In what alternate reality has Bridget existed where I'm the villain in our story?

"And he was so mad that I had *one* little indiscretion," Bridget says. "But I heard she's going behind his back with this photographer she was [BEEP] before he found her."

I press the screen to stop the clip. I can't hear any more right now. My temples literally throb with suppressed rage.

"Why'd you turn it off?" Lotus asks.

I glance down at her with a frown.

"Babe, she's—"

"A bitch," Lotus says sharply, staring at the screen in the dim light provided by the city lights beyond the car. "But she can't hurt us."

She tosses the phone onto the seat beside me and holds my face between her hands. "We know the truth." Her eyes pierce mine. "You know I would never cheat on you with Chase or anyone."

"Of course," I answer immediately. "I trust you completely."

"And we know that I'm not almost your daughter's age." She teases me, chuckling. "Though there's eleven years between Simone and me, too. Should I call you Daddy?"

"You're laughing?" I ask incredulously.

"What do you want me to do? Cry? Pout? Throw a tantrum? There will be people who watch that, feel sorry for her, believe her lies. We can't control it. All we can do is live our lives and refuse to let it come between us."

I dip my head to kiss her, caressing her jaw with my thumb.

"Thank you for being so cool about this circus act." I heave a frustrated sigh. "I'm not. I hate having my privacy invaded and having lies told about us, about you. Doesn't she even think about how hard it will be on Simone? Dragging us back into the tabloids like this?"

The thought of my daughter being set back after the small steps forward she's taken infuriates me. Despite her progress, I know she's still emotionally fragile, and so many transitions, so much pressure and attention? It's bound to wear on her.

"Fuck!" I expel the word harshly and slam my hand on the console between us. "If this hurts Simone... God, why can't Bridget just—"

"It'll be okay. Whatever comes, we'll deal with it."

"This is the last thing I want to be thinking about when I only have a day with you before I have to fly back."

"Then don't think about it." Lotus leans in to kiss me, slipping her hand between my legs to squeeze my dick.

"Damn, babe," I rasp into the kiss.

"I had to distract you somehow." She laughs against my lips.

"Distraction or not, you woke the sleeping beast. Now you have to handle it when we get upstairs."

I ask the driver to drop us off in the private car garage in case there are any more reporters lurking. I tip him, grab our bags, and half-limp as fast as I can with this hard-on to the elevator. As soon as the doors close, Lotus strains up on her toes to kiss my jaw and suck my earlobe. I kiss her so deeply we're both out of breath by the time the doors open for my floor.

Once inside, we drop the bags, and Lotus wraps her arms around my neck and her legs around my waist. I walk back to the bedroom, my hands full of her ass. She scatters kisses over my face.

When we reach my bedroom, the light is already on. Weird, since I haven't been here in weeks. I'm mesmerized by the passion, the love in Lotus's eyes as she slides her legs down to the floor. She turns toward the bed.

"Oh my God!" she gasps.

I look past her, and my heart stops and then sprints in my chest. Simone is on my bed, asleep. She looks so peaceful that at first it doesn't compute. The open, empty bottle by her hand. My daughter's preternatural stillness.

"Moni?" I rush over to the bed and shake her. "Simone, baby, wake up."

She doesn't stir. She's so cold. Fear squeezes my heart until I'm sure it's hemorrhaging.

"I'll call 911," Lotus says behind me, horrified panic in her voice.

I don't feel panic, though I know this is serious, but an eerie calm descends as I answer the operator's questions. Yes, she's breathing. She's taken a bottle of her mother's pills, but I don't know how many. The EMS team arrives quickly, loads Simone onto the stretcher, and rolls her out of the apartment building. In the ambulance, she stops breathing, and they intubate. Watching them force a tube down my daughter's throat, my icy wall cracks, and terror, panic, anger—they all rush in on a tidal wave. Bright lights and the screaming siren, muted before by my shock, flood my senses.

God, my baby girl. Simone.

"Moni," I mutter, paralyzed by my helplessness.

Lotus squeezes my hand but doesn't cease her persistent whisper. Psalm 35, what she was repeating last night. Tears course over her cheeks, and she shakes her head.

"It wasn't you," she says, her voice thin and reedy. "It wasn't you. It was…"

She doesn't finish that thought. She doesn't have to but resumes her urgent whisper. I have no idea what to say or believe. What to think. Could Lotus have been right? Could last night, her premonition or whatever it was, have been about Simone?

As soon as we reach the hospital, they wheel Simone out of sight. She's breathing but still hasn't regained consciousness. They have to pump her stomach.

A tube down her throat, her stomach being pumped. I'm caught in my worst nightmare, and I can't wake up. Can't even stir but watch uselessly like some spectator trapped behind a glass partition separating reality from fiction.

"Bridget!" Lotus says, her tear-filled eyes wide. "You have to call her."

"Shit." I pass a shaking hand over my face. I dread having to break this to Bridget, but I'm also struggling to keep my temper under control. The lies she told, the scrutiny she exposed our family to *again* for her own gain—it's all fresh in my mind. And the pills. Her name's on the bottle of pills Simone took.

My conversation with Bridget is brief, terse, almost stoic in spite of her hysteria. It has to be. If I allow one emotion, compassion, through that wall of ice, they'll all overtake me—trample my intention to save recriminations for later. For after Simone is out of the woods.

I'm seated in the waiting room, gripping Lotus's hand like it's a rope thrown over the side of a cliff, when Bridget arrives.

"Kenan, oh my God." She's dressed simply in jeans. No makeup. Sneakers. None of the camera-ready glamour I've gotten used to seeing since she's been filming *Baller Bae*. Her face is streaked with tears.

I stand to greet her, and she flings herself into my arms. My teeth grind together, and I bite back all the questions, the accusations, and instead awkwardly pat her back.

"Where is she?" she asks, pulling away to search my face.

"They're working on her now. They were pumping her stomach." I hesitate. "The pills she took—it was a bottle of yours. Did you notice it was gone?"

Her eyes transform from wide and teary to slitted and enraged.

"You can't be blaming me," she snaps. "If this is anyone's fault, it's yours."

She glances down to Lotus still seated in the waiting-room chair.

"And hers." She points one long finger at Lotus, her voice rising. "This was Simone's cry for help, for attention. When she needed her father most, *you* came and ruined everything."

"That's enough," I snap. "If you're gonna point fingers at anyone, it should be at *yourself*, Bridget. You think it's coincidence that Simone tried this the night your train wreck of a show aired? The very night you dragged all the shit that drove us into counseling in the first place back out? Have you considered that?"

"No, I haven't, because I wasn't the one missing in action when she needed me most. Where were *you* when she needed you? With *her*." She jerks her head toward Lotus. "So get off your high horse, Kenan. Maybe we've both failed her lately, but at least she didn't have to wonder if she was first with *me*."

"God, that's so unfair," I say. "We've been apart for almost three years between separation and divorce, and this is the first time I've dated anyone."

"But Simone wants us back together," Bridget says. "Maybe now you'll believe her."

"We can't do that. We can't tailor the world to her like that and you know it, but we can help her deal with reality. And you've undermined that at every turn, encouraging this fantasy that we might get back together."

"I wish both of you would just shut the hell up," Lotus says tonelessly from her seat.

Bridget and I stare down at her, our mouths gaping open.

"Excuse me?" Bridget's hands go to her hips, and indignation jerks her brows up.

"I know what it's like to think the adults are all crazy," Lotus says, shaking her head. "To feel like no one is considering what's best for you. She doesn't need the two of you at each other's throats. She needs you *both* by her side."

Lotus takes my hand and looks up, holding my stare. "This isn't about you, Kenan. It *can't* be. It has to be about Simone."

Her eyes cool, harden like volcanic rock when they shift to Bridget. "It's not about who is wrong or right because if it was, believe me, Bridget, you'd be wrong."

"Who do you think you are?" Bridget takes a step closer to Lotus. Before I can insert myself between them, Lotus stands and, even several inches shorter, manages to look Bridget right in the eyes.

"I'm cutting you some slack because they're shoving tubes down your daughter's throat," Lotus says, her tone darkening. "But you have one more time to put your finger in my face and step to me."

Bridget draws a deep breath but takes a step back, wisely retreating.

"Look," Lotus says, her gaze moving between us. "This isn't about me either. We all have sacrifices to make until Simone is better. I'll do my part."

What the hell does that mean? What sacrifices?

I'm about to ask her when the doctor comes down the hall and tells us we can finally see Simone. I follow the doctor, eager to see my daughter and to start the healing she needs. At the last moment, I turn back to the waiting room, intending to ask Lotus to wait for me.

But she's already gone.

My first sight of Simone almost brings me to my knees. There's a machine monitoring her vitals and an IV running into one thin arm. The pallor of her skin, usually glowing golden, is a sickly gray.

Her heart is broken in her eyes.

How the hell did I miss that? That fathomless sorrow in my baby girl's watery blue eyes—has it been there all along? What if we had been delayed coming from the airport? What if we'd gone to Lotus's apartment instead of mine? What if I'd gotten stuck in typical New York traffic? A thousand scenarios fly through my mind like bats, the dark wings casting shadows on a day that could have ended with me standing in a morgue instead of in this hospital room.

"I'm sorry," Simone croaks, tears rolling over her cheeks. "I just…" A sob shakes her, and she turns her head into the pillow, her eyes squeezed shut.

"Moni, it's okay." My voice comes out strangled, and I take a moment to compose myself. "We'll sort it out tomorrow."

"Yeah, rest," Bridget says, stroking Simone's hair back from her face. "We'll talk about everything later."

"I know I shouldn't have done it." Simone hiccups. "I just wanted it all to stop. The fighting and the tweets and the posts on Facebook. Some kids from school were tagging me. It all started again."

Rage simmers under my expressionless face as I listen to how my daughter was tortured by our choices and insensitive people who didn't stop to think how a careless tweet might push an emotionally fragile girl over the edge.

Bridget's sob pulls me from my thoughts. She grips the bed railing so tightly her knuckles show white through the skin. I cover her hand. The same helplessness torturing me swims in her teary eyes. For once, we're on the same page, though it's a terrible one in our story—stained with our regret, dog-eared by our pain. To the two of us, Simone is everything. It's the common ground we lost sight of on our battlefield. Neither of us speaks, but at our daughter's side, we broker a silent détente.

The door opens behind us, and Dr. Packer enters. All the times she told us to be careful, told us Simone wasn't doing well, told us it wasn't about us, twist through my memory. When I look into the therapist's eyes, I don't find judgment or censure. Only kindness and concern, but I don't need her to condemn me.

I can do that to myself.

CHAPTER 42
LOTUS

"Kenan's here," Yari says from my bedroom door. "You sure about this?"

I stare unseeingly at the interview notes for next week's gLO Up podcast. I'm not sure I'm ready to do what needs to be done. I may not be strong enough.

"Yeah." I stand and walk past her. "It's the right thing to do."

"Maybe not. Maybe you could—"

"I know what I'm doing, Ri."

"Okay, well, I'm going to meet Pedro for dinner," she says. "But if you need me to stay—"

"No, go. I'm good." I force a smile and head toward the living room. She slips out, and I brace myself for the conversation ahead.

As soon as I see him, I want to dash back to my bedroom and hide under the covers. I can't do this. Who am I kidding? He's magnificent. It's not just the regal, raw-boned face or the brutal beauty of his big body. The compelling sexuality. It's the way those austere lines soften for me. Only for me. The love that blazes in his eyes. Only for me.

"Hey." He stands from the couch and brackets my waist with his hands. I duck my head, avoiding his kiss. He stiffens and peers down at me, rubbing his hands over my arms.

"What's wrong?" He cups my face, tracing my mouth with his thumb.

"Um, Kenan," I start and then falter. My resolve, so steely and set before he came, wavers, melts with him standing so close. He burns right through it without even trying. He's just standing here, being him, loving me. How do I turn away the man I love more than anything in this world?

"How's Simone?" I ask, putting a few inches between us so I can think.

His expression shutters, but not before I detect the pain and guilt there. "She's recovering well, physically."

Everything is tight. The hard slope of his shoulders. The corners of his mouth. The hands knotting at his sides. "There's a three-day hold on…"

He clears his throat before he ejects the next words.

"Suicide attempts," he says, his thick brows jerked into a frown. "There's a psych eval and then…we'll see. She, uh, apparently told Dr. Packer she'd like to move back to Cali and live with me. Since she's only a month into the school year, it shouldn't be too hard to enroll in her old school. Get back to her old routine."

I go still, searching his face for clues. "And what about Bridget?"

"She'll stay in New York to finish *Baller Bae,*" he says, a sardonic twist to his lips, "and then come back to San Diego. Since I'll be on the road so much for the season, I asked my mom if she might be willing to move in with us and give Simone some stability."

His every word only solidifies that my instincts were correct. And on some level, he'll agree with me, but not at first. Not yet. I have to convince him.

"Kenan," I say, forcing myself to look up and meet his eyes. "I think we need some time apart. A break."

He doesn't blink or even seem to breathe for a few seconds. I expect an explosion once my words have sunk in, but instead he meets my words with implacable calm. "No."

One word lands with blunt force in the room, but there's a subtle tightening where he touches me, on my arm, at my face, like he's prepared to hold on if I try to pull away.

But I have to pull away. "Yes, Kenan, I—"

"I said no," he cuts in. His mouth settles into a hard line. His face is a stone wall. His eyes, black diamonds, are sharp enough to cut through glass. "No break. No time apart."

"You haven't heard me out."

"What the *fuck* could you possibly say to make me believe I shouldn't be with you?" he demands, his voice finally gaining heat, volume.

"Simone not only needs you, Kenan, she needs you to be apart from me." I pull out of his hands, turn my back on him. "Especially if she'll be living with you. It doesn't have to be forever. It can be—"

"Not only is it not forever," he shouts behind me, "it's not at all. This is ridiculous, Lotus."

I whirl around to face him. I can get loud, too. I can get mad. Anger is easier to deal with than the ache even the thought of walking away from him brings.

"Your daughter tried to kill herself, Kenan." I pound my chest. "At least in part because of me. Because of us. How do you think that makes me feel?"

"Lo—"

"Me," I slice in, our voices clashing like swords. "The girl whose mother chose another man, an awful man, over her."

"If you would—"

"Me, who never felt first with my mother, who always wondered why she didn't love me more than she loved him. I can't do that to another little girl."

"This is so completely different from your situation," he fires back. "You think I'm not worried? You think I'm not broken after this? Simone almost…"

His voice withers, and he exhales a quick breath. I can almost see the emotions roiling inside him, sloshing against his insides, close to spilling out.

"If she had died, a part of me would have, too," he says, his voice subdued, despairing. "And we have a lot to fix, but us separating wouldn't fix those things, and what you went through is not what she's going through. You didn't abuse anyone. Hurt anyone. What'd you do wrong? Love me? Want me?"

"I'm not saying it's exactly the same. I'm saying I know how she feels." I blink at burning tears. "Do you have any idea how many times I wanted to do what she did? To end my life if that would make the pain stop?"

"I'm so sorry, Lotus," he groans, linking his hands on his head and looking up at the ceiling. "But you have to see this isn't the same."

"I'm not talking about the reality of what we've done, of our situation. I'm talking about how she *sees* it. How it *feels* to her, which is all that matters right now."

The laser probe of his stare snaps back to my face. "And you think us breaking up will make everything better?"

"I think us *taking a break*," I emphasize, "while she gets help could make her feel like she's first with you, and that's what she needs from you and Bridget. To feel like she's your priority. Like you'd do anything for her, even stop seeing someone."

"I don't agree, and I'm not giving you up." He takes my arm. "Why would you leave me now when I need you so much?"

There's such dismay in his question, such an ache in his voice. It pricks my heart like a needle, passing through the beating muscle and piercing my soul. I love him with everything. My heart, my soul, my body, my mind. There is no part of me he hasn't laid siege to. I'm an occupied city. Completely his.

And yet I keep wondering if my mother felt so consumed by a man, even an evil man, that she couldn't do the right thing. Couldn't do the thing that needed to be done. Couldn't let him go when she needed to, when she *had* to, but chose her own desires, right or wrong, over her child.

"We're the adults," I force myself to say, even though my voice shakes, my resolve shakes. "I'm not saying it's forever."

I meet the outraged disbelief, the refusal of his stare.

"I can't be away from you forever," I say softly. "You already know that, Kenan, but I am saying for now, for her, let's just step away from this. At least for the season. As if basketball isn't enough of a distraction while you're negotiating this, you don't need me, too."

"That's where you're wrong," he says. "I need you so bad."

He pulls me in to him by my wrist, and the smell of him, the heat of him, seduces me. I close my eyes and savor the light press of our bodies together. I imagine the grind, how it feels when he's buried inside me. When will I have that again?

"I want it, too," he whispers in my ear, his hand sliding to my ass. "What you're thinking about right now. What you're remembering. I want to fuck you, too."

"Kenan, don't." It's a pathetic protest overshadowed by the way my body throbs with him so close.

"I love you," he says, his voice a wisp of sound and breath over my lips before he captures them with his. His tongue hunts for mine, seeking, seizing. My convictions fade, and I kiss him back. He groans, his hands fumbling between us and under my dress. His unfailing fingers find me through my panties.

"God," he breathes, pressing his temple to mine. "You're soaked."

"Kenan, we can't." I say it, but my hips roll into the urgency of his hand. My clit flowers under his fingers.

"Why can't we?" He kisses my neck, sucks the curve hard, and walks us a few feet back until my back hits the wall. "You're mine." He unzips his jeans and hoists me up by my thighs, pressing me to the wall.

"Did you forget?" he asks, his voice gruff, graveled. "You said you belong to me. Are you a liar?"

"No. You know I'm yours, but we need to do this for her. Can't you see that?"

"This is what I see. What I know." He jerks my panties aside and plunges inside me like a warrior charging into battle.

"Oh my God." I can't resist the call of our bodies fused together, and I rock into him, heedless of my intentions, damning my plan. My pussy clenches around him, possessive, demanding.

"That's it. Fuck me, Lotus," he breathes into the paltry space left between us while our aggressive thrusts thump my back against the wall. "Tell me whose you are, whose I am."

I score my nails across his head, sink my fingers into his neck with a ferocious desire born from desperation. When this is over, I'll make him go, and I'm not sure when I'll have him again.

"My beloved is mine," I quote, my head thrown back, tears slipping from under my closed eyes. "And I am his."

"Again." His hands tighten under my thighs, and he slams into me, the churning of our bodies furious, frantic. "Tell me again."

"My beloved is mine, and I am his." The words come louder, harder as my climax builds.

"Again! Tell me."

"*My beloved is mine, and I am his,*" I scream so loud the words scrape my throat and ricochet off the walls.

"How dare you think you can take this from us?" he growls into my neck. "A fucking break? There's no break. No separation. Tell me again."

"Oh, God. I'm yours, Kenan." I shake against him with my sobs, with the orgasm thundering through my body even as I weep. "You know I'm yours."

"And I have found the one whom my soul loves," he quotes back to me, his voice crashing into the curve of my neck. He comes, a roar strangled in his throat. A growl dying on his lips as he loses his breath with the force of his release.

We stay that way for long moments, me pinned to the wall, my legs wrapped around him, his hands gripping my thighs. I relish the wet evidence of our love, our passion. I hate that it's already sliding out of my body. Lost on my thighs. I want to hold him inside me forever.

"Don't leave me, Lotus. God, I can't take it." He presses his forehead to mine. "Not now. Not ever, but not now."

"But it has to be now," I whisper. "I'm so sorry, baby, but it has to be now."

I drop my legs, but he doesn't move, keeping me pinned to the wall. I poke at his chest, but my strength is puny beside his, and he doesn't move. I look up at him through my lashes and starch my will.

"Move," I say firmly. "Go."

"No."

"You can't stay here forever," I reason. "At some point you have to go. You're just delaying the inevitable. The sooner you focus on Simone, the sooner we can…"

"The sooner we can get back together?" He pushes my hair back and traces the shell of my ear. "We're not breaking up."

"Kenan." I blow out a frustrated breath. "We are. For now, we are. It's not forever, but it needs to happen. She failed this time. I doubt she wanted to succeed. She did it in your apartment, in your bedroom, knowing you'd be coming home. But what if she still feels like she's not getting your attention? What if she does it again?"

"She won't ever do that again." A twitch disrupts the stern line of his jaw.

"The thing about trying to kill yourself," I say, keeping my voice hard, being ruthless because I have to be, "is you get better at it every time you try."

He draws in a breath that strains the muscles of his chest in his shirt.

"Show her now, Kenan," I urge, grabbing his hand. "Show her she's the most important thing to you. Focus on her, and when the time is right, when she's better, Dr. Packer will guide her into accepting me as part of your life." I breathe a little chuckle. "Maybe one day accepting me as part of her life, too."

"I want that," he says, the look in his eyes intensifying. "I want you in her life. I want us to be a family. Lotus, I want you to be my—"

"Stop." If he says it, there is no way I can send him away. Longing swells so big inside me, I think I might burst. "Don't. Not yet."

"When?" he demands, lifting my chin. "When can I say it?"

"Later. After she's better, you can say it."

"Promise me. Promise me I can say it when she's better, and I'll give you your break."

"It's not *my* break, Kenan," I say, huffing an exasperated sigh. "It's for her, not us. That's the point."

We stare each other down, and it's reminiscent of all those times I walked into a room and forced myself to stare into the eyes of the most beautiful man I'd ever seen and walk away. I was afraid then of what would happen if I gave in to the pull between us. Then I only suspected that if I ever got involved with him, I wouldn't be able to leave. Now, I know who he is behind that rough exterior. I know his tenderness, his love, his passion, and they've exceeded my every expectation. He's so much more than I imagined he would be, and it's breaking me in half to let him go even for a season.

"Everything you've told me seems to underscore my point," I say carefully. "Simone wants to be with you. With her living in your house, this is the perfect opportunity to show her she's your priority."

He doesn't release me from the wall. I'm a butterfly trapped under glass. He studies me but still doesn't move.

"I'm flying Dr. Packer in once a week so Simone doesn't have to start over with a new therapist," he finally says. "When she determines that Simone is better and that the time is right, you'll, um…" He clears his throat, his lashes lowered and hiding whatever is in his eyes. "When the time is right, you'll come back to me?"

My unguarded warrior. Never have I heard him more vulnerable, more exposed than he is right now. I reach up to cup his face, meeting his eyes with the force of my passion, my devotion.

"When the time is right," I promise, my voice husky from the tears kept at bay in my throat, "I'll come running, Mr. Ross."

He bends and locks his elbows under my ass, picking me up and pressing his forehead to mine.

"No one touches you," he says softly, fiercely.

"No one," I agree.

"No dates."

"None."

"No flirtations or any of that shit."

"None of that shit."

He pauses, narrowing his eyes. "I'm serious, Lotus. We are not on a break. We are not seeing other people. You are not single."

"And you can tell those groupies who hang around in the tunnel after games that if they like their teeth in their mouths," I say sharply, "they'll keep their paws and their nasty little pussies away from my man. Do I make myself clear, Kenan?"

He grins, a flash of bittersweet against his mahogany skin that has my heart skipping beats and turning cartwheels, even as it breaks. "Crystal clear."

CHAPTER 43
LOTUS

"Paris next year, Lo," JP says decisively. "I want to show in Paris instead of New York."

I nod, focused on the dress design I've been working on. "That sounds good."

"Orders from the new collection have far surpassed our projections."

"That's amazing," I reply, smudging the line of the shoulder with my thumb.

"And I think I'll use that new model from Mars."

"Love it." I frown at the length of the sleeve, flipping my pencil to erase a half inch.

"And let's open the fall show with an orgy."

"Great idea." I tilt my head and squint one eye at the hem. "Orgies are so hot right…"

My head pops up, and I stare at him wide-eyed. "Wait. What?"

"I wondered how far I would have to go before you actually started listening," he says, his grin teasing.

"Very funny. I was listening."

"Oh, so you will be scouting on Mars for my next model, eh?"

"*Va te faire foutre*," I mumble, and fight a smile.

"I think that's the problem." He accessorizes a suggestive waggle of his brows with a devilish grin. "You're the one not getting fucked."

My grin falls away, and I gather my sketch pad, phone, and laptop.

"And on that note," I say, standing, "I think I'll go get some real work done."

"You miss him, Lotus," JP says. "It's obvious how miserable you are without him."

"I'm not miserable. I'm fine, and it's temporary."

"We only get so many days, *ma petite*, on this Earth. Why waste even one when you've found the love of your life?"

"What makes you think he's the love of my life?" I ask, and head for the door to leave his office.

"You're one of those creatures who only loves once and greatly, I think. So Monsieur Ross, he is it. *Ai-je tort?*"

I pause at the door, my hand on the knob.

Once and greatly. I've never been in love before, not even close, and I hope to never love anyone else. Only Kenan.

"Am I wrong?" JP repeats in English this time.

"No." Over my shoulder, I give him a wan smile, softening when I find concern in his eyes. "Probably not."

I close the door behind me and head straight for the back room downstairs. Not only do I need privacy to work, but I also need some time by myself.

The last two months have been even harder than I anticipated, but I think we did the right thing. Kenan and I have spoken a few times. His schedule has been hectic, playing games every other day, sometimes back-to-back days, and constant travel. I probably wouldn't have seen much of him anyway.

Even knowing it was the right thing to do, it was the hardest. I feel Kenan's absence not just from New York but from my life profoundly. Every part of me misses him. My body craves his touch—the way he'd push my hair back from my face or caress my fingers when we talked or trace my spine after we made love. My soul aches for its interlocking piece. My heart is pressed to my chest with a glass, straining to hear the echo of his heartbeat, but it's too far away.

I set my things down, ready to get to business.

"Where'd that pencil go?" I mutter, looking around. I pat the oversize pockets on the jumper I designed myself, and I feel a small square card inside. I go still for a second and then pull it out.

You populate my dreams. They are rich with the scent of you. Your heart is on my pillow, and I taste you in my sleep.—This one is all me

My smile wobbles. Once a week, I get a note in the mail. My weekly treasures are the brightest spots in my life, the barely legible words he handwrites to me. It's another card for my lunch-box sewing kit.

"Here you are," Yari says from the door. "I've been looking for you."

I sniff and turn away to wipe under my eyes.

"Here I am," I force myself to reply brightly, sitting down at my laptop. "Come to distract me from my job again?"

"Not this time." Yari walks over, her expression serious. "Billie resigned."

"What?" I close my laptop and stand. "What do you mean resigned?"

"Resigned, as in take-your-job-and-shove-it resigned."

"But why?"

"I had to," Billie says from the open door, her face tear-streaked and splotchy. "It's over with Paul."

Yari and I meet her halfway, and she's in our arms before the first harsh sob spills from her. God, I hate the sound of a broken heart. I've heard it so many times from women in my family who exchanged their bodies for hope of a better future, only to be disappointed time and again. From friends who trusted the wrong men—who gave them everything they wanted thinking it would make them stay, only to watch them leave. Heartbreak is a habit for some women, one I promised myself I'd never form.

"Tell us." I walk Billie over to sit on a sewing table and slip my arm around her shoulders. "What happened?"

"I came in this morning, and he told me we had to end it." Billie swipes at her nose with a trembling hand.

"Here, honey," Yari says, digging some Kleenex out of a nearby drawer.

"Thanks." Billie blows her nose and bites her lip. "He said his wife found out about us."

"Oh my God." One hand covers my mouth and the other my heart. "How?"

"I don't know." Billie shrugs and closes her eyes tightly. "But he said when she confronted him about it, he confessed everything and said it was…a fling. Nothing. He told her I was nothing."

Another sob shakes her chest and crumples her face. She hiccups the next words.

"He told her it was a slip-up, a mistake that only happened once." Billie's laugh is void of humor, full of hurt. "We've been together over a year. He took me to Aspen for our anniversary. How could he lie that way?"

"He's a liar," Yari says, her voice brittle. "He lied to his wife, and he lied to you. It's what he does. I know you're hurting, but it's for the best, Bill. You can do better than that. Better than him."

"She's right, Billie," I say, a little more gently, but no less direct.

Billie nods, her usually neat red hair mussed and falling around her shoulders, as if she's been running her hands through it. "I almost feel like I knew it would have to happen like this. Like I brought it on myself."

"How do ya figure?" Yari asks.

Billie settles curious green eyes on me for long seconds.

"What?" I ask. "Why are you looking at me like that?"

"At my birthday party," she says. "You said be careful what you wish for. Why'd you say that?"

I blink at her, searching for some explanation that would make logical sense to them. "No reason." I run a hand over the back of my neck. "Why? What did you wish for?"

"A baby. I wished for a baby to force his hand, to make him choose," she whispers. Her eyes fill with tears. "I know it's the oldest trick in the book, but I stopped taking my pills."

"Bill, no." Yari's horrified gaze stretches wide, flicking between our friend and me. "Are you pregnant?"

"No." She looks at me again. "His wife is."

My heart drops to my feet. I don't know what made me say that. I don't always know details, but sometimes I have impressions or a strong feeling. Whatever gift I inherited from MiMi, it's not perfect or precise, like the night I sensed death near and assumed it was for Kenan but it was actually warning me about Simone.

"I wished for a baby to make him choose," Billie says bitterly. "I guess I should have specified a baby for *me* to make him choose *me*. You were right, Lo. I should have been careful what I wished for."

I can't answer the questions in her eyes to any satisfaction, so I redirect the conversation. "So you resigned."

Billie watches me for a few more seconds before nodding. "I can't work for him anymore. Not after this. I'll start pounding the pavement, I guess."

"You have a business degree from NYU," I say wryly. "And four years working for one of the hottest houses in fashion. We'll find you something."

"What if it's not finding something," Yari says, her bright eyes flashing between us, "but making something."

"What do you mean?" Billie draws her brows together. "Me? Make something? You know I can't sew or design or even cross-stitch. The only head I have for fashion is a business mind."

"Right." Yari jogs over to the table where my things are and holds up my sketch pad. "But I happen to have a friend who is very good at making things."

"Me?" I point at my chest. "No, I'm not ready to strike out on my own. I've still got a lot to learn from JP. Maybe in a year or so."

"I think you underestimate yourself," Billie says, borrowing some of Yari's excitement. "We could do it, Lo. We could start our own label."

"And your podcast has become so popular," Yari chimes in. "We could totally leverage the influence you're building through it."

I'm about to tell them what a horrible idea this actually is when Paul walks in.

Brave, foolish man.

"Billie, could I talk to you for a minute?" he asks, fixing his eyes on her and deliberately avoiding the glares Yari and I hurl his way.

"No, Paul." Billie looks at him, and I hate the weakness creeping into her eyes when their stares connect. "There's nothing left to say."

"I disagree," he replies, adjusting his glasses and clearing his throat. "Uh, ladies, maybe you could excuse us for a minute."

"Uh, Paul," Yari snaps, stepping in front of Billie to partially obscure his view, "maybe you could go fuck yourself for a minute."

"Look, I'm still the CEO of this company, dammit," he says harshly, "and you can't talk to me like that. I will not abide insubordination."

"Insubordination?" I ask, a dark chuckle rolling out of my mouth. "You have five seconds to take your ass back upstairs or your wife gets a call from me tonight with the truth, not that shit you told her to cover your ass."

"Billie, if you could—"

"One," I say, stepping beside Yari to completely hide Billie from his view.

Red mottles his winter-pale skin, and he frowns. "Look, I can explain—"

"Two," Yari says, her arms folded over her chest, her hip cocked out.

"You want a recommendation, don't you, Billie?" he asks, a cruel light in his blue eyes. "How far do you think you'll get in this industry if everyone knows you tried to sleep your way to the top?"

I walk over to him until I'm so close I can smell what he had for lunch.

"Oh, you got threats now, Paul?" I ask in a dangerously soft tone. "You don't want to threaten her because when you threaten her, you threaten me. And when you threaten me, I attack."

"You can't hurt me," he sneers, but a vein of nervousness runs through his voice.

"You sure about that?" I ask, using artificial sweetener for my smile. "You *do* know why we no longer use Chase, right? He crossed me, and it only took one conversation with JP to ensure he wouldn't be coming back. Maybe it's time JP knows you've been fucking his employees."

"You're crazy," he says, fear darkening his eyes.

"Yes, which is why if I were you, I'd run. I'm crazy enough to take great pleasure in destroying your career, that sham of a marriage, and anything promising in your future." I angle my head to Yari behind me. "What number were we on, Ri?"

"Three," she spits.

"Oh, yeah." I scowl up at him. "Three. Four. If you're still standing here at five, I start destroying shit."

With a growl that may as well be a whimper, he turns on his heel and strides from the room.

I turn back to my friends and grin.

"Chickenshit," I say with a cackle. I high-five Yari and go to do the same with Billie, but the tears in her eyes stop me. "Oh, honey. He's not worth your tears. You can do better. You'll find *someone* better."

"I know that." She sniffs and gives us a tremulous grin. "But my heart has to catch up to what's right."

I caress the small square hidden in my pocket, its words tucked away on a shelf in my soul. Doing what's right sometimes breaks our hearts. Knowing it's right doesn't make it hurt any less.

I know that firsthand.

CHAPTER 44
KENAN

"He fakes left," I tell August as we leave the practice facility. "You'll have to guard him tight, and he's a beast off the dribble."

"I got it, Glad," August replies, hefting his gym bag onto his shoulder.

"Don't give him much room. Push him back so he has to take a lower-percentage shot at least."

"I watched the same film you did." August pauses before we go our separate ways, his car on one side of the parking lot and mine on the other. "I'll be fine. We'll be fine. This is the best season start we've ever had. This is our year, bruh. Why are you so uptight?"

"Yeah, you're right. I know you got it. Just a lot going on, I guess."

"Everything okay with Simone?"

August and Iris have been supportive and know the demands I've been juggling between the season and having Simone living with me.

"Yeah, she's good, man. Thanks for asking." I chuckle. "And being here for her is exactly what my mom needed. Kenya and I were worried about her after my dad died, but taking care of Simone has given her a new lease on life. Dr. Packer says Simone's much better."

"Man, that's great."

"If you can believe it, Bridget's even been on her best behavior." I grimace. "I mean, it helps that she's in New York and not here. Who knows if our truce will hold once she moves back out west for the summer? But for now, I think we're in the best place we've been in a long time. What happened with Simone was a wake-up call for us both."

"Sounds like everything is lining up," August says, hesitating before going on. "So does that mean you and Lotus…"

"Soon." I smile, even though it hurts to even hear her name. "I think really soon."

"That's what I like to hear. You guys deserve it." August daps me up and turns to go. "Okay. I promised Iris I'd be home right after practice, so I'm gonna roll out. See you on the plane."

Tomorrow's game is the first of a pretty brutal road trip. Four games before we return to San Diego. That means a week away from home. I'll have some quality time with Simone, though, when I drive her up to this dance camp in Laguna Beach today. At least she'll be gone for a good part of my time away and will feel the impact less.

I'm clicking "the tank" unlocked when a guy approaches, his phone thrust toward me to record. I haven't had to worry about tabloids for a while, but I know a reporter when I see one.

"Glad, hey!" he yells, his phone thrust toward me to record. "You excited the *Baller Bae* season is ending?"

"I don't discuss my personal life," I auto reply. "You got a question about basketball, get a media credential and show up at a press conference after the game. Otherwise, no comment."

I climb into the car and start the engine.

"And what about Lotus?" he yells right as my foot hovers over the accelerator. "That girl you were dating this summer?"

I grit my teeth and try to talk myself out of engaging, but it's a battle lost. I roll down my window and try to ignore the satisfaction in the creep's eyes.

"What about her?"

"Well, rumor is that she's dating that photographer again," he says in a rush. "Bridget claimed she was cheating on you with him. What do you have to—"

I roll up my window and pull off.

Son of a bitch. That's what I get for giving him the time of day.

My finger twitches over the button on my steering wheel that would dial her. We've talked some. It wouldn't be completely out of the norm for me to call. We've kept each other abreast of our lives.

"Fuck it."

I hit the button.

"Kenan?"

Her voice in my car makes me want to blow off my road trip and go get her. Fly to New York and bring her home with me.

"Yeah, it's me." *Obviously it's you, dumbass.* "Uh, how you doing?"

"Good." She pauses, clears her throat. "I got your card yesterday. So you're a poet now?"

My own laughter almost catches me off guard. This summer, I forgot how much time I spend alone. How little I actually talk to people most of the time because I laughed, I talked, I felt more freely *myself* with Lotus than I ever have with anyone else.

"Not a poet exactly," I say when our laughter trails off. "A little something I had on my mind."

"I liked it," she says, her voice husky.

There's so much I want to say to her. So much she's missed, even though we've talked occasionally. But mostly I just want to know… "Um, so this reporter approached me after practice."

"Okay."

"He mentioned something about the girl I was seeing this summer dating that photographer again." I leave the unspoken question suspended over the thousands of miles separating us.

"Oh." She's quiet for a moment. "I have no idea where he got that."

I need to focus and make sure I'm clear on what she's saying. I pull over to the parking lot of a gas station and lean back in my seat, waiting for her to elaborate. She doesn't.

"Yeah, I don't know either," I finally say. "Because you know we said…"

I don't say what we said, but she knows we aren't dating other people. I trust her. It hadn't even occurred to me until that reporter planted his poison.

"Yeah, we said…" She huffs a quick laugh. "You didn't think… I wouldn't. Kenan, I haven't."

I release a relieved exhale and nod, even though she can't see me. Why can't she see me? I should have FaceTimed. God, I want to see her.

"You haven't…" She starts, stops. "Well, we said…"

"Yeah, we said—no," I rush to assure her. "I'm living like a monk."

She laughs, and I hear relief in her voice, too. "My monk."

"Your monk. Completely."

Her breath catches, and she sighs. I want to taste that sigh. If I could kiss her, I'd know what she was thinking. I'd know what was in her heart just from the press of our lips.

"I miss you, Kenan," she says, her voice breaking. "So bad."

I clench the steering wheel and clamp my teeth together until my jaw aches. "I don't want to do this anymore, Lotus. I think we can… Simone's so much better. We have her diagnosis. She's on the right meds. My mom is holding it down for me during the season." A rough chuckle rumbles from my chest. "Mama's even got Simone's hair looking good."

"That's awesome," Lotus says, a smile in her voice.

"I told my mom about you."

A short pause. "You did? What'd you tell her?"

"That I'm in love with you."

Lotus's breath hitches again, so I must be doing something right.

"I told her I want to marry you one day."

She didn't let me say it the last time I saw her—that I wanted her to be my wife—but I say it now before she sees it coming, before she can stop me.

"You told her that?" Her voice wavers and squeaks sweetly at the end.

"Yeah, and you know what she asked me?"

"What?"

"When she could expect more grandkids. With only one, she claims to need a backup."

Lotus's laugh cracks open, and a sob spills out. "I love you, Kenan Ross, and I will gladly marry you and have all the grandkids your mama can babysit when the time is right."

When the time is right.

Right.

"What I'm saying is that the time is soon, Lotus."

"Talk to Dr. Packer, and we'll go from there. We don't want to undo all the things we sacrificed already."

"She thinks you're amazing, by the way," I tell her, an unstoppable grin on my face.

"Why?"

"Because she thinks you did the right thing," I say, sobering. "In our case, she thinks it was best for Simone. All of it. Not everyone is that committed to putting their kids' needs before their own."

"But you were."

"No, you were. I wouldn't have done it if you hadn't forced the issue."

"Well, like I said, I know what it's like to feel that everyone else is more important."

Voices in the background break the spell this conversation has woven over me.

"My meeting's starting," she says. "I gotta go."

"Yeah, me, too. I have to drive Simone to this dance camp thing."

"Okay." She pauses for a second before whispering, "I love you."

"You have no idea," I reply immediately. "But I'm going to show you real soon."

"I like the sound of that."

"So do I. Love you, Button."

I'm on the proverbial cloud, feeling like some lovesick fool but not really giving a damn.

My high crashes when my dashboard displays an incoming call from Bridget. We've been civil the few times we've spoken. With her in New York, there have been thankfully few visits to coordinate, and those happened while I was on the road. Dr. Packer believes the harmony between Bridget and me is just as much a stabilizing force as me waiting to be with Lotus or my mom moving in with us.

I answer the phone and brace myself for any drama Bridget may have in store. "Bridget, hey," I say, keeping my eyes on the road. "What's up?"

"Hey, Kenan," she says, her voice filling the car interior. "How are you?"

Oh, manners. I remember these. "I'm good. What's up?" I repeat.

"The cast has an appearance in LA today," she says, her tone slightly hesitant. "I, um, thought I might swing by to see Simone."

"You know she has that dance camp in Laguna Beach," I remind her. "I'm on my way home to take her now."

"Oh, yeah. I forgot. Um…maybe next time."

"Well, LA is even closer to Laguna Beach. Pop in and see her before you go back. I'm sure it'll be fine."

"You think so?" she asks, brightening.

"Yeah. I start a stretch of road games tomorrow and will be gone for the week, so seeing one of us will probably be good for her."

"Okay. I'll text her to make arrangements." She goes quiet for a second. "She's better, right?"

The same cold-sweat fear I have—that I'll find Simone barely breathing on my bed again—resides in Bridget's voice. I find myself in my daughter's room when she's asleep and watching her breathe, like I did when she was a baby. It reassures me. Right now, Bridget doesn't even have that.

"Yeah, Bridget. She's better."

"I think we all are," she says, a smile in her voice.

"Yeah."

"She told me you're not seeing Lotus anymore," Bridget says, the tiniest flicker of hope in the words. "I'm sorry things didn't work out."

"They're actually working out fine," I reply carefully. "Lotus and I wanted to give Simone some time to recover and for me to focus on her as much as possible while the season is still so demanding."

"Very thoughtful of you." An edge blunts her words.

"Lotus's idea, actually."

Several drops of quiet form a shallow puddle of silence that starts becoming uncomfortable just as Bridget speaks again.

"I saw you with her a few times, you know," Bridget says, exhaling a breathy, bitter laugh. "There were a few shots of you this summer out doing things together. Laughing. Having fun. I barely recognized you."

"Searching hashtags again?" I ask, unable to stanch that familiar irritation.

"How else would I know what was going on in your life?"

"Why would you *want* to know?" I demand, exasperated. "I don't get you, Bridget. You have an affair with one of my friends. You throw our marriage out the window—"

"Our *marriage*?" she asks, a double-edged sword of scorn and bitterness. "Is that what you called it?"

My mother, as angry as she was with Bridget, expressed sympathy for her because we were ill-matched.

Bridget tried to crack you like a nut. For the woman you love, though, really love, it's not hard work. I didn't have to crack your father. He spilled himself with me.

God, my mother was right. I don't know that I did anything *wrong*, but there must have been some things with Bridget I didn't do right. And now I see clearly that I couldn't, would never have trusted myself, *the real me*, my inner self, with the person Bridget has proven herself to be. I don't think I was capable of it with her.

"Look, Bridget, we've been at war with each other for years, and if what happened with Simone showed me anything, it's the value of a second chance. We have a chance to clean the slate. I'm tired of fighting. It's destructive, and we both have to move on."

"With Lotus, you mean," she says, her voice subdued. "You're moving on with Lotus."

"Yeah." I meet the disappointment in her voice head-on. "With Lotus."

I ignore her sharp breath and continue.

"I've been angry with you," I admit. "For years, angry that our family, our life was ripped apart."

"I know, and I'm sorry," Bridget whispers.

"I've been angry," I continue. "But I could never understand why *you* were angry, too. You've been angry with me for not being what you thought I would be. For not letting you in, for abandoning you in our marriage."

"It doesn't excuse what I did," she says faintly. "I never meant to cheat on you. It just…"

I'm grateful she doesn't say it just "happened." Those things don't just happen.

"It wasn't all you," I tell her, clearing my throat. "It was me, too. You used to talk about the wall that came up during the season, but it wasn't only when I was playing ball. It was all the time. I'm a hard man to know, to reach."

"But not for her." Her words come out on a light breath but land with a thud.

"No, not for her." A wry half smile crooks my mouth. "I don't regret us, Bridget, because we have Simone, and she's the best thing."

"She is." She chuckles softly on the other end, hesitating before rushing on. "Can you ever… Could you forgive me, Kenan?"

I've simmered in resentment for years, and in this moment, all the pain and humiliation and awful things Bridget's affair caused me to experience rush to my mind.

Then other memories slowly start to sift in. Bridget, young and alone in a strange city with a newborn while I was on the road. So many missed birthdays, anniversaries, milestones, and times I knew there was something she needed and had no clue how to give it to her.

Bridget and I haven't been on the best of terms the last few years, but I've known her half my life, was married to her for more than a decade. She gave me my daughter. There may not ever have been a time when I loved her the way she needed to be loved, and there may not ever have been a time when she truly saw me, understood me, knew the real me, but there *was* a time when we were friends. There was a girl I met in college who walked with me through the challenging transition into the NBA, through being a father when I didn't know what the hell I was doing. Through my greatest accomplishments. I wish we could have focused on those things more instead of all the ways we failed each other, and now we have that chance.

"I'll forgive you," I say with a half-pained smile, "if you can forgive me."

I don't have to explain why I'm asking forgiveness. It's fueled her own anger and frustration and hung over us for years.

"I can do that," she says, the words tremulous. "Thank you, Kenan."

It won't be easy, and I have no doubt our anger and past hurts will resurface sometimes when we least expect it. Maybe it took this wake-up call for us to gain perspective on what's most important—that it really *is* about Simone, and that maybe for her we can set the past aside and focus on her future. Maybe for her, we can be friends again.

"Got everything?" I ask one more time before I leave Simone at the lush beach retreat where the dance camp is being held.

"Yeah." She shifts the gym bag on her shoulder. "Grandma double-checked the list they gave us to make sure I wasn't forgetting anything."

"Good. I'll call you from the road. Our first game is Toronto and then Chicago and then San Antonio and then the Lakers. I'll be back Saturday."

When I look down at my daughter, a wave of gratitude overwhelms me. The "what ifs" have tortured me ever since the night we found her unconscious on my bed. My nightmares are made from dark alternate endings, and I've jerked awake more than once to rush down the hall and make sure she is real, not some grief-induced hallucination.

She's beautiful and growing up fast. She'll be fifteen soon and won't be thinking about her old man anymore. I've missed so much. Basketball has given me a lot, but it's taken its money's worth.

"I love you more than everything, Moni." I kiss her forehead and press her head to my chest. "You know that, right?"

She glances up at me, her brows crinkling over her pretty blue eyes, and then nods.

"What?" I frown down at her. "What is it?"

"What happened to Lotus?"

I wish Dr. Packer were here right now. I'm not sure how to handle this. Simone knows I'm not seeing Lotus anymore, and I haven't talked about her at all, so I'm not sure what prompted the question.

"Uh, she still lives in New York. Why do you ask, baby?"

"You seemed...I don't know." Simone shrugs her narrow shoulders. "You seemed happier when she was around."

Damn, I miss her.

Isolation hits me with crushing force. My life is so much brighter with Lotus in it. I don't speak. I'm still formulating the best answer— one that won't unravel all that we've worked so hard to put together.

"It's okay if you love her, too," Simone says quietly.

I pull back and peer down into her face. Her eyes, when they meet mine, are sober. They've seen too much, know too much already.

"It is?" I ask tentatively.

"I want you to be happy." She swallows and looks down at the ground. "I want Mommy to be happy, too, but I know you don't make each other happy anymore."

"But we'll always love you," I say, cupping her face, "and always put you first, okay?"

She nods and offers a small smile. She's a good kid. In spite of all the shit she's been through. She's the only good thing to come out of my marriage.

"Simone," a tall, elegant woman calls. I remember meeting her at one of Moni's recitals. "The other girls are all inside. Say goodbye and join us, please."

"Coming, Madam Petrov," Simone replies before turning back to me. "Gotta go."

"Okay. Love you, Moni." I swipe my hand down her face, our familiar expression of love. She smiles, looks happy. God, let it be real. Knowing your child is hurting in a way you can't make stop or make better is the most helpless feeling in the world. You watch for any distress signal, strain to catch each sign of progress or hint of joy, with your breath held. With bated hope.

"Love you, Daddy."

We're gonna be okay.

It's a refrain playing on repeat in my head as I drive back to San Diego. I loved talking with Simone on the way up, hearing about how well things are going at school and with dance. Giving her space to tell me how the meds make her feel better. Allowing her to tell me about the days when they don't. Every word she shared, even those that were hard to hear, reassured me because she's sharing it. She's not hiding it or keeping it to herself. She's so much like me in a lot of ways, naturally burying her emotions and hoarding her thoughts.

But as much as I enjoyed our talk driving up to Laguna Beach, I revel in the silence on my drive home. It's hard to describe to someone who doesn't need it how refreshing being alone can be—not lonely at all, but alone. On this scenic stretch of highway, I have the breathtaking view of the ocean all to myself. The moon glimmers off dark-blue water as I negotiate the twists of the Pacific Coast Highway. I put on my favorite song: "It Never Entered My Mind." The opening strains of piano blend seamlessly, flawlessly with Davis's trumpet. He sandpapered every note until it was smooth dulcet tonal perfection.

Even as I relish my solitude, Lotus won't leave me alone.

"What's your favorite song to listen to when you want to unwind?"

"'It Never Entered My Mind.'"

"Well, let it enter your mind."

My laughter at the memory breaks the silence in the car, and I wish she were here beside me, curled up in the passenger seat talking about everything or nothing. I'd settle for her silence, her voice, her scent. I'd take anything of her I could get.

It makes me eager to get home—to put this road trip behind me and find a way to see her. I'll speak with Dr. Packer and figure out when we can talk to Simone, what to say. It's time to bring Lotus back into my life, into *our* lives.

I'm not-so-patiently stuck riding behind a slow truck carrying huge pipes when my headlights illuminate a chain anchoring the pipes as it pops loose. The pipe slides off the truck and toward me, headed for my windshield.

"Shit!"

I swerve, avoiding the pipe that lands in the road where my vehicle was mere seconds ago. Another pipe slips from the truck's flatbed, bouncing on an unpredictable trajectory. The entire sequence takes seconds, but everything retards to a slow-moving, terrifying crawl. Inside me, though, accelerant douses everything—my racing, pounding heartbeat, the blood rushing through my veins like river rapids, the quick, shallow breaths chopping up in my chest as my body deploys adrenaline to every vital organ.

The wheel slips through my hands as the SUV hurtles toward the guardrail. In my mind, I see Lotus clutching her little saint, her face wreathed in fear and love by the flickering light of candles, eyes fixed on me, never looking away. All I hear is Lotus's urgent recitation, the psalm falling from her lips with the determined persistence of raindrops pinging a tin roof.

It's the last thing I hear before the groan and crash and moan of colliding metal take it all away.

CHAPTER 45
LOTUS

"You ready to hit this J train?" Yari asks.

"In a minute." I glance up from the dress I'm pinning for JP. "Isn't this gorgeous?"

"Girl, yes." Yari walks farther into the fitting room where the models usually try on the clothes. I'm working from a body form, though. "What's that for?"

"A certain Hollywood actress wants to be wearing this when the Oscar goes to her," I mumble around the pins in my mouth. "We've got plenty of time since she hasn't even been nominated yet."

We share a quick laugh. I get up and stretch from the long time on my knees. "Let me grab my stuff."

My phone rings in my pocket as I'm walking back to my cubicle. Iris's ringtone.

"Hey, Bo. What's up?" I ask, motioning to Yari that we can keep walking out. "You calling to complain about how hungry my nephew is again? I've told you that formula—"

"Lo," she breaks in. "No, I, um… That's not why I'm calling."

The somber note weighing her voice down stops me shy of the elevator. Yari stops, too, eyeing me curiously.

"Oh," I say. "You sound funny, Bo. What's up? The kids okay?"

"The kids are fine." Her voice catches. "It's, um, it's Kenan, hon."

All my bodily functions pause. Or at least it feels that way. The whole building, the whole city, the whole world seems to stop for a second. I want to stay in this tiny window of time before I know how bad it is, before she tells me something that will demolish my heart and ruin my life.

"What about…" I clear my throat, but the fear doesn't move. An unbudgeable dread gathers and ties knots in my belly. "What about him? He's okay, right? Iris, he's okay?"

The silence that follows blares in my ears. I pull the phone away and press it to my chest, closing my eyes and forcing myself to listen again.

"Lotus?" Iris asks. "You there?"

"Yeah. Just tell me."

"He was in a car accident."

"But he's okay. He's alive. I'd know if he weren't."

Iris's skepticism reaches me across the phone—the same skepticism I get from Kenan. She thinks I make it up—that I've bought into some of MiMi's old-lady nonsense. She doesn't understand. She never really has.

My soul would know. I'd get goose bumps. The damn sky would open up and pour out fire. Somehow, *some way*, I would know if Kenan Ross had left this Earth.

"He's alive, yeah. He's in surgery now," Iris says. "But it's serious. You need to come. August is chartering a flight to get you here as quickly as possible."

"Okay." My body is all over the place. My heart has splintered into a million shards, but my mind is so incredibly focused, as if I'm watching this all from an observation tower. It's not happening to me. It can't be happening to him.

Yari calls Billie, who meets us at the airport. I swing by our apartment and grab my stuff. A few items of clothing, my lunch box, salt, candles, Saint Expedite. I'm fully prepared to make a fool of myself. I'm braced for skepticism and accusations of lunacy, but I refuse to give a fuck.

My friends have never seen this side of me. They watch me carefully as I sit in my seat, clutching the little figure in my hand and reciting Psalm 35 until my mouth is dry and cottony. I take up the litany in my head, barely blinking or breathing. I frantically assemble everything MiMi ever told me about life, about death, and healing. The afterlife. The diaphanous walls that separate time from eternity—how they fall without notice and the ones we love can so easily slip from this life into the next.

"Help me, MiMi," I whisper with my head pressed to the cold window as we fly above the clouds. There's no sign of pink. No cotton candy in the sky. "You said I have your heart. I truly believe that's all I need. Don't let me miss the things our eyes can't see. I need you."

Salty tears run hot and fast into my mouth, and I pray around them. I open my little lunch-box-cum-sewing-kit and pull out all the notes Kenan sent me. There's one I need. One I cling to.

"Place me like a seal over your heart, like a seal on your arm; for love is as strong as death,
its jealousy unyielding as the grave.
It burns like blazing fire, like a mighty flame."
—Song of Solomon 8:6

"Love is as strong as death," I mutter, my eyes wide, not seeing the ocean below. "Love is as strong as death. Love is as strong as death."

I've forgotten my friends and only realize they're still there when we land. Worry knits their brows and tightens their expressions. They think I'm losing it.

"Come on," I say without further explanation. "Let's go."

The ride to the hospital is a blur. I don't look out the window or make conversation or pretend I'm not worried. I don't have time to accommodate people's concern, their doubt. In the Uber, I press my forehead to the headrest of the passenger seat and close my eyes, blocking out the sounds of the city and erecting an impenetrable wall around my faith, my beliefs, my wild notions of life and death and what's possible. I'm prepared for anything. I dive so deep inside myself searching for the heart MiMi left me that it's as if *she's* in the car with me, not my friends. Her heart is my inheritance. My birthright. I take silent, certain possession of it.

"Um, we're here," Billie says.

I open my eyes and nod. A light rain falls as the car pulls up to the hospital's emergency entrance. The three of us get out, bringing our suitcases with us. When we reach the waiting room, August and an older woman I don't recognize are the first ones I see. Mack Decker, the front-office executive whom I've met at a few functions with August, sits in the corner with a phone pressed to his ear. Iris rises from the boxy waiting-room chair. At the sight of my cousin, the fragile hold on my composure slips, and a sob flies free from the cage of my chest.

"Bo," I cry brokenly.

Iris crosses the room immediately, and her arms close around me, the comfort we've expected and given each other since we were kids flowing between us like a balm. My tears soak her hair, and I let myself go limp. I share my heart's heavy burden, drawing strength from her she doesn't even know she has.

After a few seconds, the pattern MiMi braided into my hair so long ago tingles, eyes in the back of my head deciphering the weight of someone's scrutiny.

I turn from Iris's embrace to face Bridget. Her cheeks are wet and splotchy, but resentment still burns in the ice-blue flame of her stare. She doesn't want me here, but she would have to drag me from this hospital to get rid of me, and were she of a mind to listen, I'd advise her not to try.

Movement behind her distracts me from our stare-down. The last time I saw Simone, she was unresponsive and EMTs were shoving a tube down her throat, intubating to save her life. Her face is so pinched with worry, she doesn't look much better now. She slips one thin hand into her mother's, I suppose an act of solidarity against me, the sworn enemy. I can't be angry at her—can't blame or hate her. She's the most precious thing in Kenan's world. I long to hold her. His blood runs in her veins. She has his mouth, his cheekbones, his DNA. She's the closest thing to the man I love in this room, and if she'd let me, I'd give her a bone-cracking hug and lavish her with kisses.

"Hi, Simone," I say instead. I'm braced for rejection but will settle for indifference. Before she can mete out either, a white-coated man holding a clipboard strides into the waiting area. He eyes the small group assembled and speaks, sounding weary.

"Kenan Ross's next of kin?" he asks, inquiring brows lifted.

"Here," the older woman I don't know says, standing and stepping forward. "I'm his mother."

Another person who shares his blood—a woman Kenan wanted me to meet. I never imagined it would be under these circumstances. Not in my wildest dreams or tortured nightmares.

"And I'm his wife...ex-wife," Bridget amends, pushing the hair back from her face, making the wedding ring she insists on wearing glint under the harsh fluorescent light. "This is his daughter. What can you tell us?"

I step closer to hear what he says because fuck them all if they think they'll shut me out.

"He came through the surgery well," Dr. Madison, according to his name badge, says. "He's strong, that one. He swerved to avoid the pipes and miraculously sustained few injuries when his car collided with the guardrail. The trauma sustained by his torso, though, caused extensive internal bleeding. We have it under control, but it's tricky and has to be monitored closely. If not stopped, it could cause brain damage, cardiac arrest, and any number of organ dysfunctions."

"But it's under control?" I ask, ignoring the three sets of Ross women's eyes that shift to me at the question. "He'll be okay?"

I see him making the calculations. If the older woman is Kenan's mother and Bridget and Simone are his "wife" and child, then who am I?

Bridget gives me a flinty look. "I really don't think—"

"Lotus is Daddy's girlfriend," Simone says, watching me with unblinking eyes. "She needs to know, too."

Bridget's mouth drops open, but Kenan's mother brushes her hand over Simone's hair in a caress and looks at me.

"He's talked a lot about you," Mrs. Ross says.

She wants more grandkids.

I bite my lip, beating back the fear that I'll never be able to give them to her. I nod jerkily, unable to form words, and look back to the doctor, silently urging him to go on.

"So yes," he addresses me and my question. "But we aren't out of the woods yet."

"When can we see him?" I ask.

When can I see him?

I need to lay eyes on him, to see that massive chest rising and falling at regular, reassuring intervals.

"He's just out of surgery," Dr. Madison says. "It'll be a while."

He turns a concerned look on Simone, who seems to be fading, her eyes heavy. "You've all been here for hours. This would be a perfect time to go home. Catch a shower and a few winks. By the time you return, you'll be able to see him."

Simone shakes her head, her chin setting to a stubborn angle. "No, I want to—"

"Dr. Madison's right," Mrs. Ross interrupts gently, firmly. "We'll run home, shower, lie down for an hour, and come back."

"But Grandma—"

"Listen to your grandmother." Bridget puts an arm around her daughter's shoulder. "It's just for a little while."

Simone's shoulders droop, and she wears her disappointment in every line of her body.

"We'll talk when I come back," Mrs. Ross says to me through a tired smile. "We have a lot to learn about each other."

"I'd like that," I reply. My eyes drift back to Simone, disconcerted to find her staring at me.

"You love him," she says, a statement, not a question. There's a sobriety to her that reminds me so much of her father, my heart reaches out to her like hands stretched toward a fire, seeking warmth.

Maybe it's unwise, maybe it will unravel all that we've worked to make right for her these last few weeks, but Kenan said she was better and we were close, so I'll take him at his word.

"I love him very much, yes," I answer, struggling to keep my voice steady.

"He loves you, too," Simone whispers. Tears gather over her blue eyes, an ocean of fear.

"He's going to be fine," I say to her, holding her stare and hoping she feels my faith. "He will."

She stares back for a few seconds before dropping her head to her grandmother's shoulder.

"Let's go, Moni," Mrs. Ross says. "The sooner we go, the sooner we come back."

Simone nods and trails after her grandmother toward the exit.

Bridget doesn't follow them but stands her ground in front of me. We eye each other, neither wavering or backing down.

"When he pulls through," she says, her voice stiff, "you be better to him than I was."

Shock holds me completely still for a moment, and then I draw a breath. I don't speak because anything I say to the woman who lost the best man I know would be wrong, inadequate. There's no consolation prize on Earth that could satisfy me if I lost Kenan. I don't know if Bridget still actually loves him or just regrets that someone has assumed the place in his life she forfeited. Either way, it's obviously hard, so I nod, silently assuring her that he'll have my very best. Without another glance, she walks the path Simone and Mrs. Ross took.

"We'll be back," she says over her shoulder, rounds the corner, and disappears.

"You go home, August," Iris says. "With Michael and Sarai. Relieve the sitter. I'll let you know when he's awake."

I'd forgotten August was here—forgotten Yari and Billie, curled up in hard chairs, nodding off to sleep. August gives me a quick, reassuring squeeze and then leaves.

"Hi, Lotus," Decker says. "Not sure if you remember me."

"Yes, I remember," I say, managing a smile and accepting the hand he offers. "And Kenan's talked about you a lot, Deck."

"Same." Decker squeezes my hand. "I need to go report back to the team but wanted to at least say hi." He leans close enough to whisper, "He's a great guy. He'll make you happy."

Tears prick my eyes, and my smile widens. "I'm gonna make him happy, too."

Decker smiles down at me. "He deserves that."

And then he's gone. The room is quickly emptying, everyone taking Dr. Madison's advice, but I cannot leave. I won't.

"You okay?" Iris asks, studying me closely.

"Yeah." The exhaustion I've ignored since we landed in San Diego falls on me like a pile of rocks, but I don't want to go to sleep. "I think I'll grab some air to clear my head."

"I could use some fresh air, too," Billie says, standing.

"I'll come with," Yari says.

"I'm gonna call the sitter." Iris fishes her phone from her jeans pocket. "I know August is on his way home, but I need to talk to her myself."

"We'll be right back," I tell her.

Once outside, the "fresh air" Billie needed is a smoke break. Yari and I step a breathable distance away from her noxious puffs. It's later than I realized. Or rather, earlier. It's morning. We arrived in the middle of the night, and the sun has already started its climb, illuminating another day. A vise cross-stitched from anxiety and fear still grips me by the throat, but with each passing second, I breathe easier. He's not out of the woods yet, but he will be. Barring any complications, he'll recover. I cling to that and try to clear my mind of the scenarios that tortured me while I tried to reach him.

"Glad the rain stopped," Yari says, leaning against the brick wall a few feet down from the glowing tip of Billie's cigarette.

"I know." Billie takes a long draw. "It supposedly never rains in Southern California."

I'm about to agree when I hear it. The faintest whisper I've learned to trust.

Look up.

And I see what I've only ever seen once before. The thing most never witness once in a lifetime, I've now seen twice. Colors set aflame, an omen streaking through the clouds. A fire rainbow.

"No." The word ejects itself from my body. A denial. A rebuttal to the sky's prophecy. "No."

"What?" Billie asks. "No what?"

I don't answer. I can't. I sprint back to the hospital entrance and down the hall, my legs and arms pumping, my heart exploding. I barrel around the corner and into the waiting room. Iris sits there alone, still chatting with the sitter, I presume.

"Iris," I say in a rush of breath and terror, "something's wrong. I have to go to him right now."

Eyes widening, she says a hasty goodbye and disconnects the call. "But the doctor said—"

"I don't care what the damn doctor said," I scream and start down the hall I saw Dr. Madison take, dragging Iris with me.

"Wait!" Iris resists, digs her heels in, and stops us. "You heard Dr. Madison. We can't see him yet."

"I need you to come with me, Iris. Please shut the fuck up and help me find him."

Yari rushes in, chest heaving. "Lo, what's wrong?"

"If you can calm down," Iris says soothingly, "and tell me what—"

"I won't calm down," I screech, ignoring their wide eyes and gaping mouths. "There's something wrong. I know it!"

Billie rounds the corner, frantically searching our faces. "What'd I miss? What's wrong?"

"Lotus wants to see Kenan now," Iris says. "But, honey, we can't see him yet. We—"

"Come with me," I beg, my voice breaking on a sob. "I need you, Bo."

Her eyes lock with mine, and something, I don't care what—my desperation, our lifelong bond, the desire to placate me—persuades her and she nods.

"I don't understand." Iris's sigh is resigned. "But I'll come with you."

"Thank you," I whisper, pulling her down the hall behind me. "Thank you so much."

I speed-walk past the reception desk, ignoring the woman yelling at me to stop. I check each room, peering through the windows and jerking open doors.

"Lotus, you can't do that," Iris hisses a warning from behind me. "I got the receptionist to wait on calling security, but you're gonna get both our asses dragged out of here."

I ignore her and keep walking until goose bumps scatter across my arms. My steps stutter, and my breath shallows as cold assaults my flesh.

"It's this one," I whisper.

I push open the door, startling the medical team with paddles poised over Kenan's chest. My magnificent man, a massive frame barely contained by the hospital bed. The specter of that night, of that premonition in MiMi's house, can't compare to the reality of seeing my beloved still and lifeless. For a moment, I have no words and can only make the wounded sound of a snared animal. I'm that trapped and helpless.

But only for a moment.

"Do it," I bark, pointing to the paddles.

"Miss, you can't be in here," Dr. Madison says gently, not

bothering to question why I've burst in on the chaos of the room. "We've done it several times."

She said you were the strongest of us all. She said all the power we didn't want passed on to you.

Aunt Pris's words drift back to me, spurring me on, building my confidence.

"You haven't done it with me here," I say sharply. "Do it again. Just do it again, please. Do it again. Do it again."

The words become a chant, an incantation tumbling from the lips of a madwoman.

"We'll break his ribs if we continue the compressions," a nurse tells Dr. Madison.

"If he's *dead*," I spit out, "will it matter if his ribs are broken? Do *something*. Please. Please. Please. *Please*."

"Okay." The doctor shifts his eyes from the equipment to the technician. "Prepare to do it again."

I grab Iris's hand and look in her eyes. "I need you to believe."

"Believe what?"

"That he'll make it," I say, barely able to see her for the tears blurring my vision. "When you were in the hospital and Michael wouldn't come, we held hands. You hadn't dilated for hours, but there was a moment when we held hands, and he came. The doctor said your body had a power surge."

"Yes," Iris says. "But it was—"

"It was *us*." I squeeze her hand. "I need a power surge, Iris. The power of an unbroken line."

"The power of a what?" Iris mumbles, consternation on her pretty face.

"Clear!" the technician yells, using the paddles and making Kenan's torso leap.

Nothing happens.

I clutch Iris's fingers in one hand and Saint Expedite in the other.

"Place me like a seal over your heart, like a seal on your arm; for love is as strong as death."

"Clear!"

And you'll always come for me, won't you?

Yes. Always.

I'll always come for you, too, Kenan.

"Clear!"

"Lotus, it isn't working," Iris says, wriggling her fingers in my tight grip.

"No, don't let go." I turn to her, desperation making my voice sharp and high. "Please don't let go. Look at me."

She does, and the fear, the despondence gathering in her eyes, I combat with faith, with the assurance I may not be entitled to but seize as mine. For him. I have to.

"Feel my words in your mouth," I tell her, hoping, praying, begging the conduit of our blood to save him. "Feel my power in your veins. It's the power of the unbroken line. Two women from our lineage together. There's power in that."

"I'm trying, Lo," she says. "To believe."

"Try harder!" I command, my voice rising above the beep of machines and the tightly contained panic of the medical team.

"No change," Dr. Madison mutters gravely.

My blood, my body, my thoughts—frenzied. "This is the biggest hopscotch of my life, Iris. I need you to *believe*."

That word *hopscotch* is holy to us, our covenant. The fear fades from Iris's eyes. And if it's not faith that takes its place, it's at least resolve. I can work with that.

"You know who I am," I whisper with tears streaming from my eyes, rivulets of desperation. My face crumples, and my shoulders tremble. My head hangs, but my faith holds strong. "This man's soul hangs in the balance. I'm here to make my judgment known. I'm here to lay a stone on the side of..."

"Clear!"

"Life!"

"Clear!"

"Love is as strong as death," I whisper. "Love is as strong as death. Love is as strong as death."

"Clear!"

"Love is as strong as death."

CHAPTER 46
KENAN

"Button."

That croaked word is all I can squeeze out from a throat as dry and burning as the Sahara.

"Mr. Ross, you're awake." A nurse with salt-and-pepper hair smiles and puts a cup to my lips. "Drink a little. Slowly."

I'm connected to at least two machines, as far as I can tell. Everything is so hazy, like a layer of Jell-O's been poured over the room. My words, my movements—everything is slowed down, and every breath costs me. I feel myself slipping back under but fight to maintain consciousness.

"Button." I say it again, but I don't know why. I can't figure anything out. Can't piece any of this together.

"How long?" I ask the nurse. "Asleep?"

"Three days." She checks a tube running clear liquid into my arm. "We had to sedate you."

"Three days?" I ask incredulously. "That's not possible."

"You rest better and heal faster asleep sometimes."

I try to sit, but sharp pain arrows across my chest.

"Shit," I mutter weakly, touching my torso.

"You have a few broken ribs," the nurse says.

"Was it a dirty play?" I ask, my voice hoarse. "Somebody kicked me on the court?"

"No, Mr. Ross." Her brows bunch in concentration while she checks the machines and tubes connected to me. "You weren't playing basketball. You were in a car accident. Your body's been through a lot. It'll take some time for all your memories to come together, but it'll happen."

"Okay," I mutter, sinking deeper into the bed.

"The doctor will want to examine you. I'll be back," she says, and leaves the room.

"You broke the rule."

That husky voice from the shadowed corner penetrates my fog, startling me. "You're only supposed to call me Button when we're alone."

"Lotus?" I try to sit, but that shaft of pain in my chest lays me out, pins me to the pillows.

"Hey, easy." She comes to my side and presses my shoulders back into the bed. "You've been through…" Her voice breaks, and I look up to find her eyes shiny with tears. "You've been through a lot," she finishes, her lips trembling in a smile.

"What have I been through? I don't even know how I got here. I was driving, right? I remember that now."

"You don't…" She closes her eyes and breathes deeply through her nose before looking back at me. "You were driving from Laguna Beach."

"Laguna Beach? Why the hell would I…" Memories sift through the fuzziness. A deadly cascade of pipes from the truck ahead of me. A crash. Glass shattering. The grind of metal.

"*Simone.*"

I force myself to a sitting position, and one of the tubes in my arms jerks against the motion.

Shit! That hurts.

"Stop." Lotus presses me back into the bed again. "Simone is fine."

"But I was taking her to…something. I can't remember."

"A dance camp," she answers, biting her bottom lip.

My head hurts. I frown, trying hard to recall any of the events leading up to the accident, but it's all a mishmash of pictures and flashes that I can't piece together into a timeline.

"It's a miracle your injuries weren't worse," she says. "You suffered significant internal bleeding."

"That he did," a doctor says from the door, followed closely by the nurse. "You are very lucky to be alive, Mr. Ross."

The doctor examines me and tells me I'll be here for at least another week, maybe longer.

"Doc, when can I get back on the court?"

Three pairs of eyes stare at me.

"Um…" The doctor clears his throat. "Your team has contacted us asking the same question. I've been in consultation with the Waves' doctor and actually have to give a press conference today reporting on your case."

That's standard when someone like me is hospitalized— someone who has a stack of insurance policies ensuring my team doesn't lose money on its investment: my body.

"We aren't sure when you'll be ready to play," the doctor hedges. "As I said—"

"Yeah, internal bleeding. I heard you, but I'm not bleeding now, right?" I ask. "So when? This is our year to make the playoffs, and that can't happen if I'm sidelined for a long time."

"Is that all, doctor?" Lotus asks, her tone as sharp as a scalpel. "I mean, do you have anything else you need from him?"

"Not at this time, no."

"Could you give us a minute then?" She plasters a stiff smile on her pretty mouth.

"Of course." He nods to the nurse, and they leave the room.

"You listen here, Kenan Ross," Lotus says, her eyes narrowed and her lips pulled into a flat line. "You almost died. Do you hear me? *Died.*"

"I get it," I say, wincing at the soreness in the rest of my body from the impact it absorbed. "But I didn't die, so I need to get back to my life. To my job, babe. I can't let my team down."

"What you *need* to do is rest and heal, and you will not be returning to anybody's court even a minute before the doctor feels absolutely confident you are ready. Who you will not let down is your daughter, who almost lost you."

Her voice breaks, and she covers her eyes with a trembling hand.

"And your girlfriend, who almost lost you and cannot," she says, tears saturating her words, "under any circumstances go through that again."

Weak as I am, I manage to pull her close. Despite the wires and tubes, she buries her head in my neck and soaks my hospital gown with her tears.

"You're right," I say into her hair, pushing it back from her face. "I'll take my time, okay? I'll be careful."

"I can't lose you." Her head shakes. Her *words* shake. "I tried to tell you."

I glance past her to the floor where something catches and holds my attention.

"Is that why there's a circle of salt around my hospital bed?" I ask, half-smiling, half-freaked out.

"They wouldn't let me use my candles." She sniffs with a weak laugh. "Fire code."

"God, they're gonna commit you, baby."

"No, they actually think I can bring people back to life."

"Why would they think *that*?"

She shrugs, her look sheepish. "Baby, I have no idea."

EPILOGUE
LOTUS

"Look at her now.
She arises from her desert of difficulty clinging to her beloved."
                                            —*Song of Solomon 8:5*

Dinner. Tonight.

I PRESS THE CARD WITH KENAN'S NEARLY ILLEGIBLE WORDS TO MY lips. It's just paper and ink, but I taste the sweetness of the man behind it. His sincerity and love wrap around me. Even when we're thousands of miles apart, I feel the protection of his arms.

It's so good to *not* be thousands of miles apart today, though. In addition to negotiating a long-distance relationship, we've been getting Simone used to us being a couple *and* maintaining two demanding careers. The last seven months have been eventful and blissful and, at times, really hard. And there's still so much transition ahead. It's good to be here in San Diego, though, even if I don't get to stay very long.

Which reminds me…

Me: Chicas! Are we ready for LA next week?
Yari: Yasss, girl! I sent you guys the list of locations we're scoping.

Billie: Got it! And I've scheduled lunch with three investors while we're there.

Yari: Lo, you NEED to ask that investor in your bed if he wants to get into your pants...the ones you design, I mean. Okurrrrr!

Me: What'd I tell you about Cardi B? LOL! And NO. I'm not asking Kenan to invest in gLO. Forget about it. Can we make sure our shit is tight so we don't have to ask my boyfriend to float us? TYVM.

Billie: Right. Let's impress these investors. Lo, did the samples make it to San Diego?

Me: Yup. They're here at Kenan's place. I'll bring them with me to LA next week. Are you guys apartment hunting while you're there?

Billie: Affirmative!

Yari: Yes, mami!

Simone's face interrupts on-screen with a FaceTime request.

Me: Gotta go. TTYL.

Yari: Deuces!

Billie: Byyyyyyyye.

I accept the FaceTime request and smile at Simone on-screen.

"Hey, lady!" I hop onto one of the counter stools in the kitchen and hold the phone in front of my face. "How's camp?"

"Grueling." Simone rolls her eyes but grins. "I *thought* I knew how to dance. I had no idea. It's a whole other level. There's no time for much else."

"At least Laguna Beach is gorgeous. I hope you get in *some* sun and surfing."

A shadow crosses Simone's face. "I keep thinking about the last time Daddy brought me up here. The accident."

Even with the terror behind us, my heart still stutters, and my hands clench where they rest on the counter.

"I know." I shake off that memory and laugh to dispel the heaviness. "He was back on the court as soon as the doctor cleared him, though. Remember? We had to practically tie him to the bed."

"Daddy was not about to miss the Waves' first playoff season."

"Hey, we might get to go to more playoff games. Maybe next time they'll win it all."

Simone's eyes brighten, and a smile breaks on her face. "*Or* what if Daddy retires?"

Kenan missed a lot with her during his career, and she obviously loves the prospect of having him around more. So do I. He's seriously considering making this next season his last.

"Maybe," I reply noncommittally. I'm sure that's a tougher decision for him than we can really understand. Probably even more than *he* can grasp until he experiences that huge void where ball used to be.

"My mom's in LA," Simone says, recapturing my focus.

"Oh really?" I keep my tone deliberately light. "Cool."

Bridget has accepted me in Kenan's and, by default, Simone's life, but she and I still aren't the best of friends. We don't actively dislike each other. It's more of a wary indifference.

"Yeah," Simone says. "She's taking some acting classes. She says NeNe left *The Housewives* and made it to Broadway. She wants to be ready."

"Good for her," I reply neutrally.

"You're going to LA next week, too, right?"

"Yeah. Meeting with investors. Looking at spaces for the shop."

"I can't wait to see your first line."

"Gah." I laugh and shake my head. "I can't believe I'm really doing this. Leaving New York. Moving out here. Starting the gLO line. Having my first show next March for LA Fashion Week. It feels like it's happening so fast and also taking forever."

"My dad'll be a lot happier when you're living out here. That's for sure."

I don't know how to respond. My design studio will be in LA because it makes more sense than San Diego. There's a richer fashion scene there—better opportunities, more celebrities—but I'll be living in San Diego to be close to Kenan and making the two-hour drive up to LA a few times a week. We've been careful every step of the way orienting Simone to our relationship. I've even sat in on a few family-therapy sessions. We want to do this right. For her, we have to.

"I'll be happier, too," I answer, "but my boss won't! JP is kicking and screaming."

The hiss of frying food snares my attention. I hop down, still holding the phone so Simone sees my face, and prop the phone against the backsplash while I stir the onions, garlic, and flour for the base of my étouffée.

"When do you leave New York?" Simone's blue eyes widen with excitement. It makes me smile that she's happy I'm coming to the West Coast.

"It'll be a few months. I'm staying in New York through Fashion Week in September to help JP. Then I'll move out here."

I stir in more flour and check the rice cooker.

"What're you making?" Simone asks.

"Baked catfish, étouffée, some fried okra."

"My *father* is eating fried food?" Simone asks, surprise etched onto her smooth face.

"I'm sure he'll be back to eating rabbit food tomorrow." I chuckle and open the oven to check the fish. "This is one night only."

"Oh, for the anniversary!" Simone sounds approving.

So she *does* know. Even though our relationship is so much better, I walk on eggshells sometimes, scared I'll break something, so I didn't tell Simone Kenan and I are celebrating our one-year anniversary. Technically, it's the one-year anniversary of our first "not a date." The start of our relationship was such a sore point with Simone, I wasn't going to mention it.

"Daddy told me," Simone says matter-of-factly.

"Can you believe he even wanted to celebrate something so silly?" I ask, keeping my voice casual.

"It's not silly." Simone's smile is sly, knowing, and curious all at once. "Did you get him a gift?"

"I did, but I'm not telling you what it is, big mouth." I wag a finger at her. "Don't think I've forgotten his birthday. So much for surprising him, thanks to you."

Simone's unrepentant laughter billows out, and she looks young and carefree. Not too long ago, we discovered her lifeless on Kenan's bed. I saw her at the lowest point of her short life. Watching her now, you'd never know that less than a year ago she was that same troubled girl.

"Talked to your grandmother?" I ask.

I turn everything off and grab the phone, heading out of the kitchen. I pad barefoot through the immaculate living room, the foyer with its soaring ceiling and massive chandelier. I knew Kenan was a wealthy man, of course, but his apartment on the Upper West Side, though luxurious, didn't prepare me for his sprawling home in La Jolla, one of the most elite parts of San Diego.

"Yeah," Simone replies, popping a piece of gum into her mouth. "She's loving the cruise with her 'girls.'" She makes air quotes and rolls her eyes.

"She deserves some time off, putting up with two bossy people like you and your dad," I joke and climb the winding staircase.

"*We're* bossy? Who basically rewrote the rules of Taboo when her team was losing?"

"Oh my God. We beat you guys fair and square." I shake my head as I enter Kenan's bedroom. "Bunch of sore losers."

"You guys had Banner," Simone scoffs. "She should count as two players."

"Yeah, well, you had her husband. She and Jared are like barracudas." I shudder. "Can you imagine if they played on the *same* team?"

"We'd never let that happen," Simone says with a straight face.

A slim, dark-haired woman comes into view on Simone's screen, standing in the doorway of her room. "Simone," she says. "It is time."

"Yes, Madam Petrov." Simone flashes her a grin before looking back to the phone. "Gotta go."

"Okay. Thanks for calling." I sink onto Kenan's California king bed smile. "And I like the hair, by the way."

Simone touches the braids streaming over her shoulder. "Keeps it neat for dance." She gives that same little secretive quirk of her lips. "Enjoy your anniversary."

Once we've disconnected, I note the time on my phone.

"Ugh," I mutter. "Still need to get dressed."

I dart off the bed and race over to the closet, pausing to reverently stroke the dress I'm wearing tonight. The full organza skirt bells out from a cinched waist and will stop just above my knees when I put it on. The sheer cap sleeves will spill over my shoulders and dust the top of my arms. I spent days embroidering lotus flowers on the bodice and hem, making it uniquely mine. And, of course, it's cotton-candy pink.

I've waited a long time to wear the dress I made for my FIT final, and I always envisioned showing it off somewhere like a premier or a fashion show—somewhere public. Everyone would ask who I was wearing, and I would proudly say I made it myself. But tonight, I wear the dress for an audience of one.

Kenan's not supposed to return from the Players Association executive board meeting for another hour and a half. Plenty of time to get ready. We could have gone out to celebrate, but we haven't seen each other in two weeks. Neither of us wants public scrutiny and speculation or to field autograph seekers all night. There was always some of that in New York, but here in the city where Kenan actually plays ball, it happens constantly.

And I want him all to myself.

After showering, I put on my dress and slip in wireless earbuds so I can listen to Billie Holiday while I put on makeup and tame my hair into a curly updo. Kenan's taste in music is rubbing off on me. I love Billie's voice but wish the lady who sang the blues had found more pink clouds in her life to chase the blues *away*. This song, "You Go To My Head," is perfect for a night celebrating the genesis of my relationship with Kenan. The lyrics tease my memories of Hook Shot and our first kiss on the Hudson, to which Lady Liberty, the Brooklyn Bridge, and a roomful of my closest friends bore witness.

The song tells the story of a woman entranced by her lover. He spins through her thoughts like bubbles in a glass of champagne. He's a sip of sparkling Burgundy brew. He intoxicates her soul with his eyes. Each of Billie's slurred metaphors lures me deeper into the past—back to that first night. Kissing Kenan changed everything. It tilted and shook my world like it was a snow globe, redistributing the stars. I hum along, remembering how my throat was still burning from the tequila when my mouth burned from his kisses.

I look into the mirror, poised to apply a matte red lipstick. My eyes collide with Kenan's in the reflection, and I almost drop the tube. He leans against the doorjamb, his hands pushed into the dark, well-tailored slacks tapered to the length of his powerful legs. The movement strains the crisp white cotton of his tie-less collared shirt across his broad chest.

"What are you doing here?" I ask, a little breathless at the handsome picture he makes.

"I live here," he replies, one corner of his decadently full lips canting up with his amusement.

I turn around and prop my bottom on the marble bathroom counter to face him. "You're early." I bite into the irrepressible smile seeing him for the first time in fourteen days elicits.

"I'm eager." He steps closer and clamps huge hands around my hips, pulling me up and into the tower of his hard body. "I've missed my girlfriend."

Barefoot, my head doesn't quite reach his shoulder, so I strain up on my toes to whisper in his ear, "Is she coming?"

Kenan pulls back to peer down at me, his eyes heavy-lidded with lust and love. His hands explore under my dress, and he strokes the sensitive skin of my inner thigh with a callus-roughened hand.

"Oh, she's definitely coming," he says huskily. "I'm gonna make sure of that."

"Don't you start." My laugh is breathy, my body aroused.

"After two weeks away," he says, bending to suck my neck, "do you have any idea how fast this could be over? We can fuck, eat, whatever you want to do. In that order."

I ignore the rush of liquid heat that starts in my belly and slides lower. "You were the one who wanted to celebrate this non-iversary," I remind him. "And we're going to do it right. I cooked dinner. We need to eat."

His fingers climb higher to tease the edge of my panties. "That's what I want to do." He brushes a finger over my damp heat through the silk, desire simmering in the dark eyes that consume me. "Eat."

Sweet child of mine. This man. My man.

I breathe deeply, hoping the cool air filling my lungs reaches other parts of my body.

"Food," I say meaningfully. "Eat the *food* I cooked. First."

I reach under the dress and place my hand over his to halt his progress. When our fingers tangle at the juncture of my thighs, the breath flooding my chest stalls, hovers around my heart, and squeezes. The first time he touched me this way, we coaxed my body to orgasm together. He watched me come. It was a sensual storm that broke over every part of me, raining on my heart. Growing my trust. Nurturing an intimacy I'd never known with anyone else. Any vestiges of playfulness disappear from his expression, and what takes its place on his face, in his eyes, steals my breath.

Is he remembering, too?

"What?" I ask, mesmerized. "Why are you looking at me like that?"

And can you never stop?

"I was thinking of the first time I saw you come," he says, searing me with a look so hot, so loving, I couldn't deny him the moon if he asked for it.

"Okay. One kiss," he whispers, inadvertently saving me from my hussy tendencies. "An anniversary kiss."

"One kiss," I agree, like I wasn't about to give him the cow, the milk, and the whole damn farm.

"Until later," he says.

I tuck that promise away in the wanton places where my body aches for him. He dips to capture my lips, and a moan rattles my ribs.

Lord, he tastes even better than I remember.

How is it possible that I want him, need him, *love* him more every time we touch or kiss?

He ravishes my mouth while his hands roam my body possessively— squeezing my butt, caressing my arms, gripping my thighs through the silk skirt. His hands slow, still. He smiles against my mouth.

"This isn't *the* dress, is it?" His question breathes over my lips. "Cotton-candy pink?"

I nod, and his gaze pours over me, taking in every inch of the silk-and-organza confection I gave my all to create. I worked on this dress until my fingers bled. My blood is in the stitches, woven into the seams. A frown pinches between his brows.

"We're just having dinner at home," he says. "I thought you were saving it for a special occasion."

I tip up on my toes to link my fingers behind his neck.

"You *are* my special occasion, Mr. Ross," I whisper, baring my soul in the look I offer him.

The frown clears, and that slow smile, the one that starts in his heart, creeps into his eyes and makes its way to his mouth. He bends and rests his temple against mine and must hear the faint sound of Billie Holiday still playing in my ear. I'd blocked out the music once I saw him, but now I tune back in to the lyrics, and they woo me again. I smile and slip one wireless bud out of my ear and into his so we can listen together.

"I like," he says, turning his mouth down at the corners and looking impressed. "Good choice. The Lady herself."

"This song reminds me of our first kiss."

He closes his eyes, a look of concentration arresting his features. He nods and tightens his hands at my waist, urging our bodies into a subtle sway to the music.

"We've never danced before." It strikes me as both silly and vitally important. A first when we're celebrating a night of firsts.

"When you move in, we can dance every night." He pulls back to catch my eyes. I lower mine first. He's alluded to me living with him before, but I want to be sure it's the best thing, the best time for Simone. He's her father, and I know he's more in touch with her mental and emotional state than I am, but I can't feel responsible for her going off the rails again. Simone likes me now. We get along great, but moving to San Diego is one thing. Moving *in* with them? Would that be too much for her?

"We'll see." I flick my lashes up to catch his eyes. "I'll be in LA half the time anyway. I've been looking at a few apartments near La Jolla."

"Stop looking," he insists, frowning. "I want you here with me."

I slide my hands over his shoulders and down his arms to twine our fingers, hoping to distract him from something we might not agree on yet. "I got you a gift!"

He angles a wry look at me. *He peeps my game.*

"Lotus, baby, we—"

"An anniversary gift." I switch off the music in our ears.

His steady stare and a few beats of silence tell me we'll revisit the living arrangements later.

"You don't want to give me the gift after dinner?" he finally asks.

"Now seems as good a time as any." I drag him by the hand into the bedroom, pushing his shoulder until he's seated on the bed. "Close your eyes."

He deliberately keeps his eyes open, going so far as to stretch them wide for emphasis.

"Kenan Admiral Ross."

"Aw, hell." He shakes his head and closes his eyes. "My mother gave you that."

"She's very forthcoming after a few drinks." I grin saucily. "Mama gave up all your secrets."

A deep chuckle shakes the broad slope of his shoulders. "I knew I should have kept you two apart."

"Keep your eyes closed," I order again, walking backward to the closet, watching him the whole time. "And no peeking."

I'm like a kid at Christmas, only instead of being eager to open my gift, I can't wait to give it.

The package is so huge, I struggle to drag it out of the closet and to the bed. Fortunately, it's protected by thick shipping paper.

Once the gift and I stand before Kenan, I wave my hand in front of his face.

"Stop waving your hand in my face," he says with a grin and still-closed eyes.

"Are you *peeking*?" My question ends on an indignant squeak.

"No, I just have the heightened senses of a bobcat," he jokes.

"Do bobcats have heightened senses?"

"Who the hell cares?" Kenan asks with good-natured exasperation, his smile widening. "Can I open my eyes now? *Shit*."

I laugh so hard I have to bend at the waist. I'm having way too much fun with this.

"Okay," I say, after I've composed myself. "You can open."

When he opens his eyes, they latch onto me and then shift to the gift, which stands about a foot taller than I do. It's large and square and shrouded in brown paper.

"Is this…" His eyes dart between me and the large square. "Did you—"

"Would you just open it? *Shit*," I repeat his curse mockingly.

He stands and covers my hand holding the gift up by the corner. Instead of tearing into it, as I assumed he would, he bends, loops his other arm around my waist, and kisses me so deeply I can't breathe and sway on wobbly legs when he's done. He feathers kisses down my chin and neck.

"Kenan," I protest weakly, trying my damnedest to stave off the horniness. "Behave. Open it."

He smiles and releases me to rip the paper away and reveal the photograph from Chase's exhibit.

"God, Lotus." Kenan looks between me and the photograph several times like he's not sure which one he wants to stare at most. "It's so beautiful. I don't know what... Thank you. You know how badly I wanted this."

"Yeah, I heard you offered twenty thousand dollars for it." I laugh and caress his face. "What a schmuck."

"Oh, I'm a schmuck?" With seemingly little effort, he hefts the huge photograph up and walks it over to prop it against the wall. He strides back to the bed, his eyes glinting with wicked intent. "Say it again."

I hold my breath, allowing the anticipation to coil between us to the point of snapping. "Schmuck!"

I take off running to the other side of the mammoth bed. He chases me, almost catches me, but I jump up, my feet sinking into the soft mattress, and leap to the other side. I feint left and right, running around and over the mattress a few times before his iron arms close around me and gently wrestle me to the bed.

"Please don't tickle me," I beg, laughing before he's even started.

"So I'm a schmuck?" He slips one arm under my back, pressing me to him and making it impossible to do anything but squirm and relish our closeness.

"No, you're not a schmuck! And you're not a grumpy old man either."

"You didn't call me a grumpy old man," he says with a frown.

"Well, I just did! Suckaaaah!"

And then his persistent fingers dig into my ribs, finding every soft, ticklish spot. I kick and flail and arch my neck and contort my body as much as possible, but he won't be deterred.

"Oh my God," I protest. "Please don't make me pee in this dress the first time I wear it."

He finally relents, lying on his side, resting his head in the heel of his hand as he watches me.

"That is the only thing that saved you." His features, already softened with humor, grow even more tender with affection. "I love your photo. It's going on that wall so it's the first thing I see every morning."

"That's not awkward or anything," I mumble, but I can't hold back my pleased grin. "I'm glad you like it."

"I *love* it," he repeats. "But soon I'll be spooning the real thing every morning when I wake up."

"Kenan, we'll see." I release a long exhale. "Let's talk to Dr. Packer. Moving in is a big deal, especially since Simone *lives* with you. I just want to make sure she is a hundred percent comfortable."

"Okay." He drops a kiss on my forehead before pulling me to sit up on the edge of the bed. "Now you close *your* eyes."

He stands, lifting his brows when my eyes remain as open as his did. "My turn."

I roll my eyes before closing them.

"Keep them closed," he calls, his voice coming from farther away but still somewhere in the room.

"They're closed, dammit," I pretend to grouse.

I'm still trapped behind the darkness of my closed eyelids when he takes my left hand and twists the gris-gris ring off. It hasn't left my finger in years. I suppress the instinct to open my eyes and grab it before it's gone.

He slowly eases it onto the ring finger of my right hand. My heart assumes a thunderous rhythm, and blood rushes to my face and throbs in my ears. Sweat sprouts out all over my body as he slides a different ring onto the finger where MiMi's ring rested before.

What if she gave me *to you? What if I'm your gris-gris now?*

Kenan's words from months ago wash over me, run through me. *You did good, MiMi,* I whisper in silent, complete gratitude.

I thought her heart was the greatest gift she left me, but no.

It's this man.

I can't play along anymore. My eyes fly open to find Kenan down on one knee in front of the bed, in front of me. A vintage cushion-cut diamond set in blackened platinum glints from my left hand. I have no idea how many carats it is, but it's huge without being gaudy. It's antique but thoroughly modern.

It's perfect.

"Kenan, oh my God." A shaky breath whooshes past my lips. I press a trembling hand to my throat. "Are you sure about—"

"I already talked to Simone," he interrupts, his voice low, fervent. "And to Dr. Packer and to my mother. They're all fine with it. Ecstatic about it." He pauses and brings my hand to his lips. "I even told Bridget."

"Bridget knows?" I gape. "How does she feel about it? How is she?"

"She's dating one of the crew from *Baller Bae*," he says dryly. "I think she'll be fine. She's known for a while how I feel about you." He shakes his head and huffs out a truncated laugh. "Hell, everyone knows how I feel about you."

"And Simone?" I ask, once more needing to be certain. "You're sure she's okay?"

"She helped me pick out the ring." His chuckle comes out deep, but I detect the faintest trace of uncertainty. "The only holdout is you. You, uh, still haven't said yes."

He looks at the ring on my finger, and his shoulders and chest go so absolutely still, I think he's literally holding his breath. Tears prick my eyes, and I blink several times, but there's no stopping them from rushing over my cheeks. My gladiator, one of the most intimidating men in the NBA—I have his heart in the palm of my hand. But it's an even trade because he has my heart, too.

I scoot forward until I'm at the very edge of the bed and my legs have to split and spread around his broad torso as he waits on his knees for me to answer. I cup his chin, lean forward, brush my nose against his, then slide the curve of my cheek against the raw-boned angle of his, and pull back to lock our eyes.

"Don't look away," I whisper, licking into the seam of those full lips. He groans, opening the way he only ever has for me.

He twines the fingers of his right hand with the fingers of my left and strokes the sparkling declaration of his love. My tears come faster, mixing with every hungry nip and ravenous lick as I taste him. It's not the rich, tangy flavor of his kiss. I taste the acceptance, the patience, and the unconditional love I've found myself seeking all my life.

I have found the one whom my soul loves.

It's all there on his lips, in this kiss, in the emotion of the dark eyes that never look away. Without breaking the sweet, hot thread between our lips or the deep, unwavering intimacy of the look we share, I whisper into our kiss the answer he's been waiting for.

"Yes."

BONUS EPILOGUE
KENAN

I'M ACCUSTOMED TO THE GLARE OF CAMERAS. I'M TRAINED TO barely squint in the shine of a spotlight I never wanted. After a decade and a half in the NBA, celebrity has become second nature. I've been trailed by paparazzi, bombarded by signature-seeking fans, and found my front door surrounded by a shoal of gossip-starved piranha snapping razor-sharp teeth at my most private parts.

But rarely have I felt more exposed than I do today when I lay one dream to rest—my career as a professional baller—to pursue a new dream.

A normal life.

Well, as normal as my life will ever be with Lotus DuPree, soon to be Ross. From the moment I met her, I recognized something wild in her. Something untamed, uninhibited. A don't-give-a-damn-ness that liberated me in many ways, too. She was and remains my wildflower. My storm.

Today, though, as I stand at this podium and tell the world I'm retiring from the NBA, Lotus is the eye of the storm—seated in the front row, my serene center in a room packed with flashing lights and avid questions.

"I'm here to officially announce my retirement from professional basketball."

A murmur crests through the roomful of sports journalists.

They didn't see this coming. Even though I've been considering it for months—years, if I'm honest—everyone knows how rigorously I train, how fastidiously I eat, how disciplined I am to always maintain elite playing condition. All the hallmarks of a man who planned to play for years to come.

And yet I'm walking away.

Not so much walking *from* something as walking *to* something. To Lotus and Simone and other interests, a life beyond the game that has consumed me since high school.

"I've been fortunate to play at the highest level for the last fifteen years," I continue, ignoring the hands already popping up like bread from a toaster. "I've done everything I set out to do. I've won two championships. Played for two incredible organizations."

I find August standing against the back wall, arms folded and a bittersweet twist to his mouth. His road to a championship is tougher with me gone, but they'll figure it out. My departure frees up a shit ton of cap space so the Waves can pursue young talent to help August.

"I've battled alongside teammates who became friends," I say, holding August's somber stare for a moment. "Who became family."

Mack Decker and Ean Jagger, our interim coach, stand in a back corner with identical hard sets to their jaws. Me leaving now is not ideal for the team, but they know it's best for me and my family. They both care enough to want the best for me even when it makes their jobs harder.

"I could not have asked for better front-office executives," I say, nodding to Deck. "Or a finer coaching staff."

Jagger dips his head in acknowledgment, his face its usual implacable mask.

"And this journey would not have been nearly as thrilling or successful without my agent." I turn to smile at Banner, who stands beside me with tears in her eyes. She's tough as cowhide, but her heart is bigger than Texas. "It's always more than work, more than the job or the game with you, B. Working with you has been a privilege and an honor."

She presses her lips together, probably to stem more emotion than she wants the cameras to see.

"Basketball has a million rewards," I continue. "But each reward comes with sacrifices."

The hard lines I've marshaled my expression into soften at the sight of my daughter seated between Lotus and my mother. Simone's blue eyes are bright, and her smile is wide. When I told Simone I was retiring, she launched herself at me. I can still feel her arms tight around my neck, holding on the way she used to when I left for road trips that took me away from home often for weeks at a time.

"I don't make this decision lightly. I know this is a dream most will never get to live out and a blessing so few ever experience."

I allow myself to look at Lotus. I haven't until now because she distracts me. Not because she is so beautiful.

Though, damn. She's so beautiful.

Painted in shades of gold and copper and bronze. Hair and skin gilded. Gleaming like polished precious metals. But her eyes, dark and sober, remain watchful. Fixed on me. As much as she knows I want to do this, need to do this, she also knows how hard it is for me to walk away. I haven't looked at her because when I do, I don't want to look anywhere else. The understanding that's been so hard to find all my life, the intimacy I never knew was missing, even in a roomful of salivating journalists, I find with her. Her smile is soft and grows wider when I pause to take her in. She nods almost imperceptibly, reminding me this connection between us never goes away. It will still be there later waiting for us, and I should finish this.

"Even with so many accomplishments behind me," I say, clearing my throat and dragging my eyes from Lotus to meet a sea of curious stares, "I have my whole life ahead, and I want to spend it with the people I love. I want them to have the best of me. As important as basketball has been, I have another set of priorities. My daughter and my fiancée being at the top of that list."

Simone beams and turns her head to share a smile with Lotus.

My girls.

They're my life, the two of them. Suddenly, I just want this finished. I peruse the rest of the statement Banner helped me draft. It's just more of the same. Reviewing my accomplishments and explaining my need for what's next. Well, I'm tired of hearing about the things I've done, and I don't need to explain to these people what I want to do now. Offering Banner a rueful smile, I fold the paper in half. She rolls her eyes and shakes her head, the corners of her lips twitching. She knows me well.

"That's all I have to say."

I slide my hands into the pockets of the tailored slacks Lotus picked out for me to wear to, I hope, the last press conference I'll ever hold.

"Any questions?"

The room erupts.

The house is still. In contrast to the circus of that press conference, the quiet is almost deafening. It could be prophetic, foretelling the silence ahead of me. Retired players often say the silence is one of the things hardest to get used to. No roaring crowd, thousands of people cheering you on, encouraging you, depending on you for their next thrilling moment. It's a glorious pressure not everyone is built to carry. As much as I enjoy my own space and solitude, there's a part of me that will miss that roar.

Simone's up in her room, door closed. Probably talking to that knucklehead she met at school. I don't like him. I don't like fifteen-year-old boys sniffing around my beautiful daughter. I was fifteen once. I wanted one thing from a girl, and that motherfucker is not getting it from Simone.

I'm scowling.

Lotus says every time I talk about him, I scowl. I make a conscious effort to loosen my facial muscles when I enter the kitchen. The clank of porcelain and silverware as Mama loads the dishwasher meets me. I walk over and wordlessly begin the prerinsing process she always insists on before a dish goes into the machine. Even when I was growing up, she rinsed the dishes before loading them.

"Double washing," I mutter, running tepid water over a plate, a small smile tugging at my lips. "Daddy used to say it was a waste of time."

Mama's hands pause over a cluster of forks she dropped into the cubby for silverware. She resumes, slipping dishes into slots with efficiency.

"Your daddy never loaded a dishwasher a day in his life," she says with a chuckle. "What did he know about it?"

Her smile doesn't last long, abandoning her mouth like it forgot her sorrow for a moment and has to recover quickly.

"I still miss him, too." I shift a bowl to make room for another plate, my voice subdued.

She flicks a glance up at me and closes the door on the last of the dishes, punching the flat-panel buttons to start the machine.

"I'll never not miss your father." She dries her hands on a dish towel and sighs. "That's the danger of finding your soulmate. Your heart has no idea how to go on without them."

There was a time my inner cynic would have scoffed at that. Even married for so long to Bridget, I never thought of her as my "soulmate." That word held no real meaning, had no context before Lotus. I wonder if everyone experiences that shock of recognition when…if…they find that person? Not love at first sight. That's a cliché that doesn't begin to encompass what I felt that day in the hospital when I met Lotus. More like the door of a secret chamber in your heart creaks open a little more every time you see them until one day the door swings wide, flooding that room with light. That's what Lotus did. She flooded my heart, my life with light when I didn't even realize I was sitting alone in the dark.

"It's once in a lifetime," Mama says, peering up at me with the slightest curve to her lips. "But you know that now, don't you? Because of Lotus."

"Yes, ma'am." I grab the dish towel Mama discarded and dry my hands, too. "I know now."

She nods decisively and wipes down the counter.

"Your father would have been proud today."

"You think so?" I ask with false steadiness, feigned nonchalance.

"He would have loved that you went out on your own terms." She props a hip against the counter and faces me. "Not because you couldn't play anymore or because of an injury. You chose to walk away. No one had to run you out, buy you out, sell you out. It was, as Simone says, a boss move."

I aim a smile her way. "She loves having you here. You know that, right?"

Mama sobers and straightens. "I was going to talk to you about that. I think I'll go home, back to Philly."

I stare at her for a few moments. I always assumed I inherited my inscrutable expression from my father, but the locked-tight mask my mother wears looks exactly like mine. I probe under it for regret, sadness, anything indicating this isn't what she wants. It's not what we want.

"Mama, stay."

She meets my mild comment with an irritated frown. "Now, what brand-new wife wants her husband's mother up in their business all the time?"

"One who has a young stepdaughter here in San Diego," I say wryly. "And a business she's getting off the ground in LA. Lotus will appreciate you being here. So will I. I may be retired, but I have businesses all over the world I need to take care of, too. And eventually, I'd like to make a move for partial ownership of an NBA team. I'll be around more, of course, but there's still a lot to do."

"But Lotus—"

"I wouldn't suggest it if Lotus and I hadn't already discussed it."

"But my house is—"

"You could sell the house," I interrupt. "Or lease it out."

"I don't want to be in your way," Mama says carefully, her eyes trained on a spot above my shoulder.

"Mama, look at me." I grab the hand clenched into a proud knot at her middle, waiting for her to meet my eyes. "We want you here. Lotus wants you here. She didn't grow up surrounded by a loving family like Kenya and I did. Her mother…"

I swallow futile anger and frustration at the thought of Lotus's mother, of how she betrayed her.

"She didn't treat Lotus well," I settle on saying. "And Lotus's great-grandmother who raised her passed away a few years ago. I think having you around would be good not only for Simone but for Lotus, too."

My mother studies me for a few seconds, eyes narrowed and her fingers tightening around mine.

Lotus and my mother come from completely different backgrounds. Our household was my mother's domain. Her husband and children were her enterprise. She applied all of her intelligence and will to making us shine. Lotus's ambitions will always reach far beyond our home. Even now she splits her time between San Diego and LA launching her fashion line gLO. Vastly different in their priorities and dreams, but an identical vein of steel runs through their compassionate middles, and they like each other very much. Lotus's own mother was a disappointment and an awful excuse for maternal love. I want to share everything with Lotus, including what I grew up taking for granted: my kickass mama.

"All right," Mama finally replies, giving the counter one last swipe before folding the dishcloth neatly. "But I want to hear from Lotus herself before I agree to stay."

"Fair enough." I pull her close and bend to kiss her cheek. "Thanks for dinner. It was delicious."

"I figured you wouldn't want to eat out somewhere and be approached every two minutes or get a lot of questions from reporters."

"You know your son."

"I should by now," she says, chuckling and pulling away to head for the arched kitchen doorway.

"Turning in?"

"Yes." She offers an over-the-shoulder grin. "Don't let Lotus work all night. She's been burning the candle at both ends getting ready for that show."

I tap the switch on the wall, leaving the kitchen illuminated by one light over the range. "I'll do my best, but she's hard to shut down once she gets going."

Mama heads to her in-law suite on the first floor, and I climb the back stairs to the bedroom I share with Lotus. When I find it dark and empty, my feet automatically turn, carrying me down the hall toward the guest room Lotus commandeered as her office-cum-studio. Half-clothed mannequins stand at attention around the room, patiently awaiting sleeves, collars, tops or bottoms to complete their outfits. Sketch pads litter the desk and an overstuffed couch. On the opposite end is a drafting desk facing the ocean through a window that takes up most of the wall.

Lotus's back is to me. In contrast to the white, flowy tank top she wears, her shoulders appear rigid and tightly held. Sleek, toned legs peek from beneath the shirt's hem. Her wild curls are tamed into a knot on top of her head. One small bare foot crosses over the other. Her charcoal pencil flies across the paper, and the sinuous lines of a dress take shape right before my eyes.

She doesn't hear me enter, or if she does, she doesn't turn. I step across the thick rug as lightly as someone my size can manage, sneaking up behind her.

"Don't even think about tickling me," she mutters, her pencil never slowing.

I drop my stealthy approach and loop both arms around her slender frame from behind.

"You're no fun," I whisper into the scented curve of her neck.

"That's not what you said last night." She chuckles and presses her back deeper into my chest but keeps sketching the dress.

"Well, my dick was down your throat. That's never not fun." I massage the tight muscle of her shoulder. "Damn, you're tense. Thought I was the one who had a stressful day."

"Deadlines. Hmmmm. That feels so good." She moans and drops her head to the side, reaching up to cover my hand with one of hers. "Were you happy with how things went today at the press conference?"

She can't see my quick shrug. "It was fine. Just glad it's over."

She turns to face me then, her dark eyes searching, probing.

"The press conference?" she asks softly. "The day? The NBA? What exactly are you glad is over?"

"All of the above." I trace the glittering crown on her T-shirt and the phrase QUEENS DO DOPE SH*T. "Is this for the new line?"

"Yeah, Yari and Billie thought it'd be cool to just release a few T-shirts and get interest going ahead of the full-scale show in March. We're selling them already." Some of the tension my fingers had kneaded out returns to her shoulders. "There's so much to do and not enough time."

"You need to relax." I press my hands into her shoulders again, seeking out the knotted muscles. "I'll have the team masseuse come to the house tomorrow."

"Do you still have that privilege now that you're no longer on the team?" Her question is teasing and light, but there's real concern in the glance she angles up at me.

"He'll come." I take her earlobe between my teeth. "Would you like to come, Button?"

"Using sex to distract me from talking about your retirement, huh?" she asks, her voice deeper, huskier.

I venture under the T-shirt and squeeze one breast.

"Is it working?"

"It is working like a motherfucker." She sinks her teeth into her bottom lip. "But I need to talk to you more than I need to screw you."

My hands still, and our eyes catch. Hers questioning even through the haze of lust I inspired with a few touches. There's no hiding from Lotus. Ever. Truth be told, I don't want to. I spent most of my life in my own head, guarding my heart. That's not who we are together.

"Your loss." I offer a small smile, pulling my hands away and taking a step back.

"Yours, too," she says softly, stepping close again and sliding her arms around my waist. "Tell me."

I pass my hands over her back in strokes that should soothe her but instead ease the knot inside me I didn't want to acknowledge. I needed this. I needed her.

"I know retiring is the right thing." I rest my temple on her hair. "For me at this time, I know it's right. I've missed a lot with Simone. She's ecstatic that I'm retiring."

I pull back enough to see Lotus's face.

"You are, too, right?"

"I'm excited for you to start a new chapter where you'll be around more for your daughter." Her grin is slightly sheepish. "And, yes, for me, too, but I haven't lived through years with you gone most of the time the way Simone has. Basketball has taken up so much of your life for so long, I know it's not easy to walk away from. I can't imagine leaving fashion in some form. It's such an extension of who I am and how I express myself. A huge part of my identity. And for you, basketball is a huge part of how the world defines you."

She's right on all counts. I nod. Not letting Lotus into my head is futile and only a matter of time. She always gets in. I want her there.

"So it may be right," she continues, her voice softening. "But having peace about a decision is not the same as it being easy."

"When I stood up there today, I felt relieved to be leaving, but tonight the house was quiet. And for the first time in my life, the quiet bothered me. It's always been an escape from how loud my life is. How I can't eat in a restaurant without someone asking me for an autograph. Or how much time I spend with a microphone thrust in my face, usually at times when talking is the last thing I want to do."

She scoots an inch closer, nuzzling into my neck and sliding a hand under my shirt to stroke my back.

"But tonight it was quiet," I say. "and I couldn't help but think I'm getting exactly what I wanted."

"And you asked if you're sure you want it?"

"Something like that," I say with a half-smile. "But I do want it. I've never been an adult without basketball, without this game taking up so much of my life, but I look forward to it. To being there for Simone. And for you."

"We want that, too."

She tips up on her toes to kiss me. It starts light but deepens, hunger and love drawing us tighter together with each stroke of our tongues and nip of our teeth. She pulls away to tug the elastic band from her hair, freeing a cloud of golden-brown curls to frame her face and shoulders. She tugs the T-shirt over her head and stands tiny and tempting in only her boy-shorts underwear. With shaky fingers, I trace the filigreed lace inked around the tops of her thighs. I get lost in the shape of her, the curve of shoulder and dent of waist and round-ness of hips and lines of her legs. I slide my hands down her back to squeeze her ass, and she clasps her arms around my neck, dragging her legs up to encircle my waist. She wraps around me. Arms tight at my neck. Thighs clenched at my waist. I set her onto the desk.

"Damn," I mutter at the sight of her. A tiny bar pierces one plump nipple. A lotus flower blooms around her belly button. "You are so—"

"So are you," she cuts in, eyes and smile lit with mischief as she tugs my shirt over my head. Our mouths rejoin, limbs re-tangle, breaths collide.

"I want you," she whispers over my lips. "I've wanted you all day."

"Yeah?" I dot kisses along the slope of her neck and shoulder.

"Even at that press conference, I kept thinking about last night."

"And this morning?" My husky chuckle feathers over her cheek.

"Yes, this morning, too. You're pretty virile for an old man."

"Old man, huh?" I trail my hand down her bare stomach and into her panties until I find the hot, wet slit and slip my thumb inside. "I got your old man."

Lotus squeezes her eyes shut and leans back with the heels of her palms pressed to the desk.

"You have no idea how hard I'm about to fuck you, Kenan Ross."

"Shit, now I'm scared." My laugh is breathless with anticipation.

"You should be." She leans forward to bite my nipple.

"Ouch! Babe, what'd I tell you about that?"

"If memory serves me correctly, it was something like…please, baby, please, baby, please."

I fit my mouth over hers. Lotus tastes as sweet as she did that night on a moonlit boat ride. Our first kiss floated on water. Our second was lit by the sun, shining through pink clouds as it set over the Hudson. And this kiss, flavored with hunger and devotion, is as tumultuous as the Pacific waves crashing outside the window.

There's something I need from her. Something she needs from me, and we take it. My hands roam frantically up and down her back and squeeze her ass. We grind at the center, at the apex of our bodies. Her, hot and soft. Me, hot and hard. We made love this morning, but our bodies don't care. It's insatiable, this bottomless need. It's a growling belly that's never quieted, never satisfied.

"I need it right now," I mutter into our kiss.

She bites my lip, soothes the sting with a sly lap of her tongue. Her legs fall from my waist until her feet touch the floor. Before I can reach for her again, she turns to face the desk, hands braced on its surface.

"From the back, Kenan," she pants, her breath and words roughened with anticipation. "Hit it from the back."

I run my palm over the silky expanse of her back, tracing the zipper following the chain of fragile bones in her spine. When I splay my hand at the small of her back, my fingers hang over the sides. My hand is that big and she is that small. I could so easily break her if I was not careful. She's so delicate and—

"Are you planning to fuck me tonight or what?" she says, slicing into my thoughts, wringing a rueful grin from me. No matter how delicate she may look, my girl is not fragile. Not breakable. Life tried to break her more than once, and she has stubbornly held on to all her pieces.

Rough and tender and filthy and sweet.

I'm sliding her panties down when the door opening down the hall startles us into complete stillness. We both glance back to find the office door standing open.

"Crap!" Lotus hisses, grabbing her tank top from the desk and bundling it to cover her breasts. My daughter's chatter, presumably on the phone, reaches us, passes us, recedes down the hall, and descends the stairs. Knowing Moni, she's raiding the fridge for leftovers. We stare at each other, holding our breath until we no longer hear her voice or her steps.

"That was close," I say.

"We've had a few close calls lately," Lotus reminds me with a grin. "We keep forgetting we're not alone anymore."

"We may need to soundproof our bedroom. God, you were howling at the moon the other night."

"You're lucky I didn't suffocate when you shoved that pillow over my face."

"You told me to do that if you ever started screaming the house down when Mama or Moni were home." My smile slips a little. "Are you sure you're okay with this arrangement? Tonight Mama mentioned going back to Philly."

"Did you tell her we want her to stay?" Lotus asks with a frown.

"Yeah, but are you sure? I mean, you're young. It's a lot of instant family. A teenage stepdaughter and mother-in-law under our roof. If you want—"

"I wouldn't have it any other way. I mean, if you're gonna keep putting it down like you do, I think soundproofing the bedroom might not be a bad idea," she teases, "but otherwise you know I love Simone, and your mom is invaluable, especially once the school year starts and things get crazy with gLO. I'll be back and forth to LA a lot. I think your mom being here will give Simone continuity and stability."

"If you're sure. And, of course, Bridget will be back on the West Coast from time to time to help with Moni."

I pause, dipping to catch her eyes, to check them for any signs of displeasure or distress.

"I know Bridget can be drama, but—"

"But she's Simone's mother, and she's actually a decent one. Believe me, I know how important having your mom around is. Especially one who actually loves you." Her expression clouds and quickly clears. "Besides, now that Bridget's dating and not trying to steal you back, we've been getting along just fine."

"Look at us, all blended family. I'm sure it'll be awkward at some point over something, but I'm knocking on major wood that things are going so well."

I glance down between us at what is still a rather impressive erection, if I do say so myself.

"Speaking of major wood…" I waggle my eyebrows and slide a hand down to the round firmness of her ass.

"Oh, hell no." Lotus slips the tank top over her head. "That ship's sailed, Mr. Ross."

I mourn the silky, nude flesh criminally covered up by fabric.

"Lotus, no." I tug at the hem of her shirt. "We'll lock the door or go to our room."

"It stays on." She tugs back, her lips, even set in a mulish line, twitching with humor. "I keep letting you distract me. I'm so far behind with the designs, Kenan. I'm glad I helped JP with that last show in Paris. He gave me every break I ever had in this industry, so I wanted to do what I could, but it delayed me starting my own thing. I'm playing catch-up."

I sober and lean a hip against her desk to glance around the room filled with mannequins and sketches and fabrics. The last few days we've focused so much on my retirement announcement, but she's at a pivotal juncture in her career, too.

"Can I help?" I ask, lifting her chin to catch and hold her eyes. "Anything I can do?"

Something clouds her expression for a second, but then she shakes her head.

"Anything, Lotus," I press. "You know I'll give you anything you need."

"Time?" she asks, chewing on her bottom lip. "What do you think about postponing the wedding? A longer engagement?"

"Anything but that," I answer abruptly, scowling.

"Kenan—"

"Lotus, no."

As soon as I put that ring on her finger, a clock started counting down inside me. You'd think after my last marriage ended so disastrously, I'd be hesitant to do it again. But it's Lotus. Nothing else I've ever had with anyone else comes near this. I feel like we've lost time already. In three years, I'll be forty. I want kids with Lotus and lots of time to raise them. I want life with her as my wife, and if I could make that start right now, I would. So a delay is the last thing I want.

"It's just a lot to plan when I have"—she gestures to the barely controlled chaos of the room—"all this going on. There's so much to do, and we have these investors, and the show is soon. I don't want to screw this opportunity up. Yari and Billie are moving across the country and betting it all on gLO. I can't let them down, either."

"I hear you. It's a lot, but the wedding can be simple. We've both been so busy, we've barely even talked about the details."

"I'm all for simple." She reaches up to cup my jaw and stroke a thumb over my mouth. "All I need is you."

A thought starts unfolding in my head. She might not agree, but it's worth a shot.

"You mean that?" I ask.

"Mean what?" Dark brows draw together over her querying eyes.

"That all you need is me."

"Well, and my dress, which I'm designing." Her grin is smug and confident. "I'm almost finished with it, actually. I started sketching it the night you proposed."

"That's good," I say decisively, warming to my fledgling idea more by the second. "You show up with the dress, and I'll take care of everything else."

Her full lips form a disbelieving *O*.

"What are you saying, Kenan?"

"I'll plan our wedding." I point to myself and then to her. "You bring the dress. Just focus on your line and the show."

"And why, for the love of black Jesus, would I let you plan our wedding?"

I laugh at that, relishing the shocked and dubious expression on her pretty face.

"You shouldn't leave it to me. We both know that would be a disaster, but leaving it to me, Iris, Billie, and Yari? Add my assistant Davis, and our wedding will be epic as hell. What do you say?"

"I'm not sure if they'll want to—"

"They will. They'd do anything for you. You know that." I dip to rub our noses together, my hands at the slim curves of her hips. "I'd do anything for you. You know that, too."

She kisses me briefly, nodding and letting her shoulders slump with the breath she expels on a deep sigh. "It would be such a relief to just focus on the show."

"I know it would, and it just so happens that as of today, my schedule opened up a lot. I find myself with some free time on my hands."

She looks almost convinced, but not quite.

"Hey, trust me. I won't let you down, or at least your friends won't let me let you down."

She chews the corner of her bottom lip. "We haven't even discussed location."

"Where do you want to have it?"

She links her hands behind her neck and glances around the room, taking in the mounds of fabric and stacks of sketches. Her brows pinch, and the tension we had worked out of her starts to tighten her shoulders again. I gently dig my fingers into her arms and shoulders, hoping I'm working a measure of the peace she brings me into her.

"Trust me, Button," I whisper. "Now, where do you want to marry me?"

She looks up, her expression softening with the love and trust we work so hard to cultivate, to keep.

"You know what?" She tips up to loop her arms around my neck. "Surprise me."

LOTUS

I'm not afraid of ghosts.

I've shared a room with death more often than I would have liked. Occupational hazard of growing up with a voodoo priestess.

The goose bumps, the raised hairs on the back of my neck, that frisson of...something not quite fully alive or human caressing my nerve endings. I'm familiar with those sensations, and like any "normal" person, I used to fear them. Not anymore. I've looked death in the face, so to speak. Death is not evil, not good or bad. It's just the vehicle that transports us from this world into the next, as much a part of life's cycle as birth, but with more baggage. Bags filled with joy and sorrow, filled with all the ways this world delivered and disappointed. History. The tail end of life that drags our hearts along.

No, I'm not afraid of death, and I'm not afraid of ghosts.

Today as I stand in front of a mirror, sheathed in a dress of buttercream silk and chiffon, I long for a ghost. Not just any of those nomad souls wandering between worlds. I long for a particular one.

I wish Mimi was here.

My hair is swept up, a few curls allowed to spill free. I don't feel the pins securing the style. Instead I feel the phantom brush of Mimi's hands roping my hair into braided patterns crowning my head. She shaped not just my hair but my character. Lessons that carried me from that spot where I sat on her living-room floor to where I stand right now. On the precipice of more happiness than I ever thought I would have.

It's my wedding day, and I'm marrying my magnificent gladiator.

How did this become my life? I went from the girl prone to randos and determined to feel nothing to the woman completely consumed with one man and willing to give him everything.

"You outdid yourself with this dress, Lo," Yari says from behind me.

"Thank you." I smile, meeting her eyes in the full-length mirror. "I hope Kenan agrees."

"How could he not?" Billie asks from beside Yari. "You look so beautiful."

I look back to my reflection, taking in the dress I lovingly sewed in between designs for our first show, which will take place in just a few weeks. JP always said construction is beauty. He taught me the importance of craftsmanship, and the sly punch of this deceptively simple dress lies in the way it's made. The bodice is corseted, pushing up my breasts and baring my shoulders. The stiffened silk molds my hips but then flows in layers of chiffon down my legs and to my feet. The back panel is nonexistent, exposing the intricate design inking my spine.

In the mirror, I split a smile between my two maids of honor. "Thank you both for everything. For helping Kenan plan this so I could focus on the line."

"Girl, that's our cheddar, too," Yari says with a chuckle. "Us focused on the nuptials and you focused on gLO, that's teamwork right there, baby."

"I didn't expect Kenan to be so…" Billie grins and rolls her eyes. "Particular."

I turn to search their faces, wrinkling my nose into an apology.

"Was he impossible?" I ask.

"Yes!" They reply in adamant unison, making us all laugh.

"I thought he'd just hand everything over to us and be on his merry way," Yari says, "but he wanted today to be perfect."

"Down to every detail." Billie adjusts the circlet of lotus petals arranged in my curls. "Even the flowers that would be in your hair. He hadn't seen your dress but wanted to make sure these would work if you wanted them."

"I definitely want them." I reach up to stroke one velvety petal.

"And do you love the location?" Yari bites into a knowing grin.

Right on time, a Caribbean breeze wafts in through the door opening to a private terrace overlooking turquoise water and powder-fine sand.

"It's perfect," I reply, walking over to the terrace and breathing in the sultry air.

"A trip to Turks and Caicos is the least Kenan could do after all the hoops he had us jumping through," Billie jokes, her lips twitching with good-natured humor. "A gorgeous destination wedding is a perk for sure."

"And Davis? Was he a perk?" Yari lifts one challenging perfectly plucked brow. "Don't think I didn't pick up on you vibing with Kenan's assistant."

"Davis?" I ask, surprised, turning my back on the gorgeous scenery to study Billie. "No way. That's awesome, Bill."

"Don't throw me the bouquet yet," Billie says wryly. "We're taking it really slow. I'm not rushing into anything after…"

She lowers her lashes and lets the words trail away. Yari and I exchange a quick glance. Paul is well in the rearview, but Billie still has some hard days. The day Paul and his wife had their new baby was one of them.

"Hey, taking your time is smart." I walk over to put my arm around Billie's shoulders. "And I for one think giving Davis a chance is really smart. He's amazing."

Billie nods and flashes us a bright smile. "He is. He's great."

She clears her throat and reaches up to cover my hand on her shoulder with one of hers. "But this is your day," she reminds me with a sweet smile. "You don't have long before you walk down that aisle."

"We are so freaking happy for you, Lo," Yari says, joining us and slipping her arms up over our shoulders.

"Nobody deserves happiness more than you do," Billie adds, blinking at the tears misting her big green eyes.

We huddle for a few seconds, pressing our foreheads together and sniffing.

"Thank you both again for everything," I say, my voice wobbling with emotion. "Not just the wedding, but for supporting me as I figured all my shit out. For believing in me and launching this line with me. For uprooting your lives and moving to the West Coast. Just for being my girls."

"We love you, bitch." Yari chokes on a teary chuckle. "What're we supposed to do? You'd do the same for us."

She's right. I'd do anything in my power for these two. Most of my family born of blood let me down, but these girls are the family I chose, and they never fail.

But I was blessed with some family I can count on, and at that moment, Iris walking through the door reminds me of that.

"Do not ruin your makeup," Iris warns, pointing at my face. "It's almost time."

I pull away from my friends to fan my face and blink furiously against the threat of more tears.

"Do I still look okay?" I ask a little anxiously.

Iris walks over and whispers a gentle thumb under my eye. Her lips tremble, and tears fill the dark eyes that meet mine. We exchange a wealth of emotion in that glance. A lifetime of love passes between us. A bond that reaches well beyond mere friendship or even blood. People always talk about soulmates in terms of romantic love, but I believe those aren't the only people fate links us to for life. I thank God for Kenan and believe we're meant for each other, but if I'd never met him, I'd still have Iris forever. Our hearts were joined before I spoke my first words or took my first steps. She's been my constant, and I've been hers.

"You look perfect, Lo," Iris assures softly.

The door opens, and the wedding coordinator pokes her head in, her smile as quick and efficient as she has proven to be. "Ladies, it's time. Let's line up."

We all move toward the door, but she stops me with a gentle hand on my shoulder. "Not you, Lo. I'll be right outside the door and will signal when it's time."

Yari and Billie send me one last tearful smile before leaving the room in rustles of silk.

"Iris." I catch my cousin's elbow before she follows the rest of them. "Hold on."

Iris's eyes when they meet mine already swim with emotion.

"Before you even start, I warned you about that makeup," Iris says, her voice cracking. "Don't ruin mine, too. There's no time for touch-ups."

"I'll try." My tear-husky chuckle breaks, and I take her hands between mine. "But I need to say this."

Iris's spine is stiff and straight, as if she's braced for what I'll tell her.

"I've always had you," I tell her shakily, our stares locked and watery. "And you've always had me."

My eyes drop to where our fingers clench. Both of us wear our gris-gris rings on our right hands now because the men we love placed new rings on the left. Mimi gave us those rings to protect us. We grew up with the strange men our mothers kept around, with the men who kept them, and we rarely felt safe. I wasn't safe. I was vulnerable and violated. Iris knows what it's like to not be safe, trapped in a cage with a rabid animal, helpless and alone. We know what it's like to be endangered, to be hunted by our pasts, but one of us always comes when the other calls.

"We did it," I whisper to her.

I don't have to explain. Iris knows what we did. Two girls from the Lower Ninth, a place that eats up and spits out innocence, found their happy ending. Not just that we each got a day for white dresses and flowers and wedding cake, but that we are whole. We are safe. We are loved. We dreamt and pursued and fought and struggled and dragged ourselves out from under the shadow of our mothers, away from their cycle of brokenness.

We survived.

"We did it," Iris echoes back to me, her smile wide and her eyes aglow with pride and tears. "I wish Mimi was here to see."

My chest grows tight, too narrow a passage to hold both my heart and the one Mimi left to me. I swear I hear two heartbeats beneath the bodice of my wedding gown. I imagine her fingers in my hair and her wise words in my ear. I touch the lotus petals circling my head.

No one has to tell a queen to wear her crown.

Mimi's words revisit me, remind and comfort me.

"Oh, Mimi's here," I assure Iris. "She wouldn't miss this for the world."

A sharp rap at the door interrupts us.

"It's time," the wedding planner's voice comes from the other side with an edge of urgency. "Iris, you're up next."

Iris makes sure her hair is still upswept and in place before kissing my cheek. "Love you, Lo. See you out there."

And she's gone. And I'm alone. Only I'm not.

As strains of music reach me in the room where I wait, the reassuring warmth of Mimi's long-missed companionship wraps around me. When I reach the oceanfront chapel's small stone foyer, a breeze whispers through the frothy layers of my skirt, and beneath the smell of salt and fresh ocean air, I find Mimi's familiar scent. And when it's time to enter, I feel her touch, a firm, gentle hand at my back, guiding me forward like she's always done.

No, I don't walk alone down the aisle. And I may be the only one who knows, but she gives me away, her pleasure with and trust in my groom as real to me as the bouquet of flowers in my hands.

I'm only vaguely aware of the small gathering of our friends and family. Of August holding their baby, Michael, now almost a toddler. Of the beaming faces of Kenya and her plus-one, Jade. Of Deck and his fiancée Avery clasping hands and smiling. Of Banner, Kenan's agent, standing with her back pressed into the broad chest of her golden-haired husband, Jared. Of JP and my friends from the fashion world, splashes of familiar flamboyance among the crowd. Simone, Mrs. Ross, Kenan's teammates—all here. Sarai waits, lovely and fidgety, beside her mother and clutches a basket of flowers. My three attendants, my best friends, sparkle, swathed in orange and fuchsia and lime silk, like cool mixed drinks for this tropical setting.

The details sharpen and then fall away when Kenan turns to face me, to track my steps up the aisle toward him.

And it's just us two.

I almost stumble as the force of his eyes on me, looking through me, steals my breath and breaks my stride. When our glances tangle, I lose the thread of time for a moment, and I'm not sure if I'm in that hospital room where I first saw him or by the water at sunset, kissing under the cover of cotton-candy clouds. Or in my magic tree, him warm and sure at my back and the bayou a murky, marshy mystery in the distance. Or are we somewhere outside time? Some place where our hearts were knit together before this world began, tied with a thread that will endure when time is done?

Are we in forever right now?

By the time I reach him, I'm trembling and laughing and crying. I can't hold back the onslaught of emotions, and we haven't exchanged even one word yet. He takes my hand and pulls me close. So close I have to tip my head back to look into his eyes. He dips until his lips brush my ear.

"You look beautiful, Button," he whispers, his voice rich with the same emotion bursting from my very pores.

"So do you, Mr. Ross," I whisper back, lost in the depth of his eyes and the timbre of his deep voice.

The priest invites everyone to take their seats and begins the ceremony. He leads us through the vows, and we repeat the things he says, but our eyes make our own promises, words we don't want to share with the people listening. When Kenan slides the platinum band on my finger, his eyes speak even when his lips don't move.

I have found the one whom my soul loves.

And I reply, a silent, secret declaration between our hearts.

My beloved is mine, and I am his.

When the preacher declares us man and wife, it's the most surreal moment of my life. I stare at this beautiful man with the bearing of a king and can't believe he's mine. Can't believe I'm his. It's still not real as we dash down the few chapel steps, hands clasped, into the balmy air. I'm still a little shaken while we take photos with the ocean as our backdrop and eat from trays of decadent food. With a silly grin, I watch our friends shuffle through the Electric Slide on a makeshift dancefloor on the beach. I feel like a bird observing from above, like my heart and every part of me that matters is still at that altar, still kneeling there, reverent, grateful.

"Are you okay?" Kenan leans down to ask me while we stand in front of a huge cake, poised to cut. His eyes aren't exactly concerned but curious, watchful.

I nod somewhat dazedly but then shake my head.

"To be honest," I tell him, clutching the knife and smiling, almost dizzy with happiness, "I keep thinking I'll wake up, like this is all a dream. It doesn't feel real yet."

He smiles and bends to brush his lips over mine.

"After we cut this cake and you toss that bouquet," he says, his voice a husky provocation, "we're getting out of here so I can make it real for you, Mrs. Ross."

Desire sparks through the happy haze, and where our eyes meet, where our hands touch over the knife, where our bodies press as we smile for the cameras and slice into the cake—every place we're connected burns. I can barely concentrate on slicing the cake I'm so aware of Kenan watching me, wanting me with an intensity that makes me squirm in my finery, itching to be free of all my clothes and naked in his arms.

"Toss those damn flowers," he whispers. "I want you to myself."

I nod my agreement and reach up to kiss him, grabbing his neck and opening my mouth over his. Our tongues duel, and we groan together. It's always there, this pulsing need between us, waiting to be ignited.

"Not so fast," Iris says, her tone chiding and eyes knowing when we pull apart to look at her. "The honeymoon can't start till you toss the bouquet."

She ignores Kenan's semi-impatient sigh and pulls me toward the cluster of women on the beach waiting for the toss. All the single ladies line up behind me. The sun sits low as we approach sunset. The sky is painted in shades of purple and pink and gold, and my breath catches at the beauty of my wedding and this day and this moment. Such a glorious sky ahead of me and everyone I love behind me. I'm so overcome with gratitude I have to blink back tears but compose myself enough to go through with this last thing before it's just me and my new husband.

"You ladies ready?" I call over my shoulder to the brightly garbed women lined up for the bouquet.

I count off and toss the bundle of flowers back. There's a chorus of squeals and laughter when I turn around.

"Eeeeek!" Yari brandishes the bouquet and grins triumphantly. "I'd be happier if the groom was already attached so I could skip the dating grind."

As expected, we all laugh, but my laughter fades quickly when Kenan joins me, taking my hand and tugging.

"Let's go before they find some other useless thing for us to do."

"These are traditions, Kenan," I say, grinning up at him. "And you planned all of this, so don't complain."

"Well, I'm done with them now," he says, some of his typical gruffness after being with too many people for too long showing. He glances down at me, his eyes gentling and heating.

"The chariot awaits," the wedding coordinator says, making her way over to us, navigating the dense sand in bejeweled flip-flops. "Or rather, your boat awaits."

I gasp and giggle at the boat pulling up to the shore.

"Ready?" Kenan asks, his eyes alight with anticipation.

"A boat?" I ask and look to where a boat with "JUST MARRIED" along the sideboards waits.

"We're getting out of here," he mutters. "Damned if I'm spending my wedding night on the same island with all these people.

I wouldn't put it past our friends to want to do things with us tomorrow."

He sounds so disgusted I have to laugh when said friends line the shore and cheer. They all hold sheer bags of flower petals to toss at us when we leave. A narrow pier juts out over sapphire waves curling seductively around the pier's slim wooden legs. The party playfully shoos us down the pier and toward the boat bobbing on the water, waiting for us. Iris, Yari, and Billie are with me, grinning and tearing up just like I am.

"I can't thank you guys enough for this day." I gesture toward the chapel and to the beach and overhead as if they special-ordered this spectacular sunset. "For everything. I love you."

"And we love you," Yari says, squeezing my hand. "But honey, if you don't get on that boat right now, I think Kenan might rip that dress off of you in front of er'body."

I didn't even realize Kenan had already boarded the boat, a look that is joy, impatience, and, yes, hunger stamped on his handsome face. He helps me down, his big hands spanning my waist and tightening possessively. He bends to kiss me, and a fall of lotus petals, cheers, and well wishes cascades over us. We wave at everyone clustered at the pier's edge. Kenan sits on the plush bench and pulls me onto his lap. I huddle into the warmth of his chest, tugging the lapels of his tuxedo jacket around my shoulders, shielding against the wind as we speed across the water.

"Where are we going?" I ask but don't really care. He could say the moon or Jack in the Box for a burger and I wouldn't care as long as we end up together, just the two of us.

"It's a private island nearby." His lips brush my ear, and a shiver skitters over my body. I stretch to subtly swipe his neck with my tongue. He glances at the driver and back down to me, groaning.

"If you don't want our first time as man and wife to be on the back of this boat," he says, nodding toward the driver, "with a witness, you'd better behave. I'm on a very short leash right now. Do you have any idea how you look in that dress?"

"This dress?" I point to the bodice but surreptitiously stroke a finger over my nipple, bringing it erect through the silky material.

"Lotus," he rasps into my hair, and I can barely hear him over the boat's engine. "I'm going to try my best to be all reverent and gentle after I carry you across the threshold, but you're making it very hard."

I squirm in his lap, grinding my silk-covered ass into his erection.

"I'm making you very hard," I whisper. "And you'd better not ruin my wedding night with that reverent and gentle shit. You'd better fuck me hard."

"Jesus." He slides a huge hand under my wedding dress and between my thighs, pushing past my panties and shoving his middle finger unceremoniously inside, circling my clit with his thumb.

"Oh my God." I collapse against his chest, churning my hips slowly into the finger fucking me. "I'm gonna come."

"I don't have a pillow for your face," he says, a deep chuckle vibrating into me. "So you'll have to keep yourself quiet."

"I bet the driver would enjoy seeing me come."

"Yes, but then I'd have to kill him," Kenan says, his smile disintegrating but his finger and thumb still working in tandem between my legs to drive me over the edge.

"Oh, God, Kenan." The words slip out trembly and breathless. "Please don't stop. I'll be quiet. Just don't stop."

I burrow my face into him under the perfectly tailored jacket and bite into the thick muscle of his shoulder, stifling the cries wrenched from my throat as my orgasm explodes from my core and overtakes my whole body. Kenan pulls his fingers away, leaving a wet trail down my thigh, just when the driver turns to us.

"We're here, Mr. Ross," he says, smiling as he pulls the boat to shore.

Still shaking, I glance up, and my hand literally flies to my mouth at the breathtaking sight. The white sand is pristine, marred not even by a footprint. Like we are the first to stumble upon the charming bungalow set back off the beach, sheltered by mangrove trees and vibrantly splattered foliage. My legs tremble from the recent earthquake in my pussy, but no need to fear. Kenan scoops me up in his arms, surprising me, making me squeal and clutch his neck.

"Kenan, I can walk," I say, breathless and absolutely content to have my feet nowhere near the ground. This whole day has felt like I was walking on pink clouds, so why should this be any different?

"And have that dress dragging in the sand?" He shakes his head and steps onto the shore, his breath not even labored when he treks up the sandy slope toward the bungalow. The sound of the departing boat drifts to us. I don't ask about clothes or suitcases or anything. One, I trust that Kenan has thought of everything because all day he's proven that fact. And two, the last thing any sane woman who has a horny Kenan Ross on a deserted island should be thinking about is clothes.

Kenan shifts me in his arms just enough to turn the doorknob. When the door swings open, I take in the beauty of the room and the delicious-smelling food laid out on the table butted up against a window with an ocean view. I take it in, but there is something much more beautiful in this room.

I reach up to trace the austere beauty of my husband's features. I caress the thick, dark slash of his brows and run a shaking finger over the sculpted cheekbones and full lips. I press my forehead to his and close my eyes, unable to stand the intensity of the love and devotion in the eyes staring back at me. For a moment, feeling unworthy of it.

"I'm yours, Kenan," I push the words past the tears burning my throat.

"And I'm yours," he echoes, not putting me down, standing still in the middle of the front room.

"Prove it." The command scrapes deliciously in my throat, and my fingers dig into his neck. "Your wife needs to be fucked, Mr. Ross."

"I'm not doing this on the floor in the living room," he says, his chuckle thinned out and husky. "We're at least making it to the bed on our wedding night."

He kisses me but keeps moving, navigating the stretch of stone tiles leading to the back of the bungalow. When we reach the bedroom, he slides my body down his until my feet touch the floor. I barely noted the details of the front room, but the cool beauty of this one captures my attention. A sheer air canopy floats above the four-poster bed covered in white linen. Pillows at the head relieve the starkness with a line of vibrant color. Dark-paneled floor-to-ceiling louvered doors are flung open to a balcony overlooking the ocean, a seemingly infinite stretch of Caribbean blue and green.

"It's beautiful, Kenan." I kick off my shoes and walk toward the open doors, the salted breeze luring me to the view.

"Not another person in sight," Kenan says from behind me, slipping muscled arms around my waist. "We are the only ones in this little corner of paradise."

His voice is even, but his breathing is slightly ragged, and he's hard as a sword pressing into my back. I reach behind me, between us, and palm his dick.

"Shit, Lotus," he hisses, his hands moving from my waist to grip my hips.

I turn to face him, the wind at my back, and reach up to slip the pins from my hair. Anticipation heightens my senses, and the curls falling over my neck and onto my shoulders are as sensual as a lover's kiss. Kenan searches my face, considers the hair I've liberated, and finally looks at the bodice of my dress, a silent command to keep going. One I'm more than happy to oblige.

"Our own little corner, huh?" I ask, turning away from him again to face the azure waters. The dress bares my back, and I know how the delicate line of ink marking my spine affects him. I reach for the hidden zipper at the small of my back, dragging it down until the dress peels away from my ass, hips, and thighs and slumps to the floor, leaving me wearing only a tiny silk thong and stockings so sheer they feel like a sigh on my legs. The intricately scrolled lace at the tops of the expensive stockings overlays the similar pattern etched into my skin. I can finally afford the real thing.

It's decadent facing the ocean, exposing myself even to an uninhabited world. With only the setting sun and the thinning clouds as my witnesses, the island whispers over my breasts in a balmy breeze, drawing my nipples into tight buds. I cup and stroke my breasts, leaning back into Kenan's chest. Something about him still being clothed, the roughness of his tuxedo against my nakedness, licks a flame inside, making me desperate to have him. I circle my ass into his groin, moaning at the hard readiness.

"Lotus," he growls into the curve of my neck, my name a warning and a plea. One of his hands covers mine over my breast, and the other hand slides down my waist until big, blunt fingers dip into the panties and unerringly find my wet, begging heat. I widen my legs, making way for his hand to palm my pussy. He plucks at my nipple, pinches my clit, and pushes up into me roughly in an unrelenting rhythm that makes me ride his hand.

"Oh my god. Sweet Jesus. Fuck. Shit. Dammit."

A litany of curses streams helplessly from my lips until my mouth falls open on a scream that travels nowhere and everywhere. My broken cry pierces the air, loud and brazen, but there's no one to hear but us.

"So good," I mutter, my head lolling back against his broad chest as the orgasm drains me, liquefies the cartilage and bones, and leaves me limp.

He scoops me up into his arms and leaves the balcony. Through slitted lids I see the large bed like a mirage. He sets me on the edge, towering over me, still dressed as impeccably as he was during the ceremony.

"Undress," I beg, my voice husky and hoarse. "I want to see you."

"Soon." A wicked grin twists those sinfully full lips. "You first."

I glance down at my naked breasts and the expanse of stomach barely interrupted by the scant silk of my thong. He gently pushes my shoulder until the sweat-dampened skin of my back meets the cool sheets. He takes one stockinged leg and bends to kiss my inner thigh. Heat zings along my leg, and I moan. His lips trace my thigh, steadily sliding the silk down in a trail of open-mouth kisses, until he reaches my foot. Slowly and with excruciating care, he rolls the stocking over my foot, pausing to suck the arch.

"Oh, yes." I ground my hips into the bed, a prelude to how very hard I plan to fuck my husband when he completes this round of torture.

He repeats the ritual of disrobing kisses on the other leg until all that's left is my thong. I'm panting, and the silk between my legs is soaked. I give in to a perverse desire to torture him as he is torturing me and slip my hand into the panties and busy my fingers beneath the silk. Rolling over the knot of nerves and fingering myself until I'm coming again so hard, eyes locked with his. I press my foot into his chest, lost in a wave of my own doing.

"Fuck, Button," he mutters, pulling my leg gently until it's flush against his chest. He tugs roughly at the thong, and it gives a satisfying rip. I watch his eyes glued to where I still dip a finger in and out of myself. He dives between my legs and grabs my hand, pulling it fully into his mouth and licking the wetness from every finger before burying his face in my folds. He separates me, his fingers deft and abrupt, exposing my clit for his teeth, lips, and tongue. The noises he makes. God, he sounds like an animal, rabid and wild and ravenous. He grips my legs, pressing them wide so there's nothing but pussy. I'm tossed by wave after wave of orgasm, the sheets clenched tightly in my fists while I crest and ebb.

His jangling belt buckle and the rustle of expensive material snap my eyes open.

"I wanted to undress you," I mumble half-heartedly because at this point, elves could prance in and strip him for all I care. I just want all that man naked. I just want that dick so bad I'm literally rubbing my thighs together, creating friction until I can have him instead.

"Uh," he grunts, quickly stripping his pants and briefs off before sitting on the edge of the bed and dragging me onto his lap, spreading my legs over his powerful thighs.

"My gladiator," I whisper over his lips, kissing him and tasting myself. I dip my head to gently suck and bite his nipples. "My king."

I take his hot, hard length into one hand while I twist his nipple with my other, mirroring how he brought me to orgasm for only nature to see just minutes ago. His head falls back, and he grabs my ass, urging me over him.

"Lotus," he grinds out. "Now."

I roll a clenched fist up and down his stiff erection, fighting a grin.

"What was that?" I ask playfully.

His dark eyes open, impatient, starving, gentle. He lifts me effortlessly, poising my body over his.

"Now."

And he surges up and in, accepting the open invitation of my body, so much smaller than his but designed, tailored for him. We gasp into each other's mouths when our bodies meld. And it's like our first kiss, this first married mating. Deep and demanding and hungry and new, a desperate discovery. Not just the physical joining, but the way our souls kiss, the way my heart clamors, straining for his through layers of skin and muscle and bone. I undulate my hips in deep waves, offering his body refuge in mine. I squeeze him between my thighs and wish time could elongate, could suspend us in these seconds where I'm starving and satisfied. I take his face between my hands, tracing the unexpected softness of his full lips set in a plane of stark, ungiving bones, and lock our eyes, showing him every part of me and demanding every part of him. Surrendering and conquering at a glance.

"Don't look away," I beg him, tears streaming unreservedly over my cheeks.

"Jesus, Lotus, never," he says hoarsely, one hand gripping my hip and the other pressing my back, pressing my breasts into his chest. "I love you so much. I didn't even know this was…"

Possible.

The word goes unspoken, but I hear it. I read it in the tears standing in my indomitable warrior's dark eyes. He defies my declaration that I didn't need reverence and douses my face, my shoulders, my breasts with kisses that are prayers. With tears that are offerings.

And it occurs to me that most will never know this rare love, the kind that circumvents time. What if we didn't find each other in this life but have found each other again? Like Moses's Red Sea, one body split down the center, separated only to meet again miraculously in the middle? What if in the beginning we were one? One lump of clay, brought to dusty life by the breath of our Creator and then cleaved into two until the time was right. Two aching, needing parts that, once separated, never felt quite whole until right now, until this moment of sacred reuniting. Flesh, blood, soul, heart, baptized in kisses and moans and tears. Not just a consummation but a reunion, sealed in vows by our lips and this kiss as we come with a crash of bodies and heartbeats.

We remain that way, lingering in elastic seconds, stretched for us to revel in one another. Still splayed across his powerful thighs, still widened around him, I press my forehead to his and, with a trembling hand, link his fingers with mine. The gris-gris ring on my right hand locks with the wedding band I placed today on his left.

"Maybe I'm your gris-gris now," I say, my voice cracked with tears and awe.

He doesn't ask if I'm reminding him of his words to me from before or declaring it to him right now, but his reply is in perfect harmony with either, with both.

"You are," he whispers into a kiss of mingled breaths and promises, his fingers, his future locked tightly with mine. And I am.

ACKNOWLEDGMENTS

Thank you always feels insufficient for this part of the journey.

The End.

The long road to reach *The End* of each story is paved with the generosity and support of so many. First I must thank the survivors who shared their stories with me as I sought to understand Lotus's hurt and her healing.

You know who you are, and I owe you a debt of gratitude.

And to Ceedee Gaddis, MS, LMFTC, thank you for crawling into Lotus's heart and mind to make sure we documented her healing journey with sensitivity and compassion.

Too many authors and bloggers and readers to name have helped me. I'll forget someone, for sure, so thank you all. I'm especially grateful to Brittany, Vanessa, Joanna, and Shannon, who lead my promo team so well and with such grace.

To the Brooklyn Mavens (IG: @bklynmavens), thank you for loving Brooklyn so deeply and sharing that love with me!

Always, thanks to my boys, my husband and son, who loan me out to my dream every day. I love you both beyond words. Even beyond my own.

Thank you for reading!

—XO

ABOUT THE AUTHOR

A RITA and Audie Award winner, *USA Today* bestselling author Kennedy Ryan writes for women from all walks of life, empowering them and placing them firmly at the center of each story and in charge of their own destinies. Her heroes respect, cherish, and lose their minds for the women who capture their hearts. Kennedy and her writings have been featured in *Chicken Soup for the Soul*, *USA Today*, *Entertainment Weekly*, *Glamour*, *Cosmopolitan*, *TIME*, *O* magazine, and many others. She is a wife to her lifetime lover and mother to an extraordinary son.

Connect with Kennedy!

Website: kennedyryanwrites.com
Facebook: @kennedyryanauthor
Instagram: @kennedyryan1
TikTok: @kennedyryanauthor
Twitter: @kennedyrwrites